The Art of the Stab

R. Jamie
Langa

The Art
of the Stab

For what's-his-face

It is to this head that the evils of deep play ought to be referred.
Though the chances, so far as relates to money, are equal,
in regard to pleasure, they are always unfavourable. I have
a thousand pounds. The stake is five hundred. If I lose, my
fortune is diminished by one-half; if I gain, it is increased only
by a third. Suppose the stake to be a thousand pounds. If I gain,
my happiness is not doubled with my fortune; if I lose, my
happiness is destroyed, I am reduced to indigence.

Jeremy Bentham, *The Theory of Legislation*

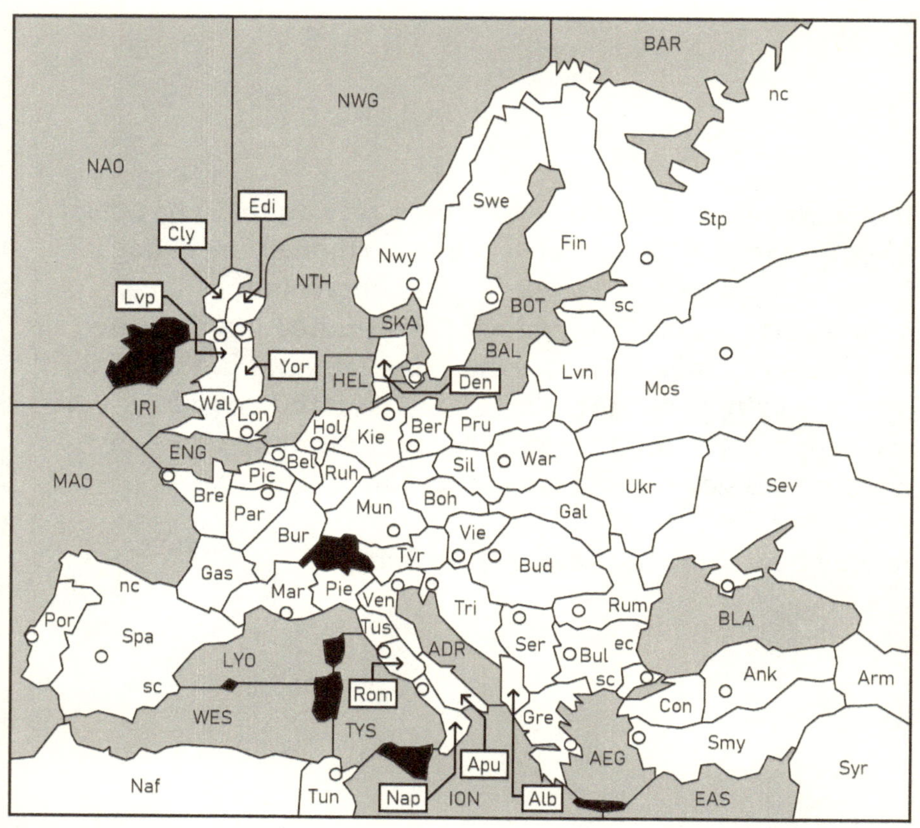

Figure 1 -- The Game Map (Circles Denote Supply Centers)

Supply Centers

Ank	Ankara
Bel	Belgium
Ber	Berlin
Bre	Brest
Bud	Budapest
Bul	Bulgaria
Con	Constantinople
Den	Denmark
Edi	Edinburgh
Gre	Greece
Hol	Holland
Kie	Kiel
Lvp	Liverpool
Lon	London
Mar	Marseilles
Mos	Moscow
Mun	Munich
Nap	Naples
Nwy	Norway
Par	Paris
Por	Portugal
Rom	Rome
Rum	Rumania
Stp	St. Petersburg
Ser	Serbia
Sev	Sevastopol
Smy	Smyrna
Spa	Spain
Swe	Sweden
Tri	Trieste
Tun	Tunis
Ven	Venice
Vie	Vienna
War	Warsaw

Other Land Territories

Alb	Albania
Apu	Apulia
Arm	Armenia
Boh	Bohemia
Bur	Burgundy
Cly	Clyde
Fin	Finland
Gal	Galicia
Gas	Gascony
Lvn	Livonia
Naf	North Africa
Pic	Picardy
Pie	Piedmont
Pru	Prussia
Ruh	Ruhr
Sil	Silesia
Syr	Syria
Tus	Tuscany
Tyr	Tyrolia
Ukr	Ukraine
Wal	Wales
Yor	Yorkshire

Water Territories

ADR	Adriatic Sea
AEG	Aegean Sea
BAL	Baltic Sea
BAR	Barents Sea
BLA	Black Sea
EAS	Eastern Mediterranean
ENG	English Channel
BOT	Gulf of Bothnia
LYO	Gulf of Lyon
HEL	Helgoland Bight
ION	Ionian Sea
IRI	Irish Sea
MAO	Mid-Atlantic Ocean
NAO	North Atlantic Ocean
NTH	North Sea
NWG	Norwegian Sea
SKA	Skagerrak
TYS	Tyrrhenian Sea
WES	Western Mediterranean

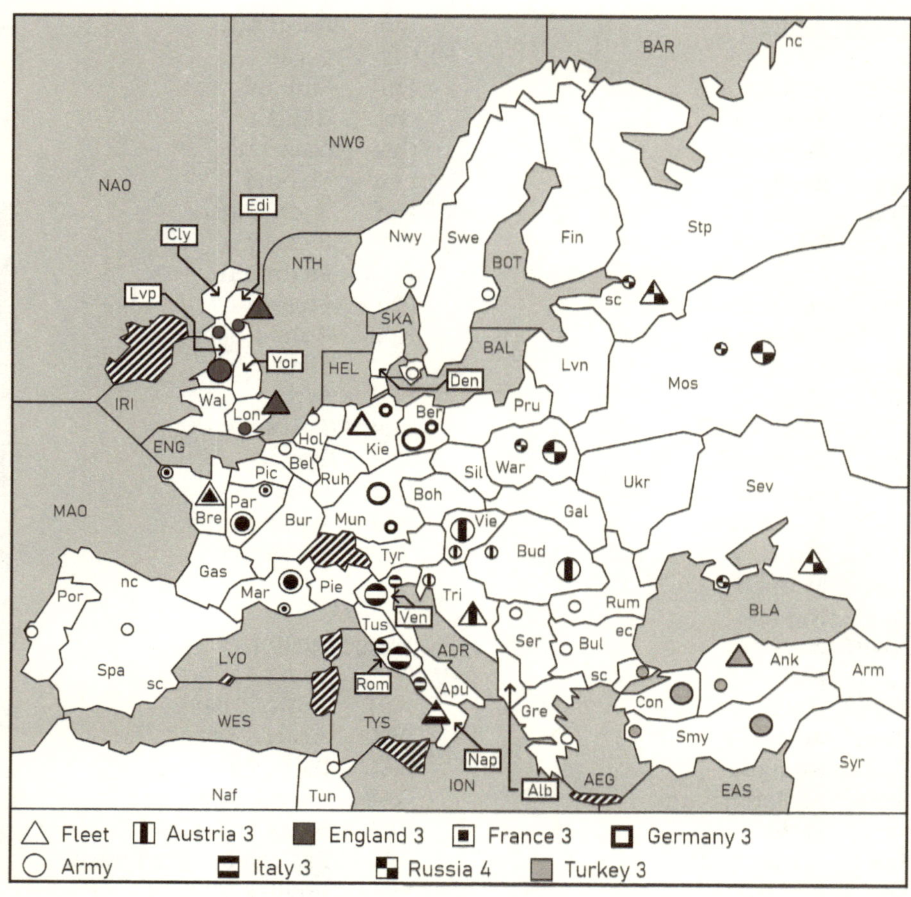

Figure 2 -- Game Map, Start of Spring 1901

Spring

1901

[The invitations and their responses]

Ollivander: All I'm saying is it's a weird subject for an oral history. Your advisor really okayed it? … Well, all right. It was just about the last time all of us would be in The City before heading off to college. Community college in Jeff's case. I asked everyone if the Wednesday after our graduation ceremony would work; Vicki phoned me to say that she was taking a pass because she wanted to spend every day she could with Nestor until her family left for vacation Friday morning.

So I told her to have him join us. I thought the call had cut out because she took a few seconds before replying, "Really?"

"Sure, why not?"

"He's not really a board game guy, you know?"

"Ask him anyway," I told her. A couple hours later she texted me that he was in. I confirmed that she'd forwarded the e-mail with the FAQ Lance composed, and we were on.

Jeffrey: Yeah, I was a little surprised. Nestor didn't really hang with us. Played some deathmatch with him remotely a few times, talked a little when he'd come by to pick up Vicki, but that was it. This was going to be the longest time we'd spend with him outside of this one all-day field trip junior year.

I was kinda looking forward to it. He was the closest thing the school'd had to a star athlete in a while. We weren't expecting to see him in the NFL, but he'd been recruited to play for a Division I team, pretty exciting, right? I had a billion questions for him, and I was hoping to catch him away from Vicki and ask them all.

Cassandra: Those guys convinced me to play a game online once. I didn't really care for it. Everyone was telling me to do stuff for them; it was confusing. When I got knocked out after five or six turns I was relieved. I could tell them I'd given it a shot and it wasn't for me.

But this was maybe the last time I was going to get to be with my best friend before we all headed out to college. I told Lance I'd go. I was dying to ask him if she was coming. The only reason I didn't was because if she wasn't, she would be off somewhere with Nestor and I wouldn't see her anyway. And so I'd want to be at Evander's with those guys to take my mind off of it.

Lance: I put together the FAQ. The rulebook, strategy guides, how to use the website, a couple of tournament highlights: stuff like that. Evander looked it over and sent it out with the invites a couple of days after we were done with our senior finals.

Evander's idea. He told me the only way we'd get the people we wanted there to attend was if they had the information they needed to get close to an even playing field.

It worked. We knew Booker and Jeff would be up for it. I had to convince Cassie, but when I told her Vicki was invited, she was in. All that was left was to get Vicki. And Nestor.

Booker: They invited me; I accepted. One moment, please, who else agreed to be interviewed? ... All six? Even Nestor?

I *am* surprised. You will have to send me a copy once you have finished writing it up. To answer your question, I had played before, but never in person. I thought it would be an enjoyable way to spend a day, and so I said yes.

Victoria: I wanted to spend every day I could with Nestor until I had to leave. I was going to say no until Evander told me to bring him along.

Some of those guys I'd known since grade school. I knew I wouldn't feel good about going off to Europe without seeing them in person one last time. I could go, play that game, say my goodbyes, and then leave to have fun with my boyfriend. All before it started to get dark.

So I called Nestor. "It's only been a day, girl. You miss me that bad?"

I laughed and told him to get over himself. "No, it's this thing Evander wants us to do at his house. The 12th, Wednesday after graduation." Then I forwarded him that e-mail and told him who else was coming.

After Nestor read it over and clicked on a couple of the links, he called me back. He was moaning about spending a full day with those guys when he could be hanging with his friends.

"It's just one day, bae. We'll be out of there by six. And then I'll thank you that way you like."

"*Damn* you thirsty. Alright, fine. Tell him I'll be there."

Nestor: After I looked at that e-mail? Read a little about that game? I knew I was going. I would've gone even if Vicki didn't.

[Obtaining permission from their parents]

Ollivander: My mother said fine, as long as we were done by six. And she was going to bring the liquor into her bedroom and lock the doors to it, her home office, and her bathroom. We'd have to use the one in the hallway.

Jeffrey: She asked who would be there, and when I told her, Mom was practically forcing me to go. She thought those guys were good influences, sure. But the other part of it? She was convinced that they could help me transfer into a regular four-year college. Become an engineer instead of just a technician.

"Or even a doctor! You could be a doctor!"

"Sure, Ma. Let me focus on my first year classes, okay?"

But she was too excited to listen. She told me to make sure to get all their contact info. "And get them on LinkedIn and connect!"

Cassandra: Mom and Dad told me to be back by six-thirty for dinner.

Booker: They said fine. It was during the daytime, a week after graduation, and so I would not have expected them to deny me permission. I do not understand why you would ask.

Lance: It was a whole big thing. My father sat me down and explained how Mom and him understood how hard I'd worked to get into a good university, but now we had to spend some time together as a family.

"Your mother is going to be really sad when you're gone, you know that? That's why I don't want you spending every waking moment with your friends this summer."

So I had to negotiate with him just to get that one f---ing day … wait, we can swear, right? … Dashes, huh? There's going to be a lot of those by the time you get the whole story down. Anyhow, he finally agreed to let me have it.

Victoria: They told me okay, but only if I had everything packed by Tuesday, the day before.

Nestor: My father was all for me going.

Said he thought it was "good wholesome fun." Actually used those words, said he was glad I was "mixing it up", spending a little time away from my usual squad.

[The morning of, before the start of the game]

Ollivander: Lance was a half-hour early, and he spent the time driving me up the wall worrying about whether Vicki and Nestor would actually show.

Just as I expected, they came last. "You are late," Booker said.

Nestor took off his sunglasses and looked at his watch. "You seriously griefing me over eleven minutes?"

Jeff bumped fists with him. "Your eyes are red, my damie. Got turnt last night?"

He laughed. "I'm sure you can imagine."

"There's bagels, donuts, orange juice and coffee in the kitchen," I said. "We'll get started in five minutes, so you can spend those imagining what Nestor's been up to."

Cassandra: Vicki and I hugged. "Hey, girlfriend!"

"Hey-ey!"

"I'm glad you came."

"I wouldn't miss it, right, bae?"

Nestor nodded to her, then tilted his head up at me and said, "Good to see you, Cassie."

"Sure good to see you too." I hoped that came off as sincere. If it didn't, Nestor didn't notice. Maybe because he was too hung over.

Booker: The sort of small talk you would expect. Summer plans, when our fall semesters began, and the like. Was there something specific you wanted me to address?

Jeffrey: Evander called us over to the living room, told us to bring our cups. We stood around the card table in the middle of the room and then he said, "All right, before we start: John Quincy Adams High, Class of 2019!"

We cheered. "Go Kestrels! Woo!" Vicki yelled out.

It felt good. I know that we'd celebrated last Tuesday at the ceremony, but that moment ... it was nice. I had good feelings for those guys, and I was looking forward to a day with all of them.

Victoria: Okay, don't judge, but Nestor got me out on Evander's back porch after we'd got our orange juices, and he showed me his hip flask he'd brought with.

"It isn't even ten-thirty a.m.!"

"You saying you don't want any?"

"F--- it. Quick, before anyone sees." And we had ourselves a couple of screwdrivers. It's stuff like that which is why I liked being with Nestor. I ... yeah.

Nestor: Evander was the only one of the five who knew s--- about sports, the only one who could *converse*. I could tell him my time running the forty, and he'd know how good it was. The others?

I don't get it. All the great teams we've had to root for in San Francisco and they're not into it?

Jeff, yeah, he was a loser, but back then I thought he was okay. Went to the games, cheered me on. He was a little extra about it, but at least he showed respect for my hard work and talent. I could appreciate that.

But those three? Every time I saw Booker he'd act like I was a stranger. Not counting that day, I can't remember the last time I talked to him for more than fifteen seconds. Cassie barely tolerated me, and I tried *hard* to get along with her, because she was friends with Vicki before we got together. Lance, though? He hated me. Salty little b---- ever since this one time freshman year.

Lance: Nestor? That's a long story.

[The rules of the game]

Ollivander: All the players start with two armies and one fleet on their home country supply centers. The exceptions are England, which starts with one army and two fleets, and Russia, which starts with two armies and two fleets.

Booker: Each year is divided into spring, fall, and winter. During the spring and fall stages, players negotiate with each other as to the moves they will make and what support they will give to other players. The players then submit their orders. These orders are resolved simultaneously. Then, if any units are successfully dislodged, the player to whom they belong will submit orders to retreat or disband it.

In winter, each player will build or disband units, depending on how many more or fewer supply centers—sometimes termed "dots" as a shorthand—he or she controls compared to the start of the year. Builds must occur on one's home supply centers, and may be deferred to a later year, if desired.

Jeffrey: Armies can occupy land territories. Fleets can occupy water territories and coastal land territories. And only one unit at a time in a territory.

Orders are either holds, moves, supports, or convoys. One order per unit per turn. Fleets can convoy armies from one coastal territory to another one. Like the army is leapfrogging using the fleet as a lily pad? But otherwise, a move is only to an adjacent territory. And you have to be able to move to the destination territory yourself to support a move, does that make sense? Give you a for instance: you can't use an army in a coastal province to support a fleet's move into the ocean.

[Examples using one method of abbreviating game orders]

A Ber → Sil	**Move** army from Berlin to Silesia
A Ruh S F Hol → Bel	**Support** fleet move from Holland to Belgium, using army in Ruhr
F Den Holds	Fleet in Denmark to **Hold**
F NTH C A Lon → Nwy	**Convoy** army from London to Norway, using fleet in North Sea

Lance: All units have the same strength as every other unit, whether they're an army or a fleet.

So a unit can only move to another space if the total number of units moving or supporting the move is greater than the total number of opposing units holding, moving, or supporting the hold.

This is where the strategy of the game comes into play. You'll have to negotiate with other players during the diplomatic phase to support your moves into other territories, or keep your unit from being dislodged. Or to hang back and let you move instead.

The thing is, you can lie. Break your promise and take advantage. The tricky part is timing and choosing your betrayals carefully.

Ollivander: A player gets a solo win by controlling eighteen supply centers. It rarely gets to that point, and instead the surviving players will agree to "split the boardtop". In other words, have a two- or multi-way tie.

There's a handful of other special cases in the game mechanic, and I can explain those as they come up. But those are the basics. The game is conceptually straightforward. Of course, that doesn't mean it isn't complex in practice.

[Who got what country and how]

Lance: After we toasted with coffee and O.J., Evander said, "Let's get started. You all know the rules; you've all created your accounts on the site. This board here is because it's easier to visualize the state of play that way."

"Hey, you got those old wooden pieces," Jeff said.

"I had to special order them. Worth every penny. Moving on, we're entering all orders online, in this room, together. You can do it with your smartphones or on that laptop on the card table in the corner if it's easier. When it comes to press—"

"'Press'?" Cassie asked.

"Communications between players. Secret or otherwise. For that, you can either message through the website with your phones or talk in person. Use the living room, the back porch, the front porch, or the kitchen for your chats.

"A couple of items not covered in the rulebook. One, you can't make deals based on anything outside the game. Like, don't promise someone twenty bucks if they support you or betray someone else. Two, no one else gets to see you enter your orders. Any questions?"

Booker raised his hand. "What is the time limit for each turn?"

"Fifteen minutes for the diplomatic phase, five minutes to enter orders. One extra minute for retreat orders, if necessary. In winter, five minutes for build and disbands. If you're using the laptop, don't hog it. Anything else?"

Cassandra: There was a little bit of drama then with Nestor's question: "Who gets which country?"

"Dibs on France," Lance blurted.

People started arguing. Not me or Vicki or Evander, but those four guys did. About who got to pick when. Until Evander grabbed seven of those little wood blocks, one of each color, and walked over to one of the end tables next to the couch, where he picked up a baseball cap that was on it.

He shook the blocks in his right hand. He dumped them into the cap; lifted it up so it was above his head; and then picked them out, one by one, and plopped them on the table in front of each of us as he said, "Jeff, you're Russia. Lance, you get England. Booker, you're France. Nestor, you're Germany. Vicki is Turkey, Cassie is Austria, and I …" There was some complaining from the guys that they didn't get to pick their own pieces out of the hat until the very end, when he finished, "I get Italy."

Everyone was quiet for a second. "You know, if you insist, we can do it again, and this time everyone gets to pick themselves."

"Not a chance," said Lance. "You're just saying that because you're stuck with Italy."

Evander sighed. "No one wants a do-over?" He looked around. "Well, s---." He put the sorting hat on his head. "Okay, let me enter the country assignments into the website for the game … and we're off. Fifteen minutes, remember." And then he went to the bathroom.

[The game begins: spring 1901]

Jeffrey (Russia): There's not a lot of interesting action on the board during the spring of 1901. People will be setting up alliances, making plans. But the actual moves are going to be to lock down those open supply centers they're closest to. I mean, if everyone knows what they're doing.

The exceptions? There's this thing called the Key Lepanto. That's Italy and Austria teaming up to take out Turkey from the get-go. But there was no way Evander would get Cassie to turn on Vicki right at the start, so that was out.

And there's this other thing that Russia and Turkey usually do. They both try to move their fleets into the Black Sea. Both moves fail, so there's what they call a "bounce". Then in the fall Russia's army in Ukraine moves to Rumania and Turkey marches into Bulgaria.

I was going to do that when Vicki asked me to come out to the front porch and help her out.

Victoria (Turkey): I skimmed those things Evander sent, and I guess I knew how to play? But I needed to talk to Jeff about it.

"Take Bulgaria with your army in Constantinople," he said. "Then move your fleet in Ankara to Constantinople."

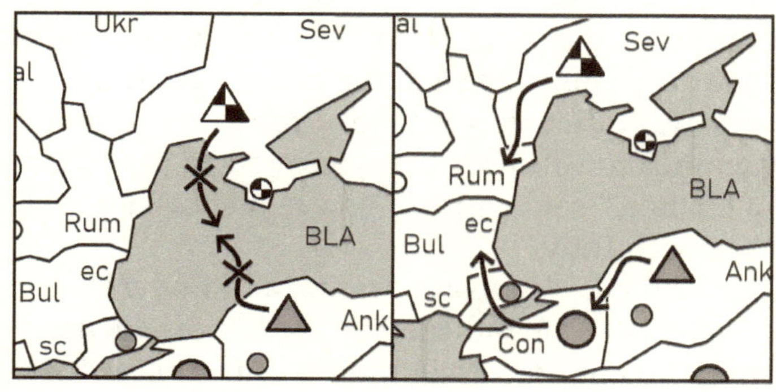

Figure 3 -- The "Black Sea Bounce" and the Proposed Alternative

"What about that other army?"

"It's up to you. Move it to Ankara if you want to make space for a build in Smyrna."

I was getting confused, so I had him show me all that on the map on my phone. "Just one thing, Vicki. If I can trust you, then I can take Rumania. Us two'll have one less thing to worry about, and we can make our moves elsewhere. Ya feel?"

"Oh yeah! I mean, what could I do even if I *wanted* to attack you?"

He squinted at me. Then he shook my hand and we went back inside.

Austria

```
A Bud → Ser
F Tri → ADR
A Vie → Tri
```

England

```
F Edi → NTH
F Lon → ENG
A Lvp → Yor
```

France

```
F Bre → MAO
A Mar → Spa
A Par → Bur
```

Germany

```
A Ber → Kie
F Kie → Den
A Mun → Ruh
```

Italy

```
F Nap → TYS
A Rom → Tus
A Ven Holds
```

Russia

```
A Mos → Ukr
F Sev → Rum
F Stp.sc → BOT
A War Holds
```

Turkey

```
F Ank → Con
A Con → Bul
A Smy → Ank
```

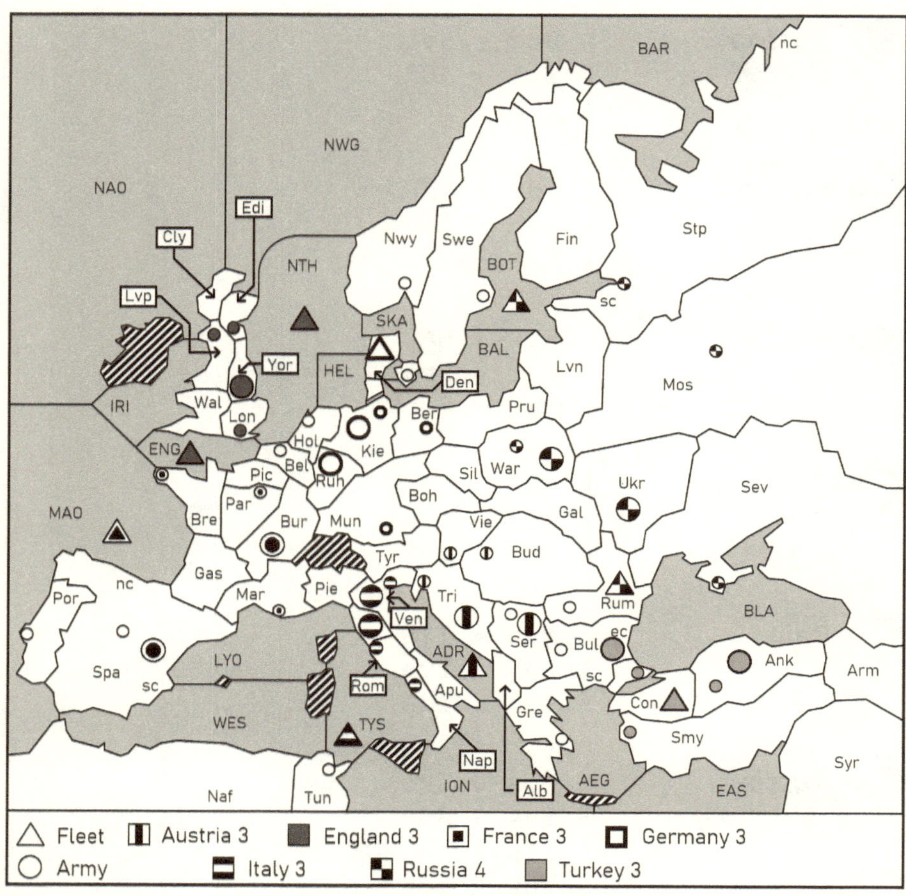

Figure 4 -- Game Map, Start of Fall 1901

Fall
1901

[Reactions to the orders of spring 1901]

Booker (France): There were two inferences I took from the first round of play. Judging from Italy's actions, there would be no Key Lepanto. And Austria's move into the Adriatic served as further confirmation that the two countries would not ally.

It was a surprise, I must confess. When Italy did not attempt to form a pact with me, I had assumed an alliance with Austria. I could only conclude that Austria decided to betray Italy immediately. Which struck me as a bold move, but too soon to be effective. Italy is the worst country in the game, but it could easily repel Austria's forces. And then Austria would be forced to defend itself on multiple fronts.

The other was Victoria and Jeffrey's front porch chat. Russia not moving into the Black Sea smacked of a prearranged agreement, if not an explicit alliance.

Lance (England): Except for those things Booker told you about, Spring was like you'd expect. The first real moves were coming in the fall.

[Diplomatic phase of fall 1901]

```
Lance>    Got a sec?
Booker>   I do. Where do you wish to talk?
Lance>    Stay in chat window?
Booker>   So Nestor is unaware?
Lance>    Y. Supt me into Bel
Booker>   Why would I do that?
Lance>    Keep from Nes
Booker>   That could be done were you to
   support *me* into Belgium instead.
   Why should I give *you* that supply center?
```

```
Lance>    U risk leavn Bur open? Nes go Ruh to
   Bur? Bad 4 u
Lance>    U there?
Booker>   I am; I was considering it. Very
   well, I will support your English Channel
   fleet into Belgium. Just keep in mind that
   you owe me a favor in return.
Lance>    Thx
```

Cassandra (Austria): Vicki looked at the board. "I'm going to powder my nose. Cassie, come with."

"I thought you ladies only did that at restaurants," Evander said.

"We never miss a chance to make out in the bathroom," she replied.

Nestor laughed. "That's my girl."

She took me by the hand and led me there. "Close the door," she said, and I did. She sat on the edge of the bathtub and patted the space next to her.

Once I was sitting, she whispered to me, "Give me Greece."

It took me a moment to realize she was referring to the country. "Why are we whispering?" I whispered back at her.

She giggled. "You never know who's listening. Come on. You can take Italy instead. I've got my back against the wall and I need those units to defend against Jeff."

I pretended to think it over. Of course my answer was yes. She squealed and hugged me.

[How Cassandra and Victoria met and became friends]

Victoria (Turkey): It was freshman year, first week. Three lesbians, one junior and two seniors, were leaning against the lockers and putting the moves on this Asian girl. She was hugging her books, looking down at the ground.

The older girls had warned me about them. They'd pretend they were spreading the news about the LGBTQ club to the froshes so they could get first pass at the fresh meat. Said it was open to "allies" whenever a girl told them she was het. No one ever taught those chickenhawks how to take no for an answer.

Cassie lifted her hand to push her hair back behind her ear, so I jumped forward, grabbed her wrist before she could wrap it back around her books and said, "C'mon, girl! We gotta go!" and pulled her off, down the hall.

One of them shouted, "You didn't get the flyer!" and I said, "Stick it in her locker!" Didn't break my stride. Cassie had to run to keep up.

When we were away from them, she thanked me. Became friends. And we stayed friends, all the way through high school.

[How Jeffrey and Lance met and became friends]

Jeffrey (Russia): We were both into anime back in junior high. I know, I know, these days a lot of people are, but we were way over the top about it. Total *otaku*. My mom hated it, because she's Chinese and not a big fan of Japanese stuff. But she let it slide because I was making friends. And the right type of friends: the smart ones who did well in school and stayed out of trouble.

Lance was way down there on the popularity scale. Lower than me, even. Did you ever see a photograph of him from seven years ago? ... Well, if you had, you'd know what I mean.

That was half of it. I'm convinced that the other half was his unlucky name. He told me once that his dad chose it because Lance Armstrong had just won his first Tour de France titles around then. Probably thought, "Sports hero. No one's going to pick on my son because his name's Lance, right?"

Then by 2012 Armstrong was dodging doping accusations. Sued left and right. And back in sixth grade, kids started calling him names.

You know the deal with name-calling: if the insults aren't memorable enough, it fizzles out or even backfires. And at first, what they came up with was pretty lame: "Lance Armstrong", "Doper", s--- like that.

Then some kid hit on "One-Nut Lance", and it took off like f---ing wildfire. Three months of that, then it was summer break.

I met him in seventh grade. He was wearing a yellow rubber bracelet, and when he told me his name, I asked him if that's why he had a Livestrong on his wrist. He held it up so I could see it. It was one of those parody bracelets The Onion sold. Had "Cheat to Win" on it. That day, after school, Lance told me all about the year before. Told me it was going to be his slogan there on out.

The kids got bored and moved on the way kids do. And no one called him "One-Nut Lance" again for a while.

[How Ollivander and Booker met and became friends]

Booker (France): There really is not that much to the story of how I met Ollivander. We were in accelerated math classes together, and there was an after-school chemistry program we both attended our freshman years. He introduced himself and asked that I call him ... Evander. I paused there because I had to remind myself not to say Ollivander. He hated the name.

His parents were British, although he had grown up in the States. They were cultured in the way many, perhaps most, Englishmen and -women who attend the top universities are. Their decision to name him after a character in the Harry Potter novels was an uncharacteristic lapse in their usual good taste.

I digress. I took a liking to him immediately. He was, in a word, worldly, in large part to his parents' influence. I remember that he was the only student in our high school with a classical music collection of any breadth. Even here at university, I do not see many students who can effortlessly traverse the worlds of high culture and popular entertainment the way he could. It is not an accident that he both taught me how to play poker and introduced me to the board game we played that day.

I spent afternoons at his apartment—this was before his parents divorced and he moved with his mother to Bernal Heights—listening to his albums and doing homework together. Those are my happiest memories of high school. It is hard to explain, but when I was with him, I felt the way one does when cresting a hill and seeing the new land that lay ahead.

His parents invited my family over for dinner three years ago, and my mother was fully taken in by their sophistication. My father? He smiled at their anecdotes and lifted his eyebrows at

Ollivander's precocity.

Eventually we took our leave. I sat in the front passenger seat as my father drove. That was when he told me that he had enjoyed himself and he was, on balance, glad of our friendship.

I did not miss the "on balance", and so I asked him what was in the pan on the other side of the scales. "It's hard to explain. There was a … quality to his banter that seemed strange to me."

"Maybe he gets it from his English parents?"

"No, not quite. It's—"

"Baby, let the boy have his damn friends without overanalyzing erry single thing," my mother said.

"We code-switchin' back to black now we away from the white folk?" I asked.

"Boy, you wait 'til we get home. I'll take a switch to yo' black a--," my father said, and we laughed. My brother took out his earphones to ask what was so funny and we tormented him for the rest of the trip with our refusals to provide him with an explanation.

… No, I am still here. I was finding it remarkable that you managed to get that from me. You are quite the skilled interviewer. I see now how you managed to get Nestor to talk to you.

[How Nestor and Victoria met]

Nestor (Germany): I had this idea when I made JV football my freshman year that being a player meant playing the numbers. Hitting on everything that moved, trying to impress by telling them I was on the team.

I had no game. Turns out I didn't need any. Number five, Constance Kwak, shoots me down right in the hall right next to her locker, and I hear laughter behind me. Two girls, one white, one Asian, are watching the whole thing. They're trying to cover their mouths with their books, like that could ever actually work.

I go over and ask, "So you thought that was funny, huh?"

The white one stops laughing long enough to reply, "No, I would never." Still smiling.

I'm thinking of telling them off, but I don't have the energy after I just got dissed and dismissed. I just shake my head and turn to walk away. That's when the white girl asks me, "Aren't you going to hit on me?"

I look over my shoulder and say, "Don't have time."

"My name is Vicki. Come back when you do."

Austria

```
F ADR S A Tri → Ven
A Ser → Alb
A Tri → Ven
```

England

```
F ENG → Bel
F NTH C A Yor → Nwy
A Yor → Nwy
```

France

```
A Bur S F ENG → Bel
F MAO → Por
A Spa Holds
```

Germany

```
F Den Holds
A Kie → Mun
A Ruh → Hol
```

Italy

```
A Tus → Tun
F TYS C A Tus → Tun
A Ven → Pie
```

Russia

```
F BOT → Swe
F Rum → Sev
A Ukr → Rum
A War → Gal
```

Turkey

```
A Ank → Con
A Bul → Gre
F Con → Bul.ec
```

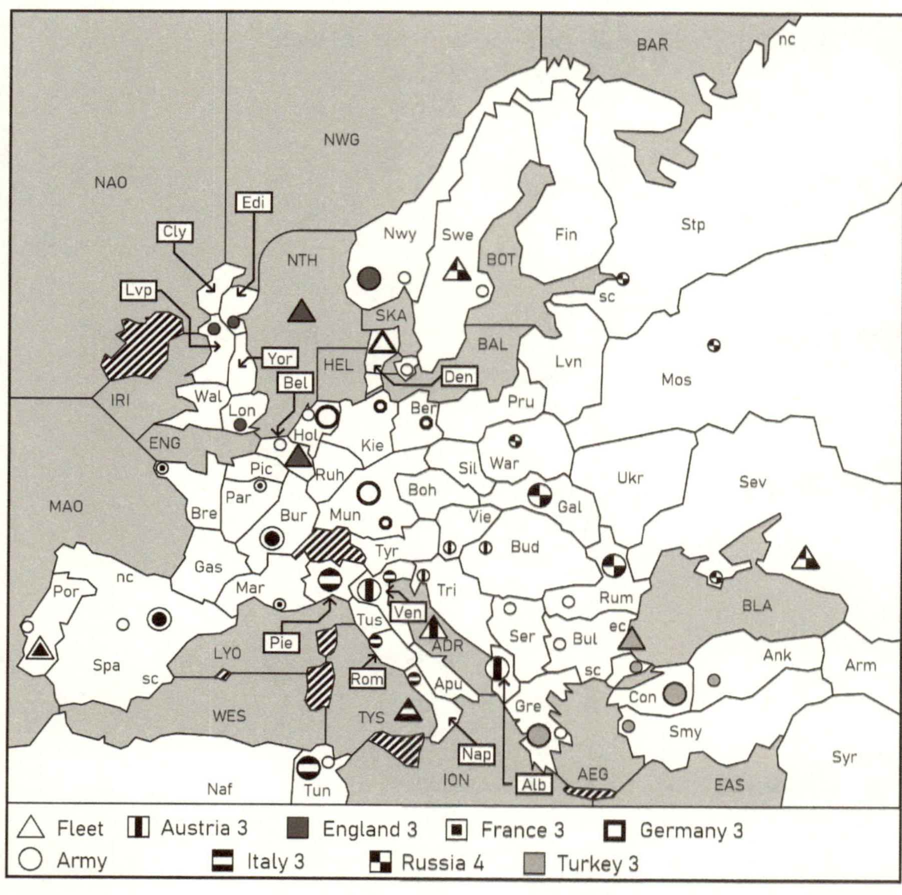

Figure 5 -- Game Map, Start of Winter 1901

Winter
1901

[Reactions to the orders of fall 1901]

Ollivander (Italy): When the page refreshed with the results of the Fall 1901 moves, I turned the laptop around so everyone could see.

First thing anyone said was Jeff asking Vicki, "You went to the east coast of Bulgaria, huh?"

"What?" She peered at the screen. "I didn't know I was doing that." This was one of those special cases I mentioned: three coastal territories have two noncontiguous coasts, and Bulgaria is one of those. Its east coast borders the Black Sea, and the south coast borders the Aegean. Vicki had moved to the coast that would potentially put her into conflict with Jeff. "So now I'm trapped?"

"No, all you have to do is move your fleet to Constantinople, then to the south coast," Jeff explained. "Two turns."

"I'm sure she'll get right on that," Lance said. "No one's going to bring up Italy? What were you thinking, Evander?"

"Bet I know," Jeff answered. "You were setting yourself up to take Marseilles, weren't you? But that would only work if Cassie agreed not to take Venice."

"Instead you f---ed him over." Nestor said. "Respect." He put out his fist for her to bump, but she didn't notice. Or pretended she didn't. She was staring at the game board on the other table.

That left Booker. He had that look he always did whenever he was thinking hard about something.

Lance (England): Evander picked up the laptop and started moving the wooden pieces, checked that he had it correct. Then the laptop dinged to let us know it was winter, and he told us to figure out our builds in the next five minutes.

We all had out our phones and were clicking away when Cassie said, "Wait a minute, I only get one? But I took Serbia and Venice!"

Booker explained it to her. "If you are newly occupying a supply center in that year, you have to have a unit in that territory at the end of the year for it to count."

She shook her head in frustration. "I just don't get this game."

"Could have fooled me," I said. "Taking Venice before the year was out? Impressive."

So everyone got two more units, except Cassie, who got one, and Evander, who stayed even.

Jeffrey (Russia): No big surprises in the builds, from what I remember. You got the play-by-play from the website up on your monitor?

Good. Okay, so I'm looking, and the only takeaway is that France put an army in Paris instead of a fleet in Brest, and England didn't build a fleet in Liverpool. Liverpool would maybe have been slightly less aggressive towards France than the London build? But I could imagine that Booker and Lance agreed to put as much pressure on Nestor as possible, so maybe Booker told Lance to build his fleets where he did.

Italy? Wait, remind me what I said. … Huh. No, that's a good point. But it was the only explanation that made sense at the time.

You know … looking at the map, it's still the only explanation that makes sense to me *now*.

Cassandra (Austria): After we got our new units on the board and it was spring of 1902, I gave Booker the sign to follow me to the back porch. He put on that quizzical look he had and with a shrug, he did.

"Are you proposing an alliance? Divide Italy's supply

centers?"

"No," I replied. "But you can take Tunisia. I won't stop you."

"That is acceptable for now, but we will have to revisit the issue soon. Did you wish to discuss an attack on Munich?"

"No, that's not it either. It's … what's the deal with Evander?"

"What do you mean?"

"I don't understand his moves. He was trying to attack you?"

Booker checked the time. "I will have to give you the short version. Under different circumstances, were Italy to move its fleet from the Tyrrhenian Sea to the Gulf of Lyon in the spring of 1902, it could support its army from Piedmont into Marseilles." He showed me on the map on my phone.

"Okay, but it'd be the easiest thing to stop him, right? You've got two armies next to Marseilles you could use to keep him out."

"It would tie up my units. Then if Italy allied with England, they could execute a pincer maneuver on me."

"Is that what he was doing? I didn't see those two talk."

"Do not forget about the chat window on the site. But this is all moot, as this plan required Austria not to take Venice. He miscalculated, and now he is in real trouble." Another look at his watch. "I have to go."

"Wait, just one thing: Evander and I didn't have an agreement. I swear."

"Whether or not you did, I have no issue with your decision. The game requires betrayals. They are only objectionable if they are ultimately ineffective or aesthetically displeasing."

Victoria (Turkey): I messaged Lance to join me on the front porch,

```
Vicki>    fr porch 2 min?
Lance>    ??? k.
```

and when he got there, I asked him if I could ask him a question.

"Anything for you, my sweet." I rolled my eyes and he smiled. "What is it?"

"What's Evander up to?"

That grin he had on disappeared. "You heard something?"

"No, I mean it's … okay, I barely get this game. I mean, bare-ly."

"Could've fooled me. You're doing really good so far."

"Yeah, thanks. Anyway, why's he losing so bad?"

Lance was wondering why I was wondering, I could tell by his expression. Finally he looked away, bit the side of his upper lip for a sec, and told me, "You gotta understand that this isn't a game like chess or *go*, where a grandmaster will always crush a novice. Force one of the ten best players in the world to be Italy, put him in a game with six halfway decent opponents, and he'll go down first if they know who he is. They'll read him as a threat and he won't get enough help from anyone at the table to stay alive.

"So that's why Evander took a gamble on taking one of Booker's territories before he or anyone else knew what was going on. Didn't work, but that doesn't mean he was wrong to try."

"Okay. I mean, I guess that makes sense."

"Sure. You want to talk about getting together?"

"An alliance? We're on opposite sides of the board."

"… yeah. No, you're right. Too soon. Well, see you inside."

[How Lance and Jeffrey met Ollivander and Booker]

Lance (England): Freshman year, I was walking down the hall to my next class and I heard someone talking about how the Terrans needed to be nerfed. Stopped me in my tracks.

It was a white guy talking to David Kim. I knew Dave from one of my classes, but I didn't know the white guy. I asked him if he was talking about Starcraft II, like I didn't already know the answer, and of course he said yes. He introduced himself, told me his name was Evander. I gave him my handle and said we should fight it out online sometime.

We spent way too much time playing. Enough that Jeff and Booker were looking over our shoulders and back-seat driving us. We started playing two on two just because it was less annoying that way. And then we decided to hang out IRL, like my mom and dad keep telling me normal people do.

[How Cassandra met Ollivander, Booker, Lance, and Jeffrey]

Cassandra (Austria): It was through Vicki. We would spend time together on weekends that first semester freshman year. She was a … I'm not saying this to be snarky, but she was a girly girl. And I loved it. It was so much fun hearing her talk about the boys she thought were hot, clothes, makeup YouTubers, stuff like that.

Then, one time in October as we were leaving school, she told me she couldn't hang out that coming Saturday. "I've got a date!"

"Oh, that's nice," I told her. "With whom?"

She started giggling. "You know that guy who was hitting on Constance that one time?"

And I replied, "Very funny. Who are you really going out with?"

"His name is Nestor, and I'm really going out on a date with him."

"Oh my God."

"What? He's cute!"

"Vicki, you know how many girls he made passes at before Constance? At least two that same day!"

That's when we ran into Lance and Jeff. Lance said, "Vicki! We're playing videogames this Saturday! My house, and we'll have a PlayStation 4 *and* an Xbox One!"

"Nerd!" she said, laughing. "Can't join you guys, because *I* have a date!"

"Oh. Well, maybe next time?"

"You know what? You should invite my friend Cassie to dork out with you."

Jeff stepped up. "Yeah, Cassie. You should come over so we can all say mean things about Vicki behind her back."

She punched him in the shoulder. "Gotta go, text me later and tell me how it went!"

My parents were going to say no, but I told them Lance's dad would be there to chaperone and they relented. And that was where and when I met Evander and Booker.

[Nestor and Victoria's first date]

Nestor (Germany): My father advances me twenty bucks from my allowance and tells me to spend it wisely. I complain that it isn't enough, try to get my mother on my side. She isn't having it either. "Be creative, *conejito*. Girls like it when they know you're making an effort."

I'm thinking maybe my grandpa will back me up, but he makes it oh for three: "Listen to your mother. Use everything I've taught you, keep your wits about you, and you will prevail."

So I fire up the internet to find the perfect first date idea for a man low on cash. That's when I hit on the Palace of Fine Arts. I tell Vicki I'll come by her place and we'll go there. She tells me her dad will drop her off and pick her up after instead. I'd be mad, but it means I won't have to pay for her Muni tickets.

One o'clock they show up, her dad looks me up and down like I'm major sus, shakes my hand and tells me to bring her back to that same spot at four.

Vicki asks me what I've got planned, and I tell her that I thought we'd walk around and talk.

"So you weren't going to spend anything on me, is that it?"

She has her arms crossed, weight on one foot, hip out to the side, like she's low-key pissed at me. I can't tell if she's pretending or not, so I figure I have nothing to lose when I tell her, "Those boys throwing money at you are trying to make up for their shortcomings, if you know what I mean."

We hear this guy say "Ha!" in a loud and deep voice before we see him and his wife coming up to us on the sidewalk. Big black guy. Points at me and says, "You damn right, *ese*."

His wife shakes her head and she says, "They teenagers. What's *your* excuse for being cheap and triflin'?" She apologizes for her husband and they walk on. When I turn back to Vicki? She's smiling.

We stroll through those colonnades and look around. "One

hundred years," I say. "It's why I brought you here. Won't you want to tell your kids you saw it on the centennial?"

"My 'kids'? How old *are* you?"

"I'm fifteen. You know what I mean. Tell anyone."

"I guess."

The next couple of hours are just talking. Mostly about school, movies we'd seen and wanted to see, you know, s--- like that. Thinking back, I can't even remember what that place looked like, because I was locked in on that conversation, the words coming out, smooth as silk. I could pretend that's because I had some great game with the ladies back then, but I already told you that wasn't it. It was ….

My grandfather, one of the books he told me about was by this guy. I forget his name, something Eastern European. Anyway, he came up with this idea of "flow". Like being in the zone where everything is just zero effort. I got that sometimes running the perfect slant so the ball just *slid* into my hands. But never like it was on that date with her.

We walk over to a coffee shop and sit down, and that's when Vicki says, "So I heard tell you're on the JV team."

"Not for long. One year, two at the most, I'll be varsity."

"Maybe I should start dating you when that happens. Play the field 'til then."

"Yeah? Maybe I'll date one of the hotter girls that'll be knocking down my door."

"So if I go steady with you now, you'll dump me when you make varsity?"

I'm tripping over my tongue, trying to think how to reply to that when I catch what she's saying. "Does that mean you want to go out with me some more?"

She smiles as her phone vibrates. "My dad's five minutes out." I walk her back and before she gets in the car and rides off, she gets up on her toes and kisses me on the cheek.

Later on, she admitted to me she was a little mad I cheaped out on her on our first date. That married couple made her come around, give me a chance. Funny how dumb luck can change our lives, huh?

[Jeffrey and Cassandra's dates]

Jeffrey (Russia): Cassie and me? We went out a couple of times, first a movie then a hike, but those weren't *date* dates. What, she say something different?

Austria
```
F ADR ◊ A Alb ◊ A Ven ◊
Build A Bud
```

England
```
F Bel ◊ F NTH ◊ F Nwy ◊
Build F Edi
Build F Lon
```

France
```
A Bur ◊ F Por ◊ A Spa ◊
Build F Mar
Build A Par
```

Germany
```
F Den ◊ A Mun ◊ A Hol ◊
Build F Kie
Build A Ber
```

Italy
```
A Tun ◊ F TYS ◊ A Pie ◊
```

Russia
```
F Swe ◊ F Sev ◊ A Rum ◊ A Gal ◊
Build F Stp.sc
Build A War
```

Turkey
```
A Con ◊ A Gre ◊ F Bul.ec ◊
Build F Smy
Build A Ank
```

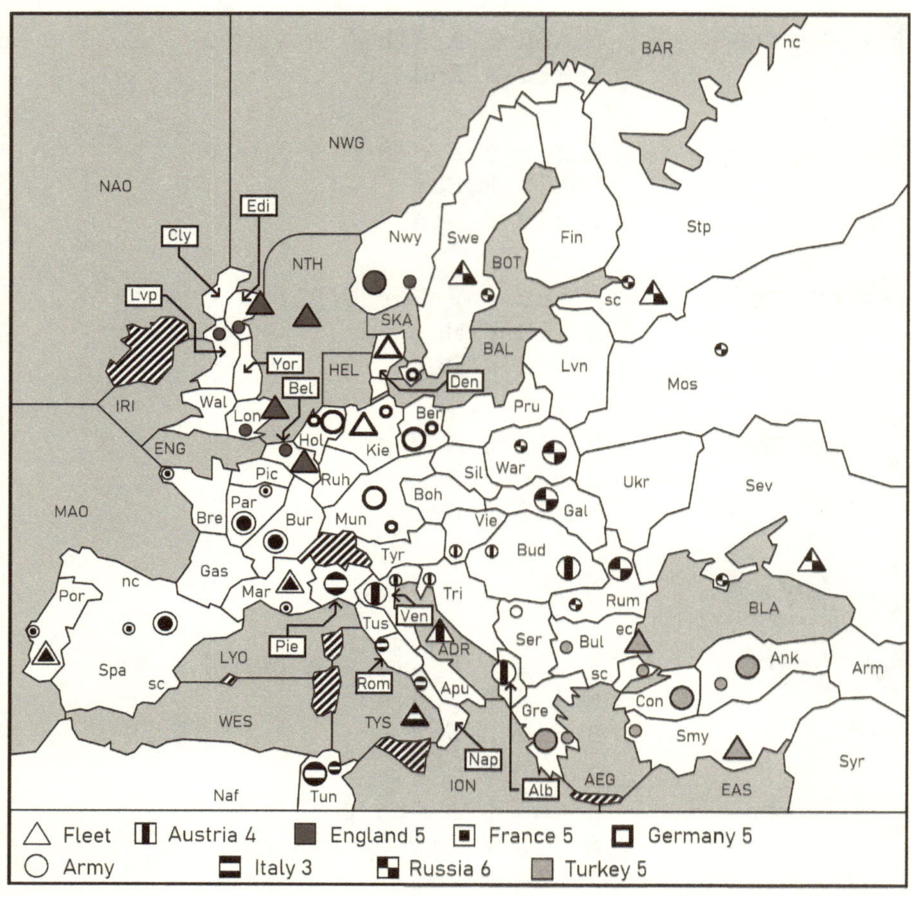

Figure 6 -- Game Map, Start of Spring 1902

Spring
1902

[Diplomatic phase of spring 1902]

Booker (France): Before I tell you about that turn, there is something that has been troubling me about this project of yours. How can you possibly hope to fashion a chronology around these events in any manner that would amount to a "history"?

    … I … I suppose you could do so, as long as the reader will not be confused by it. Well. The spring of 1902. My alliance with England was holding, and so my thoughts turned to Germany and Italy.

    I put an offer to Italy, in the hope that it would accept an alliance. But I would not rely on it to do as I asked, as it would likely be acutely focused on avoiding elimination at the hands of Austria. So I was preparing myself to accept Austria's offer of Tunis in the near term and concern myself with the rest of the Mediterranean another year.

    As for Germany, Munich appeared ripe for the taking. All that was necessary was assistance from Russia or Austria, and it would be mine by fall.

    I thought I would sound out Russia first, but Germany had beat me to it. Jeffrey and Nestor were in the kitchen, where Nestor was talking softly enough that only Jeffrey could hear. And Jeffrey listened with rapt attention.

```
Booker>  Jeffrey, do *not* make a deal with
    Nestor until you have a chance to listen to
    my proposal.
```

Cassandra (Austria): I don't know why it was bugging me, but it was. I got my chance to put the question to her while Jeff was stanning Nestor over in the kitchen. "Hey Vicki."

    She held up a finger and I waited for her to finish texting or whatever. "What's up? You want to talk about our moves?"

"Oh, yeah, we should do that. But can I ask you something?"

"What?"

"Why did Evander invite Nestor?"

"Whoa. *Rude*, girl."

"Oh no, no, no—I don't mean it like that at all. It's just, I wouldn't think he'd want to come."

Vicki looked around, made sure no one was in earshot, and said, "You know, me neither. Evander invited me, and when I said I wanted to hang with my boyfriend instead, he told me to bring him along. So I talked Nes into coming."

That made sense to me; I don't even know why I followed up with: "Hey, who was Evander going to ask instead?"

She shrugged. She was in heading back to the kitchen before I could remember to ask her about the moves.

Jeffrey (Russia): So of course I asked him what it was like to be recruited to play Division I ball. That was the coolest thing that'd happened to any of us, and I wanted to hear all about it. I would've brought it up before we started playing, but Nestor and Vicki were out on the back porch, being a couple and … doing couple things, I guess.

"UConn and Arizona State did it the same way. Coaches showed us the weight room, introduced us to the staff, all that. If you're wondering, ASU's facilities were better."

"No doubt. Pac-10 instead of … what's UConn again?"

"Independent. No conference. But the players, they took us out partying. Off. The. *Chain*."

"Yeah? Who's got the hotter girls?"

Nestor smiled. "I only have eyes for Vicki, you know that."

"So if their pitches were the same, and ASU had the better facilities, why'd you choose UConn?"

Nestor looked at his watch. "I'll tell you later. Let's talk about your next orders. You don't have the units to take me on."

"C'mon brah, I wouldn't do that to you."

"I know, relax. So instead? You got to figure out who you *are* gonna go after."

"You're going to tell me your woman's off-limits?"

"You and her go to war, that's just the game, right, *Jefe*? But you ain't lined up to attack any of her stuff. So you go after Cassie. Kick her out of Budapest, you got the units."

"What about England?"

"What are you going to do? You can't take Norway off him. Budapest. Build in the south, hold in the north, and bide your time."

Lance (England): Jeff was on his phone, typing. "Who're you messaging? It can't be Nestor: you were just talking to him."

"Oh, um … I was texting my mom."

"Fine, don't tell me. You're going to want to hear this: Nestor wants me to team up with him to take Sweden."

That got his attention. "No way. He thought you'd agree?"

"The point is to win. He'll team up with me if he can get what he needs out of it."

He scratched his neck. "So you're supporting him into Sweden? Or the other way around?"

"The idea was he'd get Sweden and I'd get St. Petersburg a turn or two from now."

"So why are you telling *me*?"

"Because we're going to set him up and grab his supply centers instead. It's a no-brainer: he's got five up in the north, and you only have two."

"And you don't like him."

I took a deep breath and got the words right in my head. "That's right. It'd be crazy to betray you just to help him."

He bit the corner of his thumb. "The fifteen minutes are almost up, Jeff. You've gotta decide now."

"If I go along with it, what orders do I put in?"

"Sweden to the Baltic Sea. St. Petersburg to the Gulf of Bothnia. And your army in Warsaw to Silesia. You give up Sweden, but it's temporary. You can take it back in the fall, next spring at the latest. Nestor will have to play defense against you, me, and Booker while he's overextended."

He chewed on his nails some more. "We got a minute left. I'll see you in the living room."

Ollivander (Italy): I watched Booker cogitate as the fifteen minutes ticked down. He was pacing in the hall, stealing glances at Jeff and Nestor in my kitchen.

Finally, halfway through the diplomatic phase, he came to me for help. "Move your army to Tyrolia."

"Why?"

"It will not do you any good now, and quite possibly it will not ever. I can keep you out of Marseilles with a single unit."

"And why Tyrolia?"

"You can help me take Munich in the fall."

"In exchange for?"

"I will leave Tunis alone, which will allow you to bring that army back to the peninsula. And once I deploy my fleets, I can aid you in clearing out your Austrian … infestation."

I told him I'd think about it, and he gave me a tight nod before stepping out on the front porch. And that's when Cassie came over.

"Okay, you've got the upper hand. I'm listening."

"I … huh?"

"You came to me to negotiate my surrender, right? You tell me what I have to do to keep you from knocking me out of the game."

"No, that's not it. Whose place did Nestor take?"

"What?"

"Vicki told me Nestor coming was a last-minute thing. So who was going to play before you invited him and he accepted?"

"That's … I … Karthik. But as it happens, he left for India last weekend, so he couldn't have made it anyway." Cassie nodded. "Why did you want to know?"

"Just curious. I don't even know why I was wondering in the first place."

"Glad we could get that settled. So about your move orders this turn?"

"Make me an offer, I guess."

"Move your army out of Venice and I'll help you take Greece from Vicki."

She took her cell out of her back pocket and looked at it. "I'll think about it." She wasn't going to do it. Betraying Vicki, even to the extent of taking a single territory from her, wasn't an idea she would seriously consider until later on that day.

"Don't take too long," I told her, and a minute or so later it was time for us to enter our orders.

[Reactions to the orders of spring 1902]

Victoria (Turkey): Let me look at the map you sent me ... okay, I remember this one. Everyone was talking. Mostly reacting to what Jeff and Nestor did.

Evander snapped his fingers. "St. Monica!"

"Huh?" I asked.

"The patron saint of drunks. Nestor, you be sure to light a candle for her." He laughed and gave Evander the finger.

"Wait, I don't get it," Cassie said.

"Nestor got lucky with Munich," Lance said. "Booker could've just walked in from Burgundy when Nestor moved into Tyrolia. If he'd also moved his army in Paris to Burgundy, he could have supported a hold in Munich in the fall."

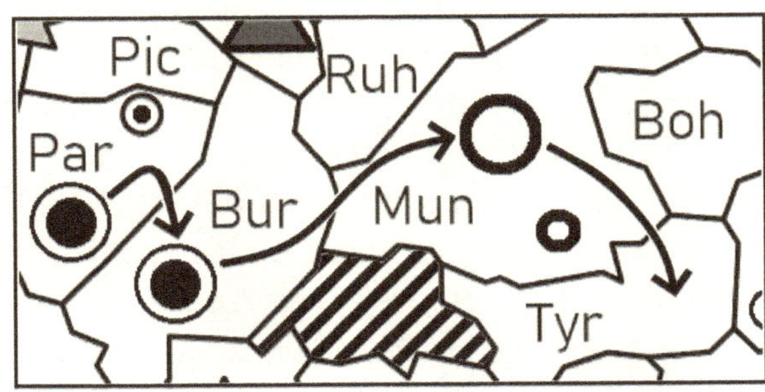

Figure 7 -- How France Could Have Taken Munich in Spring 1902

"I would not have thought to do that," Booker said. "I had assumed that Germany would have ordered its army in Munich to hold."

"But what's he doing with that army in Holland?" Cassie asked. "He's supporting Booker?"

Evander took a deep breath and launched into it. "I'm pretty sure Lance mentioned it in the FAQ, but in case you missed it, the website's code will check that a given order is valid, and it will warn you if it isn't. But it won't prevent you from entering it."

"Right," Nestor said. "Booker, that's why I asked you if you were sure."

"What? What are you talking about?" Booker replied.

"I figured it was some advanced move I didn't understand."

"What? I … you … that …" Booker trailed off.

"So Jeff," Nestor continued, "I guess you didn't take my advice."

"No, I did. See? I moved to Budapest."

"From Rumania?"

"Yeah. Why?"

"Never mind. What's with your fleets in the north?"

Then everyone got quiet, staring at the screen. Evander moved the pieces on the board and said, "Fifteen minutes."

[Lance's father talks about his son]

Lance's father: For quite some time, I debated with myself whether or not to respond to your e-mail. Obviously, I don't have the first-hand knowledge necessary to discuss my son's actions that day. However, I will share with you what I told him when he asked permission to spend that day with his friends. You and the audience for your oral history can decide if my inference is valid.

About six and a half years past, I shared with my son something I had once read in my youth: suffering is not ennobling.

The context for that is that my son was bullied in grade school. Objectively speaking, it wasn't that bad in the sense that it never got physical. But it was unrelenting for a little while.

And he took it out on us. Had his anger, his insults, been directed only at me, it would have been one thing. But his mother couldn't manage to respond stoically. She was truly and deeply hurt by it all.

His demeanor had improved considerably by the summer's end before his seventh grade. This was, I judged, as receptive as he would ever be for a heart-to-heart talk. I connected the dots for him: he had redirected the abuse he had been dealt at his mother and me. We had held our tongues in the past, but he couldn't again mistreat the ones who loved him the most. Nor should he meekly accept those slings and arrows, as it would not make him a better person.

Jump ahead to his freshman year. There was an incident in the first semester, the news of which managed to make its way back to me. I was informed that Lance had held his own without having to throw even a single punch. I felt the pride I imagine other fathers have when their children score touchdowns, hit home runs, and the like. And I felt certain that the seed I had planted in him had flowered and borne fruit years later.

How much easier life would be if only people conformed to the simple models we have in our minds. My son had been bullied, and he was hateful to us in return. And so when he stood up to bullies, he should become a loving son, correct?

Well, not quite. It took me some time, too long, really, to find that my words were not a cure. Not because he acted in the way he had in the past, quite the contrary. After that speech of mine, he was obedient to a fault; he took his studies seriously; he never missed a curfew; and he had no more unkind words for either of us.

But soon we learned that the anger wasn't gone. He had instead turned it inward. He would punch his desk at odd intervals, when there was nothing that could possibly serve as a provocation. His mother found him weeping at the kitchen table late one night. And she, in turn, took it quite hard. Even harder than before.

Therapy was the inevitable next step. And there were adjustments that followed. We let him have more time with his friends, but we insisted that he spend that in their physical presence, not just online shooting at them.

And because it seemed to work, we didn't question our luck. There's something you should know: you will become deeply, deeply superstitious when you are a parent. When things go smoothly, the idea of changing anything in your child's life will fill you with dread.

Lance did really well in school; you don't get into Harvey Mudd without displaying a real aptitude for math and science. More than one of our friends confessed to wishing their kids were more like our son. As I said, he was deferential, studious, prompt, and never openly hateful to us. And he was no longer crying or hurting himself.

But once my wife and I were through the worst of it, we wanted a little more. We wanted to feel like a family: mother, father, and son. We wanted to spend that time before he left us being happy together. I wasn't going to refuse him one day with his friends a week after graduating. All I wanted him to know was how much he meant to us and how important every moment we had left would be.

He took it very badly. He kept insisting that he had looked forward to that day for weeks, that it was the most important thing to him, and he would never forgive us if we failed to let him have it. I had to use everything therapy had taught us about de-escalation to talk Lance down and let him know he had our permission, as long as he saw where we were coming from.

The materials you sent me, if I can take them at face value, lead me to believe that there was something we all, even the psychologist, missed. The anger and the cruelty he had displayed years prior weren't gone. Merely waiting.

Austria

    F ADR C A Alb → Apu ◊ A Alb → Apu ◊
    A Ven → Rom ◊
    A Bud → Ser -- Failure, Attack str. inadequate
        Retreat to Tri

England

    F Bel Holds ◊ F Edi → NWG ◊
    A Nwy Holds ◊
    F Lon → NTH -- Failure, Attack str. inadequate
    F NTH → SKA -- Failure, Attack str. inadequate

France

    A Bur → Ruh ◊ F Mar → LYO ◊
    A Par → Pic ◊ F Por → MAO ◊ A Spa → Gas ◊

Germany

    F Kie → HEL ◊ A Mun → Tyr ◊
    A Hol S A Par → Pic -- Failure, Order invalid
    A Ber → Sil -- Failure, Attack str. inadequate
    F Den → SKA -- Failure, Attack str. inadequate

Italy

    F TYS C A Tun → Nap ◊ A Tun → Nap ◊
    A Pie → Tus ◊

Russia

    A Gal S A Rum → Bud ◊ F Stp.sc → BOT ◊
    F Sev → BLA ◊ A Rum → Bud ◊ F Swe → BAL ◊
    A War → Sil -- Failure, Attack str. inadequate

Turkey

    A Ank → Arm ◊ F Smy → EAS ◊
    F Bul.ec → Rum ◊ A Con → Bul ◊
    A Gre → Ser -- Failure, Attack str. inadequate

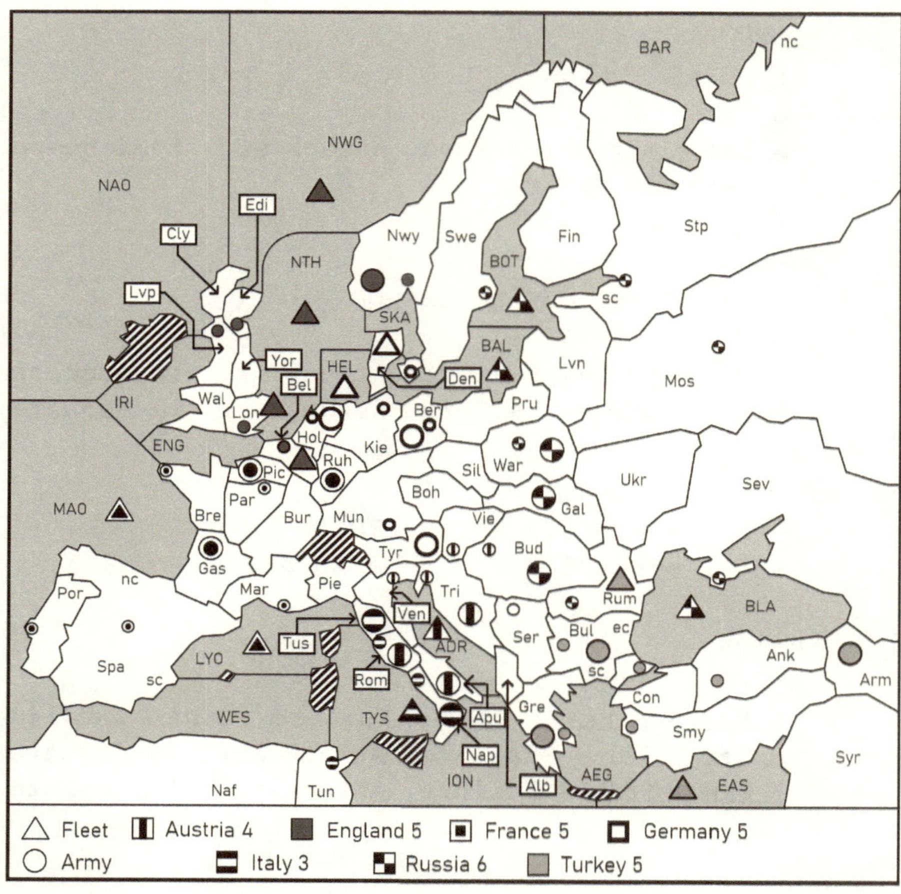

Figure 8 -- Game Map, Start of Fall 1902

Fall

1902

[Diplomatic phase of fall 1902]

Jeffrey (Russia): I looked at the game board and counted all the ways I'd screwed up. One, I should have tried moving my army in Galicia to Budapest with support from my army in Rumania. It wouldn't have worked, because Vicki's order to move her fleet from Bulgaria to Rumania would have cut support ... yeah, that's another one of the rules. Don't beat yourself up, the game's confusing as b---s sometimes. But I'd still have Rumania.

Two, I should have moved my army from Warsaw to Ukraine. And three, I shouldn't have moved my fleet from Sevastopol into the Black Sea. Two and three combined to make one big f---up.

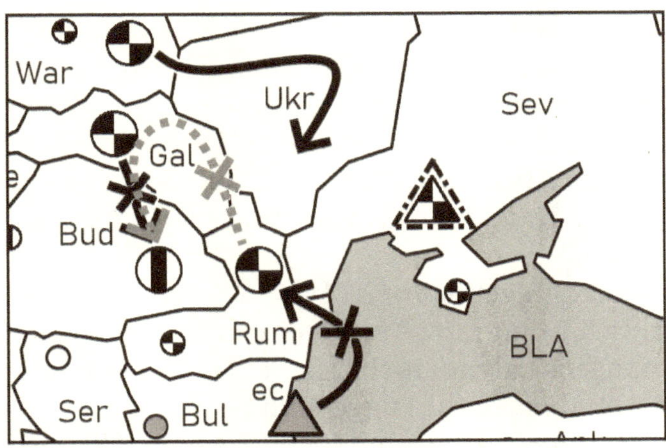

Figure 9 – Orders Russia Failed to Make in Spring 1902: (1) Didn't Move with Gal, Support with Rum; (2) Didn't Move War to Ukr; (3) Didn't Hold Sev

So I was about to finish out the year in worse shape than I should've been in, unless I got lucky and Vicki made the exact wrong moves for her. When I did the math, I thought, best case, she and I would both be up one, but worst case, she'd be up two and I'd be flat on the year. And there's no way Nestor wouldn't know I was up to something with my fleets and me trying to move my army into Silesia. But at least I didn't have to worry about England, right?

Booker (France): I had been avoiding it, but it was time to speak with Nestor. He was out on the front porch, taking a sip out of a stainless steel flask.

He held it out to me. "Want some, Data?" I should explain: people started calling me Data during my junior year. Finally I decided to look to Wikipedia's disambiguation page for the explanation: Data was a robot in one of the *Star Trek* series. Weak tea, as far as insults go. I cannot imagine why anyone would think that would bother me.

"No thank you. Do you want to explain what that was?"

"What what was?"

"I never told you to put in that support order. Why on Earth would I?"

"I guess I misunderstood."

"You know that is not true. We never spoke; we never messaged. There was nothing to misunderstand at all."

He flopped his free hand around, as if to say he was giving up on trying to convince me. "All right. You want to talk moves?"

"Very well. Have your armies in Berlin and Tyrolia hold where they are."

"And what do I get out of it?"

"Nothing," I told him. "But seeing as how you are deciding to put in nonsensical orders that fail to benefit you in any way, I thought I would make the suggestion."

Nestor held up his flask in mocking salute. "That's the spirit."

Ollivander (Italy): One counterintuitive thing about the game dynamic: the worse you're doing, the more eager people are to make deals with you. Up to a point, that is.

Booker came back inside and made his pitch. "We need to take out Austria and then Turkey."

"'We'?"

"If you believe there is some other person who can help you come back from your current … predicament, I urge you to team up with her."

"Guess it *would* be a 'her'," I said. "What's your offer?"

"You let me get my fleets through to the Ionian Sea and beyond. If you move your fleet back to the peninsula, it will not be necessary to transit through Tunis."

I paced around, looking at the ground. "There really is not much more than that," he said. "I will be moving from the mid-Atlantic to the west Mediterranean as preparation." He looked at his watch, gave me an impersonal wave goodbye, and walked back to my kitchen.

Cassie was next. "Hey."

"Hey. Shall we negotiate?"

"Um, I guess. What should I do?"

I sighed. "You don't really get this game, do you?"

"I really don't. Well?"

"All right. You have the Vienna, Venice, and Trieste supply centers. You took Rome, but lost Budapest. So you're going to have to keep Germany and Russia out of them."

"And you too."

"Yes. I'm in a position to retake Venice. You have three units that you can move to those three territories." I walked over to the map and showed her.

She thought it over. "But then you can squeeze me out of Rome."

"True. That's what happens when you get overextended and you don't have ironclad alliances to protect your flanks."

Cassie ate up another thirty seconds staring at the board. "Is that what happened to you?"

"Huh?"

"You're in trouble, right? I mean, maybe there's some strategy I'm not getting, but it doesn't seem like you're on anyone's side."

I smiled and replied, "Think it over. Because the only alternative I can see is to talk to Nestor and Jeff and make deals with both of them."

```
Cassie>  Jeff, you have a second?
```

```
Jeff>     Wat up?
Cassie>   Want to deal?
Jeff>     k. How?
Cassie>   I support you to Vienna, you support
   me to Serbia.
Cassie>   Well?
Jeff>     k.
Cassie>   Good. Take it now, before Nestor
   grabs it. If that happens, the deal is off.

Cassie>   Nestor, can you spare a moment?
Nestor>   make it quick
Cassie>   I want to make a trade.
Nestor>   what 4 what
Cassie>   You take Vienna with my support from
   Trieste, then you help me get Budapest next
   year.
Cassie>   Deal?
Nestor>   deal
Cassie>   You need to take it this turn, or
   Jeff will grab it.
```

Lance (England): And now I had to manage my alliance with Jeff. Things up there were balanced on a knife's edge, and I had to get those ducks lined up or however that saying goes for what I had planned.

```
Lance>    Jeff need to talk back porch
Lance>    Need 5 min dont wait til last sec
```

I got out there and bit my nails and watched the clock.

Jeff joined me with four minutes left. I wanted to yell at him for cutting it too close, and I would have, except I needed the little s--- on my side.

"He didn't go for Sweden," was the first thing he said.

"Surprised me too. I don't understand what he was thinking."

"I can tell you what he's thinking now, though. When you

didn't support him from Norway, he knew that you betrayed him."

"He betrayed me right back. You notice how he didn't move from Denmark?" I asked.

"Yeah."

"It's because he was teaming up with Booker instead."

Jeff shook his head. "No way. Whatever that f--- that support order was, it wasn't teaming up."

"Okay, but here's the thing. You saw them out there talking, didn't you? They're definitely planning something *now*. And between the two of them, they have the units to force me out of Belgium."

"Yeah … ain't nothing I can do about that."

"Except take Germany's other dots from him. We start with Holland."

Jeff took our sweet time thinking about it. Finally f---ing asked, "What do I do?"

"Okay, move your fleets into Sweden and Prussia."

"Prussia? Why Prussia?"

"You want it close to Berlin, but you can't take it this turn. If you try, he'll know you're against him."

"What about my armies?"

"Do whatever you need to with your other units, but hold in Warsaw for now so he doesn't get too suspicious. You can move it to Silesia spring of next year if we need it there."

There was a minute left on the clock when he said okay. My a--h--- unclenched and we headed over to the living room.

[How Lance met Victoria]

Jeffrey (Russia): They met in grade school.

[What Victoria was like in grade school]

Jeffrey (Russia): Okay, in high school, Vicki was the approachable hot girl. You know the type, right?

Well, back in grade school Vicki was the approachable maybe

kinda halfway cute if you squinted just right girl. If she'd been as good looking back in grade school as she ended up being in high school, she'd never have had the time of day for a guy like Lance. She might have even piled on when everyone started calling him "One-Nut".

When Lance introduced me to her in seventh grade, she was still that one girl who ran with a bunch of dorks. I don't know if I was able to see it when Lance couldn't because I met her later on, but I could tell she wanted to be a regular girl, doing regular girl things. Having girlfriends to talk girl stuff with. Being with handsome guys instead of with us. I mean, could you blame her?

And she was on her way. Her braces would be coming off before she was in high school. And she was … I'm trying to figure how to say this so I won't sound like a perv. How's about: "She was blossoming into her young womanhood."

I was talking with someone who knew us from some of the classes we were all in together. He told me that the best metaphor to describe Vicki was that she was like a mirage.

… "Simile"? Fine, simile, whatever. You'd think that she was close. Just a little further, wait a little longer, and she'd be near enough to touch. But the thing that you didn't get until it was too late was how she was moving away from you even faster. And then you had that moment like you were a cartoon cat turning into a giant lollipop with "SUCKER" on the wrapper in great big capital letters.

[Reactions to the orders of fall 1902]

Nestor (Germany): Oh, I *definitely* remember that one. I'm looking at the screen, all that action in the south. I don't get Vienna like Cassie promised, and after checking out all those little arrows, I figure out what happened. She lied about supporting my move from Tyrolia, so when Jeff tried to take Vienna too, we both bounce.

I find out later from Jeff that she promised to support him too. Slick move Cassie made. Back then, I'm surprised she had it in her to pull that trick on us.

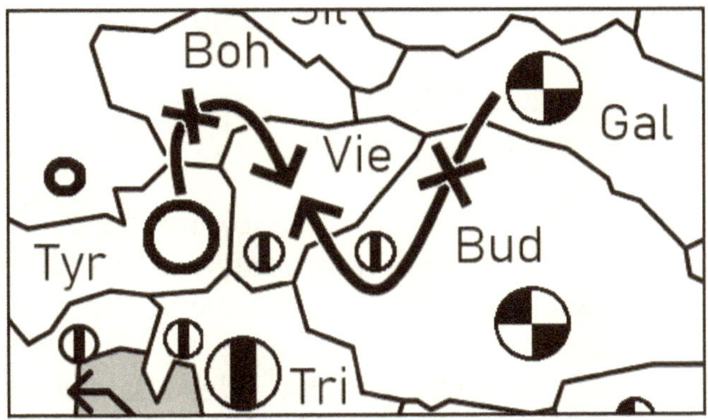

*Figure 10 -- Germany (Moving from Tyrolia) and
Russia (Moving from Galicia) Bounce in Vienna*

Jeff's having a bad year. He'd tried to take one of Vicki's supply centers from her because he knew she had the juice to take Sev from him. ... Sevastopol. "Sev" for short. You're the one who wanted to write about this, so f---ing keep up.

He could have taken back Rumania and kept her out of Sev with his fleet in the Black Sea. Sure, she'd get Serbia, and he wouldn't get Vienna. But it would've been better than the mess he's in because he thought hoping hard enough would make everything would work out somehow.

That's just the south. He really, *really* messed up in the north.

Cassandra (Austria): Jeff was clutching the sides of his head, taking half a step in every direction. But none of them would return him to the time before he made those mistakes.

"I'm sorry," I told him. "I broke my promise."

He stopped and looked at me. "No, *you* did what you had to to defend your territory. It was *him* who ... who ...." He turned and faced Lance. "You got me with my back to you so you could slip that dagger in, right between my shoulder blades. I'm such a f---ing idiot."

Lance reached out to put a hand on Jeff's shoulder. Jeff jerked it away and ran for the front door. I flinched when he slammed it behind him.

We stood in silence until Evander said, "Someone needs to talk to him."

"Why?" Vicki asked. "Can't we let him cool down first?"

"He lost two units this year. He needs to enter his disband orders."

Vicki offered to text him but I shook my head. "I'll go out and tell him. I don't have to do anything this turn, right?"

Evander nodded. "Just him and Vicki and Lance. The rest of us can take a five minute break."

I went outside. Jeff was on the sidewalk. His arms were crossed and his chin was down on his chest. He wasn't mad anymore. But the look on his face … it was like this one time the two of us …. It's a long story.

He heard my footsteps and said, "Hey."

"Hey. Um, Evander said you have to do something about your units? I don't remember what, exactly."

He took out his cell and started touching his screen. Gave it one last look and shoved it back in his pants pocket. "Are you all right?"

Jeff shook his head but he said, "Yeah, I'm okay."

"Isn't this just the way the game goes? We pretend to be buddy-buddy and then attack when they aren't expecting it?"

"I know, all right? It's … I feel so *stupid*. And I *know* it's only a game, and that makes me feel even dumber for taking it so hard."

I gave his shoulder a tentative touch, and when he didn't move it away, I rubbed his back. "You want to go? We could just leave."

He was so surprised at my offer he forgot how unhappy he was for a second. "You'd do that?"

"If you want me to," I replied.

I was hoping he'd say no. Eventually he did. "Let's go back inside. I should be a good loser."

And before I could catch myself, I said, "That's the spirit."

 *Austria*
    A Apu S A Rom → Nap ◊ A Rom → Nap ◊
    <u>F ADR → Tri</u> -- **Failure, Attack str. inadequate**
    <u>A Tri → Ven</u> -- **Failure, Attack str. inadequate**

 *England*
    F Bel Holds ◊ F Lon → NTH ◊
    F NTH → SKA ◊ F NWG → Nwy ◊ A Nwy → Stp ◊

 *France*
    A Gas → Mar ◊ F LYO Holds ◊
    F MAO → Wes ◊ A Pic → Bur ◊ A Ruh Holds ◊

 *Germany*
    A Ber → Mun ◊ F Den Holds ◊
    F HEL → Kie ◊
    <u>A Hol → Ruh</u> -- **Failure, Attack str. inadequate**
    <u>A Tyr → Vie</u> -- **Failure, Attack str. inadequate**

 *Italy*
    <u>A Nap Holds</u> -- **Failure, Hold str. inadequate**
      <u>Disband</u>
    <u>A Tus → Ven</u> -- **Failure, Attack str. inadequate**
    <u>A TYS → ION</u> -- **Failure, Attack str. inadequate**

 *Russia*
    A War Holds ◊ F Bal → Pru ◊
    F BOT → Swe ◊
    <u>F BLA → Con</u> -- **Failure, Attack str. inadequate**
    <u>A Bud → Ser</u> -- **Failure, Attack str. inadequate**
    <u>A Gal → Vie</u> -- **Failure, Attack str. inadequate**

Turkey
    A Arm → Sev ◊ F Rum S A Arm → Sev ◊
    <u>F EAS → ION</u> -- **Failure, Attack str. inadequate**
    <u>A Bul → Con</u> -- **Failure, Attack str. inadequate**
    <u>A Gre → Ser</u> -- **Failure, Attack str. inadequate**

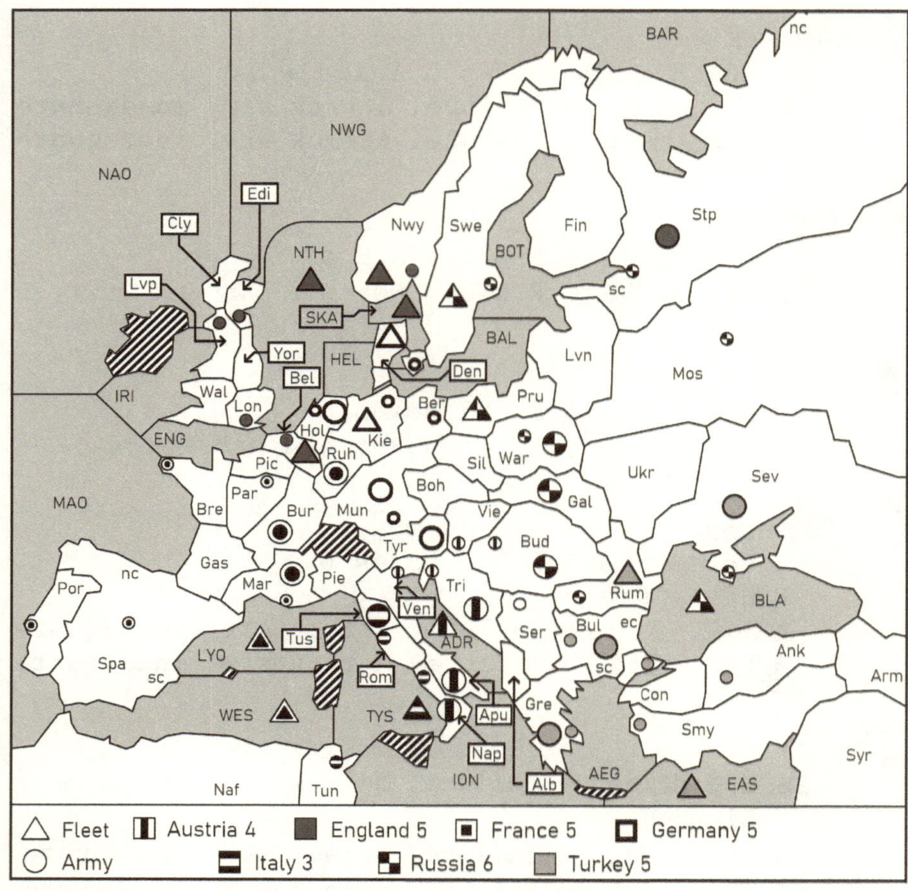

Figure 11 -- Game Map, Start of Winter 1902

Winter
1902

[Cassandra and Jeffrey's first date]

Cassandra (Austria): I didn't realize it *was* a date at first. Those guys started talking about seeing *Creed* when it came out, and Jeff convinced me to go. Then everyone else backed out until it was just us two.

I told my parents about it. My parents are pretty conservative. I don't mean that politically, but they *do* vote Republican. They even voted for Trump. When I asked my father how he could do that, he told me that he knew the president hated Vietnamese people, but he hated black people more, and that was the important thing.

But they were also conservative in the other sense. I was going out to a movie in the middle of the day, but my mother was convinced that this was merely a brief prelude to being ravished by Jeff.

She asked every question you could imagine. Eventually she got around to Jeff's parents. That's when I told her Jeff's father was no longer in the picture.

That was the sort of thing she was hoping I'd say. She blathered on about how he came from a broken home and how awful his parents were that they couldn't stay together. I got angrier and angrier until I screamed at her that Jeff's father died in a car accident when he was only ten.

My father heard and came into my bedroom. He was wagging his finger at me, and that's when I erupted. I was shouting "F--- you" at both of them, and when they threatened to ground me, I was screaming, "F--- you, ground me!" at the top of my lungs back at them.

They left my bedroom. I didn't come out until the next morning. Without another word ever passing between us about it, we'd managed to come to an agreement to forget it ever happened, an uneasy truce preferable to any resumption of hostilities. So when the day came for our date, all my mother told me was to be home by six and keep my cell with me.

It was fun, being with him. After the lights came up, he was blinking away tears but still smiling. He asked me if I liked it, and I told him yes. I didn't, it was so violent that I had to cover my eyes at times, but he was just so *thrilled* by it that I didn't want to bring him down.

He knew I was lying, so he started teasing me. "You're telling me you didn't like seeing Michael B. Jordan with no shirt on?"

"It was okay, I guess."

"Girl, you *lie*." I laughed at that. He took the bus back with me. I had a half hour before I had to be home, so we went to a coffee shop a couple of blocks away and drank hot chocolate and talked.

"It *is* kind of a guy movie," he admitted. "But the rest of the story? I mean, without the boxing?"

That's when I remembered. That huge fight with my parents and until that moment I hadn't managed to make the connection to the movie I'd seen an hour before: Jeff and the main character both lost their fathers. But there's no way I could've brought it up with all those people around. He reached across the table and touched my hand with the tips of his fingers. "Tell you what, I'll make it up to you. You pick what you want to do on our next date."

It was ten 'til six, so we walked back to my apartment. At the door I told him I'd think of something. He kissed me on the cheek before I could pull away and he said he'd see me Monday.

[Cassandra and Jeffrey's second date]

Cassandra (Austria): Let me see … the weekend after Thanksgiving 2015. I told Jeff I wanted to go hiking in Fort Funston. He moaned about how cold it would be, but he acquiesced in short order.

My parents wanted me back early that Sunday. Four o'clock. Jeff picked me up at eleven and we headed out. It took more than an hour to go those five miles, but he spent the bus ride bouncing with excitement, chattering about our freshman year so far. I barely had to speak to keep the conversation going.

When we disembarked and walked to the park from the final bus stop, the conversational pace slowed to a crawl with our huffing and puffing. From time to time I stole glances at him. You see, Jeff didn't exactly cut an athletic figure during his high school years, and I thought that maybe the hike would be too much for him. But instead he was lit from the inside as we made our way to the battery emplacements and then on to the beach.

We stopped at an overlook and watched the waves come in under the mist. And for perhaps a minute, I took in the beauty of it all: the water, the sand, the sun, the rolling hills patched with green. That was when the sweat from my exertions cooled on my body and I shivered and held myself to keep warm.

Jeff had taken off his sweatshirt, although I was unaware of it until he wrapped it around me. I turned to thank him, and that's when he kissed me on the lips.

Before he could do it a second time, I stopped him and delivered the speech I had brought him to that place to give. I liked him, but there was no chemistry. And he was a great guy, and I really hoped he found someone who adored him as much as he deserved to be.

I meant it all, but he just looked more and more crestfallen with every word I uttered. I took off his sweatshirt and draped it over his shoulders.

That was where he fixed me with that look, the one I told you about before, the one he had after Lance betrayed him playing that damned game. Bereft. Alone. Unable to imagine that a happier time would ever arrive.

That walk back to the bus stop was excruciating. He was a few steps ahead to avoid having to see me. Bringing up the rear I took in his slumped shoulders, his now-plodding gait. For the rest of that date I kept hoping that he would recover from the humiliation I dealt him. He didn't, not even by the time the bus got to his stop. He stood up, shook my hand, and left.

When I returned home, I told my mother that I had broken up with Jeff. She looked at me and with icy disinterest replied, "That's nice."

[Reactions to the orders of winter 1902]

Ollivander (Italy): They were as you'd expect. Lance built in London. The only reason to choose Edinburgh would be to move to the Barents Sea to support his army in St. Petersburg, but Jeff wouldn't have the units to dislodge him anyway unless he abandoned Sweden. Liverpool? If you have to build a fleet in Liverpool that early on, it usually means France is knocking at your back door and you're in deep trouble.

Vicki built an army in Constantinople and a fleet in Smyrna. Solid choices, the ones I would have made if I were her. When Lance and I were planning this, we argued over how far ahead she would be by this stage of the game. Two years in and I was on the winning side of that argument.

Jeff was the only one of those three with a real decision on his hands. Of course he was going to disband his Black Sea fleet: it would be of no use to him without a unit on a neighboring coast. So then he had to decide which of his other two fleets and three armies to dissolve. And he picked his army in Galicia.

I thought he might get rid of the fleet in Prussia instead. Keeping that unit meant that he wasn't planning on giving up on his northern holdings. And that meant Lance would have his work cut out for him.

Lance (England): That Russian fleet in Prussia? I expected it. Jeff was going to do whatever he could to take back St. Petersburg from me. Until that happened, I'd have an extra fleet to work with. And I definitely had plans for it.

[Nestor and Victoria's second date]

Nestor (Germany): It was the Saturday right after the first one. Some old black and white movie she wanted to see. The price was right on those tickets, so that was good. That theater was near where she lived, so she told me to come by, pick her up, and we'd walk over.

I text her outside her place, she tells me to ring the bell and her dad'll let me in. He opens the door and shifts the newspaper from his right hand to his left and shakes and he tells me Vicki's getting ready and she'd be out in five and have a seat while I'm waiting.

He sits down in his chair across from mine and it's twenty questions time. I knew this was coming eventually. I just didn't think it'd be on the second date. He starts off easy, stuff like if I grew up in Cali, how school's going.

All of a sudden he reaches across himself and picks up a pen on the table on his left side. "Wait, maybe you can help me out with this." He puts his glasses on and looks down his nose at the newspaper. "'Thirteenth century poet'. Four letters, third one's an 'm'. Any ideas?"

I shrug and he asks about football, how that's going for me so far and if I think the Niners are going to do better than eight and eight in the 2015 season. I say JV's fine so far and the Niners are gonna have a bad one.

"My hope was you'd tell me otherwise, but I'm afraid you're right." Looks at the paper again and says, "'Well-suited name'. Six letters, starts with an 'e'."

"You know you can just Google those, sir."

"That would be cheating, now wouldn't it?"

"But asking me isn't?"

He smiles at me and replies, "Not as long as I share the credit with you." Starts asking about what music I like. Gives me a funny look when I tell him I like all types, like he knows it's a bulls--- answer. He wants me to give a "for example", so I mention Kendrick Lamar. Nice safe choice, at least in San Francisco. Back over to the crossword: "'Foxy'. Seven letters, blank 'u' blank 'p' blank blank blank."

"I think giving you words that mean 'foxy' is going to get me in trouble."

He laughs. "Fair enough."

Moves on to my favorite books, TV shows, movies. I tell him I was reading *The Catcher in the Rye* in English class and liking it so far. Threw in *Watership Down*.

"The book or the movie?" he asks and I tell him both.

He checks out the paper and says, "This one's a real head-scratcher: 'Named'. Six letters, starts with a 'y', ends with a 't'." And before I can reply, Vicki's bedroom door opens.

Later on, Vicki and I are at the movies, and before they start playing the trailers, I bring up her father and all his questions.

"That's what he does."

"You mean being a dad and all?"

"No, I mean that's his job. He's a psychologist. Like he profiles businessmen for companies looking to hire."

"He was reading me."

Vicki rubs my forearm and smiles. "Sorry, shoulda warned you. He made me wait in my room for five minutes so he could do his thing."

"How'd I do?"

"You're the first guy I ever dated. He's got nobody to compare you to."

The lights go down and the movie starts.

Victoria (Turkey): I remember this bit, just because it was so *weird*. My dad made me wait for five minutes before coming out.

When my phone buzzed to let me know it was time, I went to the living room and my dad and Nestor stood up. Dad opened the front door for us and I walked out first. Nestor shook hands and said goodbye.

"It was a pleasure talking to you, Nestor," my dad said.

And Nestor replied, "Yclept. Y-C-L-E-P-T."

Austria

```
F ADR ◊ A Apu ◊ A Nap ◊
A Tri ◊
```

England

```
F Bel ◊ F NTH ◊ F Nwy ◊
F SKA ◊ A Stp ◊
Build F Lon
```

France

```
A Bur ◊ F LYO ◊ A Mar ◊
A Ruh ◊ F WES ◊
```

Germany

```
F Den ◊ A Mun ◊ A Hol ◊
F Kie ◊ A Tyr ◊
```

Italy

```
A Tus ◊ F TYS ◊
```

Russia

```
A Bud ◊ F Pru ◊ F Swe ◊ A War ◊
Disband F BLA
Disband A Gal
```

Turkey

```
A Bul ◊ F EAS ◊ A Gre ◊
F Rum ◊ A Sev ◊
Build F Smy
Build A Con
```

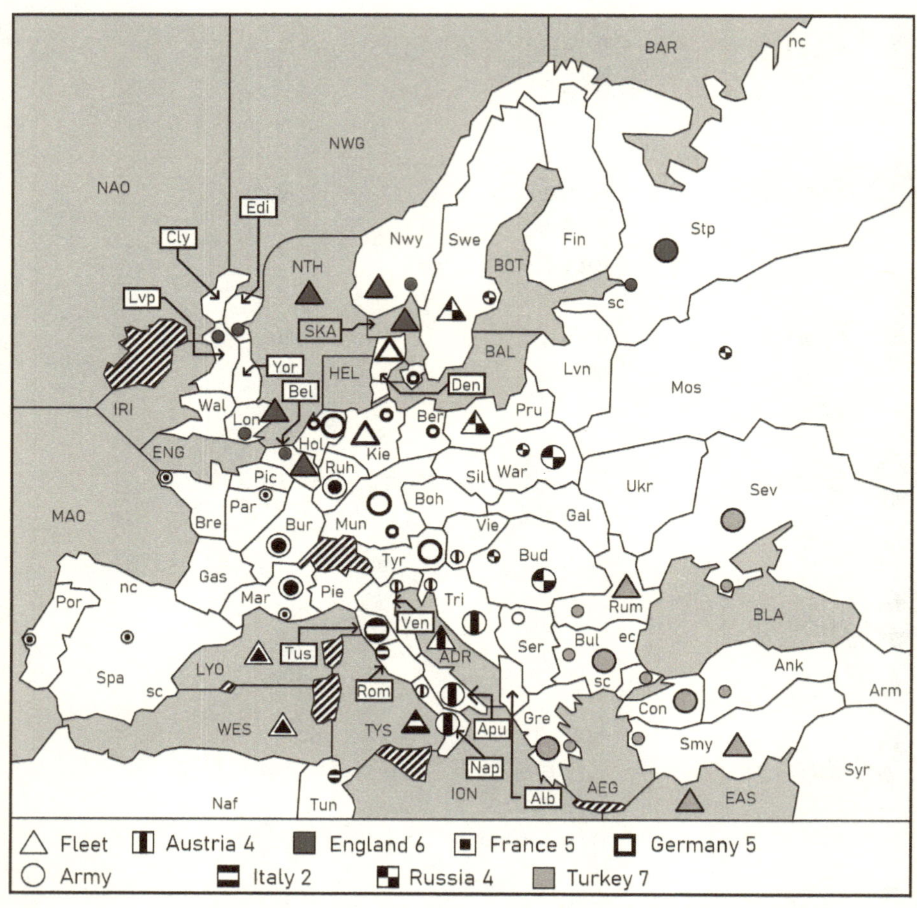

Figure 12 -- Game Map, Start of Spring 1903

Spring
1903

[Diplomatic phase of spring 1903]

Jeffrey (Russia): Wait, before we go on, I gotta ask: how many pages is this gonna be when you put it all together, anyway? You said you're getting all seven of us to do interviews, and you're writing about a lot more than game day, so …

… but … all right, here's why I'm asking. After that last time on the phone? I Googled "oral history", and those articles aren't that long. … Right, so how're you gonna handle all the one-on-one talks we had? I mean, those shorter ones can be all "I said", "he said", "she said" and then kinda put a summary, but this one's gotta have actual … what's that word I'm thinking of? … "Dialogue", yeah. But there's no way we remember the exact words, so how—

"Verisimilitude"? And your prof's good with that? … Well, okay, I guess. Evander told us that he'd be ordering lunch after that turn. Wanted to know if Chinese food was okay with everyone. No one said it wasn't, so he put a takeout menu on the table next to the laptop and told us to look it over and tell him if we wanted anything special.

I took in the board and made sure I had all the important bits down in my head before I looked around for Nestor. He wasn't up front, so I headed back to the kitchen, and out the window is where I saw him and Vicki on the back porch. She was all rubbing up against him, and he was smiling. I was thinking maybe he'd be in a good mood, so I opened the door and knocked on it, still inside the kitchen.

"Hey," I said. "Got a sec, Nes?"

Vicki gave him a kiss and broke free from him. "Come on out,

Jeff. I was heading inside anyhow." And then it was me and him out there.

Nestor was still smiling when he asked me, "What can I do for you, *Jefe*?"

"I need your help."

"Okay, and why do you need my help?"

"Lance's got fleets in Norway and Skagerrak, and he can force me out of Sweden, so I—"

"Nah. That's *how* you need my help. I want to know *why* you need my help."

"I … I don't get it."

"You have two other units up there: a fleet and an army. You could've held St. Petersburg and backed up your fleet in Sweden, all by yourself. So I'll ask you again, why do you need my help?"

I wanted to tell him I give up, but there was something on his face behind that smile. Like being able to answer the question was part of the price.

Well, I rolled it around in my head until I got what he meant. "Lance convinced me to help him take you down. Split your dots between us. It's why my units were too far away to protect my supply centers."

Nestor nodded. "There you go."

"Look, I'm sorry I betrayed—"

"Uh uh. That's not it. Don't be sorry you tried to double-cross me. Be sorry you were dumb."

I could feel my ears burning from the humiliation and anger. "You heard what I told Lance in there. You think I'm not kicking myself?"

"You are *now*. I want to make sure you don't forget the lesson you just got taught. Because Lance is gonna come back to you wanting to make another deal. Telling you that this time it'll be different."

"And I'll tell him to f--- off."

Nestor sighed. "*No*. This is still you being dumb. When he does that, you make him think you'll go along with it. Sell it like a pro. Then you f--- him *over*."

"All right. I will. If I get the chance."

Nestor straightened up off the wall and took a couple steps towards the door. "Good. I'll support you in Sweden. At least in the spring. And you support me in Denmark with Sweden."

I nodded my head off, I was so relieved. "I owe you big. I'll do my part and drive him out of St. Petersburg."

"We'll talk more in the fall, *Jefe*," he said.

Booker (France): I sat in the kitchen and watched Nestor, Vicki, and Jeff make their trips to and from the back porch.

Nestor asked me, on his way to the front of the house, "Spying on us?"

"Yes," I replied. "I would not pretend otherwise."

"Reading lips? What you figure out?"

"Nothing. Of course, that is still what I would say had I managed to learn something."

Nestor snickered at me and made his exit just as Cassandra came in. "Booker, I was hoping to talk to you."

"Shall we agree to attack Germany next turn? We could force its army out of Tyrolia."

"Um, sure," she replied. "Can I ask you a question?"

"Certainly."

"What's Karthik like as a player?"

Cassandra had been in her own separate world that morning. It was not surprising that she was uninterested in the game being played right then, although I was finding it slightly irritating that I could not count on her to care enough to execute the plan I had in mind.

What *was* unexpected was that question. "Why is it you ask?"

"So Evander told me Karthik couldn't make it?"

"Yes, Karthik is in India with his parents. You must recall how he told us on April Fools' Day?" She shook her head from side to side. "How confused we all were until he assured us it was not a prank of some sort?"

She didn't respond, so I broke the silence with, "Is something wrong?"

"Wait, then why invite him to play?"

"Karthik? He was never invited, as far as I know."

"But …." Cassandra craned her neck back to inspect the hallway. "Evander told me that he was. And Nestor took his place."

"*Evander* said that? Are you sure you heard him correctly?"

She furrowed her brow. Instead of answering, she took her leave of me.

Ollivander (Italy): All I wanted was a glass of water, but Booker waylaid me in the kitchen and asked me about his proposal from last year. "I mean, I'll try to get my fleet back to the boot, but Cassie's got two units she can use to keep me out of Rome."

"You could move it into the Ionian Sea."

"Vicki would bounce me out."

"Very well, what about the Gulf of Lyon? Our fleets could rotate."

"What would I get out of it?"

"You would survive to next year. And then I would help you take back your home supply centers."

I took a sip and asked, "And what would *you* get out of it?"

Booker laced his fingers on my kitchen table and replied, "A reliable ally in the Mediterranean. Cassandra would never betray Victoria. Nor *vice versa*."

"You sure?" I took out my phone and checked the time. "I'll think it over." Left before I could hear his reaction to that.

Lance (England): Good 'ol Boring Booker made his way over to the game board with maybe two minutes left before we had to enter the orders for spring that year. I tilted my head back to the kitchen and we headed over.

"Nestor talk to Jeff?"

"He did."

"And?"

"I do not know. Jeff was slightly less agitated afterwards, but that could simply be because he had time to calm himself."

I gave it ten seconds and told him, "I'm going after Sweden."

"Not Denmark?"

"No, I'll take it in the fall."

"What if he is supporting Sweden from Denmark?"

"Don't think he will. He knows Jeff isn't a reliable ally, so why help him now?"

Booker leaned his head a little to the left. "In any event, my armies are irrelevant to that struggle."

"Yeah, but you've gotta expect your unit in Ruhr to be squeezed out by the end of the turn, unless you support from Burgundy." I checked the time. "Decide quick how useful it is to keep it there, because we have thirty seconds."

And Booker made it to the living room with five to spare.

[Reactions to the orders of spring 1903]

Nestor (Germany): Hold on, let me check the map … this was a bad, bad turn for Boring Booker.

He doesn't even notice right away. Evander's smacking his forehead. "S---, I was supposed to move that army to Rome! How'd I mess that up?"

"Wouldn't make a difference," I tell him. "Cassie would just bounce you out with hers. Then she'd take it in the fall."

"Still." He turns to Booker and says, "I notice you took Tunis."

Booker makes this noise in his throat like he's some stuffy professor and says, "Evander, you gave me no choice in the matter. I knew you were not going to move your fleet out of the way. How long did you expect me to wait?"

And Jeff says, "Booker?"

"And maybe I kept my fleet there because I knew you wouldn't hold up your end," Evander replies.

"To what purpose? How could you possibly have benefitted from the orders you *did* enter?"

"*Booker*," Jeff says again, and this time he's got his attention. "What's with the English fleet in Picardy? What are you and Lance up to?"

Victoria (Turkey): Nestor started laughing, I remember that. I checked out how everyone else was reacting while I waited for someone to explain what Jeff meant.

Booker's mouth was open, like he couldn't believe it.

Jeff? From the time he found out Lance moved into ... hold on, let me see the map ... St. Petersburg, he'd been unhappy. I mean, even *after* he came back inside. You could see it on his face. For one, he was never good at hiding his emotions. But also, I'd known him for a while, and I got to see him sad a *lot*. So I knew what he was feeling.

But when he was looking at the screen just then, it was like all that washed away. He was calm. No, wait, that wasn't it. He had the face of a guy who found out that he didn't have to worry about whatever it was he was worrying about. You know?

Total luck I saw this one: Lance and Evander checked each other out the corners of their eyes. Like the look *was* the message. But I couldn't figure what that message was.

And Cassie? She was looking at Evander, so she caught it too. Then she saw me looking at her and she went back to staring at the screen.

Cassandra (Austria): Nestor was doubled over, gasping for air, tears streaming out of his eyes. And Booker had regained enough of his composure to close his mouth.

Evander said, "Okay, Nestor. We get it."

Nestor took a couple of breaths and slapped a hand on Jeff's back. "You ain't the only inhabitant of Dumba--ville any more. Feel better?"

Jeff smiled. "Honestly? Little bit."

Nestor noticed how Vicki was still confused, and said, "Those English fleets in Picardy and the English Channel?" She nodded. "One of them is going into Brest in the fall. Booker's about to lose himself a supply center. If—"

"Don't listen to him, Vicki," Lance broke in to say. "He doesn't know what he's talking about."

"If he'd paid attention to what happened to Jeff, he could have moved his armies to stop him." Lance responded with a dismissive flip of his hand in Nestor's direction. "You don't want to take my word for it, *querida*? Ask Booker."

Everyone but Lance looked over to Booker. He didn't say a

word. He didn't have to: we could see the muscles in his jaw flexing under his dark brown skin before he walked off.

While he was making his way to the kitchen, I thought about something I'd seen maybe a minute earlier. Lance and Evander shared this *look*. And at first I thought it was about Booker, some deal they'd made.

But looking at that map after, that made no sense to me. Evander would be eliminated by the end of next turn. Lance didn't help him. He couldn't have even if he wanted to.

Evander moved those little wooden blocks around on the board. He scratched the back of his head, checked the laptop screen, and said, "Fifteen minutes."

Booker (France): It is not much of an admission that the action in the upper left quadrant of the game board during the spring of 1903 took me by surprise. I had thought that I had succeeded in hiding my reaction then, but if the others tell you otherwise, I would have to accept that I failed in that instance. After all, our perceptions are least veridical when focused on ourselves.

I mentioned to you that Ollivander taught me how to play poker. You will have to believe that I did not distinguish myself at any of the variants we played simply because it did not interest me overmuch. Beyond the questions of game theory optimization, there really is not anything there to care about. And soon, as software completely supplants even the best human players and computer-assisted cheating becomes endemic at the tables, there will be no honest money to be made from it.

But there is one aspect of the game that I excelled at, according to those I played with. My poker face is top-notch: I do not give off tells. Any gestures and facial expressions I make are deliberate. You and your audience should understand that the game we played that day was the rare case where my usual *sang-froid* failed me.

I imagine that this claim may come across as boastful and a bit ridiculous. If so, I do not particularly care. The reason I mention it to you is that you asked why it is I came to be known as "Boring Booker".

My poker face, my boring image: they did not come to me naturally. They were instead very carefully cultivated.

Austria

    F ADR S A Tri → Ven ◊ A Apu → Rom ◊
    A Tri → Ven ◊ A Nap S A Apu → Rom ◊

England

    F Nwy S F SKA → Swe ◊ F Lon → ENG ◊
    F NTH → Bel ◊ F Bel → Pic ◊
    <u>F SKA → Swe</u> -- Failure, Attack str. inadequate
    <u>A Stp → Mos</u> -- Failure, Attack str. inadequate

France

    A Bur → Mar ◊ F LYO → Wes ◊
    A Mar → Pie ◊ F Wes → Tun ◊
    <u>A Ruh → Kie</u> -- Failure, Attack str. inadequate

Germany

    F Den S F Swe Holds ◊ A Mun → Tyr ◊
    A Tyr → Vie ◊
    <u>A Hol → Ruh</u> -- Failure, Attack str. inadequate
    <u>F Kie S F Den Holds</u> -- Failure, Supp. disrupted

Italy

    A Tus Holds ◊ F TYS S A Tus Holds ◊

Russia

    F Pru → Liv ◊
    <u>F Swe S F Den Holds</u> -- Failure, Supp. disrupted
    <u>A Bud → Ser</u> -- Failure, Attack str. inadequate
    <u>A War → Mos</u> -- Failure, Attack str. inadequate

Turkey

    A Gre S A Bul → Ser ◊ A Bul → Ser ◊
    A Con → Bul ◊ F EAS → ION ◊ F Rum → BLA ◊
    A Sev Holds ◊ F Smy → AEG ◊

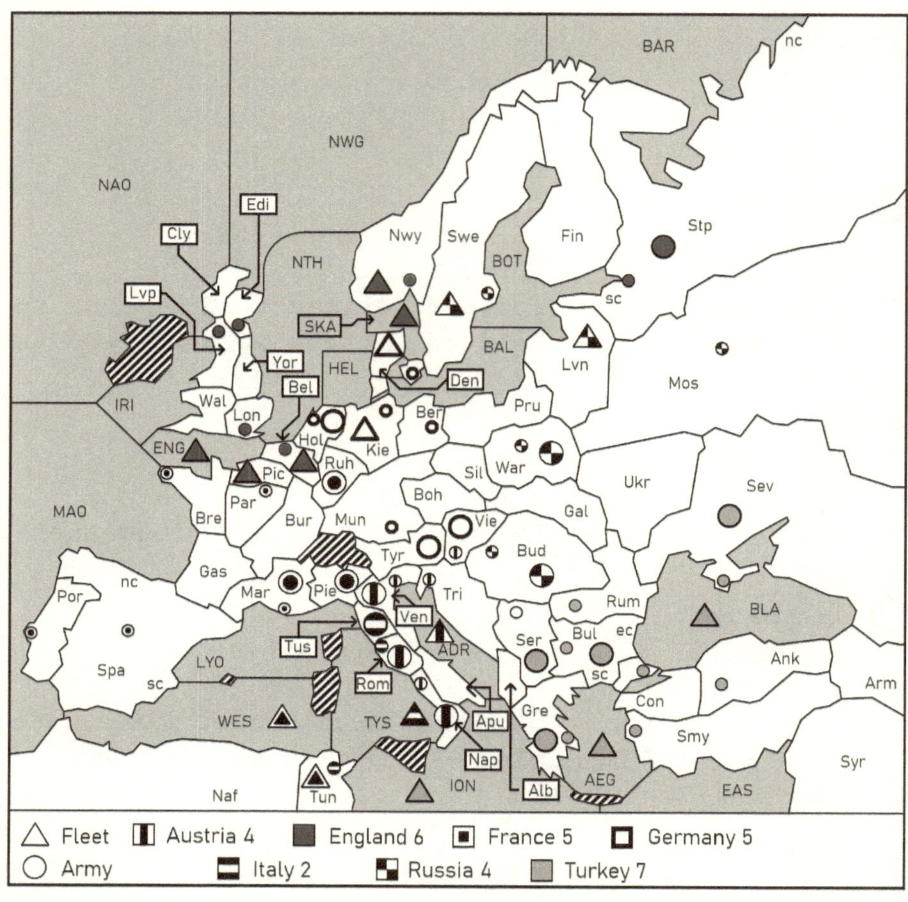

Figure 13 -- Game Map, Start of Fall 1903

Fall

1903

[Diplomatic phase of fall 1903]

Nestor (Germany): Lance double-times it back to where Booker is licking his wounds. He wants to be first in line to make a deal with him, looks like.

I decide to wait. After all, I'm pretty sure Lance'll s--- the bed one way or another.

Lance (England): Booker was at the sink, hands curled over the edge, staring out the window at the side of the next-door neighbor's house ten feet away.

I thought I'd give an icebreaker a shot: "Not much of a view that direction."

He turned around and crossed his arms. Stared at me like I was a wallpaper sample. And waited. Booker was really good at making you feel small when you said something stupid.

"I wasn't going to break our pact."

"You very clearly were going to do just that."

I'd ran back to the kitchen to talk him down before I thought through what I'd say. So I stammered for a bit until I got this out: "I don't know what I could say to convince you."

"*I* do. Explain exactly how your orders in the spring had any design other than to take supply centers from me."

He had me. I flopped around the kitchen for a bit and made a bunch more random noises with my mouth trying to come up with a speech that would fix things with Booker, until finally I gave up and went with, "I was only going to take Brest. One dot, that was it."

That was when Nestor and Vicki walked in, on their way to the back porch. Hand on the knob, Nestor said, "Let me know when you're ready to talk terms, Booker." Then he shut the door with them on the other side.

Booker took a step to join them. "One is enough."

"I know, I know. I just needed to bring an army on the continent so I could bring it to Burgundy. Through … through Picardy. Then I'd be able to help you take Munich."

"Except it is instead your *fleet* that is in Picardy."

"I screwed up. I meant to build an army in London last winter, but I fat fingered it." He took another step and I slid between him and the door. "Wait, I have to take Brest to get another army. And get my fleet out of the way. But I can give it back once I've done that."

He nodded once. Not the way you do when you agree. More like the way you do when you've heard something that's obvious bulls---. "Or you could leave your fleet in Picardy where it is and move your fleet in the English Channel to the North Sea to support my army's move from Ruhr to Holland."

I shot a glance behind me, through the back window, at those two. "Nestor needs to think our alliance is broken," I whispered. "It's part of the plan."

Booker treated me to a disappointed shake of his head. He crossed his arms again and waited for me to get out of his way.

Jeffrey (Russia): The way I'd figured it, I didn't need to talk to anyone that turn. Except maybe Nestor, make sure he'd still support me in Sweden. That's why I was chilling out in the living room with Evander and Cassie.

"So what're you going to do this turn?" Cassie asked Evander.

He made this sort of "I give up" motion with his hands. "It doesn't matter. Unless you move one of your armies out of my home supply centers and let me retake it, I'll be eliminated in the winter."

Cassie stared at the board for a while. "I could do that for you," she said.

Evander wasn't expecting that. Neither was I. "You would do that?" he asked.

"*Why* would you do that?" I asked.

She looked up at Evander. "How do you think the game would be different if it was Karthik instead of Nestor?"

I waited a couple seconds for Evander to answer before jumping in myself: "He's got a lot more experience with the game, Cass. But I don't think he would've done better with Germany. I mean, except for that time Nes put in that screwed-up support order. Karthik wouldn't make a rookie mistake like ...."

If you're wondering why I trailed off mid-sentence, it's because Cassie was looking at me when I started talking, but she went back to giving Evander the hairy eyeball halfway through.

Evander pointed at me. "What he said."

"He must have been disappointed to have to decline your invitation."

"Wait, what?" I said. "Why'd you invite Karthik when you knew he'd be in India?"

He shot his eyes back and forth between me and Cassie like he was watching tennis. Settled on her and said, "I didn't invite him."

And all Cassie did was keep looking until Evander walked away.

```
Jeff>     Support Sweden?
Jeff>     U there Nes?
Nestor>   yes
Nestor>   deal
Nestor>   talk 2 u @ lunch
```

Booker (France): The door to the back porch hit Lance's left elbow when Victoria opened it.

"Whoops! Sorry, Lance."

From the way he winced, I suspect it struck his ulnar nerve. "It's okay." He attempted a smile, which materialized as a grimace, and stepped aside. "My fault for standing there."

"Yes it was," I said as I walked out. Nestor was on his phone. Typing, it seemed. He held up a finger, a gesture for me to wait.

Soon it dawned upon me: whatever he was doing was performative, meant to apprise me of my insignificance. I fixed my gaze at a point two inches to the right of his right ear and several feet behind him.

And it was a full minute later that I heard him say, "What's up, Booker?"

I looked at him then, as if I had not realized he was there until he spoke. "Oh, just taking the air."

He pocketed his phone. "Heard you're off to Princeton in the fall."

"You heard correctly."

"Thank God for affirmative action, huh?"

"Why do you ask?"

"It's how you got in."

"You believe so?"

"You think you would've made it in if you were white?"

"Most definitely."

"What if you were Asian?"

I could discuss affirmative action in undergraduate admissions for hours. I know this because I have done so. What I cannot do is discuss it briefly and do it justice.

With that caveat firmly in mind, let me say this. My academic credentials were just fine. My grade point average was high, I garnered a good number of fives on the advanced placement exams, and I scored well on the necessary standardized tests.

But barring Westinghouse medals, math and science Olympiad team membership, and the like, academic accomplishment alone is no longer enough for most applicants. If you are not a "disadvantaged minority", you have to play a musical instrument at a virtuoso level or excel in a sport or have made millions of dollars off of an "app".

And the one point of consensus in the debates I took part in was that what counts as a remarkable résumé is a bar set higher, far higher, for Asian-Americans than for white people. It is the only way to keep these institutions from completely losing their ... let us say "historic character".

Nestor's attempted rhetorical ploy was to pit me, as a representative at-large for African-Americans, against Asian-Americans. To stand up for myself would be tantamount to denying the very real disadvantages they face. To not do so would be to denigrate myself. Thus was the nature of Nestor's cunning: his insults were well-aimed at the weakest points in his opponent's psyche.

"I can connect you with the admissions department and you can put the question to them."

"Uh huh. You out here seeking an audience?"

"'Audience'? Do you fancy yourself a king, Nestor?"

"No, I 'fancy' myself Emperor Wilhelm the Second. You want to deal or not?"

"Tell me, what possible deal could you make that I would be interested in?"

"I can support you into Belgium. All you got to do is ask."

He was not going to support me into Belgium. And even were he to do so, Lance would rebuff any move using his fleet in Picardy as support. Nor would he support me into Venice, were I to suggest that alternative. The futility of attempting an alliance with Nestor had become clear to me in that moment. If only I had thought it through earlier, I could have spared myself the sojourn.

I lifted my index finger and parted my lips slightly, as if I were about to speak. Then I opened the door and went back inside.

Cassandra (Austria): It was like Nestor had set up an office out there on Evander's back porch. Booker and I nodded to each other as we crossed paths in the kitchen. And I remember thinking that for something that was supposed to be a fun leisure activity, this board game was pretty much misery alternating with drudgery.

I took a deep breath, counted to three, and exhaled as I opened the door, where Nestor treated me to a condescending smile. "Cassie."

"Nestor."

"You wanna *Anschluss*?"

"That's World War *II*."

In a blink of the eye, that smile became a contemptuous scowl. "The idea of the *Anschluss* dates back to the late nineteenth century."

"Oh."

"Yeah. Oh. Tell you what, why don't *you* explain to me why you're out here."

"I guess I need help with Booker."

"Mm hmm."

"And I think you do too."

"Maybe."

"Can you help me?"

The smile creeped—and it *was* creepy—back onto Nestor's face. He lowered his head and paced a tight circle on the porch.

My attention wandered until the rhythmic squeaking of the boards ceased and Nestor said, "I'm going to move my army out of Vienna."

"Why?"

"So that you'll have one more unit to build in the winter."

"In exchange for what?"

"Like I said, *Anschluss*. You're going to help me take Booker's territories away from him. I ask you to support me against his armies, you do it. I ask you to convoy my armies to Tunis, you do it."

That's when I asked the question I came out there for in the first place: "Did you know that originally Evander was going to invite Karthik instead of you?"

He squinted at me. "Who's Karthik?"

"You don't know him?"

"No." I got the impression he wasn't lying. And at the time, I still had no idea what it was that was bothering me and why I couldn't let it go. "Stop stalling, Cassie. We got a deal?"

I took out my phone and looked at that map. I guess I was starting to get the hang of that damned game, because I asked him, "Your army in Vienna. You're moving it to Bohemia, right?"

He shrugged. "Haven't decided."

"Sure you have. You don't have any choice. If you don't, Booker will take Munich spring of next year. All he has to do is bring his army up from Marseilles to Burgundy and his army in Ruhr will support his attack from Burgundy or *vice versa*. Unless you have two armies of your own next to Munich."

"So?"

"So you aren't moving your army out of Vienna for my sake. You're doing it for yours."

"Except if I stayed in Vienna, I'd get to build myself an extra unit. I could just put it in Munich and then I wouldn't need an army in Bohemia."

"He'll attack your army in Tyrolia with his in Piedmont. Then you can't support your army in Munich and he'll push you out."

"No he won't. He's gonna need that army against Lance."

"Then *I'll* attack your army in Tyrolia with my army in Venice. Booker still takes Munich from you."

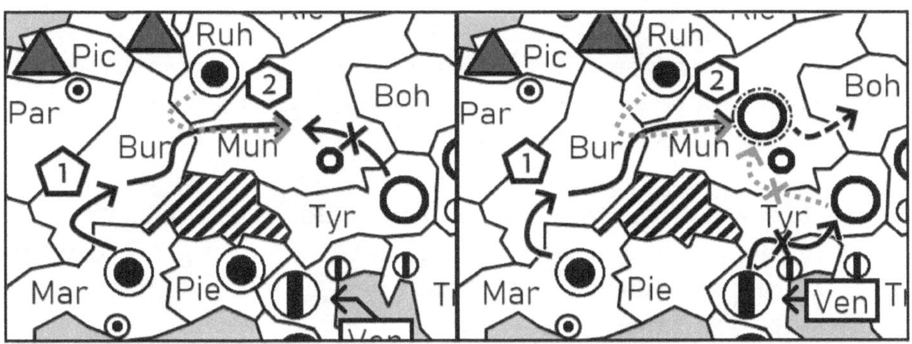

Figure 14 -- Cassandra's Argument as to Why Germany Needed to Move Army in Vienna to Bohemia [Left] France Moves (1) Mar to Bur, then (2) Bur to Mun Supported by Ruh; [Right] France Moves (1) Mar to Bur, then (2) Bur to Mun Supported by Ruh as German Support Tyr to Mun Cut by Austrian Ven to Tyr

"I'll move my army from Tyrolia to Bohemia so you can't attack me and cut support."

"Then maybe I'll occupy Tyrolia and attack you from there."

"I'll bounce you out."

"With your army in Vienna? If I decide not to move, you'll be the one who ends up moving their army. And like I promised you, you'll be out of Vienna."

He was getting ready to explode. "Booker's never gonna figure it all out. I don't need to move anything."

"I'm going to recommend it to him."

"Yeah? That's your threat if I don't move out of Vienna?"

"Like I said, you have to move out of Vienna anyway. You're not doing me any favors; I'm not going to pretend you are. And

I'm warning Booker no matter what."

So much of that day has stuck with me, even now, months later. And one of the indelible moments occurred then. The anger on Nestor's face disappeared and something like ... *enlightenment* replaced it. It happened in all of three seconds while I watched.

Nestor said, "You don't see it, do you?"

"See what?"

"How you're gonna be thrown under the bus."

"As long as it's Booker and not you doing the throwing, I think I'll be okay with it."

Nestor treated me to a beatific smile, an expression I had never seen him wear before. "Not Booker." And left me to think about it, out on Evander's back porch.

Ollivander (Italy): Lunch was coming soon, and so was my exit from the game. People were filing in to the living room with minutes to spare. Booker and Cassie shared a look. Which wasn't surprising, but it was interesting.

Otherwise it was quiet. The calm after the storm and before the next one. At the fifteen-minute mark, I called time and told people to put in their orders for the fall.

◆ *Austria*
    F ADR → Tri ◊ A Ven S F ADR → Tri ◊
    A Nap S A Rom Holds ◊
    <u>**A Rom S A Nap Holds**</u> -- **Failure, Supp. disrupted**

◆ *England*
    F Pic S F Bel Holds ◊ A Stp Holds ◊
    F ENG → Bre ◊ F Nwy S F SKA → Swe ◊
    F Bel S F Pic Holds ◊
    <u>**F SKA → Swe**</u> -- **Failure, Attack str. inadequate**

◆ *France*
    F Tun S F WES – TYS ◊ F WES → TYS ◊
    <u>**A Ruh → Mun**</u> -- **Failure, Attack str. inadequate**
    <u>**A Mar → Pie**</u> -- **Failure, Attack str. inadequate**
    <u>**A Pie → Tus**</u> -- **Failure, Attack str. inadequate**

◆ *Germany*
    F Den S F Swe Holds ◊ F Kie → Ber ◊
    A Vie → Boh ◊
    <u>**A Hol → Ruh**</u> -- **Failure, Attack str. inadequate**
    <u>**A Tyr → Mun**</u> -- **Failure, Attack str. inadequate**

◆ *Italy*
    <u>**A Tus → Rom**</u> -- **Failure, Att. str. inad.**
    <u>**F TYS S A Tus → Rom**</u> -- **Failure, Supp. disrupted**
        Retreat to LYO

◆ *Russia*
    A War → Mos ◊
    <u>**A Bud → Rum**</u> -- **Failure, Attack str. inadequate**
    <u>**F Lvn → Stp.sc**</u> -- **Failure, Att. str. inadequate**
    <u>**F Swe S F Den Holds**</u> -- **Failure, Supp. disrupted**

◆ *Turkey*
    A Bul S A Sev → Rum ◊ A Sev → Rum ◊
    F AEG → ION ◊ F BLA → Con ◊ F ION → Alb ◊
    <u>**A Gre → Ser**</u> -- **Failure, Attack str. inadequate**
    <u>**A Ser → Bud**</u> -- **Failure, Attack str. inadequate**

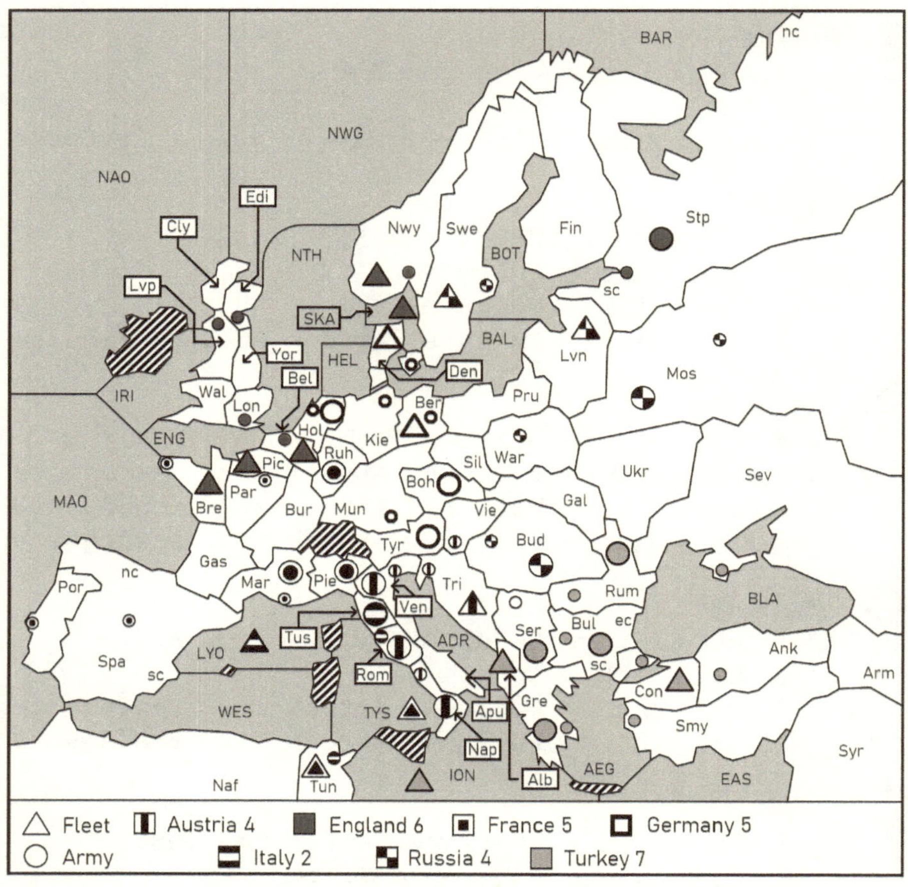

Figure 15 -- Game Map, Start of Winter 1903

Winter 1903

[Reactions to the orders of fall 1903 and builds of winter 1903]

Jeffrey (Russia): Me and Lance and Vicki and Evander were just spectators. All the action was with Cassie, Nestor, and Booker.

"You didn't tell him," Nestor said. Talking to Cassie.

She looked up from the laptop. "I did. He decided he needed his units elsewhere."

"Tell who?" I asked, and Cassie and Nestor said "Booker" right at the same time.

"Jinx! Buy me a coke!" Lance chimed in. One thing about Lance: he'd say random s--- and expect people to react like it's the funniest thing ever. That time everyone ignored him, which was usually the best move when he did that.

Nestor waited until he was sure Lance was done before replying to Cassie. "Don't believe you."

"Why not ask me?" Booker said.

He opened his mouth to reply, stopped. He smiled and then he said, "I don't think she needs your help to answer. Do *you*, Booker?"

We had another moment of silence with everyone waiting for someone else to say something until Evander stepped to say, "Vicki, Cassie, and Lance: you have builds this turn. Hurry up and put them in before the five minutes are up." Then he walked over to the board and removed his two pieces.

Ollivander (Italy): After those three did their thing, I decided it was time to bring up my idea, see if people went for it. "So now that I'm officially eliminated, I'd like to make a suggestion about the game."

"Too late for rule changes," Lance replied.

"You want to let our host finish, Lance?" Nestor asked.

"Thank you, Nestor. It's not so much a rule change as it is a rule addendum. Here it is: when a player gets eliminated, he or she can be an advisor for another player who's still in the game."

Booker's turn to ask, "Which player?"

"I was thinking the player doing worst, judging by the number of units they have compared to the start of the game."

"Which is me, right?" Jeff said.

"Right now, yes. But you can turn me down and then ...."

"There is a three-way tie between Cassie, Nestor, and myself," Booker said.

"In situations like that, we can flip a coin or roll a die or something. Well? What do you all think?"

"I don't like it," Lance said. "You're in a position to tell Jeff—"

"If I agree," Jeff cut in.

"Fine, tell whoever everything you discussed with the rest of us. It's an unfair advantage." People were nodding, murmuring their assent. Even Nestor.

"Except any player can do that right now." People started talking over each other. Lots of shaking heads. Not Vicki or Cassie. Vicki was studying her cuticles and Cassie was looking around. Not just at the board and at us, she was scanning the rest of the room too. I was starting to think I needed to keep her under close surveillance.

I raised my hands for quiet. When I got it, I said, "We can work on the honor system. The advisor promises to look at the situation as if he or she just came in." That seemed to allay most people's misgivings.

"I don't know," Lance replied. "I don't think you can forget that easy."

Jeff is usually a "go along to get along" kind of guy, or at least he was when I knew him, but he was out of patience with Lance. "Are you saying Evander has to sit on his hands in his own house for the rest of the day? Seriously?" That got nods from the others.

"You're just saying that because you're the one who'll get Evander on your team."

"Know what, Lance? If this is what it takes to shut you up, I'm turning it down. Evander, get out your dice and we'll figure out who you're gonna help instead."

"No, not yet," I said. "First of all, does anyone other than

Lance have an objection to my proposal?"

People shook their heads no, except for Vicki, who was still making sure her nails weren't chipped or something. "Now. Jeff, you get first right of refusal, then it's on to Cassie, Booker, and Nestor. Would you like me as an advisor?"

Jeff locked eyes with Lance and said he would. "Then that's that. The food should be here any minute, so I'm hitting Pause on the game. We'll start 1904 at one-thirty sharp."

Cassandra (Austria): Evander put those new pieces on the board so we could all see. That's when Lance said, "Holy s--- is Vicki doing well."

"Nobody puts baby in a corner," she said.

"Is that from something?" Jeff asked.

She dropped her jaw in mock horror. "From *Dirty Dancing*! It's a classic!"

Jeff held up his hand, palm facing her, a little like Drake in that meme, and said, "Okay, boomer." People laughed at that. Even Booker cracked a smile.

Vicki scowled. "*Nestor* liked it, didn't you, bae?"

"Oh, sure. Absolutely," he replied, laying it on thick like he was humoring her. Vicki caught on that he was making fun of her, and she gave him and Jeff the finger with each of her hands. More laughing.

"Hey, I really like the color of your nail polish," Lance said.

"Thanks! Let me give you a closer look," and she swung her arms around to give him the double birds. And we laughed even harder. I smiled just now, thinking back on it. I kind of wish we'd all decided to crown Vicki the winner right then and there and went out and seen a movie instead.

Anyway, we broke up into our individual discussion groups while we waited for lunch to arrive. Booker caught my eye and tilted his head towards the hallway. I joined him there.

"So why *didn't* you move to Burgundy?" I asked him.

"Once you explained it to Nestor, there was no need. With Germany's armies in place, I would never take Munich."

"So instead you tried to go into Italy?"

"It was a temporizing move. I will be redeploying those armies to counter England's push."

"What a jerk he's been."

Booker lifted his eyebrows slightly and bobbed his head left and right, weighing something in his mind. "As I said, the game requires double-dealing. The trick is in the timing. Too soon and you earn a reputation for dishonesty. Too late and you have already lost."

"Okay …"

"England has burnt its bridges. France and Russia were its only plausible allies in the game—"

"What about Germany?"

"Nestor," he said. He didn't have to explain to me what that meant. "Despite that, England is in a solid position, second only to Turkey. Whether or not it is a winnable one remains to be seen."

"Got it."

"Now let me ask you: what will *you* do? Work with Germany to take down Turkey? Or *vice versa*?"

"Oh, I don't know. I haven't planned it out." Booker was about to respond when I asked, "Does this game seem weird to you somehow?"

"In the way that a game with three complete neophytes would be, yes."

"You mean me, Vicki, and Nestor?" He nodded. "We're doing pretty good."

"Due largely to Italy's complete collapse. It allowed you to take the peninsula and its supply centers. And that, in turn, allowed Turkey to move into Serbia and Greece."

"That's my point," I said. "You were sure I went back on a deal with Evander? *I didn't.* I just blindly attacked him and I got lucky. Don't you think that's weird?"

Booker raised his right arm, palm facing up, like he was giving me his agreement. "Ollivander has played badly, which is unusual, I grant you. Beyond that, what we are seeing simply is not that far out of the ordinary. Now, may I bring you back to strategy?"

"Sure, I guess."

"Are you willing to join forces with me?"

"Yes."

"Even if that means we use them to attack Turkey?" I couldn't bring myself to answer him. "I thought not. I will leave you with one piece of advice. You cannot attack me with your one fleet. The only way you can successfully attack Nestor in Tyrolia is if you move your fleet into the Adriatic Sea and move your armies in Venice and Rome into Trieste and Venice. But then you will be vulnerable to attacks from my fleet in the Tyrrhenian Sea."

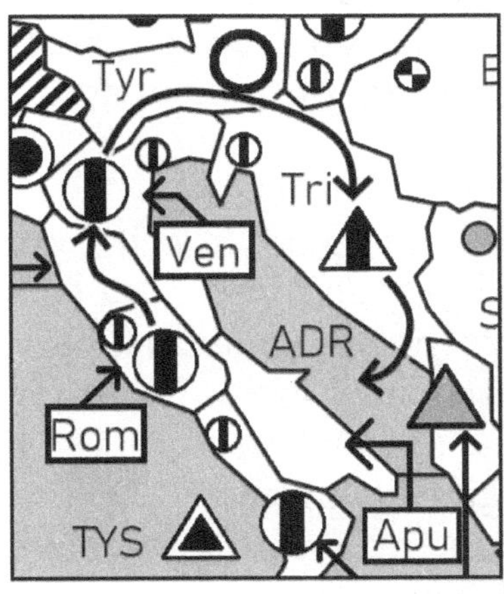

Figure 16 -- Booker's Proposed Unit Rotation for Austria:
Tri to ADR, Ven to Tri, Rom to Ven

"Maybe you could ... not do that? Don't attack?"

"I could. But in exchange for what, Cassandra? What will you give *me*?"

"I'll attack Nestor like you said."

Booker took out his phone and unlocked his screen. "In and of itself, that will not help me. But it will have to do for now." He gave me a nod and I went out to the front porch.

As I passed the living room, I remembered that there was something that was bothering me. Something I'd seen there. I gave it another once-over, but nothing was jumping out at me, so I kept walking.

Nestor (Germany): So I decide I'll gamble on Booker being able to understand what's in his best interest. I mean, that's got to be the upside of being boring like that, right?

I see Cassie finish up with him and I head over. He's on his phone. I say, "Hey, Booker," and he puts up a finger and gets back to texting.

So I whip mine out and open up the message window in the game.

```
Nestor>  All right, Booker. Read this. You
   didn't believe I'd support you into Bel. Now
   I'm going to ask you to support me instead.
   Get off of your phone and ask me why you
   should do that.
```

It works. He sees it and puts his cell away. "You have my attention. Why should I support you into Belgium?"

"Lance is a bigger threat to you than I am, that's why."

He waits for me to explain why. I wait for him to ask. That's a mistake, because he's too much of a speed bump to get tired of standing around. I give up and say, "Look at the board, Booker. Think about Lance losing a unit and me getting one. Even if I built an army in Munich, is that worse than Lance keeping all his units?"

He takes his cell back out and checks the map. I mean, I assume. "It is a matter of timing, but, yes, you building an army in Munich would certainly be worse than Lance keeping all of his units."

And now I have to bargain with him. "What if I agree to build a fleet instead?"

"That only works if I can trust you to do that."

"Why wouldn't you? When did I lie to you?"

"When you claimed that I asked you to support a move from Paris to Picardy. From Holland."

"Fine. If I admit that it was a lie, will you support me into Belgium?"

Booker tips his chin up a half inch. Just enough to notice. "I would think the easiest way for you to find out is to come clean and see how I react. Try it."

That's when I see it. I see the why behind him being boring. It's his armor. He's so afraid of being embarrassed, of people making fun of him that he'll never stick his neck out. He's too proud to take a chance and risk falling on his face with everyone watching. It must have taken everything he had not to react when I laughed in his face earlier.

I was going to keep looking for his Achilles heel, that one … yeah, ha ha, very f---ing witty and clever and s---. Like I was about to say when you interrupted me, that one thing that'd make him snap before the day was up. I'd be doing him a favor: for once in his life he'd actually do something interesting.

I tell him, "I give up. Maybe you'll figure out how badly you're playing this game when Lance takes your supply centers from you, one by one. When it happens? Don't come crying to me."

[Victoria's family talks to her about Nestor]

Victoria (Turkey): Second semester freshman year and me and Nestor are spending a lot of time together. My mom is asking me about him, and I'm trying to answer her without really saying anything.

Dad overhears us one time and tells Mom that we should invite the Martinezes—that's like a tongue twister—invite them over for dinner. I've got my hands over my ears, shouting, "Too soon! Too soon!" He thinks it's funny, backs away, shouting "All right! All right!" at me.

My sister gets involved, well, kinda. She tells me Mom told her to talk to me, get the rundown on Nestor. Be a big sister her last year before she's off to college. I tell her we're just dating; she asks me off the record what the deal is; I tell her same story as before.

Mom doesn't buy it, so she gets me alone for The Talk. I tried to make it stop; I explained that we have Sex Ed in school. She wasn't going to let up, though. First thing she did was pick up a compact from my desk and put the mirror in front of me.

"We haven't even started yet, and already you're blushing."

"It's *embarrassing*, Mom."

"No, Honey, you're *embarrassed*. There's a big difference. And that's why you're not ready."

And I yelled out, "We're not having sex!"

"I am so happy to hear that, but we're going to talk about birth control anyway. You will learn how to use condoms. And we'll discuss getting you on the pill."

I would have said anything to make it stop. That's why I agreed to tell her the moment I became sexually active. You know she made me put a condom on a banana? Twice, because I messed up the first time.

Dad did his version of The Talk the very next day. Asked me, "How's it going?"

The way he said it, I knew. "Mom told you, didn't she?"

He admitted it right away. "My question for you is a little different. What do you like about Nestor?"

I tried to brush him off, but it wouldn't work. He wanted to know. "Why's it so important, Dad?"

"Because you're getting serious with him, aren't you? He's important to you, and that's why it's important to me."

After I thought about it I told him I'm on top of the world with him. I walk through the halls at school and I feel like a queen, knowing he's my boyfriend.

Then he asked, "And Nestor knows you feel that way?"

And I told him of course he does. He nodded and that's all he's got to say about it for a while.

Austria

```
F Tri ◊ A Nap ◊ A Rom ◊
A Ven ◊
Build A Vie
```

England

```
F Bel ◊ F Bre ◊ F Nwy ◊
F Pic ◊ F SKA ◊ A Stp ◊
Build A Lon
```

France

```
A Mar ◊ F Tun ◊ A Pie ◊
A Ruh ◊ F TYS ◊
```

Germany

```
F Ber ◊ A Boh ◊ F Den ◊
A Hol ◊ A Tyr ◊
```

~~Italy~~

```
Disband A Tus
Disband F LYO
```

Russia

```
A Bud ◊ F Lvn ◊ A Mos ◊
F Swe ◊
```

Turkey

```
F Alb ◊ A Bul ◊ F Con ◊ A Gre ◊
F ION ◊ A Rum ◊ A Ser ◊
Build A Ank
```

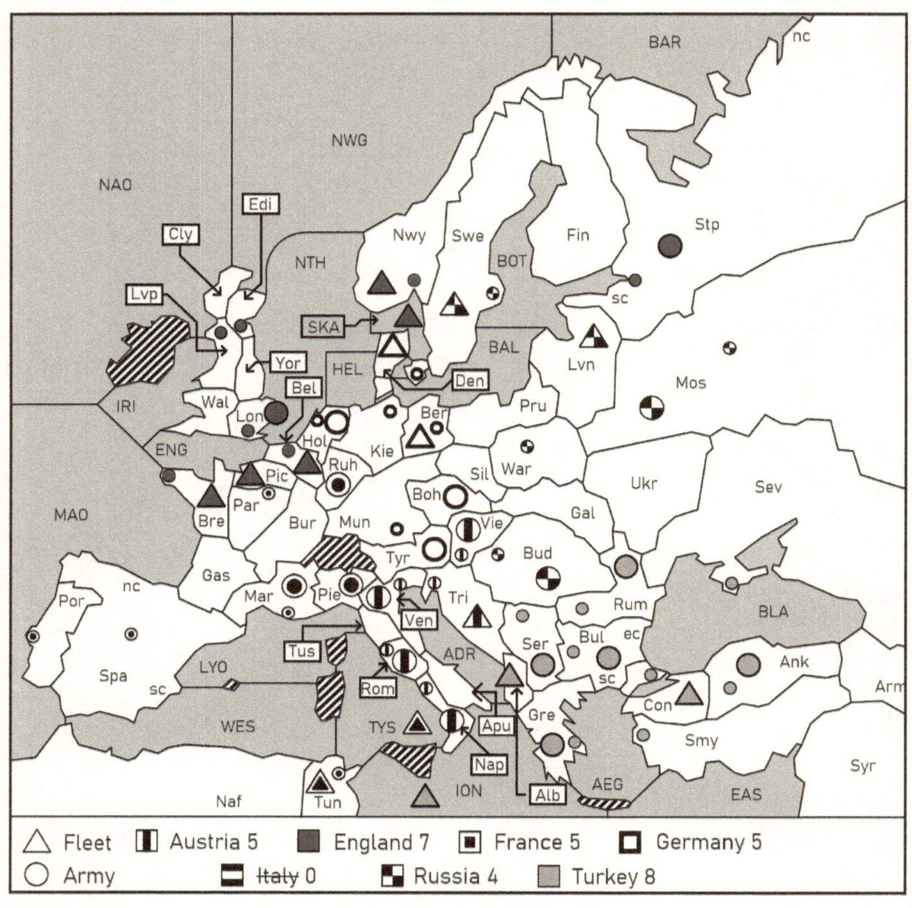

Figure 17 -- Game Map, End of Winter 1903

Lunch Break

[The chat during lunch break]

Jeffrey (Russia): Lunch came just before one. Evander brought all those bags of food to the kitchen and set everything up buffet-style.

He caught Booker discussing the game with Lance and he laid down the law: "Complete moratorium on deal-making until one-thirty. We can wait a half hour, people." No complaints when he said that, not even from Lance.

We all got our food and crowded around the kitchen table, started talking about summer plans. Evander asked, "So what's your itinerary, Vicki?"

"France and Italy. My father wants to see the big museums, my mother wants to see the sights."

"The Louvre and the Uffizi, I take it?" Booker asked. She nodded. "Where else besides Paris and Florence?"

"Rome and Venice. Mom loves wine, so Provence. We're keeping it a little loose, so we might make London before we go. You guys need to follow me on Instagram so you can see my pics!"

I didn't have an account. I took out my phone and made myself a note to get one and look her up.

"Anyone else going anywhere this summer?" Lance asked.

Nestor (Germany): Booker tells us how his family's off to the Hamptons, la di f---ing da. "A friend of my mother's from her college days invited us. Only two weeks."

"Tokyo," Lance says. "Three weeks for us. I am so psyched. I'll be sure to bring you some cool stuff, Jeff."

I'm watching Jeff like a hawk while Lance says that. Jeff gives the smallest smile and nod he can and still be nodding and smiling. Plays it off like he's too busy chewing to say thanks.

Everyone's quiet, eating that Chinese food, when Booker asks if anyone else got a summer reading list from their college.

Cassandra (Austria): "I did," Vicki said. "I'm planning to ignore all of it while I'm in Europe."

"And read them when you get back?" I ask.

"*Hell* no," she says, and there's some laughter in the room.

"I guess this is a private school thing?" Jeff asks.

"No, Victoria is going to the University of Massachusetts at Amherst," Booker explains. "A public university."

Lance says, "Well, Harvey Mudd's private, but we don't have a lot of summer reading. Just a few essays."

People look at Nestor, who shrugs and tells us he doesn't know, he needs to check his e-mail and see.

"Yeah, they have some suggested readings for us," Evander says.

"Really?" Lance asks. "Ann Arbor's got, what, forty thousand students?"

"Forty-six."

"Okay, forty-six k, and they have a reading list for incoming students? All of them?"

"Well, UMass has thirty, and they have one, according to Vicki. I'm in the honors program at the school, so maybe that's why. I didn't check the e-mail too closely to see if it's just for us or for everyone."

"How about you, Cassie?"

"Oberlin's got a reading list. My parents are adamant that I read everything on it, with all the money they'll be spending on my schooling. My sister warned me that they quizzed her on her list two years ago when she got hers. She didn't exactly pass." People chuckled at that.

"Your parents are old school," Lance said.

"I suppose," I said, a little quietly. "I'm looking forward to reading it all, so they didn't have to warn me."

And there was one of those conversational silences. Then Evander snapped his fingers. "I can't believe I almost forgot to ask. Nestor, tell us all about UConn. They've got to have a lot of things planned for you, right?"

Nestor leaned back his chair. "Yeah. They have me coming in early."

"Even though you're redshirted? They *are* gonna redshirt you, right?"

"They are."

"Vicki, I got a billion more questions, sorry."

"It's okay," she says, without looking up from her phone. "Lots of people do."

"Are they slotting you as a wideout when you're eligible?"

"That's the plan. Maybe special teams for kickoff returns too, but they're saying I shouldn't count on it."

Evander hopped up and sat on the counter next to the sink. "All right, this is what I've been wondering. It was either UConn or Arizona State, right? Why UConn?"

Nestor shrugs. "Why not?"

"I mean, talking football only, ASU's the better school, right?"

"UConn ain't nothin' to f--- with either."

Jeff jumped in to say, "Hol' up, I checked it on Wikipedia. ASU has a lot more wide receivers in the NFL than UConn does."

"That won't do me any good if I don't get my starts." Nestor put all four legs of his chair back on the floor. "Set it aside. Anyone here knows what the average height is for wide receivers in the NFL?"

"Six feet, one inch," Booker said, and we all turned to look at him.

Nestor's eyes got wide for a moment, surprised that Booker knew. "That's right. I'm five-ten. There's some short guys in that position, and five-ten isn't *that* small. But I know the odds aren't great. So I'm going to school to learn and I'm on the team to pay the bills and open doors. Make contacts."

"And if you actually get to play, that's more doors," Evander said. "Sensible plan."

"Not to mention, UConn's only an hour and a half away from UMass," Jeff added. "That's got to be a plus, right, Vicki?"

Vicki finally looked up from the screen in her hands. "What? Sorry, I didn't hear you. I was checking the 'Gram."

Nestor checked his watch. "I'm going to beat the rush to the bathroom," he said, getting up.

"TM*I*," Vicki said.

"Sorry, *querida*," he replied. He pulled out his wallet and dropped a twenty on the table.

Evander picked it up. "Nestor, I got this." But he was already down the hallway.

Jeff got up next. He grabbed his dishes and put them in the sink. "There's enough for seconds, if you want," Evander said.

"Nah, that's okay. I'm going to catch come rays out front before the next turn starts." And he headed off.

I counted to ten in my head and after bussing my plate and chopsticks, I walked out front to join Jeff. Before I could say a word, Nestor opened the door and stood next to us.

Jeff was looking out at the street with that hangdog expression again. Like before, but not as bad. "Are you going to move down to Santa Clara?" I asked.

He shook his head. "I'll be staying with my mom and ridesharing there and back."

"Commute's gonna be a killer, man," Nestor said.

Jeff finally turned to look at us. "Yeah. But what can I do? I can't afford a separate apartment there with my own car. And my mom ...."

Nestor nodded. "You're not alone, *Jefe*. My older brother's living at home too, working as a mechanic, saving up to move out. We've been sharing a bedroom, and he's happier than s--- to be having the room to himself when I'm gone."

"Oof," Jeff said.

"Three bedrooms, one bathroom. For me, my brother, my mom and dad, and my grandfather. I only joined the football team so I'd have a place to shower." Jeff laughed at that; I gave it a polite smile.

Nestor leaned against the railing and pointed at Evander's house. "How much you think this place goes for?"

From where we were standing, we could see the living room through the front windows. It was constructed at least thirty years ago, but you could tell the interior had been renovated sometime in the last fifteen. The wood on the moldings looked expensive to me, and the windows were triple-paned and practically new.

But those weren't the important thing: location, location, location. It was a house in The City, in a good neighborhood, with three bedrooms, two bathrooms, and a garage. "One and a half million?" I guessed.

Nestor shook his head. "One point seven five *at least*. I got bored, checked this neighborhood out on a real estate site."

Jeff let out a low whistle. "Damn. Maybe Evander's mom is renting?"

"I don't think a lot of these houses are available for rent," I told him. "This could be the rare exception, though."

"Don't *feel* rented to me," Nestor replied. It didn't to me, either. The full bookcases, the tchotchkes on the mantle, the sofa end tables with their flower vases on the other side of that window: everything just fit in that room like it was a permanent home. I remembered thinking that it must be nice, knowing that there was a place you could feel was your own, that you could return to if things went really wrong in your life.

"How does anyone have enough money to own a place like this?" Jeff wondered.

"Maybe Evander's folks got a mortgage, who knows. But you know what's crazy? Evander probably doesn't think he's rich. He's got a house, but everyone on TV in those shows has one. And when people think 'rich', it's all about those reality shows with billionaires like the Kardashians and the real housewives of all over the place. So in his mind, he's middle class." Nestor checked his watch. "We're starting again in five minutes. See you inside."

If Evander had never seen a reality show in his entire life, I wouldn't have been surprised. And if you asked him directly, he likely would admit to being upper class. But that wasn't the same as how he reflexively saw himself, and I suspected that Nestor was right, that Evander's default mental self-image was of a middle-class young man, about to attend a state college.

You're wondering about the other three? Booker bore himself in the manner of a Boston Brahmin. If anything, he probably thought of himself as belonging to a higher socioeconomic stratum than he actually inhabited. And that despite the fact that both of his parents were and are highly-paid professionals. I imagine that he's currently finding his fellow freshmen at Princeton far too déclassé for his taste.

Vicki—and it pains me to say this given our friendship throughout all of high school—cared about status to a near-pathological extent. She wanted to fit in, but into the top echelon of popularity. And by the end of senior year, she had done just that. But it's a bit like balancing on top of a large rubber ball in that there is no stable resting point. Instead one must constantly remain in motion to keep from falling off. And, of course, the horrible irony is that that sort of furious striving runs the danger of seeming low-status. So had you asked her, she would likely vehemently reject the notion that she was "middle-class". Because that's uncomfortably close to being a "basic b----" who's trying too hard.

Then there's Lance. He saw himself as more sinned-against than sinning. That's not a self-image that's really compatible with thinking of oneself as belonging to the economic upper class. Because those people are comfortable, and Lance was not. It's a miracle that he managed to do as well as he did in high school, given the amount of time he spent nurturing his perpetually simmering resentments. One of which was formed freshman year, shortly after I met him.

[The "One-Nut Lance" incident]

Jeffrey (Russia): This was 2015, middle of November? Don't hold me to that, but for sure it was first semester of our freshman year.

Our high school was about half Asian, a quarter Hispanic, a tenth white, five percent black, and the rest mixed. You know, like me. It's a pretty good school, but it's not Lowell or even Wallenberg. I'm not saying it couldn't have happened at those places; what I'm doing is bringing all that up because maybe it'll help paint you a picture?

Okay, it's after our last class of the day. Lance and I are walking down the hallway near our lockers, and five Hispanic guys are walking the other way. Freshmen and sophomores, but we don't know that then. One of them notices Lance, elbows the one next to him, and points and says something in Spanish. And Juan—that's the guy who got elbowed; I'd have to dig out my yearbook to figure out the names of the others—says out loud, right when they pass by, "Check out One-Nut Lance!" And the other four start laughing.

Lance? I swear he only takes one second to react. He steps across, does a one-eighty, and while he's walking backwards, he grabs himself and claps back with "You been dreaming of my junk, *maricón*?"

Ollivander (Italy): I wasn't there. What I can say about it is something I read once on the internet. A commenter in some thread on … I want to say Reddit, but I could very well be mistaken, related a story from his days in Chicago. Every so often there were fist fights outside his high school. And with every one, there was the inevitable crowd circling the combatants, jostling for the best view.

But the sidewalk isn't a boxing arena. Once the spectators are two rows deep, all everyone else sees are the backs of people's heads. What you figure out quick is that you have to come early, when the two are squaring off, puffing up their chests at each other, trading threats, what have you.

That internet commenter laid out the peculiar, yet completely unassailable, logic of these confrontations: the crowd is a necessary element. If two men fight, and no one's there to witness it, did it really happen? What bragging rights could one possibly claim?

And they serve another purpose. Left to their own devices, the two might come to their senses and walk away, muttering insults and each warning the other that he'd better watch his back. Thus, when the circle closes and there's literally no way out, there will be a sharp shove from behind if the madding crowd concludes that their hearts aren't yet in it. That commenter claimed that, in his experience, the punches *always* followed.

All right? Now that I've explained all of that, what do *you* think happened after Lance said that?

... Not even a guess? ... No, not upset, just disappointed. Here's what followed. Juan's four friends dealt him the equivalent of that push: they treated Lance's riposte as if it were the most devastating slam imaginable. Laughing, exclaiming "Daaamn!" and "Oh snap!". Asking Juan if he was going to take that from the white boy. Leaving him no choice but to escalate if he wanted to save face. And the only way out would be through. Metaphorically speaking, that is: the ring hadn't formed just yet.

Booker (France): I am not sure that the percentage of Latino and Latina students at John Quincy Adams High School is as crucial to understanding that altercation as Jeffrey would have you believe. It is twenty-five percent at Adams, ten percent at Lowell, and fifteen percent at Raoul Wallenberg.

And whether or not those numbers were and are enough to create a different interracial dynamic than that of other high schools in the unified school district, the reason behind why things progressed in the manner they did laid elsewhere. On any other day, there would have been a hall monitor to step in after the initial insults were traded and drag Juan and Lance to the principal's office. The quarrel might be quashed, or the hostilities merely postponed, but there would be nothing more to see in that hallway.

That hall monitor had been called away fifteen minutes prior to the incident with Lance. A pipe had burst in the girls' bathroom on the opposite side of the building and school security was redeployed to keep the students out of that area until the situation was under control.

Keep that in mind. The subconscious expectation that an adult would intervene before things went too far was being subverted with every second that passed.

Cassandra (Austria): The footage that made the rounds was from someone perhaps twenty feet away. The audio was pure cacophony. Nothing of what the main characters in this play were saying could be made out. However, the anonymous videographer had held their phone up above their head, so the view was reasonably

126

unobstructed.

What Juan and Lance did next was as ritualistic in its way as Thai kickboxers performing *wai khru ram muay* or sumo wrestlers sipping water, throwing salt, and clapping hands.

Jeffrey (Russia): Juan spent ten seconds being sour. Then he slowly twisted his head and looked to his left, then his right, and then he was facing front again, that frown turned upside down into this evil grin.

"The f--- you say to me, f-----?"

Lance pushed his arms through the straps and his backpack fell offa him. "I said you're itching for my d--- up your a--."

Time stretched out in my head while the crowd went wild. Juan wasn't tall, wasn't swole, even grading on a curve for a frosh. But compared to Lance, he might as well have been The Mountain. Lance was skinny. Not "lean", skinny. At least two inches shorter. If he'd ever been in a fight before, he didn't tell me about it. He was about to be hurt *real* bad.

That's when I heard someone shout "Juan!" from down the hall. Someone with a Mexican accent. The crowd parted and Nestor walked up.

Victoria (Turkey): I don't like to think what would've happened if Nestor and me hadn't been there. This girl Grace I went to junior high with was running in our direction, away from this crowd in the hallway. She shouts, "Lance is about to fight!" as she goes by.

I don't even wait. I pull on Nestor's shirt sleeve and tell him he's got to do something. Nestor rolls his eyes, but when he sees the look on my face, he takes one big breath and pushes people out of the way like they're the other team on the football field. And he stops and shouts out, "Juan!"

Lance (England): Vicki'd introduced me to Nestor once before that, so I knew who he was. I just didn't know what the Hell he was doing.

From the way he reacted, Juan knew him too. Or maybe just

knew of him, I didn't f---ing know. He'd been making fists and was crouched like he was about to rush me, but he opened them up and stood straight when he heard his name. Then Juan pointed at me and spat out angry words in Spanish. Nestor nodded, but he looked at me out of the corner of his eye and said something, also in Spanish, and all of a sudden Juan's four friends burst out laughing. Juan cracked a smile, like it was so funny he couldn't help it even though he was pissed.

Next thing I know those five were about to stroll away like nothing happened. Juan jerked a thumb at Nestor and looked at me and said, "You lucky you got a friend, One-Nut." That's when I heard ████████████████ boom out, in a voice like a thunderclap, "What's going on here?"

[Note: ████████████████ agreed to provide the following statement under the condition that he or she be identified solely as an individual who was employed by the San Francisco Unified School District and who was working at John Quincy Adams High School at the time of the incident in question.]

████████████████: We had a pretty good idea who the troublemakers and problem children were going to be before their first day of school freshman year. We would all divide up their disciplinary records and read through them to come up with that list. And where it was obvious there had been something left out because the SFUSD was afraid of a lawsuit, we would call their junior high and get those details off the record.

Lance didn't raise any red flags with any of us, so I was surprised that he was ready to "throw down", as the kids say. *Inside* the school, no less. I had a coworker deal with Juan while I took Lance aside for a talk.

"What was that?" I asked him. "What happened?"

He kept his head down and his gaze aimed at his lap as he shrugged. At least *that* was predictable. I didn't see many kids who could make eye contact when they were about to receive their yellings-at. "C'mon. Run it down for me."

So he did. Later on I checked his story with some of the kids who were there, but I already knew he was telling the truth. "Lance, why would you use words like that?"

"He called me a f----- too."

"That's no excuse, and he only did that in response to you calling him *maricón*. Anti-gay slurs?"

"Only one."

"One is already bad enough, and you know it. Besides, that 'd--- up your a--' line makes two."

That's what put the steel in his spine. He straightened up and said, "Then I'll go to the LGBTQ club and apologize to them."

Not the sort of resolution we wanted at all. That afternoon had been utter chaos: a pipe had burst on the other side of the building. So the monitor assigned to that hallway and the attention of the guard scanning the security camera feeds were understandably elsewhere. Making what would have been a non-event into an incident on the cusp of requiring reporting to the SFUSD administration.

If that happened, the school's statistics for that sort of thing would be worse by one. Our principal would be called upon to explain it. Yes, ultimately it would blow over. In the meantime, however, we could expect the school's administration to make our lives miserable with completely unnecessary "corrective actions".

The goal, therefore, was to ensure that there wouldn't be a second act in Juan and Lance's drama. "Let's not worry about that for now, okay? Why couldn't you let it go?"

"Because, ▮▮▮▮▮▮▮▮▮▮, I wasn't going to let myself be called 'One-Nut Lance' for the next four years."

"Even if that meant getting beat black and blue?"

"Yes."

I sat for a while, trying to read him. He held my stare long enough that *I* became uncomfortable. I got up and paced.

That was when I decided to level with him in the hopes that that would work instead. "If this doesn't stop here, it will end with your expulsion."

Lance went back to staring at his lap. He shrugged. "And the possibility of legal action against you and your parents." He didn't have a reaction to that, at least none I could see. "So you need to promise you won't let yourself be baited again."

He shrugged again and replied, "As long as no one calls me 'One-Nut Lance', sure."

I told him to stay put. I walked out and conferred with … my counterpart: let's call this person "Sam". Sam explained how Nestor Martinez had managed to convince Juan to lay off out in the hallway. Juan told Sam he'd leave Lance alone, his only condition being that he not have to apologize. I told Sam that would work as long as Juan wasn't expecting an apology from Lance. Sam went in to check and shortly after texted me that those terms were mutually acceptable.

I returned to give Lance the happy news. Happy for me, that is. Lance's response was to nod once before leaving. Sam and I hung up our negotiator hats and called it a day.

We kept close watch on both of them for a while after that. Thankfully, neither one was a problem going forward. Is that all you wanted to ask?

… I may not have related what we said verbatim, but it is pretty close. I taped my conversation with Lance at the time, and shortly before this interview I listened to it and took notes.

… No, I never bother with that. Anyone who takes California's two-party recording law seriously is a sucker.

Jeffrey (Russia): For a while afterwards, everyone was asking me all about it. I guess they figured that I was Lance's cornerman or something and I had the inside story on it. And I told them all the same thing: Juan insulted Lance, Lance insulted him back, Juan insulted him again, Lance insulted Juan again, Nestor came by and before anything else could happen, ██████████ was on the scene and made sure nothing did. Giving out no details so they'd lose interest and leave me alone. Most people did right away, but those ones who kept on me I'd say sorry, ask someone else who was there.

With Cassie, though, I tried to be as helpful as possible. … It was before we went and saw *Creed* together, yeah. Now that you mention it, she *did* say it was weird that everyone was planning to go to a movie about fighting, but I didn't make the connection. Anyway, she had me walk through all the details from Juan's first words to when the video started. And then she wanted my commentary on the footage.

We spent a half hour going over two minutes. I told her it wasn't exactly WorldStarHipHop material, and then I had to explain *that* to her. Finally the other end of the phone went quiet, and that's when she sent me a link to a YouTube video. It's from this movie *Taxi Driver*, and it's that actor Robert DeNiro when he was young, standing in front of a mirror. It's like he's talking to someone trying to f--- with him, and he's doing this quick draw with a gun up his sleeve.

"You're saying Juan was like that guy in the movie?"

"Lance," she said.

"*Lance* was like that guy? Wait, what made you think of that clip in the first place?"

"I watched a video of a critic explaining the importance of Martin Scorsese's films, and that was one of the scenes he discussed. Lance's actions brought Travis Bickle to mind."

I surfed to the Wikipedia article for *Taxi Driver* and read the plot section out loud until Cassie stopped me to say, "I'm not saying Lance is like the character."

"Okay ...? Then what?"

"I'm saying Lance rehearsed. You noticed how quickly he reacted? How he didn't stumble over his words? While walking backwards? And how was it that he knew that Spanish swear word?"

"I don't know ...."

"The backpack. Look at how quickly he got it off. I feel certain that if you were to try it right now with yours, you would get hopelessly tangled in the straps."

I thought it over. "Maybe he practiced those lines. But he just got lucky with his pack, Cass. You don't know Lance like I do, okay? He hasn't been working out or sparring or anything like that. So why would he be figuring out the fastest way to get ready for a fight he was a hundred percent gonna lose?"

She didn't have an answer to that.

Nestor (Germany): What I think about it? Lance was going get beat down *hard* by Juan and both their lives would've gone to dark places. I step in and defuse that situation.

And most everyone knew it too. A whole week after all that, people are praising me for my quick thinking, for doing the right thing. Not just students, either. Teachers, too. And Coach.

"Most" doesn't mean Lance, though. 'Bout a week later, me and Vicki are leaving school, and Lance and those guys and Cassie are standing around outside. Vicki stops to say hi, and there's this awkward silence because it's the first time since all that, and everyone knows it.

Finally Lance says, and this is it exact, "I never did thank you for stopping that fight." I tell him he's welcome and he immediately twists his head away and down.

Vicki talks to those guys a little more then we say goodbye. And I'm back home before it hits me: Lance didn't actually thank me. Ungrateful punk-a-- b----.

Lance (England): Damn right I didn't thank him. I didn't ask for his f---ing help. The whole reason I was ready to trade blows with Juan and get the s--- kicked out of me was because I wasn't going to let anyone insult me and get away with it. All Nestor accomplished was to make sure that was exactly what happened, and in front of all those people.

On top of that, there's what he said to stop the fight. I don't speak Spanish, but I don't have to to catch some words. And I heard Nestor the F---ing Molester say *"uno pelota"* loud and clear. Later on, I asked someone if it meant what I thought it did. One ball. That's what he was saying to get them laughing and what made Juan back down.

I had this hunch, but I had to be sure. Months after, middle of the second semester freshman year, I got my chance. I saw three of those five, including Juan, outside, and I took my shot. I started walking up to them, and one guy tapped Juan on the arm and pointed at me. They all turned around so they were facing me, Juan in front, chest puffed out.

"The f--- you want?"

"Who told you about One-Nut Lance?" I asked him.

Juan was unsure why I asked. Like, was I trying to start s---
with him? But he pointed to one of his two friends.

And I asked that guy, "Okay, who told you?"

He was confused. I found out why when he answered,
"Nestor." Looking at me like it should've been obvious. He
wasn't wrong.

I nodded, said thanks to both of them and walked away.

Ollivander (~~Italy~~): That's what Lance told you about why he was
ready to fight? And why he didn't thank Nestor?

… No, not lies. More like half-truths.

[What Cassandra is studying in college]

Cassandra (Austria): This isn't to criticize your process, but you
must apprehend just how far afield your inquiries have led you,
that you are now asking that question of me. Very well.

I spoke of my parents' conservatism, a word that immediately brings to mind its political and social connotations. But there
is also the sense it which it means cautious and deeply opposed
to risk. They are that too.

The not-really-a-joke joke about Asian parents is that there
are only four career choices that they consider acceptable for their
children: doctor, engineer, professor, and lawyer. Mine aren't
keen on law school for me, now that the profession is glutted
with graduates from now-defunct diploma mills. And with each
passing day, academia proves itself to be less and less of a viable
path for anyone seeking a decent living.

With the two remaining options in mind, Oberlin was near
the bottom of their list. I pointed to their 3-2 program for engineering; I assured them that there exist graduates of that college who are now doctors. That wasn't quite enough to over-
come their concern that the school was an untrustworthy hippie
enclave designed to lead good girls like me irrevocably astray.
What ultimately persuaded them was the financial aid package,
a much more generous one than any other school was offering.

My parents are not so terribly well-off that they could ignore that consideration.

Now, I don't recall what grade I was in when the teacher asked us what we wanted to be when we grew up. I do, however, know what my answer was, because I wrote it down, in my careful handwriting which garnered praise from adults, on a sheet of light blue construction paper with a black marker. I wanted to be a detective.

Not even remotely one of the four. But my mother and father had a cunning plan. They taped that paper onto the side of our refrigerator and encouraged me relentlessly. At an age when other girls would get dolls, they were giving me a magnifying glass and a cheap microscope. Then making me watch educational videos on optics, because "a good detective learns how all his tools work." My parents aren't big on inclusive pronoun use, as you might have already surmised. And from there, it was on to biology. My father told me about forensic entomology and had me looking at ants under my microscope and learning about how botfly infestation of corpses has been used to determine time of death. The Huỳnh family may be conservative, but what we are not is squeamish. Chemistry was next. I may have been the only kid in school with a latent fingerprint kit, luminol, and a UV light.

In the meantime I read book after book featuring boy and girl detectives. My mother found a cheap set of those Nancy Drew novels, the old hardcover ones with the yellow spines. I devoured the Encyclopedia Brown mysteries. My father and I would watch Basil Rathbone play Sherlock Holmes in those ancient movies while my sister rolled her eyes so far up in her head that I thought they would get lost.

They were first to cry Uncle. For my tenth birthday, a friend got me a child-sized deerstalker hat. I was overjoyed, judging from the video of that party. The camera panned to my parents and their nonplussed expressions. All their friends' children were into Harry Potter and loved nothing more than pointing wands at each other and shouting out nonsensical approximations of Latin. Which was just as weird in its own way, but it came with the consolation that they would grow out of it when they realized that their incantations were nothing more than gibberish and real-life sports entailed actually running and not flying around on broomsticks. That wasn't a silver lining that my parents could rely on in my case.

After the kids had left and everything had been cleaned up, they sat me down and asked me if I still wanted to be a detective when I grew up. And with all the enthusiasm of a ten-year-old, I said I did.

My mother buried her chin in her hand and thought. And when she was done, she told me to research what it would take to become a detective and then relate my findings to them.

People I've asked the question of are divided, fifty-fifty right down the middle, as to whether my mother's instruction to me was an act of unconscionable cruelty. Because what I quickly determined was that there was no way I could be a detective. I knew I would never pass the physical requirements in most locations. Most law enforcement agencies had scrapped minimum height rules, but my uncorrected vision was poor and I wasn't all that athletic and I suspected I never would be.

As for forensics, I found out that it was nothing like the TV shows. There was no real crime solving done on that end. The reality of that work was deeply unsexy, involving monotonous testing and no opportunity to innovate, except perhaps at the very heights of that profession.

My parents doggedly asked me about it, once a week for two months until I told them what I told you. I asked them if they were happy now that I was giving up on my dream. They assured me I would find another one.

Right. Some people thought my parents should have waited it out. What was the harm in nurturing my childhood aspirations for a little while longer? And then, if it turned out to be necessary, gently breaking it to me instead of forcing me to find out the truth for myself?

The others thought my mother handled it as well as any parent could. I had to find out eventually that I wasn't going to grow up to be a detective. Should she have waited another year for me to come to that conclusion? Two? And wasn't it just keeping me from finding what my real calling was?

A few were surprised that it worked. Getting a ten-year-old to understand how her dream would never come true by having her investigate on her own? If you count yourself in that category and it seems overly precocious to you, I suppose all I can say in response is that I've always been pretty realistic about things. You could ask my family. I don't mean that literally, by the way: we agreed at the outset that you would not be talking to them.

Moving on. Even after that realization was forced on me, I kept reading mysteries and detective stories. I became interested in true crime and briefly considered becoming a journalist. Until I found out how miserable being a journalist was in the twenty-tens and how it would be even worse in the future.

Sophomore year of high school I convinced Vicki and those guys to dress up as Mystery Inc. for Halloween. You know, from Scooby-Doo. Naturally, I was Velma. Vicki was Daphne, Jeff was Scooby, Lance was Shaggy, Evander was Fred. Booker was the villain, in a Dracula costume with his hands in cuffs and Evander holding his mask. If you're wondering about the optics, it was Booker who chose that role. He felt that playing an arrested criminal dressed up as a monster still managed to be less humiliating than any of the other options.

And somehow, I don't quite know how, that dress-up make-believe scrubbed the last remnants of those gumshoe fantasies out of my conscious mind for a while. I poured my time and attention into my classes and the requisite extracurricular activities. The little time I had left to think was spent mulling over what career I wanted and how college would help me have it.

At this moment, I am in that 3-2 engineering program, as I promised my parents I would be. Engineering is about building in the broadest possible sense: the materials, the tools, the design rules, the architecture. I ... I don't want you to get the impression that I believe there's anything wrong with that. I'm doing reasonably well in my first-year math and science classes, maintaining the required GPA so far. And at times I feel the same satisfaction of solving problems that the other students do. That's the answer to your question. This is what I am studying in college so far.

But I don't want to build. My childhood imagination, stamping its feet in a tantrum, has loudly reasserted itself: I want to solve mysteries. Perhaps become a semiotician and decode the signs and symbols that people create, whether accidentally or purposefully. Maybe be an anthropologist or sociologist. The school lets you design your own interdisciplinary major, so if I only read enough, learn enough, I can maybe put it all together and form something that makes sense. Stitched like Frankenstein's monster, demanding that humanity acknowledge its life to be as precious as any other's.

And I could perhaps find the solution to puzzles that no one even knew existed until I discovered them. There you go: somehow I've managed to bring your question back around to that day we played that damned game. When all this is done? When you have composed your oral history from our seven interviews? Then you can thank me for doing your thematic heavy lifting for you.

Spring
1904

[Diplomatic phase of spring 1904]

Ollivander (~~Italy~~): With three minutes to spare, I had the dishwasher going and the kitchen cleaned up adequately for the afternoon.

Vicki had found Nestor and was leading him by the hand to the back porch. "No game talk until one-thirty."

"Yeah, that's totally what we were going to do out there," she said. Nestor winked and shut the door behind him.

I went to the living room. Passed Booker in the hallway. "Keeping an eye on those two?"

He shook himself out of whatever trance he was in. "Oh. Hmm. No, I was thinking about ... something."

"Well, keep calm and carry on." Lance, Cassie, and Jeff were standing around in the living as I came in. Jeff tipped his head back and lifted the fingers of his right hand up two inches in a sort of half-wave.

I came over to stand beside him. "You and me, Jeff."

"You got any ideas?"

"Not until one-thirty," Lance said.

Jeff sighed and took out his cell to check the time. "Are you having fun, Cassie?" I asked.

"I'm still trying to figure it out," she replied.

"Don't be embarrassed. The game has its nuances."

She peered at me through her thick lenses. At my forehead, which was weird, even for her. "Do I have something on me?"

"Urr, um, no," she said. "Sorry, my mind was wandering."

We listened to the clock on the mantle ticking. The time it showed on the day of the game was off by more than a full hour: it ran slow, losing five minutes every two weeks. I used to correct it every Sunday evening.

My dad was the reason I stopped doing that. I went to his apartment on one of his custody weekends, and he brought it up. After dropping me off two weeks prior, he had lingered on the porch and caught me adjusting the time.

I told him of my weekly ritual. "Why do you ask?"

"It's a booby prize of sorts. It's almost completely worthless in monetary terms, but your mother thought otherwise."

"Why?"

"I also used to reset the time every week. Like father, like son, I suppose. I had bought it cheaply at an estate sale my first year at university.

"It became an object lesson in sunk cost. Every month I would set it forward ten minutes or so, and from time to time I would rub linseed oil into the wood, clean the glass, and remove the tarnish from the brass. As if it were a valuable antique."

"But why wouldn't you fix the timekeeping mechanism itself?"

"I could buy three digital wristwatches now that would keep better time for less than the repair would have cost then. The clock served as a fetish item, you see? My ministrations thus forming my own personal sacrament.

"Your mother never asked; I never explained. The reason for our break-up in miniature. When we did divorce, she insisted that every item be accounted for. I lied about the clock's price and she, having seen the attention and care with which I treated it, believed me. Thus your mother absolutely *insisted* she must have it. The mediator allowed me my full record collection as a consolation prize. And I bought that metronome—the one right there—for whenever I miss the sound the second hand makes."

I asked my mom about it afterwards. She gave it an impassive backwards glance and said, "It's a clock. It looks good on the mantle. Who cares?"

There you have it: two lessons in sentimentality from my parents.

"Annnnd … it's one-thirty," Jeff said. I unpaused the timer on the website and we were off.

Jeffrey (Russia): I got my mouth open, but before I could say a word, Evander said, "Front porch."

He looked through the windows to make sure nobody was

nearby and gave the all-clear. "Okay, so what do we do?"

"Budapest will be hard to hold for long without nearby support."

"Okay, so I get help? Who?"

"We can ask Vicki, but there's nothing in it for her to hold off on taking it from you."

I take out my phone and look at that part of the map. "Wait, I can take Sevastopol with my army!"

"How does that help you with Budapest?"

"She can't take Sevastopol except with her army in Rumania. But then she doesn't have the support to take Budapest from me, right?"

"Not with those units, no. But Vicki will deploy her units in Ankara and Constantinople to take it."

"She can't do that until next year at the earliest. By that time I'll have a build that I can put on Moscow to support."

Ollivander stared at the clouds for a while. "Wrong, end of this year if she gets moving now."

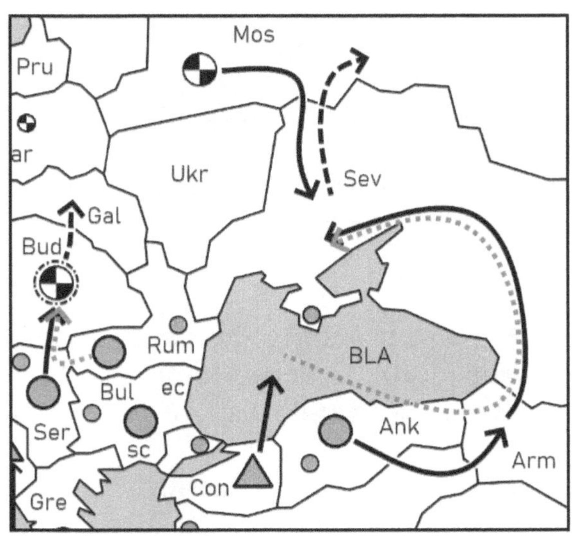

Figure 18 -- How Turkey Could've Taken Bud and Retaken Sev by End 1904 If Russia Had Taken Sev in Spring 1904: Arm to Sev with Support from BLA Fleet, Forcing Russian Army in Sev to Retreat (dashed line) in Fall 1904; Ser to Bud with Support from Rum Army, Forcing Russian Army in Bud to Retreat

He laid it all out for me. "And on top of that, if you try, you won't be able take St. Petersburg back," he added. "That army either goes to Sevastopol or supports your fleet to the south coast."

He was right. "But maybe it's worth trying?"

"Even assuming you get a build this turn and she somehow doesn't take Sevastopol from you right away, you'll have to make it an army in Moscow if you want to keep it from her. You can hold her at bay for a season or two, but that's it. In the meantime, you're weak in the north and without Nestor's help, you can't hold Sweden."

I brushed my right foot back and forth along one of the wood planks. Looked at it and thought. "You're saying I need to make a deal."

"At least one, yes."

"Cassie for Budapest."

"Sure. And Lance."

"No. F--- that s---," I said.

Evander put up his hands, kind of like, "Wait, wait," and said, "I get it. But you could convince him to move out of St. Petersburg and let you hold Sweden."

"I won't talk to him."

"Well, this is your lucky day, because you've got me to talk to him for you."

It wouldn't've made any sense for me to say no to that. "What's he going to want in return?"

"Let me ask. You talk to Cassie."

Lance (England): I was watching the two of them outside because I didn't have anything better to do that turn. When Jeff walked towards the door, Evander caught my eye and waved me over.

Jeff scanned the living room for Cassie on the way back to the kitchen. I headed out the front door to talk to Evander.

"So?"

"Give Jeff St. Petersburg and let him keep Sweden."

"What's in it for me?"

"Okay, let's say there's no deal. He pushes you out of St. Petersburg with his Moscow army. He holds Sweden with help from Germany."

"Right, which is what you want me to do for him anyway."

"Except that he can then move that fleet into the Gulf of Bothnia then squeeze your army in Finland until it pops. Then Norway would be next to go, as long as he's got Germany's help, and I think that's a given."

I thought it over. "But if his fleet is in St. Petersburg ...."

"Then he can't take Finland," Evander said. "Or Norway, because he's on the south coast."

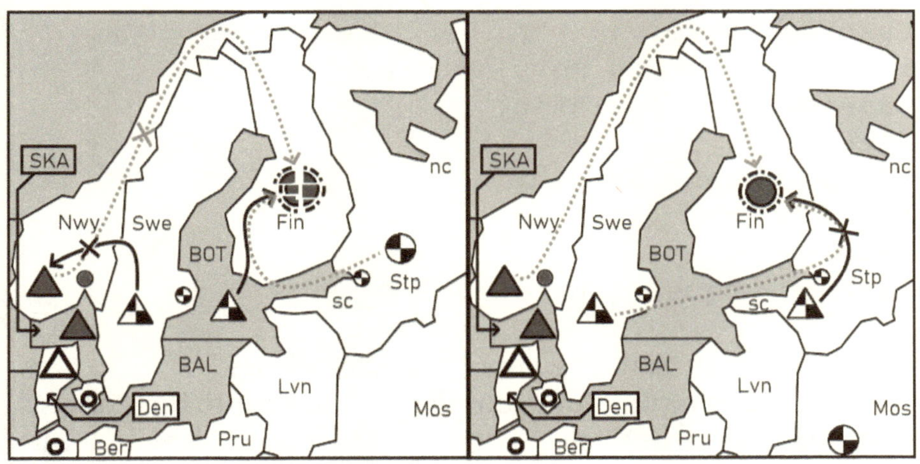

Figure 19 -- [Left] Russian Fleet Forces English Army in Finland to Disband; [Right] English Army in Finland Successfully Holds with Support from Norway

"And you can ask him to move his Moscow army to a mutually beneficial location."

I looked at the map on my phone. "Warsaw."

"Warsaw. Can I tell Jeff we have a deal?"

"Okay. Deal."

"One thing? If I were you, I wouldn't renege on it, not this season. If you do, Jeff will go to Nestor and tell him outright that all his units are his to order as he pleases, I'm sure of it."

"Not this season. Bet."

Cassandra (Austria): Booker was in the kitchen, sitting with his chin in hand and elbow on the table. He stood up when he heard me enter.

"It has been a half hour or so since we spoke. Would you like me to remind you?"

"I ...." My phone beeped to let me know I had a message. "Could you hold on a moment?"

```
Vicki>    sex to talk?
Vicki>    *sec*
Cassie>   Sure.
Vicki>    i gotta move into adr
Cassie>   The Adriatic?
Vicki>    y
Vicki>    cant say why
Vicki>    ok?
Cassie>   Okay.
Vicki>    squee! luv u gurl
```

"Sorry about that. Yes, could you remind me?"

"It is very simple. Move your fleet in Trieste into the Adriatic. Move your army in Venice to Trieste. Move your army in Rome to Venice."

"Right. And I attack Nestor this turn?"

"Attack Germany's army in Tyrolia with yours in Vienna. If I am right, you will cut the support to the army in Bohemia and it will be unable to enter Munich."

"I ... okay."

"Cassandra. It is in my interest to attack you on the Italian peninsula. I do not want to do that, but you have to help me."

"I *said* 'okay'."

Booker regarded me for a moment before replying, "I apologize. I misunderstood your response. Thank you, Cassandra."

He walked off and I took his seat. It was when I started absent-mindedly playing with my bangs that I recalled staring at Evander's hairline a few minutes prior. I had managed to make him uncomfortable doing it.

I had played it off as me zoning out, Cassie being Cassie again. But that wasn't the case, not exactly. It was as if his forehead was important somehow. Sitting at that table, I decided I had to have been wrong. After all, when has that part of someone's body ever reminded anyone of anything?

That's when Jeff came by. "Cass! Hey, got a minute?"

"Sure."

He sat across from me. "I need you to support me in Budapest."

"Support you?"

"With your army in Vienna."

I got out my phone and navigated to that area. "What about Nestor's armies next to me?"

"They can't both move against you, 'cause then Booker takes Munich, right? I bet you anything he tries to move his army in Bohemia there. And you can attack his army in Tyrolia with your army in Venice, see?"

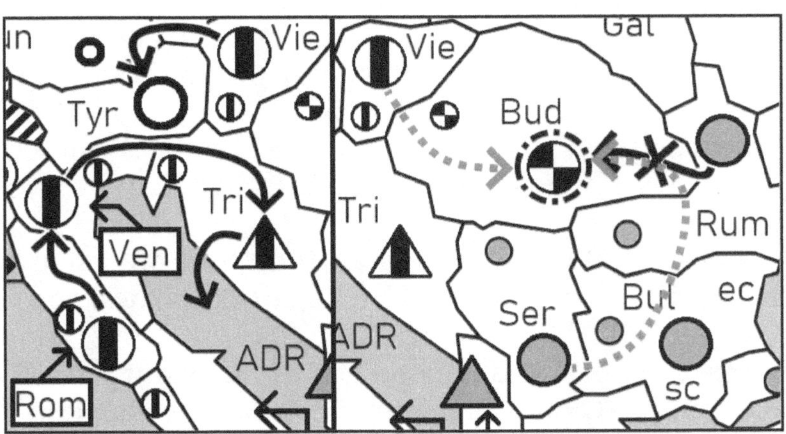

Figure 20 -- Proposed Orders for Austria: [France, Left] Vie Attacks Tyr, Tri to ADR, Ven to Tri, Rom to Ven; [Russia, Right] Vie Supports Bud Hold

I shook my head. "I don't know ...."

He gripped my wrist. "You gotta! If you don't, Vicki takes it from me!"

I looked down at his hand. He released mine. "Sorry, I got excited. What do you say?"

"Are you seriously asking me to help you stay in the supply center you took from me?" He hung his head, abashed. "That's kind of insulting."

Jeff took a few seconds to find his words: "But it's okay if Vicki takes it?"

"That's different. She's not taking it from *me*."

He tapped his fingers nervously on the table until his phone chimed. He scrutinized it briefly before standing up. "Ask her if she'll return it to you once it's hers. Let me know what she says." He crossed to the back door, knocked twice, and exited.

Victoria (Turkey): As soon as Nestor and I were out on the porch, I snuggled up to him.

I made some purring noises. Told him, "I am going to miss this when I'm in Europe."

"Wish I could be here when you get back."

"I know, I know. Tomorrow I'll give you a day you'll never forget."

Nestor chuckled and I felt it rumble through him. "That'll hold me 'til you get to Massachusetts."

I grabbed his left wrist and twisted it so I could see his watch. "Two minutes. Or we could cheat and start talking about the spring now."

"No, *querida*. When we win, they won't have any excuses."

Fine by me. I rested my head back against his chest and waited.

"Three ... two ... and here we go." He took out his cell and started typing. "Okay, your army in Ankara to Smyrna. Your fleet in Constantinople to the Aegean. Your army in Rumania to Budapest, and your army in Serbia supports that move."

"Wait," I said. I got out my phone. "What if Jeff moves into Sev ... Sevas ...."

"Sevastopol. You can call it 'Sev' if you wanna, that's what most players do. He still loses Budapest. Takes you a little longer, but you'll get him out of Sev and it'll be yours again. Promise."

"'kay."

"Where was I … your army in Bulgaria to Rumania. Your fleet in the Ionian to Tunis. That's not gonna work, but you try it, just in case. That leaves Albania and Greece." Nestor thought it over. "Do this. Text Cassie, tell her don't move her fleet into the Adriatic. That's where you're going with yours. Then you move your army in Greece to Albania."

I started texting her. "What if she says no?"

He looked at his screen, trying to figure that out. Turns out he didn't need to, 'cause Cassie said yes.

"Great," he said. He tapped a couple more times and I got all that on my phone. "You got all that?" I nodded. "You're gonna start moving those units, help me take out everyone else, one by one."

"'kay." I smiled. You know, when I told Evander me and Nestor were coming, I didn't think it'd actually be *fun*. But I was having a good time, moving my pieces around, being Queen Victoria of Turkey. Wait, did they have queens? … "Sultana"? That, then.

Nothing else to do for ten minutes, so I clung to Nestor until Jeff came knocking.

Nestor (Germany): Jeff peeks his head out the door. "Can I talk to you, Nes? Sorry, Vicki."

Vicki kisses me on the cheek, peels herself off. "No problem, Jeff. See you inside, bae."

Jeff looks through the window, so I do too. No one in the kitchen 'cept Cassie, spacing out at the table. "Coast is clear, *Jefe*. What can I do for you?"

"Evander's worked out this deal. With Lance."

I nod. "Lay it out for me."

He does. "Warsaw, huh? Ain't surprised."

"You're not?"

"He wants your armies moving west instead of south. Rolling into Silesia and Prussia."

"Then attacking you."

"That's the idea. What do *you* want to do?"

"I want to f--- him over like he did me. I don't even know if he's going to hold up his end."

I think it over. "My guess? He will. He can afford to give you a truce 'til the fall. Assume that, and tell me if that changes anything."

Jeff shakes his head. "No. I can take Sevastopol and hold in Budapest."

I look at the map on my phone again. "If you got Cassie's help. Do you?" Doesn't answer me. Doesn't have to, because his face says no for him. "So at best you break even. Hold Budapest. Or you lose it and get Sevastopol instead. But in that case? Vicki will scramble her units and kick your a-- right out again. Might take a year, but she will."

He nods, and from the way he does, it's like he's hearing it a second time. I'm betting Evander told him the same thing. "I'm gonna cut to the chase and give you my advice. Do exactly what they say: fleet to St. Petersburg, army to Warsaw. I'll support you in Sweden through the end of the year at least. Keep his units up north in a holding pattern."

Jeff thanks me and leaves me on the porch. I start planning out my moves for the spring.

Booker (France): My situation in the spring of 1904 was a mess; there was no avoiding that fact. Very soon England would be convoying an army to Picardy, where it would be a chronic irritant, ready to take Paris should I ever let my guard down. Its fleet in Brest was two spaces away from my supply centers in Spain and Portugal and three from Tunis.

My decisions that spring were relatively straightforward, but only because my hand was forced. My army in Marseilles would have to move to Spain. And my army in Piedmont would have to move to Marseilles to take its place. That would be the only way I could be sure Spain and Portugal would remain mine.

My fleets in Tunis and the Tyrrhenian Sea were not properly situated to drop anchor on the Italian peninsula and take Austria's supply centers there. So my plan was to push forward into the Ionian Sea for the time being and reassess in the fall.

The only difficult choice I faced was what to do with my army in Ruhr. I would need an army in Paris or next to it to keep England's army from jumping the Channel and taking it.

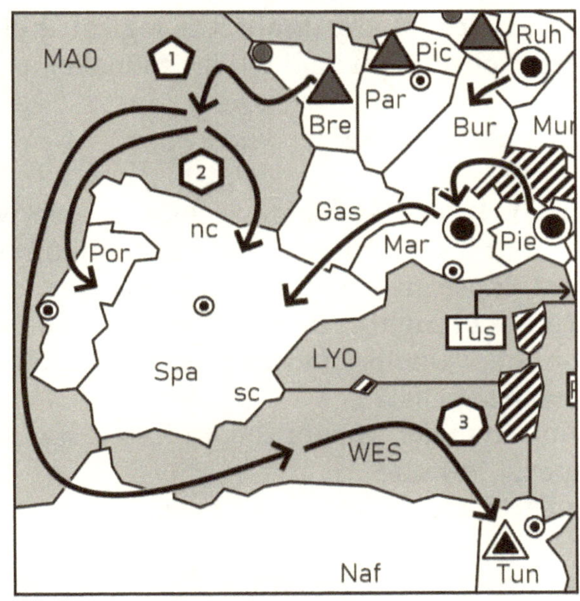

Figure 21 -- Reach of English Fleet in Brest in 1, 2, 3 Moves and France's Planned Countermobilizations in that Spring

The one bright spot of the condition I was in at that moment was that I did not need to move to Burgundy right away. Were I to take and hold Munich, I could build an army in my capital city before the English army could reach it. And even if I failed to do so, I could reach Burgundy with that army as the enemy army came ashore in Picardy. England would be stymied in that theater of operations.

Except that that best case scenario, taking and holding Munich, would be an ephemeral victory. I would have that extra army only until Germany retook Munich, which would be by the end of 1905, barring a miracle or sustained cooperation from Austria.

The alternative would be to support Germany's move into

Belgium, as had been requested of me. I could wait until fall to do so, as long as I moved to Burgundy this season. This attack would be almost certain to succeed, as England would not expect that I would support such a move. And the result would be that the country posing the most immediate threat to me would lose a unit. This was, without any doubt, the logical choice, the one any disinterested observer would tell me to make.

[Lance's discussion with Booker re: Nestor]

Lance (England): It was f---ing crazy how people were s---ing Nestor's d--- about that thing with me and Juan. But what really drove me nuts? Those guys wouldn't take my side.

The last time I brought it up to all of them we were playing Starcraft II online. "*Uno pelota*! How do you think Nestor the Molester knew to say that?"

"Stop trying to make 'Nestor the Molester' happen. It's not going to happen," Jeff said.

"Seconded," Evander said. "And even assuming you heard that right—"

I cut in and told him I definitely did. "Fine. But so what? Nestor heard it from someone, just like Juan did. He brought it up because that's what the fight was about."

"How did he know that? Huh? How?"

"He overheard it. Or someone told him before he stepped in. Or Juan told him. Again, so what?"

I told them I was right there, and Juan didn't tell Nestor. "How do you know?" Jeff asked.

"Because I didn't hear *uno pelota* from Juan, that's how."

Evander jumped right in to shoot that down. "And Juan didn't use any other slang term for testicle? Or even the Spanish word for 'nickname' and Nestor knew what Juan was referring to? Over the noise of the crowd you're sure of all that?"

Booker hadn't said anything. "Help me, Booker. You're my only hope."

He told me he didn't have an opinion about it one way or another. But said it like he wasn't going to be coming around to my side, so I might as well shut up.

Okay, remember how months later Juan's friend confirmed what I f---ing *knew*? That Nestor was the one dishing that tea, telling people about "One-Nut Lance"? Well, I was good and ready to rub it in those guys' faces. But because Booker was maybe more open to hearing me out, I was going to run it by him first. I asked if I could come by his place on a Sunday, and when he said okay, I went over and filled him in.

And his reply was, "Jeffrey and Ollivander seem to think you are jealous of Nestor."

"Him? Why would I be?" Booker didn't answer me, so I plowed ahead. "Booker, have you ever heard of the Flowers of Edo?"

"No."

"Tokyo, starting around sixteen hundred and going on until the mid-nineteenth century, would have these major fires every twenty-five years or so. Edo was the name for both the city and that period, and those 'flowers' were the flames."

"Hmm."

"And you can bet that firemen were a big deal. *Hikeshi* is what they called them back then. They had different groups, almost like sports teams. Well, of course a lot of those *hikeshi* got swelled heads. They'd get drunk and brawl in the streets. And some of them even started fires. To drum up business, but also so they could look like heroes putting them out."

"I will stop you there. I see the analogy you are attempting." I tried to reply, but Booker held up his hand to stop me. "Nestor could not have possibly told Juan's friend in the expectation that things would happen as they did. It is a coincidence that he managed to be present and put an end to your altercation at the crowning moment before a punch could be thrown."

"Fine, but even then, it's like … it's like he's getting credit for putting out the fire he accidentally caused by tossing a lit cigarette into a pile of dry leaves. Who knows what f---ing stunts he'll pull later on, now that he's got that reputation?"

Booker gave me a nod like he was saying he bought it. Not gonna lie: it felt good that someone finally saw it my way. "Were

I to tell you something, would you promise not to share it with anyone?"

I promised. I guess I'm breaking it here, but with everything that already happened, it doesn't really matter, right? "I do not care for Nestor. He has addressed me more than once as 'Boring Booker'; he has asked me to do his math homework for him. Not directly, of course: he requested I provide a step-by-step explanation of nearly every problem assigned to him. His feigned helplessness was nauseating."

"Yes! You see? It's the same thing!"

Booker stood up and waited for me to do it too. So I did, and he said, "Now that you recognize this behavior in Nestor, you are forewarned."

"I don't need to be forewarned. I need to know how to deal with him getting to play hero at my expense. What do I do with that?"

Booker opened his front door, making it real f---ing obvious our talk was over. "You let it roll off of your back. What else *can* you do?"

Austria

```
A Nap → Rom ◊ A Rom → Tus ◊
F Tri S A Ven → Tyr -- Failure, Order invalid
A Ven → Tyr -- Failure, Attack str. inadequate
A Vie → Boh -- Failure, Attack str. inadequate
```

England

```
F Bel Holds ◊ F Bre → MAO ◊
A Lon Holds ◊ F Pic → ENG ◊ A Stp → Fin ◊
F SKA → Den -- Failure, Attack str. inadequate
F Nwy → Swe -- Failure, Attack str. inadequate
```

France

```
A Mar → Spa ◊ A Pie → Mar ◊
F Tun → ION ◊ F TYS S F Tun → ION ◊
A Ruh → Mun -- Failure, Attack str. inadequate
```

Germany

```
F Ber → Kie ◊
F Den S F Swe Holds -- Failure, Supp. disrupted
A Boh → Vie -- Failure, Attack str. inadequate
A Hol → Bel -- Failure, Attack str. inadequate
A Tyr → Mun -- Failure, Attack str. inadequate
```

Russia

```
F Lvn → Stp.sc ◊ A Mos → War ◊
F Swe S F Den Holds -- Failure, Supp. disrupted
A Bud → Rum -- Failure, Attack str. inadequate
   Retreat to Gal
```

Turkey

```
F Alb → ADR ◊ A Ank → Smy ◊
A Bul → Rum ◊ F Con → AEG ◊ A Gre → Alb ◊
A Rum → Bud ◊ A Ser S A Rum → Bud ◊
F ION → Tun -- Failure, Attack str. inadequate
   Retreat to Apu
```

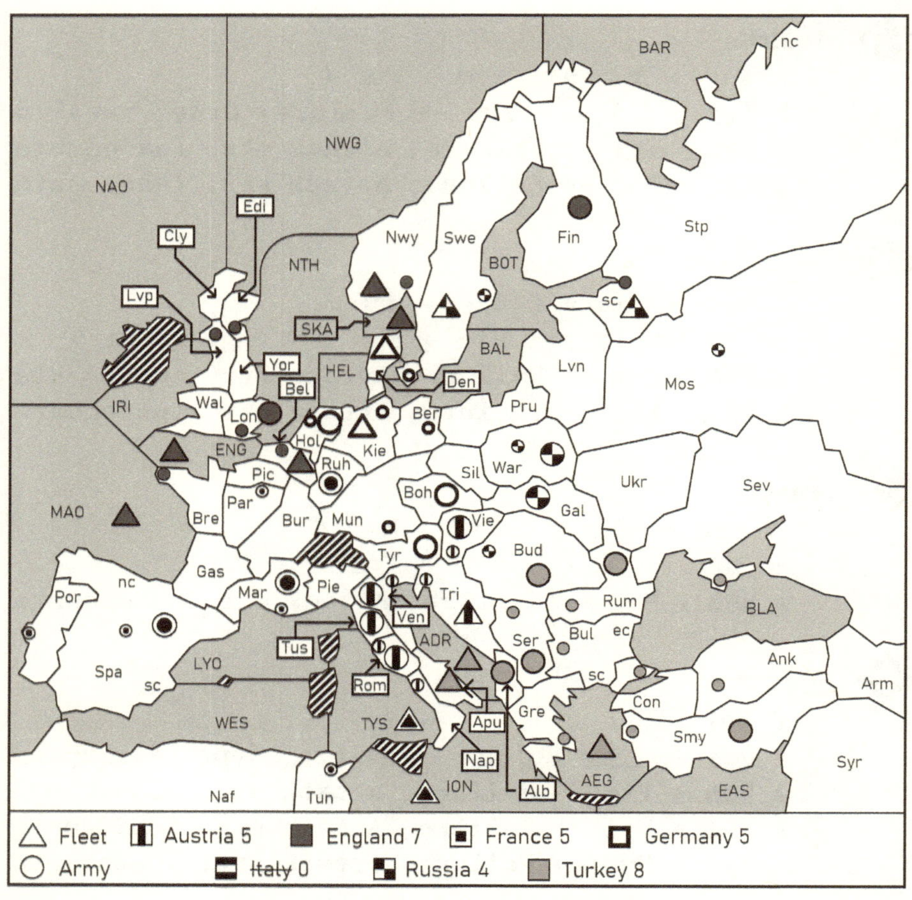

Figure 22 -- Game Map, Start of Fall 1904

Fall
1904

[Reactions to the orders of spring 1904]

Victoria (Turkey): Which one is this? … Okay, hold on …. What I remember was Booker and Jeff being salty at Cassie.

"When you replied 'okay' to my request, Cassandra, what exactly did you mean?" Booker asked.

"I attacked Nestor. That's what you wanted, right?"

Nestor plopped down on the couch, big grin on his face. "S---, I wish I had some popcorn. You got any, Evander?"

Booker ignored him. "I wanted you to move your fleet into the Adriatic Sea to make room for your Venetian army. And move your Roman army to Venice."

"But that wouldn't have happened anyway. My boats would have hit Vicki's boats, and I'd've stayed where I was."

Booker looked over at me, then back over at her. "You were on your phone during our discussion. Messaging Victoria."

"Hey! You don't know that!" I said. That was dumb. I totally gave it away.

Cassie didn't even try to deny it. "So what if I did? You told me that's part of the game."

"No. Strategic double-crossing is. What offends is the pointlessness."

"Maybe you just don't see the point."

"Then show me. Show me what you managed to obtain from keeping your fleet where it is nearly useless."

Cassie shut down the way I'd seen her do when her mom yelled at her. Booker shook his head and sat down on the opposite end of the couch from Nestor.

"I know what she got out of it," Jeff said. Then he waited.

"Well? You've got our complete attention," Lance said. "What's she getting?"

Jeff turns to me and smiles. "Vicki, you're going to give Budapest back to Cassie, right?"

"I … huh?"

"What I don't get is why you didn't tell her to take it with her army in Vienna and support it with one of your armies."

Evander pointed at the laptop. "They were probably afraid Nestor would steal Vienna with one of *his* armies. And he would've if only he'd attacked it with Tyrolia and supported with Bohemia. But I'm sure it'll happen any season now, right, ladies?"

"Let's just start the fall turn," Nestor said.

Lance nodded. "Yeah, why waste time?"

"Not for another minute and a half," Evander replied. "In the meantime, let's figure this out. Okay, so Vicki's going to have to move out of either Serbia or Rumania to make room for her army in Budapest. Then Cassie can move in from Vienna."

Booker stood up and checked out the screen. "First Germany needs to be removed from Tyrolia and Bohemia." He looked over to Cassie. "Otherwise it can simply take Vienna from you, and you will see a zero net gain of supply centers."

"You're gonna need my help with Bohemia," Jeff said.

Cassie didn't hear. I don't think she was just pretending not to, either. For a while there, the only sounds in the room were Evander moving the wooden pieces on the board and the clock above the fireplace ticking.

[Diplomatic phase of fall 1904]

Jeffrey (Russia): "Fifteen minutes," Evander said, and that's when Cassie walked over to me and asked if we could talk.

"Sure." I waved to Evander and Cassie started shaking her head no.

"Just you, me, and Booker," she said.

Evander heard that. "I'm okay with that if you are, Jeff. I'll go talk to Nestor and Lance in the meantime."

I said fine and Cassie was chasing after Booker. "What do you think that's about?" I asked Evander.

"Trying to work out a multi-way deal?"

"But then why wouldn't she get Vicki to join us too?"

"Probably because there's no point getting her involved until she's sure she has your support." By that time, Cassie had dragged Booker back to the living room. When we were finally all out on the front porch, he asked what she wanted.

"So Lance is England."

"Yes ...?" I said.

"You're France," she said, pointing at Booker. "Jeff, you're Russia. And Nestor is Germany."

"Okay ...?"

"Jeff, I'm bringing it up because there's something I don't understand."

I did this thing with my hands, like I was telling her to spit it out. Cassie was moving around her mouth and scrunching her eyebrows, trying to put the sentence together in her head. Booker glanced at his watch.

Finally she said, "If you had to make a guess at the start of the game, before we made our first moves, who Lance would attack, who would it be?"

Booker made a big show of sighing. Well, a big show for him, anyway. "I had assumed you called us together to make a deal."

"Look, just ... just humor me, okay?"

I answered, to get whatever this was over with, "I would have expected Lance to attack Nestor first."

"Me too," Cassie said. "It's clear he doesn't like Nestor."

"And Germany doesn't have the greatest position. It's not Italy, but it's *surrounded*, right?"

I noticed Booker was shaking his head no. "That conclusion is founded on the assumption that its neighbors are all enemies. Until your clumsy maneuvering at the end of 1902, England could not be sure you would act against Germany."

"But I did, though," I said.

"You did. I made a similar blunder. I assumed that my alliance with England against Germany was a solid *entente cordiale*. That was wrong, clearly." Booker turned to Cassie and told her, "Lance is playing the game as it is meant to be played. He has set aside any personal aggrievements in order to take quite a strong strategic position."

"But he doesn't have any allies," Cassie replied.

"Not at this juncture. But as I told you before, he requires none." Booker checked the time again. "I would very much like to move on to discussing our moves for this fall, but I also desire an end to this, so the floor is yours. Explain why the answer to this question should be meaningful to us."

Cassie ran the tip of her index finger along the edge of that sticker on the glass next to the front door, the one warning people they had security cameras. Meaning the one in the doorbell, was my guess. "There's something going on here. Some pattern, under the surface."

"In the game?" I asked. "What is it?"

"I don't know."

"Let us try this one final time, Cassandra," Booker said. "You found Italy's moves suspect. Although I agree with you that Ollivander's execution was wanting, the outcome was not particularly unusual. You now say that England's actions are suspect. They are not; there is no pattern that connects the two."

"Well, what about if Evander losing helped Lance?"

"That simply is not the case. I took one of his supply centers; you took the others. If Italy's quick exit is to be considered the equivalent of so-called 'chip dumping' at a poker tournament, then *you* would be the main beneficiary of the collusion."

Booker's phone ringed then. He took it out and tapped the screen. "Nestor wants a word. Did you want to discuss the fall orders? Or request Russia's help in holding Vienna?"

Cassie was staring at something far off, or she was acting like she was. Me and Booker gave up and went inside.

Cassandra (Austria): I wanted to tell those guys there was no point in talking about the next moves, or teaming up, or anything like that until we figured out what was going on. By then I knew something was. The problem was I didn't know *what*.

I rubbed my finger over that sticker on the glass, the one that said, "NOTICE: AUDIO AND VIDEO SURVEILLANCE MAY BE IN USE ON AND IN THESE PREMISES" next to a pictogram of a security camera. Then I went back inside.

Jeff and Evander were huddled in the living room. Lance was leaning against the wall in the hallway, busy with his phone.

I went to the kitchen and poured myself a glass of water. That's when Vicki came in from outside and sat at the kitchen table. "Umm, hey," I said.

"Hey, what's up, girl?"

"So that thing with Budapest …?"

She nodded. "Oh, yeah, totally. I can't do it this year. You get it, don't you?"

"I … okay, but maybe you can help me out some other way?"

"Sure! Okay, you know how I had to move into Apulia? Because Booker pushed me out?"

"Yes."

"I'm going to get out of there. I've got it all planned out. Here, let me show you." She got out her phone and starting pointing.

"Can you also move out of the Adriatic so I can move my boats out of Trieste?"

"You know what? Sure! I'll move it to Albania."

"But you have an army there."

Vicki gestured to me to come closer. "I'm moving it to Greece," she whispered. "Don't tell anyone, okay?"

I didn't know who I wasn't supposed to tell or why it would make any difference, but I crossed my heart and hoped to die.

Booker (France): After a fruitless chat with Cassandra, I headed to the back of the house in response to Nestor's summons. I suppose I knew what he would be asking already. But I went nonetheless. We had an enemy in common in the game, and I needed his assistance more than he needed mine.

I opened the back door and stepped onto the porch. "Hello, Victoria. You wanted to talk, Nestor?"

She freed herself from his embrace and went inside. "So you tried to take Munich from me."

"I knew it was unlikely to succeed. But I thought it worth a try."

Nestor took out his phone and unlocked it. "You gonna help me take Belgium?"

"Unfortunately I cannot. England will be convoying an army into either Brest or Picardy this turn. I need to move my army from Ruhr to Burgundy to keep him from moving into Paris."

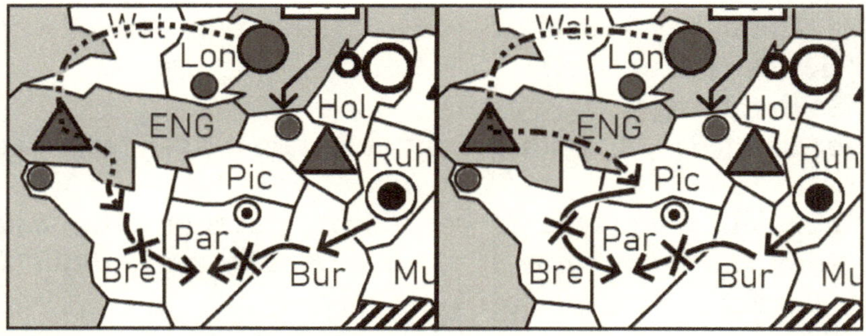

Figure 23 – English Convoy of London Army to Brest [Left]or Picardy [Right]; French Move from Ruhr to Burgundy; Subsequent Bounce in Paris

"You don't know he'll do that."

"It seems nearly certain. But I will pledge this to you, here and now: if by some miracle he does not do so during this turn, I will support your move from Holland to Belgium."

Nestor had been leaning against the wall, but he stood upright to reply, "You know what else is certain? You're gonna lose."

He smirked at me. I suppose he imagined that observation was a devastating blow to my ego. "It seems likely," I replied.

"Unless you join the winning team."

"I doubt that Turkey would agree to a partnership."

"I meant me."

"Why you?"

That smirk grew. "Because Cassie won't help you. You said so yourself"—he checked his watch—"ten minutes ago. And you think Lance's gonna make his own Normandy landing this turn. Jeff's too far away. That leaves me."

"I cannot fault your logic, Nestor. The problem is, I do not trust you."

"Why not? I haven't shivved you in this game, not once."

"You lied about that support order from Paris to Picardy."

Nestor opened his arms, as if to welcome me into his embrace where Victoria had been moments before. "All right. I admit I lied, we got an alliance? Forget about supporting me into Belgium this turn, I'm talking in general."

I considered it for a bit. "No. It is not enough."

He dropped his arms and angled his head to one side. "Don't say I didn't offer."

A bemusing incident occurred just then: before I could take my leave, Cassandra barged out onto the porch. She scanned every inch: the wall, the door, the railings, the eaves above. Then she went right back inside. I looked to Nestor for an explanation, but he seemed as confounded as I.

Ollivander (~~Italy~~): "So how'd your chat with Booker and Cassie go?"

Jeff shook his head. "Don't ask. Can we talk about Nestor first?"

"Sure. He wants you to support him from Tyrolia into Vienna. With your army in Galicia."

"What about my army in Warsaw?"

"As long as you don't push forward into Silesia or Prussia, he's okay with whatever you want to do with it."

"I'm thinking I move it into the Ukraine."

"Just 'Ukraine'. Ukrainians don't like it when you put a 'the' in front of it."

"Really?"

"Yeah, it has to do with Russian imperialism. You can wiki it if you're interested."

"Yeah, I'll get right on that. But Sweden?"

"Okay, you need to move your fleet in St. Petersburg to Finland."

"Why do I want it there?"

"You don't. It's just to disrupt his support. And you hold in Sweden."

"Nestor's gonna support me?"

"He said he would. I believe him, because there's nothing in it for him to let Lance take Sweden."

Jeff looked down at the game board. "Then maybe he helps me take Budapest next year?"

Nestor wasn't going to do that, for super obvious reasons. But there was no need to get into that with Jeff just then. "We can worry about that later. But now all that's out of the way, what *did* you three talk about out there?"

"Cass asked us if we were Lance, who'd we attack first."

"I … huh? Why? No, wait, wait. First tell me how you replied."

"I told her I would've gone for Nestor first, because Germany's weak. Booker said Nestor's only weak if he doesn't have any allies next to him, and I couldn't really be counted on to betray him."

I thought about how to answer that. "Until you did."

"I tried to, anyway. Booker said what Lance has been doing has worked like a motherf---er for him so far."

"Well, yeah. So why did she ask?"

"Who knows with her. She's convinced something's weird about the game."

"Weird? Weird how?"

"Let's me see if I can remember it. Okay, you losing real fast is part of it."

"I had Italy. Italy's not great unless you're a top-level tournament player."

"And Lance not attacking Nestor's the other. What she was tryna get at made no sense to me. Booker neither."

I took a few slow breaths. Then I made a mental note to set aside a few minutes in the upcoming spring to try to talk Cassie down.

 *Austria*

    A Ven Holds ◊ A Tus → Pie ◊
    <u>A Rom → Nap</u> -- Failure, Attack str. inadequate
    <u>F Tri → ADR</u> -- Failure, Attack str. inadequate
    <u>A Vie Holds</u> -- Failure, Hold str. inadequate
        Retreat to Boh

 *England*

    F Bel Holds ◊ A Lon → Bre ◊
    F MAO → WES ◊ F Nwy → Swe ◊
    F ENG C A Lon → Bre ◊ F SKA S F Nwy → Swe ◊
    <u>A Fin S F Nwy → Swe</u> -- Failure, Supp. disrupted

 *France*

    A Mar → Spa ◊ A Ruh → Bur ◊
    A Spa → Por ◊
    <u>F TYS → Nap</u> -- Failure, Attack str. inadequate
    <u>F ION → Gre</u> -- Failure, Attack str. inadequate
        Retreat to EAS

 *Germany*

    A Boh → Mun ◊ F Den Holds ◊
    A Hol → Ruh ◊ F Kie → Hol ◊ A Tyr → Vie ◊

 *Russia*

    A Gal S A Tyr → Vie ◊ A War → Ukr ◊
    <u>F Stp.sc → Fin</u> -- Failure, Att. str. inadequate
    <u>F Swe S F Den Holds</u> -- Failure, Supp. disrupted
        Retreat to BOT

Turkey

    F AEG S F Apu → ION ◊ F Apu → ION ◊
    A Bud Holds ◊ A Rum → Sev ◊ A Ser → Rum ◊
    A Smy → Arm ◊
    <u>A Alb → Gre</u> -- Failure, Attack str. inadequate
    <u>F ADR → Alb</u> -- Failure, Attack str. inadequate

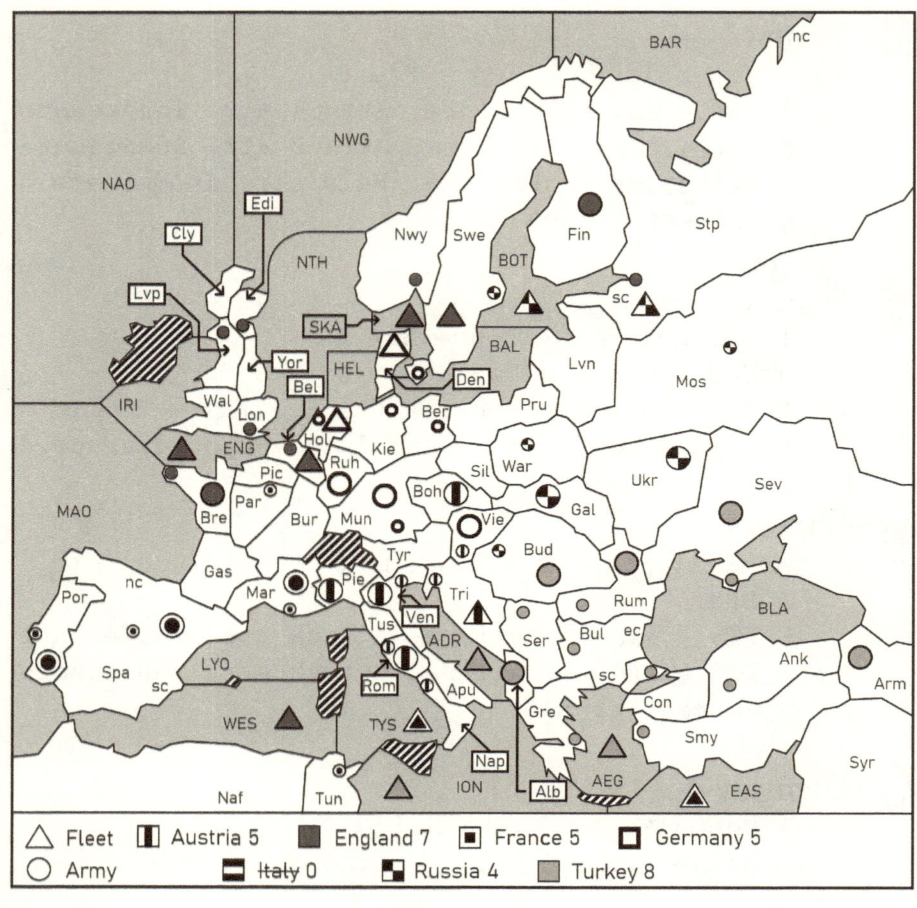

Figure 24 -- Game Map, Start of Winter 1904

Winter
1904

[Reactions to the orders of fall and winter 1904]

Lance (England): People were getting kicked out of territories left and right that season: Booker, Cassie, and Jeff all had to enter retreat orders. After they did, people looked at the map and that's when people *really* started talking.

"Hey! Everyone!" Evander shouted over everyone. "Five minutes for your builds and disbands! That's Nestor, Cassie, Jeff, and Vicki!"

Nestor got really excited looking at the laptop screen. He took out his phone and started typing like crazy. Then Vicki's phone beeped.

And to top it all off, like it wasn't already crystal f---ing clear to everyone else that they were exchanging messages, Nestor raised an eyebrow at her and Vicki smiled and touched the side of her nose with the tip of her finger.

Booker (France): I considered it a stroke of good fortune that I held even that winter. I doubted that the same would be true by the end of 1905.

The move into Piedmont was as close to an open threat that Austria would make in the game. With England stationing a fleet in the Western Mediterranean and an army in Brest, my units in the west were in parlous condition.

My fleet in the Eastern Mediterranean would be disbanded in the spring, there was no question. For its one build, Turkey had chosen a fleet in Smyrna. It was idiocy on my part to retreat deeper into enemy territory instead of back to my supply center in Tunis. Even a rank novice would not have made a mistake such as that.

And so when the winter's orders had been executed, Nestor started openly gloating. "That fleet of yours is going *down*. My girl's gonna sink your battleship." Then he laughed at his attempted witticism.

I counted to three in my head and replied, "I think Victoria is fully capable of speaking for herself, Nestor. Would you not agree?"

"Leave her out of this," Cassandra said.

"Was that directed to me or Nestor?"

Ollivander stepped towards the center of the room and held his hands out to his sides, as if he were separating invisible combatants. "Hold on, everyone. Whether you like it or not, this is part of the game. People will speculate as to future orders; others will attempt to elicit direct answers."

It upset Cassandra to hear that from our host. "And we have to sit around and take it?"

He walked back to the laptop. "Spring of 1905 begins in three minutes and forty-five seconds. Keeping the time in mind, anyone who doesn't want to discuss the fall and winter past is free to go elsewhere."

And so Cassandra did. We listened to her footsteps in the hallway and then the bathroom door swinging on its hinges and clicking shut.

Jeffrey (Russia): I waited until that thing with Cassie was over to say, "I guess you decided not to support me in Sweden, Nestor."

That took him down a couple. "Yeah … about that, fam."

I think he was expecting me to interrupt, so that was it from him.

"Big mistake, counting on Nestor," Lance said.

"Anyone ask you what you thought?" Nestor shot back.

Lance's one nut was a big brass one, because he asked, "Anyone think I need your permission to speak?"

That time it was Evander *and* Vicki getting in the middle and telling those two to simmer down.

Nestor put his hands up and said, "Whatever. This is beneath me." Lance rolled his eyes, but he was quiet after that.

And when everyone was done talking that time, I tried again. "Nestor, you were gonna say something?"

He pointed out the front windows. "Talk outside?"

So that's where me, him, and Evander went. "Who wants to speak first?" Evander asked.

"You know what? Let me," I said. "Look, Nes, it's okay. I get it. Maybe we didn't have a straight up … what's it called?"

"Non-aggression pact?" Nestor suggested.

"Yeah, that. But there didn't have to be, and I tried to get clever with you. F--- you over. You got me back."

"Naw, that's not it at all."

"It's okay, Nes. I deserved it. All I'm saying is, no hard feelings."

Evander sighed. Nestor touched his forehead, like what I was saying was giving him a migraine. "*Jefe*. I f---ed up not supporting you from Denmark."

"You don't have to apologize."

"Naw, that's not what I'm saying. I mean, yeah, I *am* sorry. But I'm telling you I f---ed up the order. I accidentally chose Hold instead of Support. I still don't know how it happened, no lie."

"If that's true, why didn't you apologize to Jeff as soon as you noticed?" Evander asked.

"Yo, this is between me and him."

"I'm Jeff's advisor. I need to be able to tell him if I think he can trust you now. Unless he orders me otherwise, I'll be asking questions."

"Fine. All right. Truth was I was embarrassed. I thought I could catch you later, away from everyone, and do it then." He read our faces. "You don't believe me. But believe the board. It didn't help me to let Lance take Sweden. And now he's going to take Denmark, because I f---ed up and built in Berlin instead of Kiel."

Evander and Nestor were both looking at me. "Like I said, Nestor, it's all good."

That really got to him. He was stepping all around, trying to get that frustrated energy out of him through his feet. He stopped and asked me, "It's like you *want* to believe I f---ed you over on purpose instead of me just f---ing up. Why? What is it with you, homes?"

I didn't have an answer for him. Then all of a sudden Evander shouts, "The bathroom!" and runs inside.

Victoria (Turkey): So it's me, Lance, and Booker in the living room. Lance was sitting on the couch, eyes closed, breathing hard through his nose, loud enough for me to hear it. Booker caught my eye and asked me if we could make a deal.

"Honest? I don't know what you can give me that I want. Nes was right: I'm finna smash your fleet."

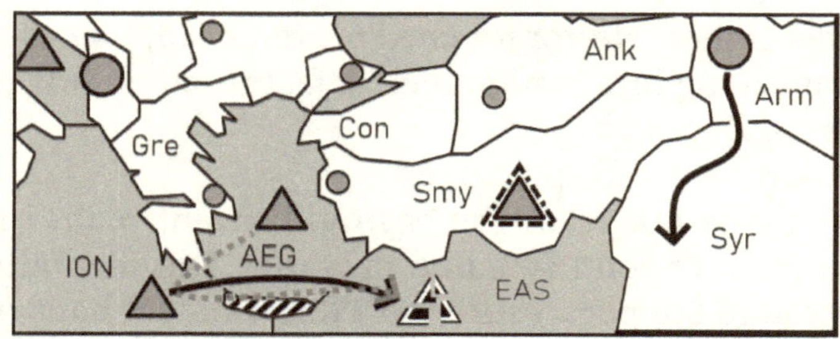

Figure 25 -- How Turkey Would Be Able to
Force France's Fleet to Disband in Spring 1905

Booker scratched his chin. "If you let me move back to the Ionian Sea, I can keep England occupied."

Lance's eyes flew open and he shook himself like he couldn't believe it. "Skrt! Right in front of me, Booker? Really?"

"Yes. Well?"

"That one fleet of his down there isn't going to do anything to me, Booker."

"Yeah, nice try, Booker."

"Every supply center he takes from anyone anywhere will inevitably be aimed at you."

"Lance isn't *that* far ahead of the rest of you."

"Not yet. Give him time and a free hand, however ..."

That got Lance on his feet. "Don't fall for it, Vicki. He's up to something."

He turned and faced Lance. Lance was bobbing up and down like he was nervous and a little bit pissed.

Booker, though, it was like he was looking at a piece of abstract art on the wall at a museum. Just kind of taking Lance in, you know? And I asked the question I'd been wanting to for four years but never got around to: "Hey, Booker. How come you never get riled up? What's your secret?"

[How Booker got his nickname]

Booker (France): I was twelve when my father and mother told me that they wanted to have The Talk. Not the one that euphemistically uses birds and bees to explain sexual reproduction. This was instead the one concerning law enforcement and African-Americans. My parents had decided that my father would go first.

The first part was boilerplate, my father said. "You didn't need to hear any of that, Son. Your mother and I know you're a level-headed young man. Between you and me? I was rehearsing for your little brother, two years from now."

But when I thanked him and got up to go, my father told me, "Slow your roll, young blood. We got more to discuss."

The second part was, to put a concise label on it, a How-To. "I'm supposing you won't be studying any philosophy until college, less'n things have changed since I was in high school. So I'm going to tell you a little about two schools of thought. Stoicism and Buddhism." He leaned to one side in an attempt to peer into the living room. "Close the door."

I did. "Why'd I just do that?"

"Your mother, bless her heart, gets a little sensitive about religion. Like I told you, she'll have more to say later on."

"Okay. Stoicism and Buddhism?"

"There's some important differences between them, but I'm going to focus on something they agree on. A Stoic and a Buddhist will both tell you that anger is, unambiguously and without exception, useless.

"And I'll tell you this: they're right on. Now, I'm bringing this up during The Talk because getting mad and staying mad at the police is how black men—not always, mind you, but too often—land in jail. Or worse. In the end, it don't matter how 'justified' their anger was, or how badly those police behaved. You remember Professor Henry Louis Gates Jr. getting arrested?"

I remembered. I was nine, but it was the talk of our household for some time afterwards.

"He was shouting in his own home. Then that damn cop tricked him into yelling out on his porch, and that was all the excuse he needed to slap the cuffs on." He pointed at me. "Don't you let them bait you."

"But … how's *anyone* supposed to keep their head when that happens to them?"

"It's hard work. But here's the other thing those philosophies have in common: they believe in the value of detachment. Now usually they mean detachment from desire, right? But you can be detached from other emotions. Doesn't mean you don't have them. It means you don't nurture that negativity, you don't stoke those flames."

My father decided that was a good time for an intermission. We got some water, used the bathroom.

"You all done? My turn?" my mother asked.

"Not just yet, baby. Me and Booker got some more talking to do." She looked at her watch and told him to hurry up.

Back inside my bedroom I asked, "But if it's that simple, how come everyone doesn't do it?"

My father sighed. "Some people think if they're angry, they need to give a beatdown to whatever got their dander up. How the Hell you gonna do that in this world? Where you got fools f---in' with you on the internet?"

"Whoa. You just used the f-word."

"I did. That's the other reason I wanted you to close the door. But that was for emphasis, you feel? Not 'cause I got so mad I swore. The other reason, like I said: it takes doing. You know how there'll be times I'll just sit in my room, hands on my thighs, eyes closed? That's me practicing."

"Practicing?"

"Buddhist meditation. I'm not telling you it's the only way. Only that it's how I get *my* calm."

He had some more to say on that. He gave me some other advice, such as the value in speaking slowly and deliberately. "You get loud? Talk fast? It feeds that beast. Starve it. Practice breathing slow, that helps too."

He pulled out his phone to check the time. "Your mama will kick down that door if'n I don't finish up soon. One last thing. Some people gonna call you boring if you don't shout and dance around like a damn fool. Let them. You'll still feel sad, happy, angry, all that. And when you're with the people you love, the people you trust, you can let those feelings ride a little and show on the outside some more. Okay?"

"Okay." As you already know, I took his advice to heart. The other kids did deem me boring, as you know. Before that, they tried to stick me with the nickname "Booger". I systematically deprived it of oxygen by refusing to acknowledge it in any way, and that is how I ended up being called "Boring Booker" instead.

... I nearly forgot, thank you. My mother kept it short. She brought in a laptop and played me a clip. It was Wynton Marsalis, teaching a class to young musicians. There was a boy, about the same age as I was back then, playing the trumpet, and playing it well, I thought.

Marsalis said that he could tell that the trumpeter was cool. And by "cool", he meant that his expressive range was completely non-existent.

She clicked Stop and said, "Your father's got his wisdom. But that advice he gave you? Are you never going to let people out in the world see what's on the inside when something takes you by surprise? How much are you going to miss out on that way?"

As for the rest of it, she told me that I could meditate all I wanted as long as I never forgot that Jesus loved me. And she left me with this bit of advice: "Soon we're going to get you a phone with a camera. Get used to recording whenever you think someone's going to lie about you later on. And don't let anyone know you're doing it if you don't have to, no matter *what* California says about 'two-party consent'."

[Cassandra's visit to the bathroom]

Cassandra (Austria): I didn't need to go to the bathroom, but it was the only room in Evander's house I could lock the door to so I could be sure to be left alone for a little while. The way Booker and Nestor were talking about Vicki like she wasn't even there had made me feel terrible. And I felt it again, like I had all day: there was something really, really wrong with that game.

I sat on the closed lid of the toilet, willing myself to feel better, telling myself it would be over soon and I could go home. Three times I repeated, softly so it couldn't be heard through the door, "I resolve not to let all this affect me."

It may seem corny to you, but that pep talk I gave myself provided me with enough strength to leave the room. I had put my hands on my knees to lever myself up out of my seated position when I heard the knocking at the door. And then Evander's voice, saying, "Cassie? Open up. Cassie?"

And that tenuous equanimity was gone, like that. I looked around, inexplicably panicking. "I ... I ... hold on!" I shouted.

More knocking. "Cassie, I really have to go bad. C'mon!"

"Just a second! Gotta wash my hands!"

"Hurry up!"

I wouldn't have even thought to search the room, but there was something in his voice that got me wondering. I flushed the toilet so it wouldn't be so suspicious and I started looking. Nothing behind the shower curtain except shower stuff. No medicine cabinet.

Yet still more knocking. I spun the taps open.

It was in the cabinet under the sink that I saw it. That Giants baseball cap Evander had put the pieces into to decide who was what country. In the center was a velvet bag with a drawstring, half-filled with cotton. And sewn around the edge on the inside were loops of string, seven of them, each the perfect size for holding one of those wooden blocks.

Austria

A Pie ◊ A Rom ◊ F Tri ◊
A Ven ◊
Disband A Boh

England

F Bel ◊ A Bre ◊ F ENG ◊
A Fin ◊ F SKA ◊ F Swe ◊
F WES ◊

France

A Bur ◊ F EAS ◊ A Por ◊
A Spa ◊ F TYS ◊

Germany

F Den ◊ F Hol ◊ A Mun ◊
A Ruh ◊ A Vie ◊
Build A Bur

Russia

A Gal ◊ A Ukr ◊ F Stp.sc ◊
Disband F BOT

Turkey

F ADR ◊ F AEG ◊ A Alb ◊ A Arm ◊
A Bud ◊ F ION ◊ A Rum ◊ A Sev ◊
Build F Smy

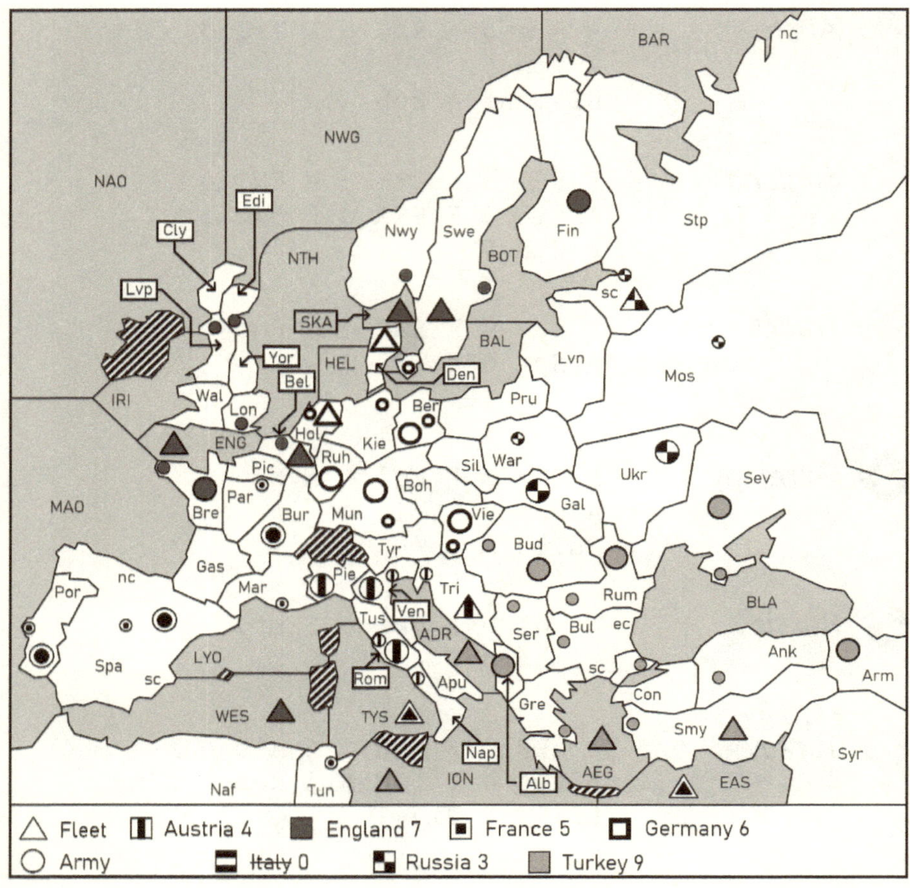

Figure 26 -- Game Map, Start of Spring 1905

Spring
1905

[Diplomatic phase of spring 1905]

Nestor (Germany): So that was weird. Me and Jeff, we look at each other, wondering what the deal is with Evander.

"When you gotta go, you gotta go," Jeff says.

"Never had to go that bad that fast."

"Me neither. Say, you feelin' sick?"

"No. You?"

"I was thinking maybe he got food poisoning? But we all had the same thing for lunch."

Jeff walks in. I hang back a minute and when I do follow, I catch Cassie opening the bathroom door. Maybe Evander doesn't have to go that bad after all, because he's taking a couple seconds to look inside before going in. Cassie walks out and the door slams on her a--.

So now us six are in the living room. I ask Cassie if she's feeling okay.

"I'm fine." Confused why I want to know. Jeff tells her his idea about the food we ate. She doesn't say anything to that.

I get out my phone to kill some time, and thirty seconds later, Booker says, "I think we should discuss our moves now and not wait for our host." Jeff's about to complain when we hear the flush. Fifteen seconds after that, Evander's back with us.

"False alarm," he tells us. Looks to Cassie and says, "Sorry about that."

Vicki gets off the couch and we go to our spot on the back porch.

Booker (France): "Spare my fleet and I will explain," I told her.

"Nah, I don't want to know that bad."

Lance was relieved to hear Victoria reject my offer. And that was how things stood until all of us were once again in the living room.

There was only one other person worth talking to in the

spring of 1905: Cassandra. She remained in the living room after our little crowd dispersed; I took a seat at the other end of the couch.

I was about to enter into negotiations with her when it became clear from the expression on her face that she was, as she had been for most of the day, not truly present. And so I asked her if she was feeling all right.

She swiveled her head towards me while the rest of her remained where it was, as it was. Picture it in your mind, and perhaps you will get an idea as to how unsettling it was. The realization dawned upon me that something *had* changed with her. She was occupying an entirely different mental space from minutes before.

"Like I said, I'm fine."

An answer which left me no choice but to forge ahead, so I did: "Then let us discuss our orders for the spring. All I ask is that you stay out of Marseilles."

"And in return …?"

"In return for that your army in Piedmont will have a free hand in defending against Germany's predations. That and the Venetian army are the only two of your units that have any degree of mobility right now."

She faced front again. And smiled. A bit ruefully, I thought. "Germany. Do you know that Nestor warned me? I thought he was talking about you, but he told me no."

"Warned you about what, specifically?"

"He was right. Imagine that." Cassandra shook her head, as if erasing the memory. "I'll think about it."

Which meant no. Demanding that she provide me with a straightforward answer would be bootless. So I left and pondered my limited options.

Victoria (Turkey): "What were you guys talking about out there?"

"I messed up, *querida*. Put Jeff in a bad place."

Nestor explained it to me. I rubbed his arm and told him, "It's just a game."

"If I didn't take it serious, everyone'd be insulted. Phones out, let's get it going." He moved his finger around on the screen. "First things, message Cassie. Tell her—"

```
Vicki>     hey gurl
Cassie>    Hey.
Vicki>     im clearing out buda 4 u
Cassie>    Thank you.
Vicki>     gonna take 2-3 turns
Cassie>    Okay.
Vicki>     Nes gonna tack u in tri
Vicki>     ill support u
Cassie>    Good. Thank you.
Vicki>     gotta go bye!
Cassie>    Talk to you soon.
```

"Why'd I tell her all that?"

"We're going to put on a show now that we're finally touching with Vienna and Budapest. Can't let everyone think we're teaming up."

"I think everyone already knows, bae."

"Keep 'em guessing." Nestor sent me all my orders. "Any questions?"

"Wow, I'm really going to attack you?"

"You up for it?"

I made sure no one was peeking through the kitchen window and I kissed him. Whispered, "That's what *she* said."

Jeffrey (Russia): Evander and me, we went to the kitchen and he'd got the chair out and his a-- was halfway to the seat when he stood all the way up, patted his jeans pockets and told me to hold on.

Nes and Vicki were out on the porch, like always. I watched them through the window. They were huddled together like it was cold outside instead of afternoon in June. And I remember ... I remember being jealous of them. They weren't alone. I thought they were so lucky to find love like that so quick.

Huh? ... Okay, "envious". I took out my phone and surfed until Evander returned. "Sorry about that. I needed to talk to Lance."

"What's there to say after he took Sweden from me?"

"Nothing, as it happens. I put the ball in his court, said it was up to him to make us an offer."

"And?"

"He couldn't come up with one. The only comment he had for me—for us—was that he was planning to order his army in Finland to hold, and you might as well do the same with your fleet in St. Petersburg."

"Sure. Whatever. My armies?"

"The way I see it, you have three options. One is you move them back to Warsaw and Moscow."

"I can see Moscow, but not Warsaw."

"My feelings exactly. Two is you move from Ukraine to Moscow and from Galicia to Ukraine. A defensive rotation."

"Okay, maybe. What's three?"

"You try to take Rumania. Attack with Galicia, support with Ukraine."

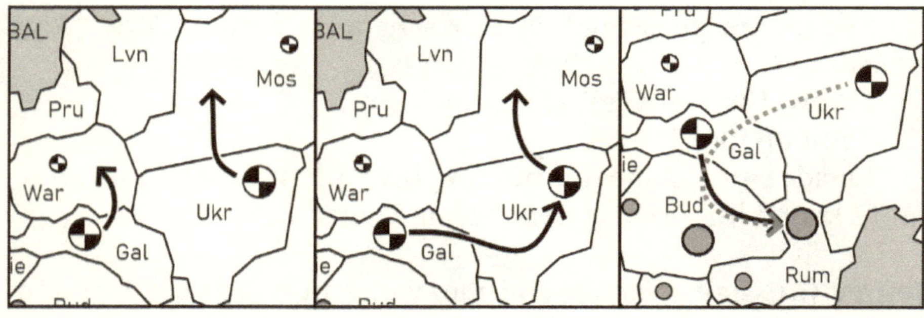

Figure 27 -- Suggested Russian Army Orders: [Left] Gal to War and Ukr to Mos; [Center] Ukr to Mos and Gal to Ukr; [Right] Gal Attacks Rum with Support from Ukr

"How's that work? You don't think Vicki will hold in Rumania and support with Sevastopol?"

"Or with Budapest. It's probable, even likely. But if she instead tries to take Moscow this turn, there's the possibility of you sneaking into Rumania or Sevastopol this year."

"Win one, lose one?"

"Except Vicki's army will be without any backup. You'll have cut her off from it."

I gamed it out in my head. "But isn't there an option four? We talk to Vicki and see if she's cool with giving me a dot?"

"In exchange for what? Jeff, I've got to level with you: you're in bad shape. Right now, I'm just trying to keep you from losing any more supply centers."

"Yeah." I sighed. "Man, if only Nestor hadn't decided he was going to get me back by letting Lance take Sweden, at least I'd have a fourth unit."

Evander squinted at me. "Jeff, I believe Nestor. I think all it was was him screwing up the order."

"Like he did when he supported Booker?"

"No. I don't know what the Hell that was supposed to be. Anyway, one, two, or three. I leave it to you to decide." He pointed at me like his hand was a gun and headed back to the living room.

Cassandra (Austria): Three long seconds I was frozen, staring at the inside of that baseball cap. Then Evander banged on the door again.

"Just a second! Washing my hands!" I fumbled out my cell to shoot video of it, trying to get it from all angles. Five seconds of that, then I shoved it back in my pocket, put the cap back in the cabinet, closed it, rinsed my hands, shut off the taps, and opened the door.

I caught him mid-knock. He looked down and to the left, where the cap was stashed under the sink. Then he barged in and I got out.

The door shut behind me, and those twenty-odd steps back to the living room felt like I was slogging through the water at the bottom of the ocean. Evander picked who would play which country. He got me out of the bathroom because he was afraid I would see the cap and reveal his secret.

What he didn't know was whether or not I had found him

out. He was probably cutting out the loops of thread and getting out the velvet bag. That pouch was fastened to the cap somehow. I didn't find out how, exactly: I didn't have enough time to. Evander was in the bathroom, making sure the evidence would be gone. But, I told myself, that was okay, because I had the video.

The other five were exploring their theory that he'd been taken ill by the food we all ate. Nestor asked if that's what had happened to me, and I told him no, I was fine.

I took a spot on the corner of the couch and put it all together. I had thought something seemed out of place in Evander's living room earlier in the day, but I had it backwards: the cap was the only item out of place, and once he had removed it, there was nothing unusual left to see. His forehead *was* reminding me of something: how it was covered by a baseball cap that was nowhere to be seen after the start of the game.

But some pieces weren't fitting. Why Evander decided to lose. Whose place Nestor took if Karthik was never going to attend. And the cameras. That decal on his front door, the one with the surveillance notice, maybe that was part of the plan? If it was, I didn't know how.

Time was of the essence; I forced myself to move on. Whatever I did next, I was going to need to show the video to someone. So I took out my phone to watch it, and that's when I discovered I'd only hit the Record button once, and that was when I thought I was stopping the recording. So I had a fraction of a second with a handful of blurry frames with the baseball cap, followed by video of the inside of my pants pocket.

I hit Stop and put it away. If I had loudly and openly confronted Evander right then and there, there would have been an end to his scheming. Instead I had tried to be clever and ended up with nothing to show for it.

 *Austria*

```
A Ven Holds ◊ A Pie → Mar ◊
A Rom Holds ◊ F Tri Holds ◊
```

 *England*

```
F Bel S F ENG Holds ◊ F SKA → Den ◊
A Fin Holds ◊ F Swe S F SKA → Den ◊
F ENG S F Bel Holds ◊
```
<u>**A Bre → Par**</u> -- Failure, Attack str. inadequate
<u>**F WES → Tun**</u> -- Failure, Attack str. inadequate

 *France*

<u>**A Bur → Par**</u> -- Failure, Attack str. inadequate
<u>**F TYS → Tun**</u> -- Failure, Attack str. inadequate
<u>**F EAS → AEG**</u> -- Failure, Attack str. inadequate
   <u>**Disband**</u>

 *Germany*

```
A Ber → Kie ◊ F Hol → HEL ◊
A Mun → Tyr ◊ A Ruh → Hol ◊
```
<u>**A Vie → Tri**</u> -- Failure, Attack str. inadequate
<u>**F Den Holds**</u> -- Failure, Hold str. inadequate
   Retreat to BAL

 *Russia*

```
F Stp.sc Holds ◊ A Ukr S A Gal → Rum ◊
```
<u>**A Gal → Rum**</u> -- Failure, Attack str. inadequate

 *Turkey*

```
F ADR S F Tri Holds ◊ A Alb → Ser ◊
F AEG S F ION → EAS ◊ A Arm → Syr ◊
F ION → EAS ◊ A Sev S A Rum Holds ◊
F Smy S F ION → EAS ◊
```
<u>**A Bud → Vie**</u> -- Failure, Attack str. inadequate
<u>**A Rum S A Sev Holds**</u> -- Failure, Supp. disrupted

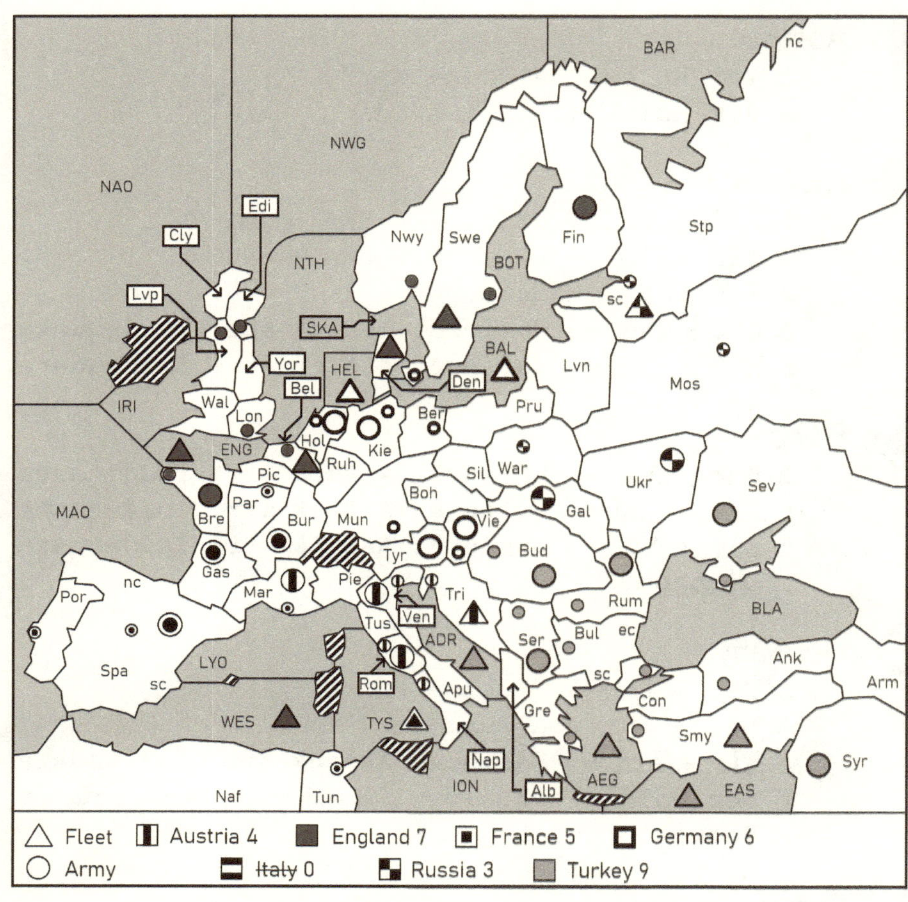

Figure 28 -- Game Map, Start of Fall 1905

Fall
1905

[A note as to the quality of gameplay]

Booker (France): I no longer have an appetite for the game; I doubt I ever will regain one. You understand. But here at university there is a small cadre of hobbyists who meet in person on a regular basis to play. On a whim, I showed them the game through to 1905, and asked what they could infer about us from the orders entered.

The vast difference in experience was evident, and only occasionally were they impressed. They likened it to a chess match between an intermediate player and a rank beginner, in that much of it was, to their eyes, ugly and workmanlike. Even if one ignored the most egregious snafus.

There was plenty they had to say about each player—if you wonder, they felt I did not acquit myself creditably with my play. Perhaps this will interest you: they ranked Germany highest, despite it being only in third place at the end of the year. One analyst was certain that the country was helmed by a seasoned diplomat.

It was at that point that I took my leave. I do not know what they would have made of the following turns.

[Reactions to the orders of spring 1905]

Lance (England): I've gotta wonder what Jeff was thinking when he said, "Whoa, look at the action in Austria!" like he was surprised at Vicki in Budapest making a move on Nestor in Vienna. I'd like to believe that he was being facetious to make a point, but the guy was just so gullible sometimes.

I asked him, "Jeff, for f---'s sake, you do know those two aren't really fighting, don't you? It's like play-acting or ... what's that word? From professional wrestling?"

"Kayfabe," Cassie said.

"What's that?" Evander asked.

"It's their term for the storylines behind the supposed rivalries between wrestlers."

"It is totally rando you know that, Cass," Vicki said.

Cassie looked down at the floor. "That's me. Totally rando."

Nestor lifted his arms in the air and walked around like he was soaking in everyone's applause after catching a football. *Exactly* like that: I've had to watch that a--hole do it while the school cheered him on. "That's right, everyone: Lance has us all figured out. Booker? Cassie? Jeff? Factor that into your calculations and s---."

Vicki laughed. Evander and Jeff did too. Nestor dropped his hands back to his sides and faced me. "What's the matter, Lance? Aren't you happy I'm admitting you're right?"

What a d--- he was. Jeff was the one who cooled things down by changing the subject. "Cass, nice move into Marseilles."

"I suppose this means you are allying with England?" Booker asked.

Cassie still had her head down. Her eyes were making tiny movements, left and right, like she was reading the grain on the wood planks at her feet. Everyone stopped and watched her. "You okay, Cass?" Jeff asked.

She looked up at Evander. "Where are the cameras?"

Ollivander (~~Italy~~): "Sorry, what? Cameras?" I replied.

"There's a sticker on your front and back doors. A notice of surveillance on 'these premises'."

"We have one of those doorbell cameras." Booker pursed his lips and walked over to see for himself.

"What about the back porch?"

That got Nestor and Vicki's attention. "Hold on, no one told us there's a camera out there," Nestor said.

"Afraid I'm going to upload the video of you two to Pornhub's Cuddling category?" They didn't find that funny. "Relax.

The camera isn't outside. We used to have it there, but we decided to move it in, on top of the cupboards. It can catch anyone coming in through the door or window, but that's it."

Booker returned in time to ask, "Why did you move it?"

"The angle was no good. Useless for identification purposes. Now a diligent thief can steal our plants, but that's it, pretty much."

The lovebirds relaxed. "Okay, we've got another minute or so left before the fall diplomatic phase starts—"

"What about the audio?" Booker again.

"What's that?"

"'Audio and video surveillance' is how the notice reads."

I took a deep breath. "Although those cameras have audio recording capabilities, we haven't enabled it. But I thought it was prudent to cover that ..." I struggled for the right word momentarily "... contingency."

I took in their reactions, one at a time, ending with Cassie. She was staring at the game board. Which reminded me to move the pieces to match what was on the laptop.

[Diplomatic phase of fall 1905]

Booker (France): I had moved my armies eastward, for the alternative would be to play defense on two fronts. As a result, my units were precariously placed. If I had five supply centers at the end of the turn, I could build an army in Paris or Brest and block England's further expansion into my home territories.

But that would require me to guess right more than once. And it would require Cassandra to willingly vacate Marseilles. Or instead to not order her armies to Naples and Rome.

Lance had come to that same conclusion, and was attempting to play mind games with me. "Where you think my fleet's going? Spain or Tunis?"

"I do not know."

"How about my army in Brest? Should I go to Paris or Gascony?"

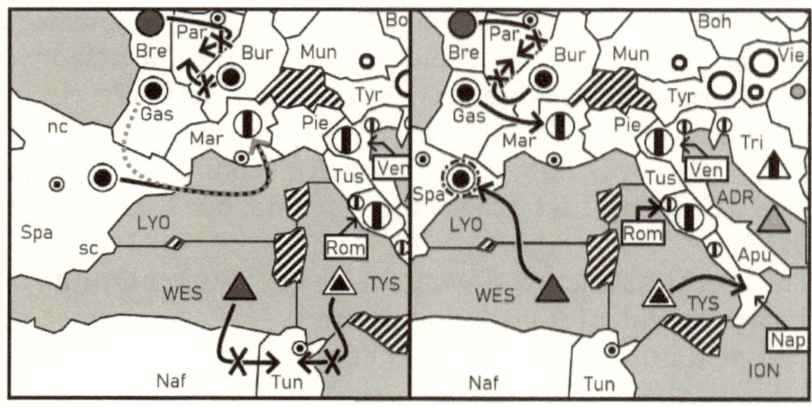

Figure 29 -- Potential French Orders If It Predicts That [Left] England Will Move Fleet to Tunis, or [Right] England Will Move Fleet to Spain

"Again, that is up to you. I cannot understand why you are asking me."

"I'm letting you know that it doesn't matter what the answers are. You're about to go down to four dots."

"It is entirely possible. Is there anything else?" I gave him a moment before crossing the room to talk to Cassandra. Lance followed.

"May we speak?" I asked her.

She looked from me to him. "Both of you?"

"My preference would be to talk to you alone, but it is for you to decide."

Cassandra rose to her feet. "Outside." Lance tried to join us, and she added, "Just Booker."

On the front porch, before I could speak, she asked, "Which country is best?"

"Do you mean right now? Turkey, in both the number of its units and its strategic position."

"No, I mean in general. The game is starting, you have first choice. Which one?"

"Either England or France," I reply. "Can you explain why you are asking? Quickly, please."

She stood in silence. I waited briefly before telling her, "I would like to make a suggestion to you. Move your army out of

Marseilles."

"Why?"

"You will need it to be in Piedmont in the spring. Otherwise, Germany will take Trieste from you now and then Venice at the start of next year." I took out my phone to show her.

"That's not true. I can support my fleet with that army."

"But then I can take Naples with my fleet in the Tyrrhenian Sea, like so." I opened the game board on my phone to show her.

"I'll just move my army in Rome."

Of course, were she to do that, I could take Rome from her. "Is there *anything* I can do to convince you to let me have Marseilles?"

Perhaps five seconds ticked by before she replied, "Can you tell Lance we're done if he wants to talk to me?"

I rapped a knuckle on the living room window and waved Lance towards us.

We passed each other on my way to the back porch. That time, his mien was serious. Jeffrey and Ollivander were at the kitchen table, on their phones. I knocked on the back door and paused for a decorous few moments before opening it. "Nestor, thirty seconds of your time? My apologies, Victoria."

"Everyone else calls her Vicki, *wey*. Why you bein' so fancy?"

She hit his shoulder, playfully. "Stop that, Nes. I like it when he says my name. Sure, Booker, come on out."

We traded places and Nestor asked me what I wanted.

"Two things. You might be able to take Trieste from Austria this turn. I cannot guarantee it, but the army in Venice might move to Rome. If you do decide to, support with—"

"Support with Tyrolia and take it with Vienna. You want to give me some credit?"

"I … yes. The other comment is that if I have five supply centers at the end of this season, I will be able to support you into Belgium."

"So *now* you want an alliance?"

"Not an alliance, at least not yet. This is a one-time offer of aid, with no strings attached."

Nestor checked his watch. "Anything else?"

"Which unit are you using to retake Denmark?"

"Baltic."

I nodded. "That is the move I would make as well. Well, I thank you for your time, Nestor."

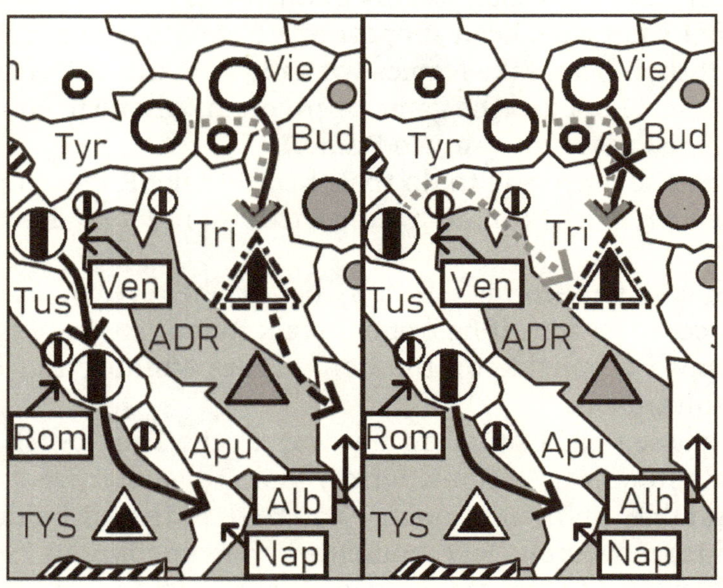

Figure 30 -- German Attack on Trieste If Army in Venice [Left] Does Not Support or [Right] Does Support

Nestor (Germany): Booker leaves and Vicki comes back to me. "Hey, bae."

I look at my watch, tell her it's time to discuss our moves. "First, I need you to message Cassie for me."

She gets out her phone. "What you got in mind?"

Cassandra (Austria): Lance came out to join me on the porch. "You know," he said, "this is the first one of these talks we've had today."

It hadn't occurred to me until he brought it up. Everyone else had visited at some point. Except Evander, unless you counted that one time right before he got eliminated. "Huh, you're right."

"Wait, I gotta ask you: what's the deal with the cameras?"

"Oh. Just making sure."

He wasn't buying it, I could tell. "Okay, if you say so."

"Which country is best?"

"Well, Vicki's ahead right now, so Turkey."

"No. I mean, if you could pick any country at the start of the game, which one would you?"

"France, no doubt. You remembered I tried to call dibs on it?"

"But Evander gave you England."

"I'm not complaining. Second place so far."

I thought it over. If that was true, Evander handed Booker the best starting position in this game. "Which one is the worst?"

"Italy. Austria's pretty bad too." I thought some more. Lance interrupted my reverie to ask if we could discuss our moves.

I told him to go ahead. "Booker wants you to give up the territory you won so he won't have to give up any of his. I even have to tell you not to do it?"

That's when I got another message on my cell from Vicki. I gestured to Lance to hold on.

```
Vicki>    hey gurl
Cassie>   Hey.
Vicki>    k, imma get out of adr u can come in
Cassie>   But then Nestor will take Trieste.
Vicki>    nah cuz imma move in from bud
Cassie>   Budapest?
Vicki>    y
Vicki>    gonna boop w him
Cassie>   Boop?
Vicki>    bounce
Vicki>    and yr boat b free!
Cassie>   Oh, okay.
Vicki>    luv u gurl
```

"Sorry."

"No prob. Tell me exactly what Booker wanted you to do?"

"He wanted me to move my army out of Marseilles. Back to

Piedmont."

"I knew it. Why would he ever think you would agree to that?"

I told Lance what Booker told me: how I'd need it to protect against Nestor. Lance was screwing up his face in disbelief with every word. "And he threatened to take Naples?"

"I said I'd just move my army in Rome to stop him."

I could see something dawn on Lance. But I didn't know what. "Look, let me suggest what moves you should make."

I studied my screen. "But won't I lose a … what do you call it?"

"A supply center? A dot? Yes, but maybe there's no way around it. Booker will get Marseilles back, but I will take Spain from him. After that, we can team up and take him down. What do you say?"

I couldn't confront Evander. I had already tried to talk to Jeff and Booker. And Nestor would have mocked me for taking so long to see it.

That left Vicki and Lance. I trusted Vicki, you have to believe I did, but she was winning. I was afraid I'd make her feel bad.

So it was Lance or nobody. "Lance, there's something I have to tell you."

He put on a look of concern and asked me what. I told him all about the baseball cap. His jaw dropped. "Do you have it?"

"Last I saw, it was in the bathroom. But then Evander went in …."

"Yeah. And that video doesn't show anything?"

"You don't believe me?"

Lance tucked his left hand in his right armpit and buried his chin in his right. "I don't know. It's … what's the point, though? He throws the game, or tries to, to *Booker*? Why?"

"I don't know."

"And what do you think he's doing with Jeff now that he's advising him? That doesn't fit in at all."

"That doesn't matter. I know what I saw."

"I'm trying to figure out how that would work. He picks up those seven pieces, picks up the baseball cap, and he puts them into those loops so he doesn't lose track?"

"No, I think he already had seven *other* pieces in the loops. He picks up seven more, then the cap, then shakes them in his hand and dumps them into that velvet bag in the middle and pulls it shut with the strings—"

"What's with the cotton? In the bag?"

"To keep them from clacking against each other would be my guess. Then he gives us all the pieces he's already picked out. He's memorized which piece is where and he's practiced it over and over to make sure he gets it right."

Lance widened his eyes and exhaled. "It's unbelievable. I mean, not 'I don't believe you' unbelievable, but ...."

"Yeah. What should I do?"

He shoved his hands in his pockets and rocked back and forth on his heels. "One suggestion, you call him out in front of all of us."

"I don't know about that."

"Me either. The other one I got is you and me do it."

"Or I do nothing. At least for now."

"Nothing?"

"If I'm right about what those things in the cap were and why Evander rushed me out of the bathroom, then they're gone now. The only way the evidence is still there is if he really did think he was going to have an accident in his pants and I read him wrong."

Lance took out his cell. "Five minutes."

"Maybe we convince someone else and then confront him."

"Cassie, you haven't even convinced *me*. I'm sorry. Wait, one thing. Even if we do nothing for now, we don't let Evander out of our sight. Maybe he slips up and that's when we'll get the chance to drop the bass on him and Booker."

Jeffrey (Russia): Yeah, I didn't have much to do that turn. My fleet held, and I moved my armies back. Biding my time, like Evander told me I had to do.

There was four minutes left before we had to enter our orders and we were all already in the living room, waiting it out. That's when Cassie said, out loud, "We should take some pictures!"

Vicki was all for it, more for her Instagram page or whatever. I never did get an account, I should do that. Anyway, Cassie grabbed Vicki's arm and said, "You should get that black Giants cap! The one Evander had! You'd look so cute!"

"Yeah!" Vicki replied. "Evander, can we get your cap?"

Evander was staring daggers at Cassie. Annoyed he had to get up and walk over to his bedroom. But he dragged his a-- out of that chair in front of the laptop and got going.

"Vicki, I'm going to powder my nose," Cassie said.

"Ooh! Good idea, me too!" and then the three of them were in the hallway.

I leaned over to tell them to hurry up, and I noticed Evander pass by his bedroom door and go into the bathroom in front of those two. Then on the way out, he handed the cap to Vicki.

I don't even know why I thought to ask him, "The baseball cap was in the bathroom?"

"Um, yeah, why?"

"No reason. I didn't notice it in there."

Evander got back to the chair and took his sweet time getting comfortable in it before answering, "It was in the bathtub. I went to the bathroom to splash some water on my face, that cap was in the way, and out of frustration I tossed it over the shower curtain rod."

"Mystery solved," Lance said.

Okay, here's something only my mom and this therapist I saw for a while know. I got this weird image in my head about a month after my father died, and ever since, whenever the shower curtain in a bathroom is closed, I always open it and look. And then close it right after.

You want to know why I'm telling you? Because I used the bathroom at Evander's twice, once in the morning, once right after lunch. And that baseball cap wasn't behind that curtain either time.

 *Austria*

    A Rom → Nap ◊ F Tri → ADR ◊
    A Ven → Rom ◊
    <u>A Mar Holds</u> -- Failure, Hold str. inadequate
        Retreat to Pie

 *England*

    F Bel Holds ◊ F ENG → MAO ◊
    F Swe → Nwy ◊ F WES → Spa.sc ◊
    <u>A Bre → Par</u> -- Failure, Attack str. inadequate
    <u>A Fin → Stp</u> -- Failure, Attack str. inadequate
    <u>F Den Holds</u> -- Failure, Hold str. inadequate
        Retreat to Swe

 *France*

    A Spa → Mar ◊ F TYS → Tun ◊
    A Bur S A Spa → Mar ◊
    <u>A Gas → Par</u> -- Failure, Attack str. inadequate

 *Germany*

    F HEL S F BAL → Den ◊ F BAL → Den ◊
    A Vie → Tri ◊ A Kie S F BAL → Den ◊
    A Tyr S A Vie → Tri ◊
    <u>A Hol → Bel</u> -- Failure, Attack str. inadequate

Russia

    F Stp.sc Holds ◊ A Ukr → Mos ◊
    A Gal → War ◊

Turkey

    A Sev S A Rum → Ukr ◊ F ADR → Alb ◊
    F AEG → Gre ◊ F EAS → ION ◊ A Rum → Ukr ◊
    F Smy → EAS ◊ A Syr → Arm ◊
    <u>A Bud → Tri</u> -- Failure, Attack str. inadequate
    <u>A Ser → Bud</u> -- Failure, Attack str. inadequate

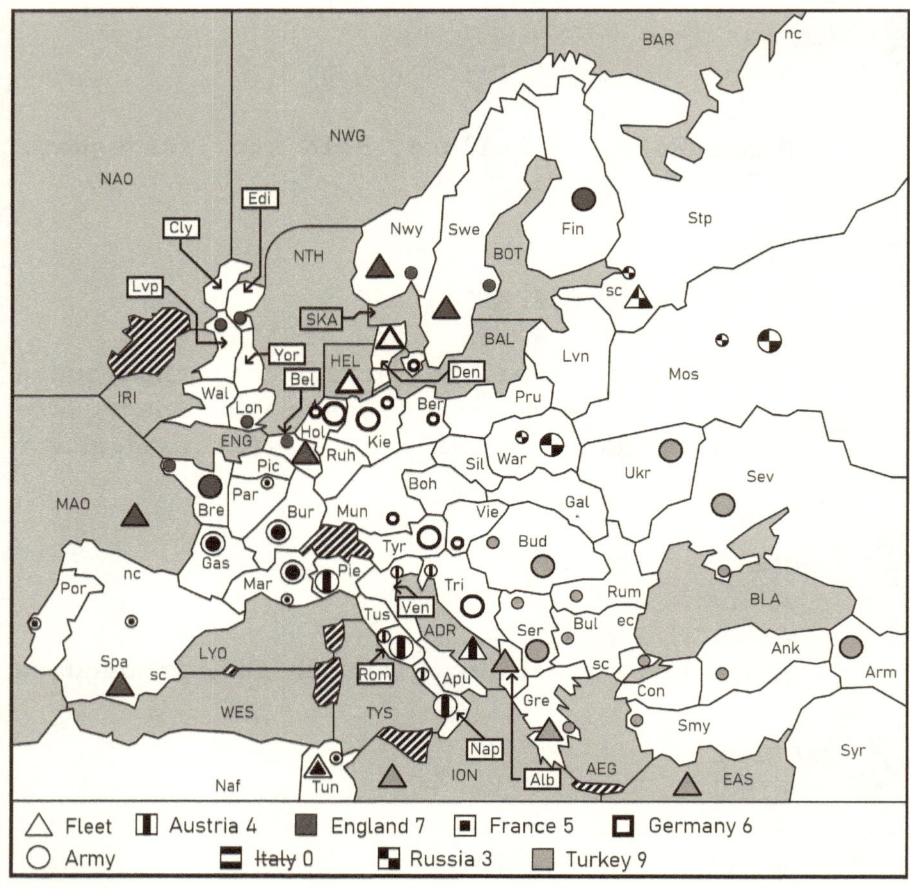

Figure 31 -- Game Map, Start of Winter 1905

Winter
1905

[Nestor's statement at the outset of our interview]

Nestor (Germany): "Thank you"? Go f--- yourself. Don't f---ing pretend I'm doing you a favor. I'm doing this because if I don't you're putting some s--- like "Nestor Martinez declined to be interviewed for this article" that's gonna make me look even worse.

... No? You saying if I tell you don't print anything anyone says about me, you won't? ... Then shut the f--- up. Don't pretend this ain't anything except extortion.

[What Nestor's grandfather taught him about the Vietnam War]

Nestor (Germany): Back in high school I did okay. C's in math and science. B's in English, mostly. But I did really well in history. I even took European history advanced placement and earned myself a 4 on the big test.

Got that from my grandfather. Sixth grade my teacher gives us an assignment, write three pages about the Vietnam War. I come home and my mother, she tells me I should talk to my *abuelo*, because he was actually there.

I didn't even know that, because he never mentioned it. Didn't have pictures or medals or anything like that out in his bedroom. Well, I go to him and he says, yeah, he did two tours stationed at Biên Hòa Air Base, thirty klicks west-northwest of Saigon. He left for home late nineteen seventy, and two and a half years after that the U.S. handed the ARVN the keys to the place and bugged out.

When he finds out why I'm asking, he says I can get three pages' worth easy off the internet. So that's what I do.

Later on I ask him what it was like. He came in after Tet, but Biên Hòa still saw some action while he was there. Rocket and artillery attacks, ammo dump explosions, and airplane crashes, mostly.

I'm thinking he's holding back on the really cool stuff and—this was summer of '13, I wasn't in seventh grade yet—I ask him what Vietnam was *really* like. My grandfather gets out of his easy chair, goes to his bedroom. He's got a DVD and he's setting up the TV when my brother comes out of our room and sees what's going on. "You asked *Viejo* about the war?" And he's laughing his damn head off on the way out the front door.

That movie he's playing is *Patton*. He's got it set up to that scene where he's giving that speech with that big American flag behind him. The one where he says, "No b------ ever won a war by dying for his country. He won it by making the *other* poor dumb b------ die for *his* country." He rewinds, turns on closed captions so I can read it while I listen again.

He asks me what that was one line was about. I tell him he's getting the troops pumped up, like Coach does when we play. He asks me what that first country was and what the second country was. I ain't the best student, but even I know who fought WWII. I say America and Germany, and I ask what's that got to do with Vietnam. My grandfather flips over that box the disk was in. Asks me what year it came out.

"1970."

"Nixon watched this movie, got himself pumped up too. Decided to double down on the war. So now it's 1970. Which one's that first country and which one's the second?"

"America and Vietnam."

He shakes his head no. I remember that paper and I ask, "America and *North* Vietnam?"

"Trick question, *Nieto*. Both countries are America."

I'm twelve years old, of course I don't get it. He explains, "The people on top, the ones who call the shots, they're never the ones dying for their country. They win wars by getting poor folk on the front lines to die for theirs. Two Americas. You see?"

"I didn't know you were one of those anti-war ... what they call those?"

"Hippies?" He asks.

"Yeah, that."

"No. You wrote that paper on the war. You remember how many Americans died?"

"Fifty thousand?"

"Little more than that, closer to sixty. You know how many Americans died in the Korean War?"

I shrug. "Beats me."

"About thirty-five. That's less, but if sixty thousand is way too many dead Americans, then so's thirty-five. But we were right to fight that one. There's fifty million South Koreans who are a whole lot better off than they would be if we'd sat at home and given peace a chance. That's not even counting the cheap cars and electronics we got out of it."

"But wasn't it still people like us fighting while rich people ordered us around?"

"Or just stayed at home and didn't worry about it one way or another. That's my point. It doesn't matter what war it is, you want to be living in that first America. Be on the sidewalk, waving flags when the veterans have parades. You want to fight wars? Be one of those men in suits, advising the president and pushing around little tanks and ships on a big map in the middle of a dark room."

I'm hoping for some war stories, and this is what my grandfather tells me instead. "What, you want to hear about being 'in country'?" Then he says something in French. "That means 'it's worse than a crime, it's a mistake'. *That's* what the Vietnam War was really like."

"Who said that French s---?"

"Watch your language. I don't care, but if you slip up and say that with your mother around?" He flicks his thumb across his Adam's apple like he's slitting his own throat. "But to answer your question, there was this man, Charles Maurice de Talleyrand-Perigord. Had a whole lot of job titles in his life. He advised the last king of France. During the French Revolution, he was in their legislature and they sent him to England to try to stop a war from breaking out. Spent a little time here in America, came back to be a minister to Napoleon. Prime Minister and ambassador to England after that. Died around 1840."

"Wait, so he wasn't talking about Vietnam when he said that?"

"He didn't say that at all. Some other French guy said it, and because it was clever and Talleyrand was the famous one, people thought he came up with it. You remember that: when you're on top, you can take credit for what other people do."

My grandfather pops out that disc and puts it back in the box, starts walking to his room. "Follow me." He looks on his bookshelf and pulls one off of it. "Here. All about the wars France was in. Read it, and when you're done I'll tell you more about what Vietnam was really like."

[Reactions to the orders of fall 1905]

Booker (France): We all crowded together for a group shot. Several group shots, actually. Ollivander was forced to pause the game for a few minutes, which put him in a bad mood.

Now that I think back on it, it would be more accurate to say that it put him in a worse mood. Victoria had asked him to let her borrow his baseball cap for the photos. That not-unreasonable request was met with angry trudging to the bathroom.

I do not partake in "social media", so the largest screens I have seen them on were those of the smartphones used to take the pictures. From what I could make out, only Victoria and Nestor's faces truly seemed to convey joy. My smiles for photographs tend to be guarded; the ones I sported then were not exceptions. Ollivander's scowl from earlier was bubbling under the surface. Jeffrey seemed to be in a daze. Cassandra was smirking triumphantly, quite a change from any of her moods that day up to that point.

As for Lance, were you to pass a man on the street grinning as he did, you would grant him a wide berth.

Victoria (Turkey): "Okay? All done? No more selfies?" Evander asked. He clicked on the laptop. "Five minutes for the fall orders."

I put mine in on my phone and swiped through the pics. Cassie joined me and peeked over my shoulder.

"I was right about the cap," she said.

"Yeah, it was worth getting Evander cranky. Hey, Evander!" I tossed him the cap and he snatched it out of the air.

Booker was last. He was trying to read Cassie and Lance's faces for a minute before he walked over to the laptop and did his clicking.

Ollivander (Italy): When the orders were resolved, I told Lance, Nestor, and Cassie to do their thing for the winter.

Vicki was upset. Her arms were crossed and her right foot was tapping staccato. At first I wasn't sure who or what she was mad at. Then, when Cassie was done with her phone, Vicki whispered something in her ear.

Cassie gave Vicki a reassuring pat on the arm. It didn't do the trick, though, because Vicki started glaring at Nestor instead.

I went to Booker and asked him, "What do you think all that's about?"

"Perhaps it is not about the game at all." And then he looked me square in the face and added, "Perhaps it is instead personal and none of our concern."

Nestor finished up with his build and Vicki moved on to whisper-yelling at him. Cassie stepped in and calmed Vicki down. Playing peacemaker. I wouldn't have expected that, not from her that day.

I took the laptop over to the game board and adjusted the pieces. Those three put their drama on Pause and everyone gathered round to take in the state of play.

And I said, "Wow, how did I not notice how good Nestor's doing? Hey Nestor, how'd you manage to sneak up on everyone?"

[How Nestor trained]

Nestor (Germany): I don't know why the f--- people were surprised. We have to have our playbooks memorized front to back and execute in real time, but handling six other countries with fifteen whole minutes to plan out each turn is some big deal?

But I'll admit it: I had help. After my parents say okay, I tell my grandfather about Evander inviting me. "You read up on that game? You going to play?"

"*Sí, Viejo.*"

"No. Not *Viejo*. Look at me." He points to his eyes with two fingers, like in that movie. "You call me Coach now."

When I get home the next day, he has me drag a chair to his room. He's not making me watch a movie from fifty years ago this time, he clears his throat and gets right to it. "John F. Kennedy and Henry Kissinger's favorite board game. Walter Cronkite loved it. You better believe there are future politicians and whatnot playing it now in colleges all over the damn world.

"You get good at it, you got yourself another way to meet some movers and shakers. Get them to respect you for more than just your yards on the field. Now, this particular match two weeks from now? Who gives a … close the door so *tu madre* can't hear … who gives a s--- if you win or lose."

"What? *I* do. I refuse to lose."

"That's a good attitude, *Nieto*, but it's not always up to you. I'm going to show you the best players in the world losing because everyone around them makes up their minds that they're a threat and they got to go."

I don't like hearing that one damn bit and he can tell. "Something you're not telling me?"

It's hard for me to admit, but I get it out. "I don't want to lose to *them*. Especially not to this one *pendejo*."

I explain who I'm up against and who they are to me and he listens. When I'm done, he says, "No guarantees, but I'm going to do my best to keep that from happening. I'm going to teach you the ins and outs. We're going to watch tournaments and tutorials. You're going to play online. And you're going to take notes. You got that?"

"*Sí, Viejo.*"

He raises an eyebrow and waits. I remember and say, "I mean, yes, Coach."

Getting my head around how different those seven countries are takes me a full week. "You don't want to be Italy. Or Austria.

If you can pick, don't pick those. Pick France."

"France? Why not Germany?"

"Because Germany's got to deal with enemies on all sides. You remember how Germany handled it back in World War II?"

"They got Russia to chill."

"The Molotov-Ribbentrop Pact. You better know the name for your college classes. But that's right. Took out a bunch of countries, then France, then a year later hit Russia hard when they least expected. In the game, you better have allies if you're Germany. Those three units won't be enough to hold off everyone."

The games I play on the internet, those are rough. My grandfather is standing behind me and nodding each time I get f---ed over by someone who says they're on my side. "Get used to it, because it's going to happen." I learn to keep my cool. Then one game I'm Italy and I pull one over on Austria. I make it through to the end, split the win with France and Germany.

And then I'm telling people what to do *and they're doing it*. My grandfather looks at the map over my shoulder and tells me, "Good. This is the same lesson I was teaching you with all those history books I made you read. Showing you what leaders are like." My mother, brother, and father are eating at the dining room table, and he gestures to me to close the door. When I do, he whispers, "Your father? He's a good man. Raised you two well. Good husband to my daughter. But he will always be a follower. Don't be like him."

I promise him I won't. He squints at me, and finally he decides I'm telling the truth and we study the map some more.

The night before, me and him are cramming like it's a test. Finally, around two in the morning, he says time to sleep. He leaves me with one thing: "You got an advantage no one else does. *Tu cabra*."

"Can't you just say 'your girlfriend'?"

"Sorry, *Nieto*, I always forget how much you hate that word. Alliances are part of the game, use it. As long as you're not starting on opposite sides of the board, you two can team up and take some supply centers fast."

"They'll be expecting it, though."

My grandfather smiles, grabs me on the shoulder and says, "They've underestimated you for four years. They won't see it coming now."

◆ *Austria*

    A Pie ◊ A Nap ◊ A Rom ◊
    Disband F ADR

◆ *England*

    F Bel ◊ A Bre ◊ A Fin ◊
    F MAO ◊ F Nwy ◊ F Spa.sc ◊
    F Swe ◊
    Build A Edi

◆ *France*

    A Bur ◊ A Gas ◊ A Mar ◊
    F Tun ◊

◆ *Germany*

    F Den ◊ F HEL ◊ A Hol ◊
    A Kie ◊ A Tri ◊ A Tyr ◊
    Build A Ber

◆ *Russia*

    A Mos ◊ A War ◊ F Stp.sc ◊

◆ *Turkey*

    F Alb ◊ A Arm ◊ A Bud ◊ F EAS ◊
    F Gre ◊ F ION ◊ A Ser ◊ A Sev ◊
    A Ukr ◊

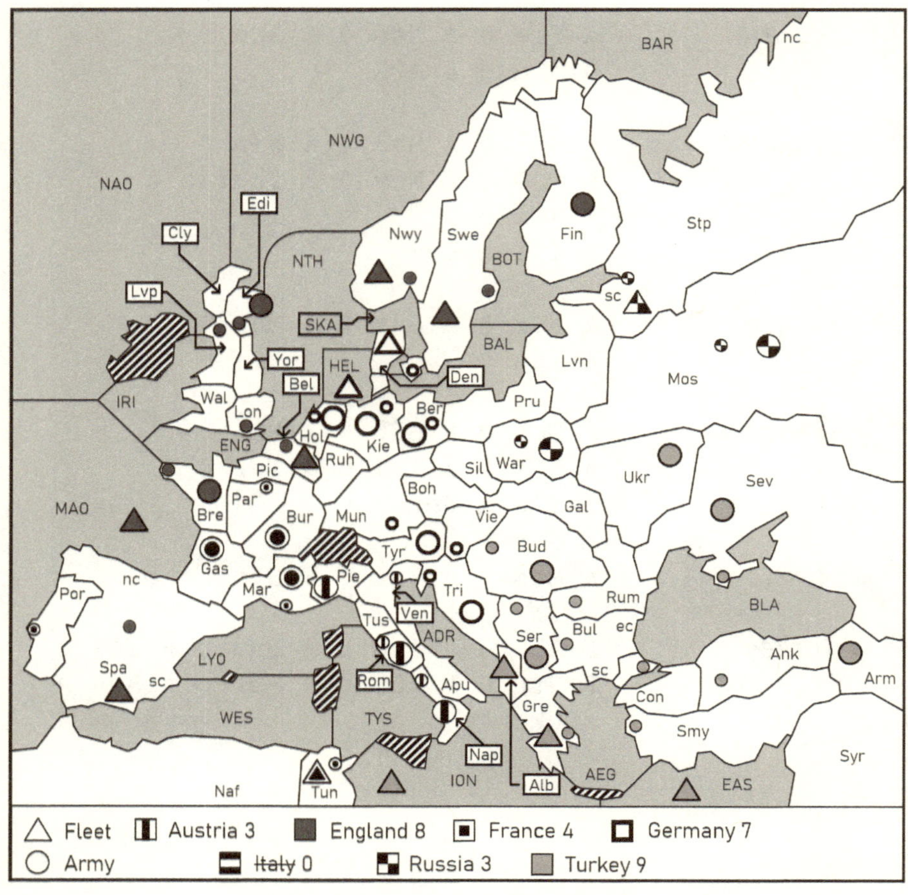

Figure 32 -- Game Map, Start of Spring 1906

Spring
1906

[Diplomatic phase of spring 1906]

Booker (France): Nestor replied, "That's a question for everyone else. Ain't like I've been hypnotizing people into letting me win."

Evander laughed and said, "Third place. Don't get ahead of yourself."

Nestor smiled and held out his hand as if his conceding the point were a small gift resting on his palm. Then there was the alarm from the laptop and the spring of 1906 had begun.

Victoria nearly ran from the room and Cassandra and Nestor followed. "I was hoping to talk to Nestor," I said.

"Vicki for us," Ollivander said. "Right, Jeff?"

Jeffrey blinked as if waking from a slumber. "Yeah."

We looked to Lance, who shrugged. "I don't know that I need to talk to anyone. Maybe Vicki. Ooh, or Cassie. We talked about you, Booker."

"This is not exactly a surprise to me."

He turned to Ollivander. "Cassie was wondering how you could be doing so badly after Evander gave you France."

They stared at each other, some subtle message flowing between them. I glanced at Jeffrey, but he was as in the dark as I.

"That reminds me, Lance. I need to talk to you too. Porch?" Lance's answer was to walk out the front door. "Jeff, you want to join us?"

"No."

"All right, I'll find you in the kitchen."

I reached it ahead of him and we took our seats at the table. Through the window, I saw Victoria speaking volubly while Nestor hung his head. As for Cassandra, only her right arm was visible from where I sat.

I asked Jeffrey, "Who do you think will win?"

He took off his glasses and started cleaning them with the hem of his t-shirt. "Beats me. You?"

"I do not know. My suspicion is that it will end in a negotiated three-way tie. If only because we cannot continue past six."

"Those three? You don't think you have a chance?"

"Even if Cassandra were to come to her senses and act in her own self-interest by allying with me, it would likely still be too late to do any good."

"Yeah. Maybe Vicki'll keep me alive."

"Or Lance will?"

"F--- Lance. You trust him?"

I struggled for a politic answer. In the end, all I could manage was, "No comment."

Cassandra (Austria): "You told me. You told me that we'd bounce off each other in ... what was that place?"

"Trieste," Nestor mumbled.

"But you took it. I promised Cassie and she had to give up her boats."

"*Querida*, she—"

"Don't *querida* me. Not now."

"All right, all right. Cassie didn't have to give up her fleet. If she'd asked my advice, I would've said get rid of the army in Naples instead."

"That's not the point. You made her lose *something*."

Nestor briefly threw up his hands in frustration before turning away and walking to the railing. Vicki squeezed my forearm and said, "We'll figure this out, I promise." And so we waited for Nestor.

Shortly after, he asked me, "Which one do you want: Vienna or Trieste?"

"I don't know."

"Because depending on which one, I'll have to move an army out of the way."

Vicki pumped a fist and said, "Yesss! You see?"

"What's the catch?"

"Same as when you asked three turns ago. You got to help me when I need it." Before I could respond, he added, "I changed my mind. It's gotta be Vienna, and you have to build a fleet on Trieste, then move it out right away and move your army in from Vienna."

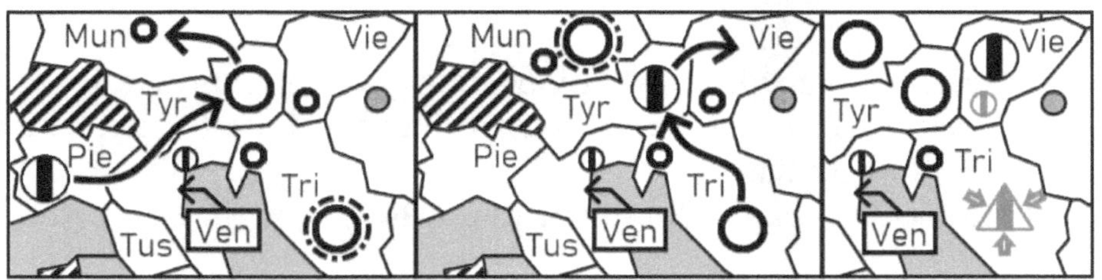

Figure 33 – Nestor's Proposed Maneuvers in [Left] Spring 1906 [Center], Fall 1906, and [Right] Build in Winter 1906

Nestor was trying to trick me. It turns out that I wouldn't have been able to build anything anywhere in the winter of 1906: not in Vienna, Budapest, or Trieste. You have to build on a home supply center that's unoccupied *and* that you control.

But I'd forgotten all about that rule back when we three were talking. I took out my phone and visualized those moves. "Why can't I build an army in Trieste?"

"'Cause that extra army is a threat to me. 'Cause you had a fleet there before, and this is you getting back what you already had. C'mon: yes or no?"

By now it must be clear to you that I didn't care about winning. How could I? The whole thing was rotten. The pieces I had remaining had value only inasmuch as they could be exchanged for the truth.

Nestor wanted an answer, and so did I. "When you told me that it wouldn't be Booker who would throw me under the bus, who did you expect to do it instead? Evander?"

"Evander? Girl, what are you talking about?" Vicki wondered.

Nestor afforded me an unfakeable look of complete incomprehension. "I don't know what that means. Yes or no."

I told him I would consider it and went inside.

Victoria (Turkey): Nestor rubbed his left cheek. "Make sure they can't see you through the window."

I put my back against the wall. "You're afraid they're going to read our lips?"

"Read our faces, more like it. You think she bought it?"

"I think so? But I don't know what we're going to get out of it."

"Make people think our alliance ain't all that and we'll see who'll try to set one of us against the other. Like Cassie. You should follow up with her."

I shook my head. "She's not going to go for that deal you offered."

"Try anyway." There was a knock on the door. "Pretend you're still pissed at me."

I opened the door for Booker. "Me or him?"

"Nestor. May I?"

"Yeah. I need some space right now anyway."

Jeff was at the kitchen table and Evander was coming down the hall. They told me how they needed my help, and out on the front porch, Evander explained how. "Don't attack Moscow."

"Why?"

"It won't help you, Vicki." Jeff nodded. "All it's going to do is give St. Petersburg to Lance."

Evander took out his phone and showed me what he was talking about. "But so what? Why do I care if Lance gets it?"

"He'll be knocking at your door, Vicki," Jeff told me. "First St. Petersburg, then he'll be in Moscow."

"No he won't. I'll be there with my army."

"What Jeff is saying is that he can do it for you. Be your man up north."

"But how's that better than me doing it?"

"He's got a fleet. You'll just have armies."

I looked at the map again. "Yeah, I'm not seeing it. Sorry, boo. Maybe you can make a deal with Lance instead?"

I went to find Cassie. She was in the living room and Lance was watching her out the corner of his eye, like he was worried about her or something. When I came in, he stopped and looked over at me instead.

"Hey, girl. I'm going to powder my nose. Join me?"

Nestor (Germany): So Vicki goes in, Booker comes out. "Nestor."

"Booker."

"You spoke with Cassandra just now. You and Victoria."

"Yes."

"Will she be moving her army out of Piedmont?"

"The f--- should I know?" I'm laying it on like I'm still salty from that fight me and Vicki were pretending we had.

Booker blinks a few times and says, "I will get right to it, then. If that army moves eastward, or even holds where it is, I will be able to support you into Belgium."

"'If'? F--- that. You already said you would."

"Contingent on having five supply centers at the end of 1905. I was quite clear on that."

I tell Booker he needs me more than I need him. "And I can take Belgium by myself in the fall. You got something else to give me? Huh?"

He doesn't, so he walks off.

Lance (England): There was a lot for me to think about in the spring of 1906, but dealing with Jeff and Russia wasn't any of it.

Evander and I walked out to the front porch. He looked through the windows to convince himself that no one was in earshot, and when he was, he said, "First things first. You're taking St. Petersburg this turn?"

"Why wouldn't I?"

"I assume you're going to need the Norwegian fleet to convoy that army out of Edinburgh. The only question is when."

"Early next year. I don't see the need to rush."

"Then that's it for Jeff. He's eliminated by winter, assuming Nestor and Vicki take Warsaw in the fall."

"Safe bet."

We stand there and listen to sounds of the traffic nearby for a few seconds. Then Evander gets back to business. "Okay, 'Evander gave you France'?"

I tell him everything Cassie told me about the baseball cap. "Where's it right now, Evander?"

He pointed to the living room and I followed the line of his finger and saw it on the floor under the table with the laptop. "See for yourself. No loops of thread, no velvet pouch."

"It's not that I don't trust you, but I'm going to check for myself."

"I would do the same."

"Are you going to confront Cassie?"

Evander made a motion with his hands, like he was weighing two things, figuring out which one was heavier. "I'm thinking no. I'll leave it to her to decide what she wants to do about … this." He checked the time on his phone. "Jeff and I are going to talk to Vicki now. Thanks."

Cassie and I made it into the living room at the same time. I picked up the cap and looked inside. Like Evander said, no loops of thread, no velvet pouch. No evidence that those things were ever there.

She was sitting on the couch, watching me. "Cassie, there's nothing here."

I took a step over to show it to her and she raised a hand to stop me. "Of course there isn't. As I told you, Evander was in the bathroom after me. He had time to fix it. Put it back. Exactly how you found it."

"I …" I did. "Done."

"Do you believe me or don't you?"

I couldn't come up with a good way to say I didn't, so I kept my mouth shut. She shook her head and said, "I never should have confided in you."

I pulled out the chair and sat at the table with the laptop, neither of us saying a word. It was a relief when Vicki pulled her out and took her to the bathroom.

Ollivander (~~Italy~~): After Vicki left us, Jeff and I stood out on the front porch. I let her words sink in for a bit.

"Is Lance going to attack St. Petersburg?" Jeff asked me.

"Yes. I thought I could convince him otherwise, but he's set on doing it right now. I'm guessing Nestor will take Warsaw and Vicki will take Moscow. Which means this is your final year."

"Well, s---."

"Yeah. We have some time left before we need to enter our orders. Want to wait out here or go in?"

Jeff chose inside. Lance was already in the living room and Booker and Nestor joined us not long after. "Those two in the bathroom?" Nestor asked.

Jeff and I shrugged. Booker and Lance didn't bother to answer. Nestor went to the bathroom and tried the door. Knocked, tried it again.

He gave up and we waited for them to come out. Thirty seconds before the end of the diplomatic phase, they did.

[Jeffrey's family dynamic before he moved to San Francisco]

Jeffrey (Russia): So in the South Bay, there's the Cupertino Union School District. All of Cupertino's in it, no duh. But also parts of the cities next to it. Like Santa Clara, where we lived back then. Houses there are more expensive *because* they're in the district. Us three, we lived in an apartment.

My dad was an engineer and my mom, when she could work, was a nurse. She's got lupus, so there're months when she's in too much pain to. Anyway, my dad did software, and he bounced around from job to job the way software guys do, you know?

What I remember was that school was getting hard for me. It's ... I'm not stupid, all right? I got okay grades in high school, B's and a few C's. But schools down there in the CUSD were seriously f---ing hardcore. At least the one I went to was. And I was starting to have problems keeping up in fourth and fifth grade.

They tried a bunch of stuff. Had me screened for ADD and ADHD. Got me tutors. And I did an IQ test, like a real one run by an actual psychologist.

I got a 104. I was happy, because that's above average, right? My mom was trying to put the best spin she could on it, saying it proved I was smart. But my dad, when he told me he was proud of me, I could tell he was ... he was *scared.*

Mom and Dad would yell at each other while I hid in my room. Some of the fights were about how my dad wasn't doing so well at work, wasn't getting promoted. And some of them were about me.

Dad wanted to move me to an easier school so I wouldn't be miserable all the time. Mom thought the answer was for me to get over the hump. Race came into it, too. My dad was white and my mom is Chinese, like, grew up there. That's why Mom was saying Dad felt that way because he was an American; Dad was saying Mom was putting me under too much pressure because that's how they did it in China.

They decided to go to a family therapist, because maybe *she* could figure out what was best for me and break the tie. Dr. Ayer—that was the therapist—talked to me alone at first. She was really nice and that room had a lot of bright colors and toys, like it was preschool. But I was still kind of scared by it all. I didn't really know what was happening, what it meant.

There's one bit of the talk all four of us had that stuck with me. Mom was going on about how this was a phase, it was temporary, and I would catch up with everyone else in class. They weren't going to leave me behind. She believed in me.

And I said, and I don't even know how I put those words together, "Mom, do you ever think maybe you believe in me *too* much?"

She burst into tears. Dad and me, we consoled her, told her not to cry. It didn't work. Over Dr. Ayer's objections, Mom begged me to take it back, swear I didn't mean it. I did. I never said anything like that to her ever again.

Austria
    A Rom Holds ◊ A Nap Holds ◊
    A Pie → Mar -- **Failure, Attack str. inadequate**

England
    F Bel Holds ◊ A Edi → Yor ◊
    A Fin → Stp ◊ F MAO → ENG ◊
    F Nwy S A Fin → Stp ◊ F Stp.sc → Por ◊
    A Bre → Par -- **Failure, Attack str. inadequate**
    F Swe → Den -- **Failure, Attack str. inadequate**

France
    A Bur S A Gas → Par ◊ A Gas → Par ◊
    A Mar Holds ◊ F Tun → WES ◊

Germany
    A Ber → Sil ◊ F Den Holds ◊
    A Tri → Ven ◊ A Kie → Ruh ◊ F HEL → NTH ◊
    A Tyr S A Tri → Ven ◊
    A Hol → Bel -- **Failure, Attack str. inadequate**

Russia
    A War S A Mos Holds ◊
    A Mos S A War Holds -- **Failure, Supp. disrupted**
    F Stp.sc Holds -- **Failure, Hold str. inadequate**
        Retreat to BOT

Turkey
    A Ukr S A Sev → Mos ◊ A Bud → Gal ◊
    F EAS → ION ◊ F ION → TYS ◊ A Ser Holds ◊
    F Alb → Ser -- **Failure, Order invalid**
    F Gre → Alb -- **Failure, Attack str. inadequate**
    A Arm → Sev -- **Failure, Attack str. inadequate**
    A Sev → Mos -- **Failure, Attack str. inadequate**

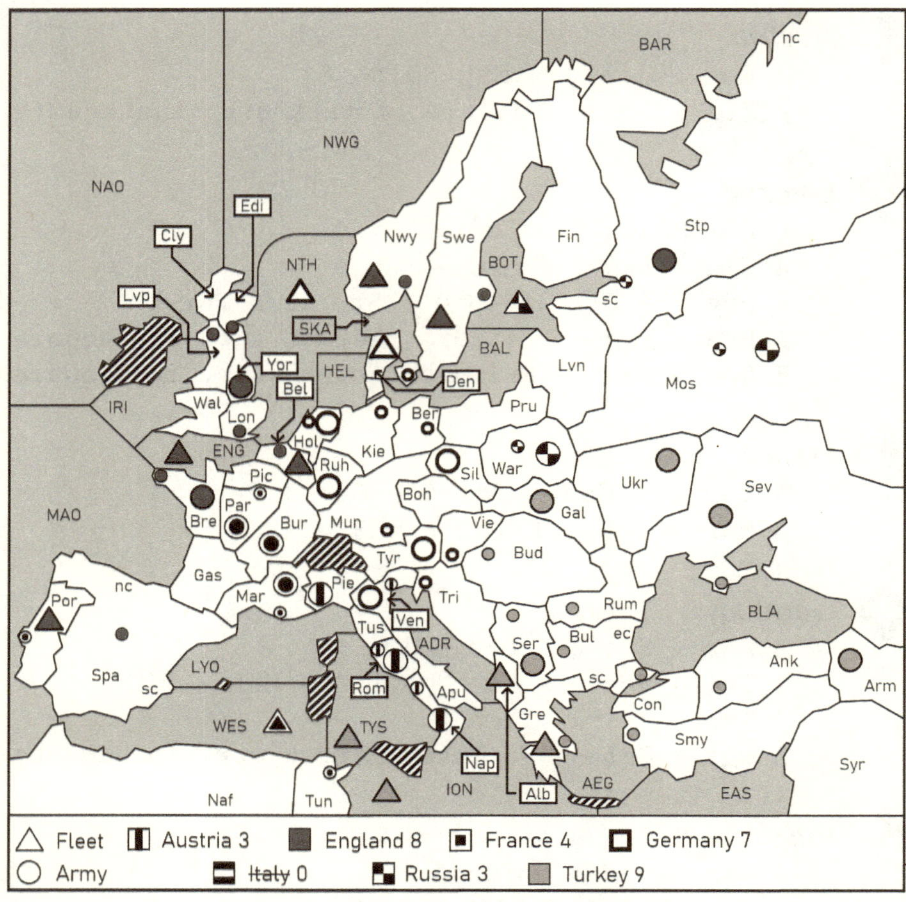

Figure 34 -- Game Map, Start of Fall 1906

Fall
1906

[Reactions to the orders of spring 1906]

Ollivander (~~Italy~~): All eyes were on Vicki and Cassie when they came in from out of the bathroom. Vicki looked dazed and worried, Cassie looked sad. Both of them lost in their own thoughts.

Nestor almost said something to Vicki—almost—before deciding against it. Those twenty seconds until the laptop beeped and it was time to enter the orders seemed to go on forever.

All right, there's something that I should explain to you about the way the game *should* be played as opposed to the way it *was* played that day. Yes, there will be open hostilities and pact-breaking in a game with experienced players. But there's usually less of it compared with what we had.

And when players are distrustful or openly fighting, you see a lot of "coin flips". These are situations where a player has a fifty-fifty chance, or a one in three chance if they are truly unlucky, of successfully defending against an incursion. That's what we were getting and in spades.

Booker had to guess correctly multiple times. Would Lance move his fleet in the Mid-Atlantic to the English Channel, or to Portugal, or would he use it to attack Gascony? Would Cassie continue to attack with her army in Piedmont, or could he move his army from Marseilles to Spain? And how many times could he successfully guess which move Vicki's fleet in the Ionian Sea would attempt to make?

After he screwed up by retreating into the Eastern Mediterranean, he was doomed to gamble out his remaining turns and lose units, one by one. Lance wasn't going to help him. Nestor wasn't in a position to. Cassie ... well, back then Cassie had her own ideas as to what game day was all about.

Lance (England): "Everyone's orders are in with ..." Evander checked the time. "... two minutes to spare."

People weren't rushing to the laptop to see. Vicki and Cassie had brought the mood down in the room. Whatever they went to the bathroom to do, it didn't make them any happier. I thought maybe Cassie was telling Vicki about the baseball cap, but I ruled that out when Vicki didn't look at Evander. She was sitting next to Nestor, resting her head on his shoulder. It was nauseating how they couldn't rein in their PDA so the rest of us wouldn't have to watch.

Evander started moving the pieces on the board. I stood up for a better look. Nestor and Booker followed.

"Looks like you're in trouble, Lance," Nestor said.

"Yeah?"

"All those supply centers of yours going down this fall."

"'All'? As in more than two? Which ones, Nestor? Count them out for me."

Nestor snickered. "You'll find out."

"Oh, no," I said. "Is *this* how we discover that you're innumerate?"

"This is immature, Lance," Booker said.

"Everyone's worried your feelings are hurt, Nestor."

Evander smacked the table hard. "*Hey*. Stop it, Lance."

"Case in point," I told Nestor, and when Evander pointed a warning finger at me, I held up my hands in mock surrender. Evander recentered the pieces he'd scattered and put the laptop back on the other table. Nestor was right that I was in trouble, though. He definitely had the units to take Belgium unless Booker helped me. And he might get tricky and attack London or Edinburgh instead.

Booker was looking over his shoulder at Cassie. He needed her to agree not to attack Marseilles so he could retake Spain. He wasn't going to get help from her though. Not while she was convinced Evander had cheated in the country draw so he could hand him France.

And I needed Jeff not to attack me in St. Petersburg or Sweden. I would have to make the case to Evander in the hopes that he could win him over on the idea.

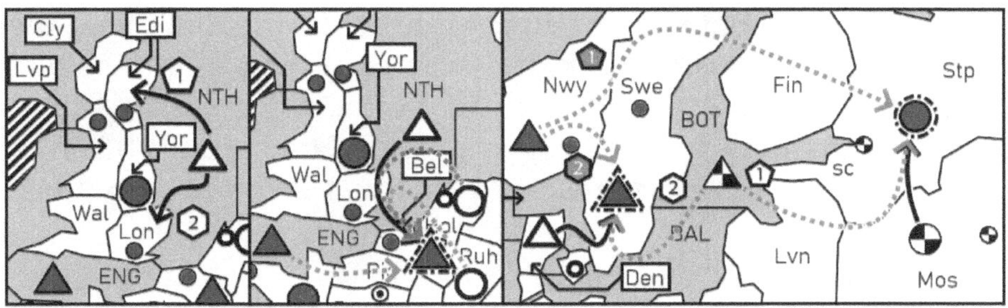

Figure 35 -- [Left] German Fleet in NTH Can Attack Edi or Lon; [Center] 3 German vs. 2 English Units in Bel; [Right] Russian Fleet Can Support 2 Attacks and England Must Decide Whether Fleet in Nwy to Defend (1) Stp or (2) Swe

[Diplomatic phase of fall 1906]

Cassandra (Austria): When fall began, I got up and left for the back porch. There wasn't anyone I wanted to talk to anymore, not in that house.

I didn't notice Booker follow me out. After that deal with Vicki and me in the bathroom, I wasn't really paying attention. It was only when he asked, "Cassandra, may I talk to you briefly?" that I registered his presence.

"Sorry, I did not mean to startle you," he added.

"I ... whatever. Fine, hurry up."

"Can you explain why you failed to keep Germany from taking Venice?"

What I wanted then were the words that would bring an end to that conversation as quickly as possible. "I don't care."

"Forgive me, but I do. I—"

"That's what I'm telling you. I didn't stop Nestor because I don't care."

"And yet you cared enough to attack my army in Marseilles." I sighed. "Cassandra, if you no longer wish to play, notify Ollivander that you quit. Your units will be given orders to hold in place. If—or rather, when—your supply centers are captured, disbands will be determined at random."

I don't get really angry a lot. This time was the angriest I had been since that time when my mother insinuated there was something wrong with Jeff because his father was out of the picture …. I didn't? Remind me to tell you about that. Anyway, I clenched my fists, lowered my head and glared at him through the tops of my eyeglass lenses. "You'd just love that, wouldn't you?"

"Come again?"

"You and Evander, getting rid of me, once and for all. You don't think I know how you got France?"

I remember the audible wet click his mouth made when his lips parted. And then how he replied, "Cassandra, I have no idea what you are talking about."

I screamed at him, "Get the f--- off of this porch." He shook his head and left. Turns out *those* were the words.

Booker (France): Nestor and Victoria were in the kitchen when I returned following my disastrous attempt to talk sense into Cassandra. It was clear they had heard her screaming at me. Nestor was taken aback; Victoria was perturbed, or, I should say, continued to be perturbed.

"Maybe you should talk to her?" Nestor suggested while I poured myself a glass of water. "Girl to girl?"

Her answer was "No. That'd only make things worse."

Nestor stopped me before I could leave. "Hol' up. That thing with Cassie: it mean you can't support me into Belgium?"

To retake Spain, I would have to move from Marseilles to Spain with my fleet in the Western Mediterranean providing support.

But I would then have to move my army in Burgundy to Marseilles to keep Austria from taking it, and Cassandra had made it clear she would make the attempt. And Burgundy had the only unit capable of providing support to Belgium.

"I suppose so. But you do not need my support."

"And you can't help Lance either, can you, Homes?"

Of course. That was what he was leading up to. "Not without forfeiting Spain."

That smirk returned. "Just makin' sure you see it."

```
Booker>  Will your fleet in Belgium be holding
  in the fall?
Lance>   y
Booker>  Is that y short for yes, or is it
  meant to be a homonym for the word why?
Lance>   yes
Booker>  Do I need to explain to you the
  ambiguity in that answer?
Lance>   yes i will hold fleet in bel
Booker>  I will support your hold from
  Burgundy.
Lance>   4 wat
Booker>  Do you mean in exchange for what?
Lance>   y
Lance>   yes
Booker>  It would be pointless to expect you
  to hold up your end of a bargain. My help is
  offered with no expectation that you will
  repay the debt you owe.
Lance>   k
Lance>   thx
```

Nestor (Germany): I was liking the setup for the fall. That little *pito* Lance? I look at the board and he's f---ed. He needs Booker and Jeff to help, but they're too weak to even if they wanted, and they don't.

Time for me and Vicki to carve them up, take what we can while we can. "You want to go out on the porch?" I ask her.

"No."

"Me either. All right, we'll do it right here," I say, and that's when we hear footsteps in the hallway.

It's Evander, and he wants to talk to me. He looks out onto the porch and decides to do it right there in the kitchen. Vicki sits down at the table and us two, we talk at the sink, keeping the volume low. "Are you seeing what I'm seeing with Lance?"

"He can't defend everything," I say.

"You got it. He's one unit short."

"What's that mean for *El Jefe*?"

"I'm going to suggest to him that he support you from Denmark into Sweden."

I take out my phone, look at the map. "No good. Lance'll support with Norway."

"One unit short. He needs Norway to support his army in St. Petersburg, because Jeff can attack with his Moscow army and support it with his fleet in the Gulf of Bothnia."

"Instead … okay. What does he want for that?"

"Don't take Warsaw. Tell Vicki not to take Moscow."

"You asking a *lot*. Also, I just can't tell her what to do."

"One turn. You can take them in the spring. Give my boy one more year."

I scratch my neck. "Let me see what I can do."

"It's all we ask. I'll instruct Jeff to hold in those two territories," Evander says and then he's headed back to the living room.

Vicki wants to know what that was about, and when I tell her, she says, "I don't know about this."

"Me neither. Let's just take them both right now. You get Moscow and support me to Warsaw?" She nods and we start working out our moves.

Jeffrey (Russia): It was the end of the game for me, and by then I was looking forward to it, because there wasn't a damn thing I could do anyhow, right?

Evander had this idea, though. I could help Nestor take Sweden. "Why do I care?"

"It's not going to keep you alive much longer, but at least you can get your measure of revenge on Lance."

"But, wait. Why don't I take St. Pete's back?"

"He'll be expecting it, Jeff. He'll use Norway to support the hold, leaving Sweden wide open."

"You sure?"

"No. But it's my best guess. So support with the fleet, hold your armies in place."

"Why I gotta hold?"

"It doesn't really make a difference. But I told Nestor you

would, and maybe we can work out a way for you to get back and have a few units through to the end of the game. Be allied with those two when they overrun the board. But they have to know you're a team player."

I thought about it, long enough that Evander got impatient and checked the time. "And they agreed not to take Warsaw and Moscow."

Evander sighed. "No. Nestor said he'd think about it and put it to Vicki. But this is the best I can do for you. You don't have any leverage to make a better deal."

"Great. Fine, whatever. Might as well."

[Why Jeffrey looks in the bathtubs upon entering bathrooms]

Jeffrey (Russia): Dad died two weeks after my tenth birthday. Maybe it was because I was young, but I didn't really get that he was dead right away. I mean, I knew it, but I didn't *get* it?

What it took was this dream I had a month after. I was back in the place we lived in when we were all together. The one in Santa Clara. It was daytime and I was walking around. You ever have a dream where you go in one direction, and you try to backtrack and everything is different? It was a two bedroom apartment and I was lost. Everywhere I was was a room in my home, but they were all … off.

When I reached the bathroom, I sat down on the toilet. Not like you're probably thinking, because my pants were on and the lid was down. Now this next part, I can't tell you why I decided to do it. It's not like I heard something or saw something. But I reached over and pulled open the shower curtain anyway.

And my dad was sitting in the bathtub. All of his clothes on. Alive. It was like there was a TV on the other side, above his feet, and he was watching.

He turned and smiled at me. "Hi, Jeff."

"Hi, Dad." And I heard my mom's voice, like she was far away. Calling for me.

"I should go see what Mom wants."

My dad, he shook his head and waved his hand back and

forth. "Stay with me a little. You ever finish that game? That one with Batman?"

"Oh. Not yet. Got to find those last question marks."

"C'mon. You never find *all* the question marks." I hear my mom again. "Are you getting outside? Fresh air?"

I don't remember what I replied to that. The window in that bathroom was on the side with the tub, so the room was getting the sunlight from outside. It was … it was so *normal.*

"Are you happy, Son?"

"Dad, why does everyone leave me?"

He said, "That's not true. *I* didn't leave you, did I?" and that was when it happened. I remembered that my dad was dead, and I wondered how come he was alive and talking to me.

A couple beats after that, my eyes opened and I was lying on my side in bed. Like I said, that's when I got it. I started crying. Mom heard me and crawled in next to me and hugged me until morning came. As soon as she could, she got me a session with a therapist up here.

What my mom and that doctor didn't get until I explained it to them was it wasn't the dream that was bad, it was the waking. When I look behind those shower curtains, it's not because I'm afraid. It's because it was so real. I know he's never going to be there, all right? It's … when I do it, I can get back to that dream for a split second. But that picture I have in my head of him, sitting there: each time it's fuzzier and more washed out than the last one. I check whenever I go to the bathroom and the curtain's closed, but I force myself to only do it once.

Because I know one day I'll pull it open and I'll look and I'll have used it all up and it'll have faded all the way away.

◆ *Austria*
    A Rom Holds ◊ A Nap S A Rom Holds ◊
    <u>A Pie → Mar</u> -- Failure, Attack str. inadequate

◆ *England*
    A Stp S A Mos Holds ◊ A Yor → Lon ◊
    F ENG S F Bel Holds ◊ F Nwy S F Swe Holds ◊
    <u>F Bel S F ENG Holds</u> -- Failure, Supp. disrupted
    <u>F Swe S F Nwy Holds</u> -- Failure, Supp. disrupted
    <u>A Bre → Par</u> -- Failure, Attack str. inadequate
    <u>F Por → Spa.sc</u> -- Failure, Att. str. inadequate

◆ *France*
    A Bur S A Bel Holds ◊ A Mar Holds ◊
    A Par Holds ◊
    <u>F WES → Spa.sc</u> -- Failure, Att. str. inadequate

◆ *Germany*
    A Hol S A Ruh → Bel ◊ A Sil → War ◊
    F NTH S A Ruh → Bel ◊ A Tyr → Ven ◊
    A Ven → Tus ◊
    <u>A Ruh → Bel</u> -- Failure, Attack str. inadequate
    <u>F Den → Swe</u> -- Failure, Attack str. inadequate

◆ *Russia*
    F BOT S F Den → Swe ◊
    <u>A Mos S A War Holds</u> -- Failure, Supp. disrupted
    <u>A War S A Mos Holds</u> -- Failure, Supp. disrupted
        Retreat to Lvn

◆ *Turkey*
    F Alb → ADR ◊ A Gal S A Sil → War ◊
    A Ukr S A Sev → Mos ◊ F ION S F TYS → Tun ◊
    A Ser → Bud ◊ F TYS → Tun ◊ F Gre → Alb ◊
    <u>A Arm → Sev</u> -- Failure, Attack str. inadequate
    <u>A Sev → Mos</u> -- Failure, Attack str. inadequate

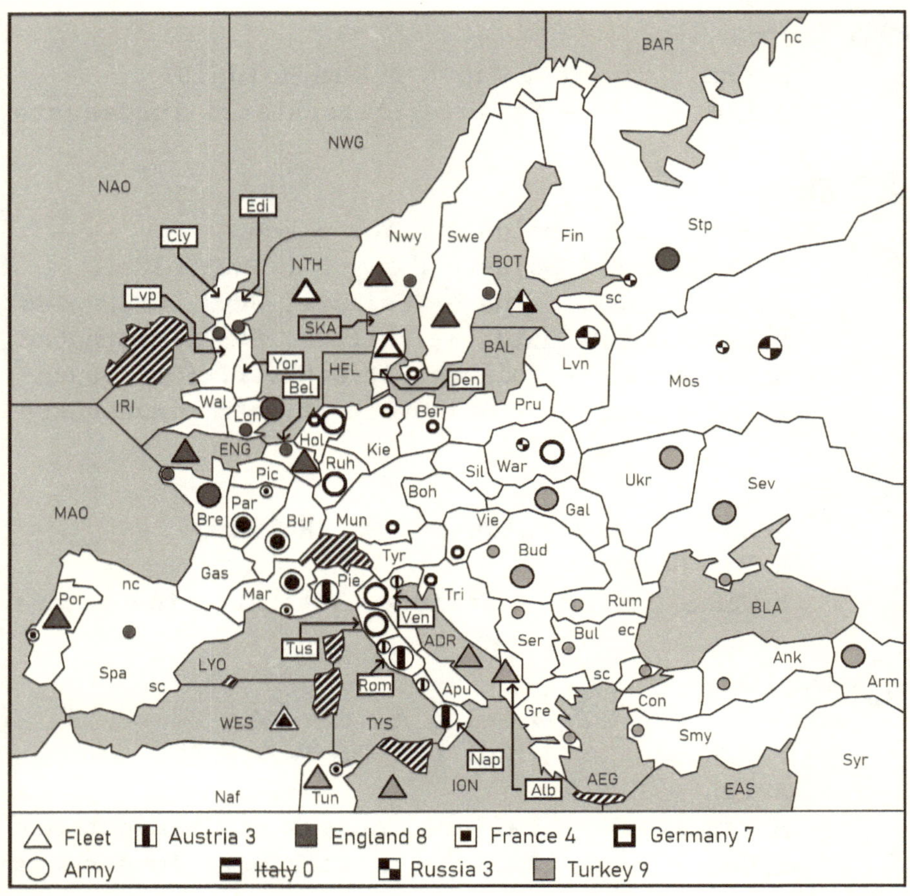

Figure 36 -- Game Map, Start of Winter 1906

Winter
1906

[Reactions to the orders of fall 1906]

Cassandra (Austria): I came in at the last second to put in my orders. I'd considered doing it from where I was, on the back porch, away from the others. But I decided my absence would draw more attention to me than a brief appearance would.

As it happened, their focus was elsewhere. Lance was grinning like the cat that got the cream and Nestor was hissing and spitting like the cat that didn't.

"Bae, you got two more. I don't know why you're upset."

"He was hoping for Belgium too, Vicki," Lance said. "But he made a mistake."

Vicki looked to Nestor to explain, but he was fuming silently. Clenching his jaw, scowling. So she looked around for someone who would.

Booker was the one who did. "He was not expecting me to support England in Belgium."

"Yeah. Your 'bae' counted wrong," Lance chimed in.

Nestor couldn't hold his tongue any longer. "I *counted* on him not going out like a little b----." Evander was ready to intervene, but Booker held up a hand to stop him. "I mean, whatever respect I had for you, Booker? It's—"

"Your respect is a worthless currency," Booker responded.

It took me three seconds to parse that sentence: I know that because I could hear three ticks of the clock on the mantle. And I could hear that because no one was speaking in the wake of those six words.

Jeff broke the silence to say, "Holy s---." Evander said, "Wow." Lance's mouth was open, and the reason I believe his response was unforced was because I was just as shocked. I couldn't recall a time that Booker had openly denigrated someone in that manner: in their presence and in front of others.

Either Nestor didn't understand the depth of the insult or he was merely pretending not to. "Pssh. Whatever."

And that should have been the end of that. Booker had been given the last word, and Nestor's half-hearted answer was hardly an invitation to press the issue. Even Lance seemed disinclined to do so.

But in the moment Jeff let himself get carried away and spoke without thinking. "'Whatever'? Admit it: ya *burnt*."

And Nestor replied, "Shut up. They only invited your fat a-- because they felt sorry for you."

I suppose he had imagined himself to be engaged in a light-hearted bout of The Dozens until he heard the venom in Nestor's voice. Jeff's smile vanished.

"All right. Enough," Evander said. "One minute until winter."

Ollivander (~~Italy~~): Nestor's comment had hit Jeff hard, filled his veins with ice water. If only that had happened to him at the outset, he might have been winning by that point in the game instead of teetering on the brink of elimination.

"Which two?"

"That depends on what you want to accomplish with the one that remains."

We were in the living room with everyone else, not a lot of privacy to be had, but I led him to the corner where the ficus tree was, and he whispered, "I want to make it a headache for Nestor. Get under his skin like Booker did."

"We're looking at a mild irritation at best," I whispered back at him. "That one unit will be gone by the end of 1907."

"I get it."

"And there's the side effect that you'll be helping Lance."

"S---s, but fine."

"Okay. Keep the army in Livonia. Scrap Moscow and Bothnia."

[Reactions to the orders of winter 1906]

Lance (England): The builds and disbands are hardly ever a big deal, but this year they were. Okay, Vicki built an army in Constantinople. Probably the play I'd've made too. She had all the fleets she could use already. Cassie disbanded her army in Piedmont, because otherwise she'd have to lose an army on one of her two remaining supply centers.

Nestor? The army he built in Munich made sense. He was just barely smart enough to make his other build a fleet, and it really didn't make much difference whether he put it in Kiel or Berlin.

Booker chose his disbands to inconvenience Nestor as much as he possibly could. It's truly f---ing amazing that he managed to piss off Booker that badly. I mean, *I* was the one who f---ed Booker over in the first place, not him.

My builds, an army in Liverpool and a fleet in Edinburgh, didn't surprise anyone, or if they did, they weren't talking. What some people weren't expecting, though, was Jeff keeping his army in Livonia instead of his army in Moscow. Jumped to the wrong conclusion about why.

[Ollivander's proposed rule change and reactions to same]

Booker (France): In the waning minutes of the winter of 1906, over the multiple conversations in the living room, Ollivander cleared his throat to get our attention.

"I want to propose a rule change," he said, and was met with sounds of disapprobation. When those had abated somewhat, he continued, "We need to shorten the diplomatic phases. As things stand, we will have time for only three more years of play. But if we make the spring and fall diplomatic phases seven and a half minutes long, we can have four more years."

"Great. Let's do that," Cassandra said.

"Hold on. I think this is a big enough change that it needs to be unanimous."

"What happens if we don't agree?" Victoria asked.

"We have to be done by six no matter what. And unless there's a general agreement to crown a winner or winners by then, it'll be decided by the number of supply centers held at the end of that season."

"So if we did that now ..."

"Then you and Lance would tie for first and Nestor would get third."

"That's some f---ing bulls---," Nestor opined. "Even if me and Vicki are allies and we have more than everyone else combined?"

"'If'?" Lance asked.

"*Lance*. Sorry, it doesn't work that way. As I said, we can work with a general agreement, but if there isn't one, counting dots seems fairest. And that's how we had it in the rules I sent out ahead of time. So all this rule change gives us is an extra year."

Jeffrey glanced at the laptop screen. "Thirty seconds until 1907."

"Are there any vetoes?"

Cassandra, Jeffrey, and I shook our heads no. Lance said, "I'm okay with it."

Victoria saw we were looking at her, awaiting her answer. "As long as Nestor's good, I'm good."

Nestor leaned back on the couch and spread his arms wide. "More years, more dots for me. Let's do it."

Ollivander clicked and typed briefly, and the alarm sounded to notify us that the spring of 1907 had begun.

[Jeffrey's father's talk with him on his tenth birthday]

Jeffrey (Russia): Dad died in a car crash driving down to Santa Cruz at night to see one of his college buddies. There's this spot on Highway 17 called Laurel Curve where if you're going south, you got to take this turn downhill? He swerved and ended up flying off the road and wrapping around a tree. Highway Patrol thinks he either got cut off by a car changing lanes in front of him or he was trying to miss a deer.

Like I said, two weeks before that was my tenth birthday. Mom and Dad had been holding back on getting me a new console for a while because of my grades, but when I woke up that morning, they surprised me with an Xbox 360. Remember those?

So after we set it up and I got to be Batman for a while, Dad comes up with a pen and a pad of paper and scruffs my hair. He watches the action, and when I mess up and get a hostage killed, he makes me hit Pause.

I'm complaining, but he promises me it'll be quick, so I put down the controller and listen.

"There's this way that people look at their lives, Son. Do you remember when I introduced you to binary trees? When I was teaching you some coding?"

I shrug. "Don't worry, I'm not going to quiz you on your birthday. That's just an analogy. You know what an analogy is, right?"

"I think so."

"In our lives, we make decisions. You can think of it like branches. You stay at home, that's one branch; you go to the store, that's the other branch. And if you go to the store and buy a candy bar, that's a branch on that branch, and if you get a coke, that's a different branch on that branch." Dad drew it for me. "You understand?"

I tell him yes. I don't remember if I was telling the truth or not when I did.

"All right, pretend you want to learn how to speak Japanese. There's some branches that will get you there quicker, like if you enroll in a language academy and go to Japan. There's some that will get you there slower, like if you take one class a year and only practice for an hour a week. At the end of both of them, you know the language. You see?"

I look at that paper and I say, "I thought each of those branches are different."

"That's what I'm trying to explain. Look, imagine I want to get from here to San Fran. Each turn or exit the branch splits, and in the end, there'll be more than one branch ending up in The City. You get to the same place, but one branch is longer than the other. Like if you go up the 880, then take the 580 across the bay, then go south on 101 until you cross the Golden Gate Bridge, that's a lot more miles than if you just take the 280 up. And like I said, the same thing can happen with life."

"Okay," I said. I didn't get it, not then, but I said it because I didn't want to feel dumb.

"Jeff, when I was young, before I had you, before I even met your mom, I wanted to get a doctorate in physics."

"What's a … what's that?"

"It's this thing you get when you've gone to school for a long time and passed a really hard test. You've got to write a book and … don't worry about it. Pretend it's a really cool medal you get, okay?"

"Okay."

"Well, I didn't make it. I got part of the way, and I got this less cool medal called a master's. But all I wanted, all I cared about, was getting that doctorate.

"Now in the branches with some examples, it's always going forward, right? Like if … okay, you're playing chess and every time it's your turn, you get a bunch of branches for each move you can make. And once you make that move, there's no take-backs. But imagine instead those are like real paths walking out in the world. You see a place where you can go left, or go right, and you do it. And if you go the wrong way? You can turn around and go back and take the other path. Some of those computer programming examples were like that, you remember."

Lance and Evander sat me down and explained binary tree travelling junior year and that's when I finally got it. Wait, 'travelling' isn't the right word. It's something else close to that.

My dad went on, "In life, you can maybe turn around if you haven't gone very far. Like, I picked this guy to be my advisor so I could get that doctorate. If I had changed my mind fast, I could have picked a different guy. But I waited too long.

"I left with that less cool medal and became a computer programmer. And I looked back at my life like I had been walking out in the world. This one path took me over a bridge. This other path was along a mountain. And another one had me walking across a dry river bed.

"And I thought, if only I had taken a different path, I'd be having that really cool medal right now. Everyone would see me wearing it around my neck, like Han Solo and Luke Skywalker at the end of *Star Wars*. You liked *Star Wars*, didn't you?"

"It was all right," I said.

My dad sighed. "When that movie came out, we thought it was the coolest thing we'd ever seen. Anyway. But I think, I can't go back. That bridge collapsed; there was a rockslide on the mountain; it rained a lot and now there's a river instead of that dry mud. I couldn't get that medal, not anymore. And that made me depressed for a long time.

"But I came to realize that it was never going to happen for me. I wasn't *ever* smart enough to get that doctorate, no matter what branch I walked. And later on, like maybe a year ago, I finally figured out that it wasn't just about where you ended up. The path you take to get there makes a big difference. You walk a long road, and no matter what direction you go, you have to be happy. Not every second, or every hour, or even every day. Sometimes you have to work hard for a little while. Sometimes life will make you sad no matter what choices you make. But if you can't find a way to be happy on that path, you have to make the first turn you can that lets you meet the people, build the friendships that will sustain you. Make you a better person while you make them better."

"Is that what you did?"

My dad looked at me and I saw his eyes were wet. He smiled a little and said, "Yes. When I found your mom and we had you, that's when I became happy. And every step I've taken since then has been a joy, because you were there."

He scruffed my hair again. "Does that kind of make sense to you, Son?"

I looked up at him. "Can this be our thing, Dad? We could talk like this every year."

My dad, he opened and closed his mouth a few times. I guess he was figuring out how to reply? But all he said was, "Sure." He kissed me on the forehead, wished me a happy birthday, and let me un-Pause.

My dad got extra life insurance through work a year earlier because Mom's lupus meant she wasn't pulling a paycheck a lot of the time and she had medical bills that the insurance didn't cover one hundred percent. We were okay for money, but that payout would have to last us for a really long while. Mom moved us up to San Francisco because she has some distant family here and because UCSF has good lupus doctors. And she thought if we were away from where we were when Dad died, it would be easier for us.

By the way, that "verisimilitude" thing you talked about? You won't need it this time. Turns out Dad had recorded us talking and set it up so the .mp3 got e-mailed to me on my eleventh birthday. And on my twelfth: that e-mail said it was in case I lost the other one. A few years ago I wrote down everything he said so I could read it whenever listening would feel like too much.

… Yeah, I'll send you a copy. … No, I never did tell Mom how Dad e-mailed it to me. She doesn't even know Dad and I had that talk. She gets weird sometimes when I bring him up. But I'll tell her one of these days.

◆ *Austria*

```
A Nap ◊  A Rom ◊
Disband A Pie
```

◆ *England*

```
F Bel ◊  A Bre ◊  F ENG ◊  A Stp ◊
A Lon ◊  F Nwy ◊  F Por ◊  F Swe ◊
Build F Edi
Build A Lvp
```

◆ *France*

```
A Bur ◊  F WES ◊
Disband A Mar
Disband A Par
```

◆ *Germany*

```
F Den ◊  A Hol ◊  F NTH ◊  A War ◊
A Ruh ◊  A Tus ◊  A Ven ◊
Build A Mun
Build F Kie
```

◆ *Russia*

```
A Lvn ◊
Disband F BOT
Disband A Mos
```

◆ *Turkey*

```
F ADR ◊  F Alb ◊  A Arm ◊  A Bud ◊
A Gal ◊  F ION ◊  A Sev ◊  F Tun ◊
A Ukr ◊
Build A Con
```

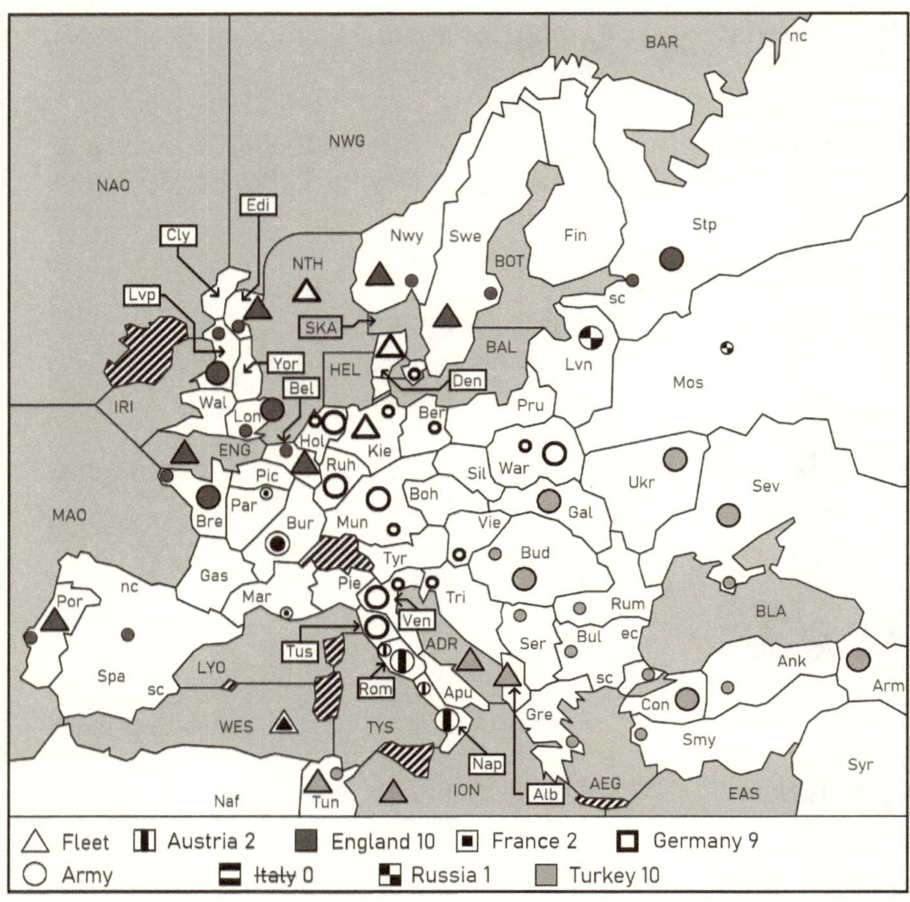

Figure 37 -- Game Map, Start of Spring 1907

Spring 1907

[Diplomatic phase of spring 1907]

Victoria (Turkey): As soon as the buzzer went off, Nestor and I ran to the back porch to make sure we'd be the first ones there. "I know Cassie's your friend, but she can feel sorry for herself somewhere else," he told me.

He got his phone out and scrolled around. I asked, "What's the deal with Jeff?"

"It took me a second, but I figured it out. He's giving Moscow to Lance."

"What?" I looked at the screen. "But how's that even gonna work?"

"It won't. If it was only you, they could keep you out, but with me in Warsaw, it's three on two. So attack with Sev, support with Ukraine, and I'll support with Warsaw. Then you move your army in Armenia to Sev."

"'kay."

"You're gonna like this, *querida*. You know about convoying, right?"

"Yeah?"

"You can convoy over more than one fleet. Like skipping a stone over water. So that army you got in Con, we're gonna send it to Tunis in the fall. Then we're gonna get your armies into Spain and France."

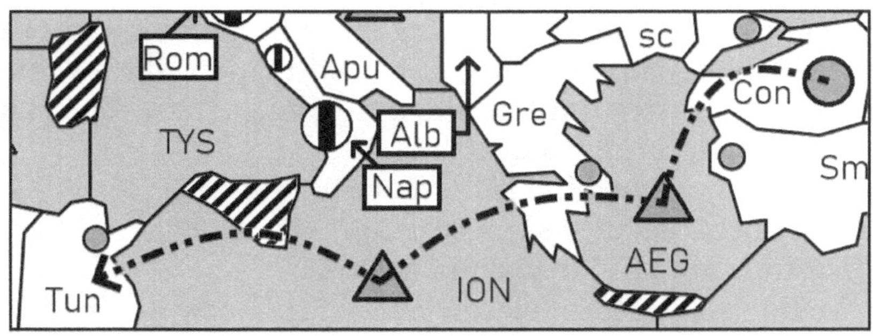

Figure 38 -- Double Convoy Proposed for Fall 1907

He showed me how that worked. "Sweet!"

"So move from the Ionian to the Aegean, from Albania to the Ionian, and from the Adriatic to Apulia. Everything else you hold."

Ollivander (~~Italy~~): I hustled Jeff out to the front porch. "Okay, move to Prussia."

"Wait, why …." He took out his phone and studied the map. "Oh f--- yeah."

"Right? Unless we get really unlucky, Nestor and Vicki will be thinking you're helping Lance take Moscow. So you'll march right in and be on Berlin's doorstep for the fall."

"And then he's gotta play defense with …"

"Munich or Kiel. I'm guessing he'll pick Munich, but who can say for sure until it happens."

Jeff looked at the screen a little longer. "But Vicki will take Moscow."

"Or maybe Nestor will. This is your last year. Then you and me will be advising Booker and Cassie."

"Weird."

"Sure. Remember, move to Prussia now. We'll deal with the fall when it comes."

Lance (England): It was getting to be a regular thing: Evander and Jeff would talk outside; Evander would get Jeff on board with his plan for the turn; I'd go out and get the scoop from Evander. I was getting sick of it, but at least I wouldn't have to deal with it after 1907.

Jeff and me passed in the hall near the front door. Right then he hated Nestor more than me, but he still didn't like me much. As long as that lasted until he was eliminated, I didn't care. I had more important things to worry about.

Evander confirmed it. "He'll move to Prussia."

"You think Nestor'll see it coming?"

"Nestor's not used to playing defense."

"Or being a real team player. Which is majorly ironic."

"He's teaming with Vicki."

"That doesn't count. He thinks she's his vassal to order around. He'll let her be up one or two now, but not at the end. He'll have to be ahead."

"You think so?" Evander asked. "I don't agree. I suspect all he cares about is winning alongside her. The order doesn't matter."

"I guess we'll see," I said.

"Yes." He checked his phone and said, "You should talk to Booker while you have time."

Booker (France): At the start of the diplomatic phase, everyone except Lance, Cassandra, and me fled from the living room to their respective corners. Cassandra was sitting on the couch, lost in her own world. Whatever had transpired between her and Victoria during the spring of 1906 had affected her strongly enough that she was seemingly still upset forty-five minutes later.

Lance opened his mouth to speak to me, then looked to Cassandra and thought better of it. He pointed to the corner of the room farthest from her with raised eyebrows, a gesture I read as "Shall we?" And so we went.

"What are your moves for spring?"

"Burgundy to Ruhr to disrupt support and Western Mediterranean to the Gulf of Lyon."

He watched Ollivander and Jeffrey make their plans on the front porch for a moment. Then he turned back to me and said, "Can I convince you to hold your fleet instead?"

"Why?"

"I bet Vicki will try convoying her armies west. If she goes to Tunis, she'll have to move her fleet out of Tunis soon."

"That could be."

"So you could bounce it out with your fleet."

"Only for one turn. Then she will support it in. And Marseilles will be inadequately protected."

"I can do that from Spain, south coast."

I thought it over. I concluded it was as good a plan as any and told Lance as much.

"I'll be taking Paris," he added.

"I vacated it in the expectation you would do so."

"And you're okay with that?"

"What is left for me in this game is to aid you in defeating Nestor."

"Those two are gonna be finishing up out there any second, but can I ask you a quick question?"

"Go ahead."

"You know why I do, but why do *you* want to see him fail?"

I replied, "Spite. Pure and simple."

Nestor (Germany): Back then I was thinking four years should be enough. Vicki and me, we'd both have more than Lance by then.

That turn, though? Spring of '07? That was me setting things up to make the real moves in the fall. I was going to put Cassie out of her misery and take her two supply centers. Then we were going to hold tight. Make everyone see how we'd smack down Lance if we had more time.

"You should talk to Booker."

"Yeah? Why?"

She takes a breath and says, "You should apologize."

"For what?"

"You said you don't respect him."

I can't tell her to shut up with that bulls---, even though I'm tempted. Instead I say, "One, that was barely anything. He rolls over for Lance, I call him on it. Two, what he says back to me? That was worse. You *know* it, *querida*."

Vicki's not happy with that. I sigh. "I'll message him now."

```
Nestor>   got a sec?
Nestor>   book?
Nestor>   hello?
Booker>   Yes, I am here.
Nestor>   took yr time
Nestor>   hello?
Booker>   Again, yes, I am here.
Nestor>   sorry i say i dont respect
```

```
Booker>  Fine.
Nestor>  you want to say sorry too?
Booker>  Nestor, you have been insulting,
   condescending, and dismissive of me the
   entire day. You apologize only for your most
   recent insult, and you expect me to pretend
   that "sorry I say dont [sic] respect" wipes
   the slate clean? It does not and I will not.
Nestor>  i tried
Nestor>  forget i say anything
Booker>  Done.
```

Vicki's looking over my shoulder, and she shakes her head when she sees what he wrote. "I gave it my best shot."

"I'll talk to him, bae."

"Why? Just let it be."

She shakes her head again. "I don't want to be responsible for leaving things on a bad note."

That's one of the things I used to like about Vicki. She cared about s--- like that. Least I thought she did.

[Victoria's sister talks to her about sex]

Victoria (Turkey): I like sex. I guess I'm supposed to dance around it a little before saying it, even now that I'm in college.

I did a lot of pretending that I didn't back in high school. At least for a while. After my mom made me put a condom on a banana, my sister Janet came back for another talk. "I know it's San Francisco, but you don't want to get a reputation, got it, frosh?" is what she told me.

"I don't even *want* to have sex yet. I told Mom that."

"That's cool. Look, when you do, you've got to be careful."

"But ... but *why*? What's the big deal?"

"Oh God, you want all the answers to that question? How long you got, Vixen?" That's her nickname for me.

"Tell me."

She got comfortable on my bed. "In high school, maybe you

can get away with people knowing you're f---ing—"

"Eww."

"—if you're popular and cute and it's only one guy. Or girl, I guess, but I never figured out the rules for lesbians, so I could be wrong. Hey, Vixen, you like girls too?"

I hit her with a pillow. "Because if you're not popular and cute and only sleeping with one guy, people are grossed out. They'll say you'll f--- anyone."

I was confused. "Okay, I get why people would say that if I slept with more than one guy. But what does being popular and cute have to do with it?"

"Because if you're ugly or lame, you'll f--- anyone. I'm not saying it makes sense, but it's how it is. Even keeping your legs closed isn't a guarantee, because of all those mean b----es who'll lie and call you a slut."

Janet saw I was confused. "Save up your questions for the end. Let me tell you about Mom and Dad."

"What about them?"

"They aren't cool with you having sex. Mom gave you the birth control talk because they're more not cool with you having sex and getting an STD or pregnant."

"I knew that."

"Okay, but here's what you've got to get with that. They're probably resigned to the fact that you're going to be f---ing Nestor—"

"Eww! Stop it!"

"*Sleeping with* Nestor. Better? But you've got to meet them halfway. You can't be rubbing their faces in it."

I asked her what that meant. "They'll give you plenty of notice when they'll be gone and when they'll be back. Nestor's got to be in and out during that time." She laughed. "Get it? In and out?"

"Gross."

"They won't ask you if you've been sleeping with him. That way you won't have to lie about it."

"Really?"

"Unless you're f---ing up at school or getting into trouble, then you're going to be grounded *and* they're going to work you over like they're detectives in a cop show."

"Dramatic much?"

"You won't know dramatic until it happens to you, trust me. That time I got home around two in the morning and tried to sneak in?"

"Oh …. Right."

"Last thing? It *is* a big deal. You don't fall in love every time you rub one out—"

"Eww, girl. Eww."

"—so why would it be different when you're actually sleeping with someone?"

"Well, yeah. Why would it?"

"Beats me. You can Google oxytocin"—Janet spelled it out for me—"if you want to read up on it, but that's barely even an answer. But it is. Different, I mean. You have sex, you run the risk of catching feelings. So you like Nestor?"

She had to drag it out of me, but I finally admitted to her, "Yes, I like him."

"Do you *looooooove* him?"

"OMG. We haven't been together that long."

"Are you his first girlfriend?"

I thought about that. "You know, we haven't even said we're boyfriend and girlfriend yet."

[How Victoria and Nestor became boyfriend and girlfriend]

Cassandra (Austria): Victoria lost her virginity to Nestor shortly after her sixteenth birthday.

She made it sound amazing. When she finished her breathless retelling, I said, "I'm so jealous."

"You'll find a guy and it'll be great. You'll see."

Victoria and Nestor started going steady a month after that.

There was a rumor going around that Constance and Nestor had had sex. With each other. After Vicki and Nestor did.

The face she put on at school was one of total unconcern. I recall someone asking her if it was true, and she rolled her eyes and brushed it aside as utter nonsense. Convincingly, I should add.

Nestor caught up with her while she and I were walking to her place after school one day. He wanted to talk to her alone, but she insisted I be there.

She didn't care about the actual sex, she told him, it wasn't as if they were exclusive. What made her angry was the humiliation of being the girl who was cheated on.

Nestor reeled at that. He said that he would never cheat on her. Constance had hit on him, then made up the story when he rebuffed her. And, he added, he was devastated that she didn't think he took what they had together as seriously as he did. He had assumed that they *were* exclusive.

Vicki sized him up and after what must have been an agonizing wait, she told him that she believed him. And they made the decision, right there, with me as a none-too-eager witness, to be boyfriend and girlfriend.

If I remember correctly, it's called a statement against interest, and here is mine: I'm certain Nestor was telling the truth when he swore to Vicki that he had been faithful. His heart was always hers to break.

 *Austria*

    A Rom Holds ◊ A Nap S A Rom Holds ◊

 *England*

    F ENG S F Bel Holds ◊
    A Lon Holds ◊ A Bre → Par ◊ A Lvp → Yor ◊
    F Nwy → SKA ◊ F Por → Spa.sc ◊ A Stp Holds ◊
    F Edi → NTH -- Failure, Attack str. inadequate
    F Swe → Den -- Failure, Attack str. inadequate
    F Bel S F ENG Holds -- Failure, Supp. disrupted

 *France*

    F WES Holds ◊
    A Bur → Ruh -- Failure, Attack str. inadequate

 *Germany*

    A Hol S A Ruh → Bel ◊
    F Kie S F Den Holds ◊ A Ven S A Tus → Rom ◊
    A War S A Sev - Mos ◊
    A Mun → Bur -- Failure, Attack str. inadequate
    A Ruh → Bel -- Failure, Attack str. inadequate
    A Tus → Rom -- Failure, Attack str. inadequate
    F Den → Swe -- Failure, Attack str. inadequate
    F NTH S A Ruh → Bel -- Failure, Supp. disrupted

 *Russia*

    A Liv → Pru ◊

 *Turkey*

    F ADR Holds ◊ F Alb → ION ◊
    A Arm → Sev ◊ A Bud Holds ◊ A Con Holds ◊
    A Gal Holds ◊ F ION → AEG ◊ A Sev → Mos ◊
    F Tun Holds ◊ A Ukr S A Sev → Mos ◊

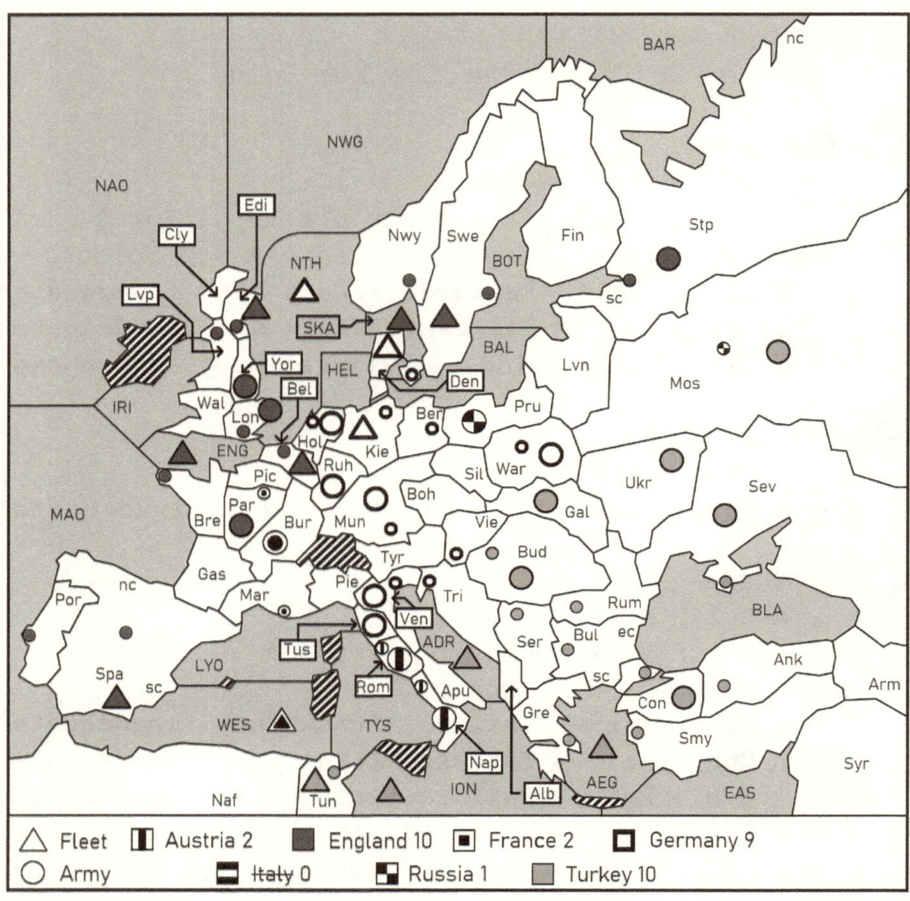

Figure 39 -- Game Map, Start of Fall 1907

Fall
1907

[Reactions to the orders of spring 1907]

Booker (France): No, that is not correct. It was *not* the case that Germany needed to occupy Berlin at the end of the year in order to avoid losing a supply center. All that was necessary was that no *other* power occupy Berlin.

At the start of the fall turn, there were three occupied territories neighboring Berlin. Germany had a fleet in Kiel and an army in Munich. And Russia had its army in Prussia.

The situation merely appeared to be precarious for Germany. There was a simple solution that would allow it to be certain to hold its supply centers against French, English, and Russian incursion: the army in Munich could be ordered to Berlin, and the army in Ruhr could be ordered to Munich.

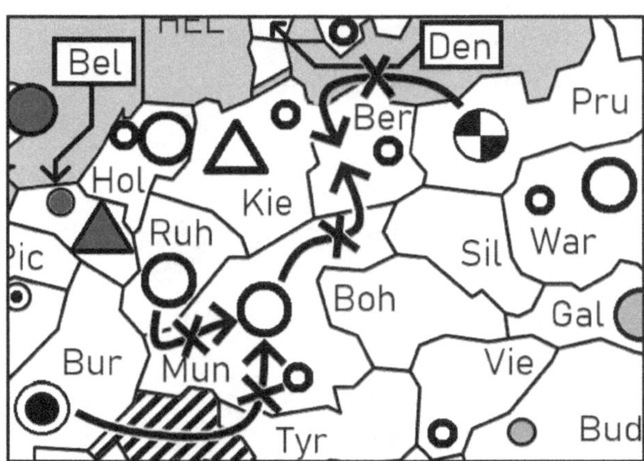

*Figure 40 -- German Moves to Prevent Berlin
and Munich from Being Taken*

Every other location had the necessary support to defend against invasion. The sole disadvantage would be that England would no longer require aid to hold Belgium. The fleet in the English Channel would be freed to convoy armies to the northern coast of France.

Would Nestor see it? Or, seeing it, would he decide to instead make a reckless gamble to grab another supply center? We all had less time to plan our moves than in previous years, after all. And he seemed agitated. That was quite unusual for him.

Lance (England): I thought Nestor was reacting to Jeff's army in Prussia. Had a scowl on, tapping his foot, crossing his arms.

It was after Evander moved the pieces on the board that I saw it. He was looking at the bottom half of the board. Italy. His two armies weren't going to be enough to dislodge Cassie's units. She was wedged in there tight.

He was going to need one of Vicki's fleets to be his crowbar. Then Rome'd be his in 1907 and Naples in 1908. It would be a three-way tie, practically. A stalemate line was building, and neither Nestor nor me were going to break it.

Vicki was looking nervous. At what, f--- if I knew. That bathroom trip with her and Cassie had been a while back; this was different from that.

Cassie, though, she had on the same face. Still focused on whatever that was with Vicki and Evander rigging who'd get what country with that baseball cap.

[Diplomatic phase of fall 1907]

Ollivander (~~Italy~~): "A minute and a half to fall," I said.

"You see it, Nestor?" Jeff asked.

"I see your last move won't do a damn thing. You have fun, though."

My phone buzzed, a text from my mother. "So it turns out we have until six-thirty. Mom's running late at work. We can make it to the end of 1911 if there's interest. Well?"

Jeff groaned. Booker sighed. Cassie kept Cassie-ing. But those three weren't the ones whose opinions mattered.

"Let's do it," Lance answered.

"Another year for me to put the hurt on," Nestor said.

Vicki was chewing the inside of her mouth. She hadn't been listening, so I repeated it all for her. "Do we have to decide now?"

"We have time."

The tone sounded from my laptop and it was officially fall. Vicki and Nestor headed off to their spot on the back porch. I tapped Jeff on his shoulder and we went to ours on the front.

"I make a move for Berlin, Nestor stops me, and that's the end."

"That's one option. You could go to Warsaw. Or to Livonia."

"Why?"

"You might get lucky. Nestor might move out of Warsaw himself to support an attack on St. Petersburg. If he and Vicki don't support a move to Livonia, you can keep them out of St. Petersburg one extra turn."

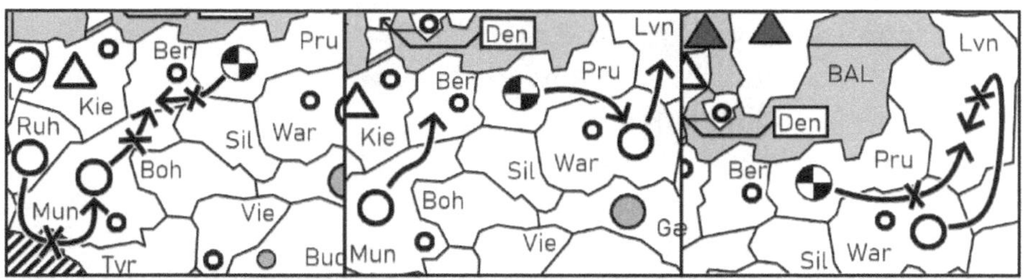

Figure 41 -- Some Russian Options and Potential German Move Orders

"Not even an extra year."

"Nope. But also? If you don't move to Berlin, then you won't bounce off of Nestor's army coming from Munich."

"Or his fleet from ..." Jeff checked his phone. "Kiel."

"He probably won't move his fleet. He does that, Lance can take Denmark. He moves out of Munich, it's another mild inconvenience for him. Maybe."

"But if he knows I'm doing that, he doesn't have to move out of Munich."

"True. If he figures you out, he'll know what to do."

"He won't."

"Nestor's sharp. Don't assume."

Jeff touched a forefinger to his temple. "I got a plan."

I waited. "Well?"

"Tell you after. If the suspense doesn't kill you."

Victoria (Turkey): "Bae, I can explain," I said on our way to the porch. Nestor shook his head and wouldn't slow down.

When we were outside with the door closed behind us, Nestor told me, "Go ahead. Explain. Why didn't you move to Apulia like I asked?"

I took too long answering. He had to look at his watch to get me going. "I couldn't understand why you wanted me to do it."

"We got to make this quick. First you move into Apulia. Then you attack Naples. I can get Rome. Then you can pull out and I can get Naples."

"No."

"What? Why?"

"I won't help you attack Cassie."

Nestor was clutching his head. "Dammit! You did it before, why won't you do it now?"

I didn't answer. I couldn't.

"We're running out of time. It's going to take me forever to do this myself, and you made me lose a turn." He started typing. "Okay, here's the orders. If I don't say otherwise, you hold."

"Okay."

He put his phone away and touched my cheek. "I'm sorry I was short with you, *querida*. But we're a team. Communication is important. For us. It's what will keep us together when we are miles apart. When we can't see each other during the week or when I'm playing an away game. You agree?"

"I understand," I said.

"We'll talk some more afterwards." He kissed my forehead and went inside.

Nestor (Germany): So Vicki's refusing to help me take down Cassie. Cassie doesn't even want to f---ing play, and all of a sudden it's really important I eliminate her all by myself?

I'm *pissed*, but I don't show it. Vicki's the love of my life, and no way I'll yell at her. Not two days before she's gone and I won't see her again for months.

I get myself a glass of water in the kitchen and think it over. Gotta keep Jeff out of Berlin. I spend the rest of those seven point five thinking it over.

And I get it. I move my armies in Ruhr and Munich. That way Jeff doesn't get Berlin, and if he tries to juke me and hold where he is, I still make sure Booker can't sneak into Munich.

There's a problem, though: I can't support my attack on Belgium with my army in Ruhr. I got my army in Holland and my fleet in the North Sea. Lance got his fleets in Belgium and the English Channel. And Booker's army in Burgundy.

If I know exactly what everyone's gonna do, I can make things hard for Lance. I'm not thinking imma take a dot off him, but damn sure he won't be getting anything off me.

Lance won't give it up. Booker won't either. But Jeff? Couple questions and I'll read the answer right off his fat face.

The clock's running down and people are heading back to the living room. Jeff's standing near the laptop, I stand right next to him.

"What's your last order gonna be, huh?"

He looks at me, says nothing. "You going into Berlin?" He smiles. "Or you finna get tricky and hold?" He smiles some more.

I step over to the board and I see everyone's watching us two. Even Cassie's pulled her head out of her a-- so she can follow the action. I'm thinking maybe I missed something, but the map around Prussia's pretty simple. And that s---s, because it means whatever's in Jeff's head is staying there.

"Your moves for fall," Evander says. "Five minutes."

Jeffrey (Russia): Before that turn, we were getting our orders in with minutes to spare. But fall of 1907, I took my sweet time. Then, with thirty seconds left I took a quarter out of my pocket and flipped it twice. Heads then tails, case you're wondering. And after that I entered my last move of the game on my phone.

Got it in with fifteen seconds to spare. When Nestor saw what I did, he was really angry. Not gonna lie: that felt good.

[Cassandra and Victoria's talk in the bathroom during spring 1906]

Cassandra (Austria): Vicki led me by the hand to the bathroom. And just like she did in the morning, she sat on the edge of the bathtub and patted the space next to her as an invitation.

The window was on the other side of the shower curtain and it faced south, and so the light that filtered into that small room was reflected from the walls of the house next to it. But even without the bulb overhead being lit, everything had a soft glow to it. The house was warm with the heat of the summer's day and the chirping of birds and the rumbling of tires over the asphalt were faintly audible. I felt the side of her thigh as she pressed against me. The atmosphere there, in the bathroom, was almost … romantic.

Perhaps that's why, when she leaned her head close to mine, her face at a half profile from where I sat, and asked if I was planning to accept Nestor's offer of an alliance, I kissed her. The angle was wrong and so I caught the left side of her lips. That actually made it not as bad as it might have been had I aimed better.

I don't know what I was thinking, or rather I should say that I wasn't. Any calculation that Vicki would be leaving soon and I would not see her for months was not at the forefront of my mind when I did what I did. It wasn't planned, you must believe me.

She didn't kiss me back. "Girl, what are you doing?"

My heart was pounding. My skin was on fire with the excitement and humiliation of it all. I stammered out incoherencies as she slid a foot away from me.

And there we sat for fifteen long and excruciating seconds. I wasn't aware that I was crying until Vicki reached for the box of Kleenex and handed it to me.

I dabbed my eyes and blew my nose. Vicki touched the back of my shoulder with a tentative hand, then rubbed it through my t-shirt. "I'm sorry. I don't know what came over me."

"It's okay, girl." Someone jiggled the doorknob. We fell silent. There was knocking and more jiggling and whoever it was walked off, towards the living room. "When did you know?"

"Since sophomore year."

She nodded. "You remember freshman year, how we met? Those lesbians trying to get you to come to their LGBTQ club?"

"As if it were yesterday."

She moved her hand back to her thigh. "It's funny, isn't it? They figured it out before you did."

I was confused by the chronology she was proposing, until it dawned on me that we were referring to different things. "It was sophomore year I knew I liked *you*."

Vicki buried her head in her hands and planted her elbows on her knees. Something about that gave it away. "You knew it. Didn't you?" I asked.

She lowered her hands. "I was kind of hoping it'd never be a thing out in the open. Like, a year at college and you'd find someone else."

"Sorry." I started crying again. She cradled me in her arms, rocked us from side to side.

And then I stopped. In my mind, I heard the klunk of the other shoe dropping. My body stiffened. Vicki noticed and asked what was wrong.

"You knew and you asked all those things of me today."

"What? What do you mean?"

"'Give me Greece.' 'Move your fleet here.' You could count on me to do your bidding."

"No. No, I wouldn't—"

"I'm such an idiot."

Vicki got off the tub and crouched on the tile right in front of me, on one knee. "It wasn't like I thought, 'I'll ask Cassie to do those things because she's in love with me and she'll do anything for me.'"

"Not consciously." I blew my nose.

"I … maybe. I don't know. But are you going to say that about everything we did together the past three years?"

"I don't know."

She stood up. "That's not fair. Tell me, what was I supposed to do, huh? Say, 'I know you're into me in a lesbian way'? What if I was wrong? What if you denied it and I ended up looking like a dumb homophobic c---?"

I got on my feet. Took off my glasses and splashed some water on my face. I was toweling off when her phone chimed. "Nestor says about two minutes 'til spring orders."

"You're really getting into this game, huh?"

"Don't hate me, but I kinda am."

"One of these days, when you get back from Europe, you should remind me to tell you something I discovered about it."

She considered asking, I could tell. Then she changed her mind and said, "I'll put a note in my phone."

"I'm not going to agree to Nestor's deal."

"Yeah, don't even worry about it."

"So I'll wait for you to help Nestor take Italy from me."

Vicki gripped both my hands. "*No.* Girl, I won't do that. I promise you I won't. It's the least I can do."

We primped in the mirror. And after we had restored some semblance of normalcy to our appearances, we rejoined everyone else in the living room.

By the way, she never did ask me what it was I found out. I never sought her out to inform her. I'll leave that to you.

 *Austria*
    A Rom Holds ◊ A Nap S A Rom Holds ◊

 *England*
    F Bel Holds ◊ F ENG C A Lon → Bre ◊
    F Edi → NTH ◊ A Lon → Bre ◊ A Par Holds ◊
    F SKA S F Edi → NTH ◊ F Spa.sc → LYO ◊
    A Yor → Lon ◊
    <u>A Stp → Nwy</u> -- Failure, Attack str. inadequate
    <u>F Swe → Den</u> -- Failure, Attack str. inadequate

 *France*
    <u>F WES → Tun</u> -- Failure, Attack str. inadequate
    <u>A Bur → Mun</u> -- Failure, Attack str. inadequate

 *Germany*
    F Kie S F Den Holds ◊ A Mun → Ber ◊
    A Ven S A Tus → Rom ◊
    <u>A Hol → Bel</u> -- Failure, Attack str. inadequate
    <u>F Den → Swe</u> -- Failure, Attack str. inadequate
    <u>A Ruh → Mun</u> -- Failure, Attack str. inadequate
    <u>A Tus → Rom</u> -- Failure, Attack str. inadequate
    <u>A War → Lvn</u> -- Failure, Attack str. inadequate
    <u>F NTH → Nwy</u> -- Failure, Attack str. inadequate
        Retreat to HEL

 *Russia*
    <u>A Pru → Lvn</u> -- Failure, Attack str. inadequate

 *Turkey*
    F ADR Holds ◊ F AEG C A Con → Tun ◊
    A Bud Holds ◊ F ION C A Con → Tun ◊
    A Gal Holds ◊ A Sev Holds ◊ F Tun → TYS ◊
    A Ukr Holds ◊
    <u>A Con → Tun</u> -- Failure, Attack str. inadequate
    <u>A Mos → Stp</u> -- Failure, Attack str. inadequate

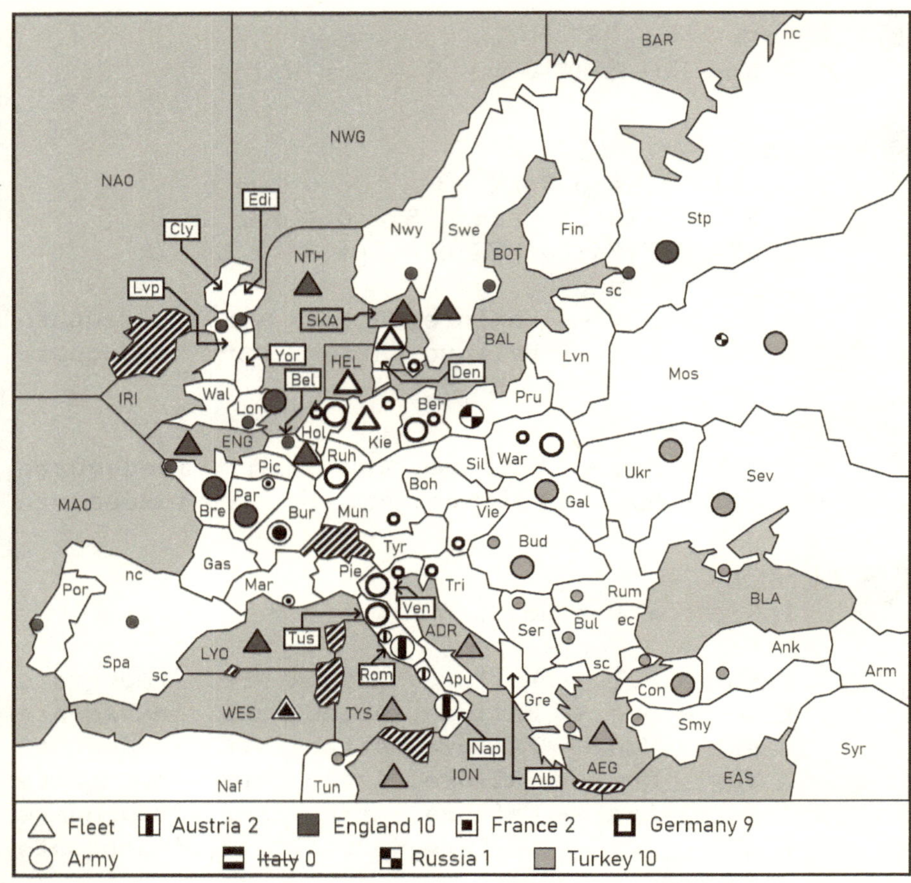

Figure 42 -- Game Map, Start of Winter 1907

Winter 1907

[Reactions to the orders of fall 1907]

Ollivander (~~Italy~~): "Yo, congratulations. Played the game five minutes longer," Nestor told Jeff. "That make you happy?"

Jeff ignored him and asked, "Evander, you and me are advisors now?"

"After winter. You won't be eliminated until then."

I made the board match the laptop screen. It didn't take long: a few years into the game, not many units can make useful moves.

And everyone gathered to look. Even Vicki. Even Cassie. Curious what the result of Jeff's coin flips was.

"Oof," Lance opined. "You must be kicking yourself, Nestor."

"I'm doing just fine. You subtract that dot Booker gave you, we both held even."

"I got another army into France."

"Yeah? And what are you going to do with it?"

"You'll see."

"Don't think there'll be anything *to* see. All that drama 'bout what his last move would be, and what? Nothing."

"I got St. Pete's."

"And?"

"Hmm," Booker said.

"You want to tell me?" Nestor asked him.

"Had you coordinated to take Livonia and hold Moscow, St. Petersburg would have fallen to Turkey this upcoming spring. But now that will no longer be possible."

Vicki scanned that side of the board. "Bae, we should've done that!"

"I suspect he spent the seven and a half minutes he had available ensuring his holdings would remain his," Booker said to Vicki. "Had the diplomatic stage been fifteen minutes, as it was earlier, I feel certain he would have noticed in time and advised you accordingly."

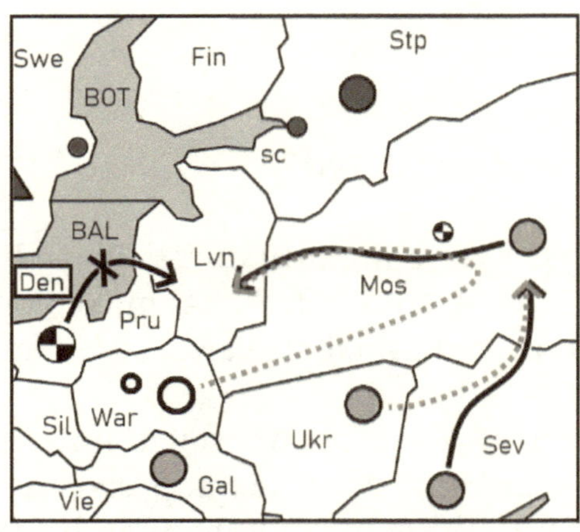

*Figure 43 -- What Germany and Turkey Could Have Done
in Fall 1907 to Enable Turkey to Take St. Petersburg in Spring 1908*

I used the moment of silence after Booker offered up his con-
jecture to tell him, Lance, and Vicki to take care of their winter
orders before the five minutes were up.

[Reactions to the orders of winter 1907]

Booker (France): Turkey's choice to build an army was unsur-
prising. A fleet would do nothing for that power, in the grid-
locked eastern half of the Mediterranean. Had our game not had
a cutoff of 1911, Turkey could perhaps line the west coast of Italy
with fleets as a prelude to an invasion of the south of France. But
it did, and given that constraint, an army would be marginally
better.

It was France and England's decisions that were the conse-
quential ones. Mine was fairly straightforward. I kept the fleet,
as it had more potential utility than the army in Burgundy.

England chose a fleet over an army. The right choice, as there
was not much that could be done with an army originating on
those isles. Liverpool instead of Edinburgh strongly suggested
that England intended that fleet for the south. It would seem
that any final fireworks, if there were to be any, would be between England and Turkey in the western half of the Mediterranean.

[Attempt at an armistice]

Victoria (Turkey): "Two minutes to spring," Evander said. "Is there an agreement to end the game?"

"Agreement?" I asked.

"Are you, Nestor, and Lance willing to call it a day?"

"What about us?" Jeff asked.

"You three don't really rate consideration. If that bothers you, neither do I."

Jeff replied by pressing his palm against his lips and making a farting noise. "Eww," I told him.

"Moving on, if you can come to terms, that's that. We have a peace treaty."

Nestor wanted to know what "Terms" meant. "Who's first, who's second, who's third."

"Me and Vicki are first."

"And Lance?"

"He loses like everyone else. We got more than half the dots, and that's not gonna change."

"No. Those aren't the rules we agreed on. Lance?"

"'In order for the game to end before winter of the final year, either one player must control eighteen supply centers or all players with at least as many units as at the start of the game must agree to the final standings.'"

"*Do* you agree, Lance?"

"No. Do it by units. Vicki and I tie for first."

"And Nestor?"

Lance looked at him. "He can settle for bronze."

Nestor shook his head. "Three-way tie?" I asked.

That time Lance *and* Nestor said no.

"Then that's that. We keep playing. And if there's no agreement by 1911, we count supply centers."

[Homecoming assembly of 2018]

Jeffrey (Russia): They *made* us go. One of the teachers? She told me if they didn't, half the school would be spending the period studying instead. But me, I'm glad they did. Getting to hang with your friends and skip a class? People needed to learn to chill and enjoy a break when they got one.

We had way too many students to fit them all on the bleachers at once, so they had four of those assemblies, one for each class. They seated us by homeroom. Karthik and Evander's was next to us and I was sitting right behind those two.

I slapped them on their shoulders. "Glad you guys are here!"

"Meh," Karthik said. "I could be getting a jump on my AP Physics homework. Like Dave Kim is right now." Karthik was all right, but he was the sort of guy who couldn't just say "physics". He *had* to mention it was advanced placement.

"How come Dave is out? Isn't this mandatory for everyone?" I asked.

"Didn't you hear? He broke a leg," Evander explained. "It'd be too awkward sitting in the bleachers with that cast."

Karthik shook his head. "Lucky b------. If I'd have known that's all it took, I would've broken mine too."

The teachers started shushing the crowd and our principal started emceeing. She was really getting into it, too. "Let's get ready to rumble!" Karthik said, loud enough for only us three to hear. Evander snickered and his homeroom teacher Mr. Yang, three rows in front and down from us, gave him a warning stare.

We were quiet until the principal introduced him: "Wearing number eighty-two, wide receiver Nestor *'El Conejito'* Martinez!"

The cheering was loud enough for us to talk again. "I don't get it. Is it just me?" Karthik asked.

"Well, yeah, it is," Evander replied. "Nestor's kind of a big deal. They're saying he's being scouted by Division I schools."

"Where his career will end."

It wasn't until our starting quarterback gave his speech and told us to make some noise that there was enough cover for us to talk. Evander said, "All of our careers will end somewhere, and I'll tell you, I'm not seeing anyone in our class who's going all the way to the top. Right now, though? Nestor's up there."

"And what am I supposed to do when it's all over for him?"

"Treat it like any other thing whose beauty is transient. Admire it, mourn it, leave it in the past."

"Leave it to you to get all philosophical and s--- about football," I said.

The band started playing then and everyone stood up. Lots of drums and horns inside that room. Big room, but they were pretty loud. All you could hear further than a couple feet away was the marching band music, which meant we could talk without Mr. Yang giving us the stinkeye. "Not everything's meant to last forever. You want to be like one of those hippies who're stuck in the Sixties?"

"I can do that without going nuts over high school football," Karthik said. "But I see what you mean." He nudged Evander and pointed across the parquet floor. Took me a second to see it was Lance, standing maybe seventy feet away. "Case in point."

I asked him what he meant by that. "Follow his line of sight."

At first glance, it looked like he was checking out the girls in the front row on his side. They let the team girlfriends sit there to cheer on their guys. "Yup, same idea there."

"Lucky b------'s got a good view," I said.

"What? I mean, yeah, he does, but that's not it. You see which one he's looking at?"

"I can't make it out from here," Evander said.

"It's obviously Vicki."

Vicki was at the end of the row, dancing to the noise like it was actual music. If Lance wasn't eyeing her, there was something else in that direction that had his attention.

"Maybe, but that's only because she's the only one he's got a clear view of."

"His face," Karthik said.

Everyone around him was getting into it. Or talking to their friends like us three were doing. He was clapping along to the beat, sure, but as far as I could tell from where we were standing, he wasn't smiling. He wasn't angry, he wasn't sad. It was like he was concentrating hard on a problem.

"What about it?" Evander asked. "He's zoning out. Thinking about something else."

"No way he's doing that. I had a crush on Vicki, you guys knew that, right?"

I didn't. Evander shook his head no. "Freshman year. You get how it is with the kinda cute girls. You think you maybe have a chance, but they end up with someone else." Karthik explained that thing I told you about the cartoon cat and how Vicki was a mirage. "And like you said, Evander: you let yourself mope for a while and then move on dot org."

"Sure."

"Not Lance, though."

Me and Evander started objecting, talking over each other. He pointed at me to go first. "We know he liked Vicki, that's not news. But that was all over after freshman year."

"You remember when he almost got into that fight?"

"Everybody remembers that."

"He used that Spanish swear word. Why would he know that?"

"Heard someone say it in the Mission?"

"Okay, why did he have it ready to go? He didn't hesitate in the slightest, did he?"

We didn't know. "I'm disappointed in you two. You know him better than I do, and the answer was clear to me right away: he was hoping to use it on Nestor."

"*That exact*—" Evander realized he was being too loud and dialed it down. "That exact line?"

"I would bet he had several practiced."

"But why?"

"In order to get Nestor angry enough to beat him up. And the reason why he'd want that was because it would utterly obliterate Nestor's nascent relationship with Vicki."

"Hold on," I said. "Then why use it on Juan?"

"My objection exactly," Evander said.

"It was a half a loaf. I'm sure in his fevered imagination Vicki would rush from Nestor's side directly to his hospital bed and nurse him back to health. Also ..."

Evander asked, "Also what?"

Karthik took a breath. "And I'm not accusing him of being

racist, but he might have found it easy to slot Juan into the role he envisioned Nestor playing because they're both Latino."

The band was on the song they always finished with, "Seven Nation Army", while we got the last of it out of Karthik.

"Say that's all true," Evander said. "How are you so certain he's not over it by now? Three years later?"

"Not only did he not get to live out his fantasy, things got twisted around so badly that Nestor came out the hero of the hour at Lance's expense. Would *you* get over something like that?"

I don't know if he was right, but I couldn't argue with his logic. The song was down to the last Whoa Oh Hohs when Karthik finished up with, "And like I said, just look at him. That's not ogling a hot girl. That's fixation."

"He'll forget about her when he goes off to college," I said.

"Well, getting away from her will definitely do him a world of good." I nodded. Evander had his face scrunched up, though, like he was trying to figure something.

And then the song ended and we clapped and yelled and filed out.

[The new teams for spring 1908]

Lance (England): The laptop dinged and Evander hit Pause. "Jeff is eliminated. Sorry, man."

"Yeah, well."

"So now you and me are advisors. Booker has one unit and Cassie has two, so he gets to pick first. Booker, which one of us do you want to advise you?"

"You, Evander."

"And Cassie, would you like Jeff as *your* advisor?"

"What can he possibly do." She sighed. "Fine, why not. Welcome aboard, Jeff."

Cassandra (Austria): After everyone else departed the living room, Jeff came over to where I stood. "'Sup."

"Sorry about that. If I didn't seem eager, it's because of the circumstances. It's not you."

"Nah, I get it. Although I bet you'd be a whole lot happier if it were you and Vicki, huh?"

"What's that supposed to mean?" I asked, a bit hotly.

Jeff held up his hands, waist height, palms towards me. "Just that you two are besties."

"Right. Of course. I'm sorry, it's this game. It's really gotten under my skin."

"Me too. That s--- Lance pulled? I want the f--- away from him as soon as we're done here."

"So *is* there anything you can do for me? Any suggestions?"

He scratched the back of his head. "Sure. Get Vicki to help you out against Nestor. You can take back Trieste and Venice."

I gave him a "get real" look and he shrugged. That was when he noticed the baseball cap on the floor next to the table with the laptop. He bent down and picked it up. Flipped it around in his hands and rubbed the visor between his finger and thumb.

He was confused. By the cap, it seemed. "Is something wrong with it?"

"No, I mean the cap's fine. You remember how ... wait, you and Vicki weren't here in the living room. I asked Evander about it being in the bathroom, and he told us he'd tossed it in the bathtub right after he got Italy."

"Right."

"Yeah. Thing is? I'm almost *positive* it wasn't there earlier. Except why would he lie about something like that?"

◈ *Austria*   A Nap ◊ A Rom ◊

◈ *England*   F Bel ◊ A Bre ◊ F ENG ◊ A Lon ◊
                 F LYO ◊ F NTH ◊ A Par ◊ F SKA ◊
                 A Stp ◊ F Swe ◊
                 Build F Lvp

◈ *France*   F WES ◊
                 Disband A Bur

◈ *Germany*   A Ber ◊ F Den ◊ F HEL ◊ A Hol ◊
                 F Kie ◊ A Ruh ◊ A Tus ◊ A Ven ◊
                 A War ◊

◈ *~~Russia~~*   Disband A Pru

◈ *Turkey*   F ADR ◊ F AEG ◊ A Bud ◊ A Con ◊
                 A Gal ◊ F ION ◊ A Mos ◊ A Sev ◊
                 F TYS ◊ A Ukr ◊
                 Build A Smy

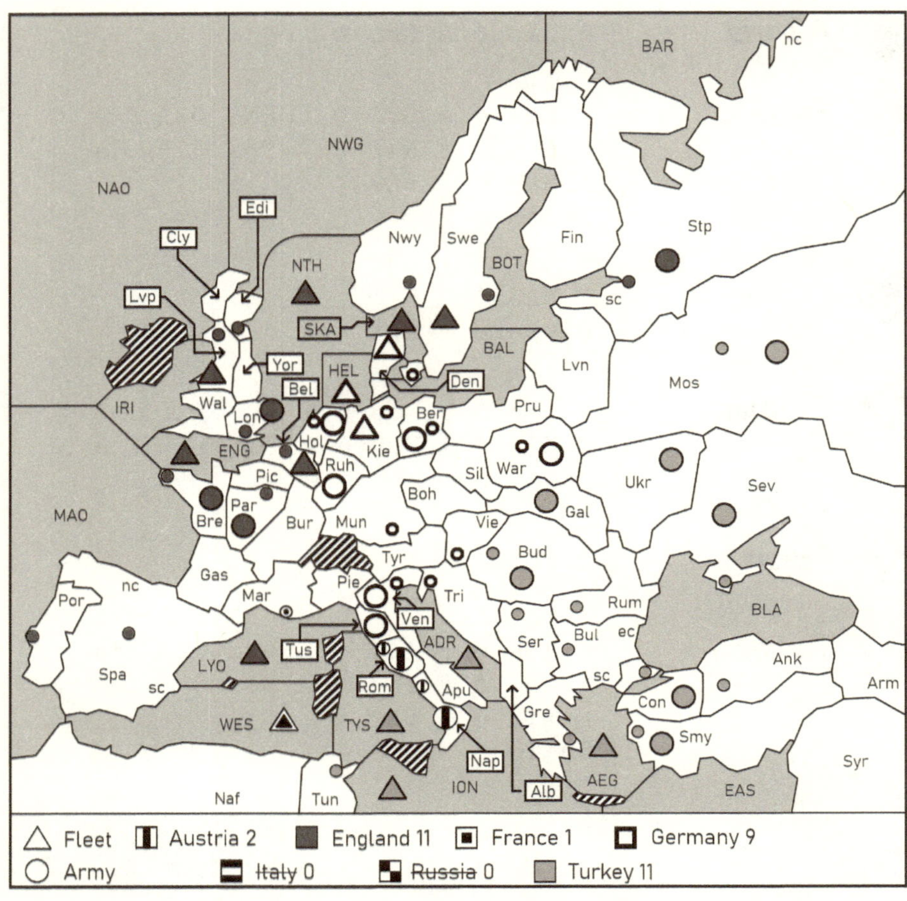

Figure 44 -- Game Map, Start of Spring 1908

Spring
1908

[Ollivander's comment on the baseball cap]

Ollivander (Italy): Sure, I took the seven game pieces I had placed inside the drawstring sack in the center of the cap to return to the living room in case anyone thought to count, but why didn't I also rip out those threads and unfasten and remove the sack itself right away? Instead of tossing it in the cabinet under the sink where it could potentially be found? We've all seen movies in which a villain could have avoided his downfall simply by paying proper attention to some minor detail. But he doesn't, and so the hero is able to prevail and the audience is torn between cheering for him and booing the screenwriters. So what's my excuse?

Well, I was just about to, when Jeff knocked on the bathroom door. I decided to shove it into the back of the cabinet and do it later. And then I forgot it was there, until I realized that mistrustful Cassie was alone behind a locked door and right next to the evidence of my perfidy. Once I rushed her from the bathroom, I carefully clipped those strings and pulled the stitches holding the sack and pocketed it all before throwing it in the tub. If you're wondering why the bathtub, I thought I should change hiding places, just to be on the safe side. And yes, that *was* dumb.

Well, I had convinced myself that I had acted just in the nick of time, until she disabused me of that notion by asking to borrow it for the pictures we took. That was when I knew that she knew.

As for Jeff, when he said he hadn't noticed it in that room, I told him the truth: it was in the bathtub; I had tossed it over the shower curtain rod. How was I supposed to know he'd already looked inside there? I mean, who *does* that?

[Diplomatic phase of spring 1908]

Booker (France): I was convinced that the only power that anyone could possibly negotiate with at that time was Austria.

That is not how the diplomatic phase for the spring of 1908 began for me. Lance asked me to join him on the front porch. I brought along Ollivander, who was nominally advising me on how to deploy my single unit. As a practical matter, however, he would serve as *aide-de-camp* for England.

"What would you have me do with my fleet?"

Ollivander looked to Lance, who clarified, "Booker agreed to let me decide on his orders here on out."

"As long as he's the one entering them into the site, that's fine by me."

"Move to Tunis. I'll move to the Tyrrhenian to disrupt the convoy's support, and there'll be a bounce."

"What's the plan, Lance? Are you thinking you can take the dot from her?"

"I'll be …." Lance's attention had been drawn to something in the living room. That something was Jeffrey, pacing in front of Cassandra and talking, fidgeting with the baseball cap.

Lance and Ollivander shared a look. I became curious enough to ask what they had noticed.

They struggled for words. It was Ollivander who managed to reply, "Jeff's talking for longer than I'd expected. Those two are up to something."

"That seems impossible," I ventured. "Unless Germany agrees to vacate the Italian peninsula or Turkey pledges its aid, there is nothing to be done except to have the armies in Rome and Naples support one another."

"Or Cassie can get help from me. Not now, but give me three turns and I can have an army in Piedmont."

I pictured the map and puzzled it over until I understood. "A three-fleet convoy from Brest. Which will come with the downside that Victoria will plant an army in Tunis."

"You got it."

"And Cassie will stay alive to the end," Ollivander said. "That doesn't concern you directly, but if you're in favor of it, Lance can keep it in mind when he negotiates with them."

It was in England's self-interest to keep Germany from taking any more supply centers. And ordinarily it would be to its advantage to take France's.

But there was a complication. The moment it took Marseilles, the French fleet would disband and England would be without support in that location until a fleet of its own could arrive from outside the Mediterranean.

Which meant that the deed would be done in the fall of 1911, when it would count for England's final tally and Turkey would be unable to use its sudden absence to its advantage. The only way to prevent my ultimate elimination would be for me to pre-emptively filch an English-occupied supply center and prevent its subsequent recapture. An impossibility, barring a serious miscalculation on England's part.

And so I resigned myself to my fate. What else could I do?

Nestor (Germany): That *pendejo* was going to take it all. Boring Booker was rolling over for him. The way things were going? One-Nut would take Marseilles and have himself twelve.

It's easy to win when people let you. Never happened for me on the field. Never happened for me in my *life*. Maybe I was gonna lose, but no way was I gonna lie down like a little b----.

"You won't help me with Italy, *querida*?"

Vicki shakes her head.

"You don't even like me bringing it up. Why? What's going on?"

Shakes her head again, that time even harder. You think *I* took things way too serious? I wasn't the only one. I'm asking Vicki to knock her friend out of the game and it's almost enough to make her cry.

I type out her orders for her and send it. She reads it and asks, "Greece?"

"We're gonna put a fleet back in Tunis. I got an idea what to do with your armies."

"Yeah, but ... why do I need an army *there*?"

"Moving them closer to the action." I smile at her. "All part of the plan."

I go inside and sit myself at the kitchen table. I got nothing to say to Cassie or Jeff until the fall, but there's time left before we put in our orders, so I try Evander and Booker.

```
Nestor>    got a sec?
Evander>   sure
Nestor>    kichen?
```

He comes by. "What can I do for you, Nestor?"

"Your guy planning to make it out of this game alive?"

"'Alive'?"

"Chill. I mean without getting eliminated."

"I haven't asked."

"Now's the time. Lance and Vicki both got eleven. Easiest way for Lance to win is to take Booker's last dot and hold everything else."

Evander was putting on a show, pretending to care about my question. Wasted half a minute fake thinking it over before he said, "I don't see how he avoids that fate."

"You do know this is some bulls---, right? Booker folded. Gave Lance all his supply centers."

"He had his reasons."

"Yeah? What are they? Lance f---ed him over first. I kept trying to get your guy to team up with me and he kept making excuses. Never *once* gave him a reason to pick Lance over me."

"The fleet in the Eastern Mediterranean. If Vicki hadn't forced its disband, he would have had the unit strength to fight off Lance. But she did, and he didn't, and he blames you."

"Why blame me? That was Vicki."

"You two have clearly been allied from the start of the game. You could have convinced her not to do it. And you should have had the good sense not to twist the knife in front of everyone."

It's so weak, I groan out loud. "He still salty about that?"

"Booker doesn't get 'salty'." Evander takes his phone out of his pocket, checks it. "The order phase is coming shortly. Let me leave you with this: these one-on-one conversations are only one aspect of the 'press'. People will draw inferences from your public statements. Keep that in mind." Then he stands up and walks back to the living room.

Jeffrey (Russia): I tossed the cap back over to where it was on the floor. "Well, whatever. If you won't ask Vicki for help, Lance is your only other option. If he moves to Piedmont and—"

"Hold on. You said the baseball cap wasn't in the bathtub earlier."

"Yeah. Anyway—"

"No, wait. How do you know?"

"I checked behind the shower curtain both times I used the bathroom."

"And just so I understand what you are saying: you're certain it wasn't there?"

I sighed. I should've lied when she asked me if something was wrong with the cap. "Like I said, *almost* certain. I didn't scan every inch, all right?"

"Why did you check? What were you looking for?"

"You know what? Forget I said anything about the cap. Can we get back to talking strategy?"

"No, no, wait. You've got to hear this." Cassie whipped her head around and saw those guys on the porch. She grabbed me by the wrist and pulled me over to the hallway where they couldn't see us. "That's the cap Evander used to pick who got what country."

"Sure, yeah."

"You don't think that's weird? How it wasn't where Evander said it was?"

"Maybe? What about it?"

There were footsteps outside. It sounded like they were coming to the door. Cassie put her finger up to her lips and they came in. Booker and Lance went to the living room and Evander went to the kitchen.

Cassie went out, all the way to the sidewalk. I was tempted to stay where I was, but I went along.

"Like I said, what about it?" I asked. And she told me she found the cap under the sink and it had a bag and seven bits of string in it. That was when Evander ran to the bathroom like he had to go really, really bad.

"I didn't see anything inside the cap, Cass."

"Like I told Lance, he took them out while he was in the bathroom. He wanted to be sure."

"You told Lance?"

"He didn't believe me."

"Four minutes. You want to know what I think?"

She could tell she wasn't gonna like it, so she didn't want to say yes to that. But she did, and I told her, "It doesn't make any sense. One, why didn't he take those things out when he went to the toilet in the morning, spring of '01? Two, why didn't he just say it was in the cabinet under the sink?"

"It *was* in the bathtub. Vicki and I saw it there. He must have hid it there after he removed the loops and the velvet sack."

"Wait, why? Why didn't he put it back where it was?" Cassie didn't say anything to that. "Three, how did he do that with the pieces to pick our countries for us? One-handed, no look?"

"He practiced, okay? He put seven pieces into the bag, pulled it shut with the drawstring, and then gave us the pieces he already had tied up in the loops. All he had to do was memorize which one was where in the hat."

"Fine, I'll give you that. But here's four: why? What's in it for him to pick who gets what? And why would he give himself Italy? I'll tell you this for free: no one would pick Italy if they had a choice."

Cassie bit her lip. "He's in it with Booker."

"If that was the plan, Evander would have held you off while he let Booker take Italy, right? Instead, Booker *and* Evander are done for. It all comes back to why, Cass. Tell me why Booker wanted to win so badly he'd cheat. And why Evander would wanna help him and then not do it."

"You don't believe me."

"One minute left. I sure don't. Not unless you get me answers to those questions."

Cassie got this hard look on her face. "Whatever you believe or don't believe, Evander moved the hat from the cabinet to the bathtub and then lied about it. You told me yourself you know it to a near certainty. Figure out why, if you care." And she walked back in.

Lance (England): Cassie and Jeff weren't talking strategy. They weren't going all the way out to the sidewalk to make sure we couldn't hear what they were planning to do with Cassie's two armies.

Cassie was going to tell Jeff about the Giants cap. Bet. She already told me. She was sure Evander was in it with Booker, so those two were out. That left Nestor. Vicki too, unless that's what those two were talking about in the bathroom that one time.

They came back at the last minute, Cassie leading the way, Jeff at her heels. I don't know what they would've looked like if she'd convinced him. But one glance at those two and I knew she didn't.

[Why Ollivander goes by "Evander"]

Ollivander (~~Italy~~): I absolutely loathe the name "Ollivander".

Yes, it's a visual train wreck: "Oliver" and "Alexander" crammed together with an extra "l" thrown in because ... you know what? I have no idea why she chose that spelling. And yes, it sounds stupid too. I had a hard time pronouncing it when I was very young, and I would shorten it to Evander. Now *that's* a perfectly fine name, one with a classical pedigree.

But more than anything, I hate it because it comes from the Harry Potter universe. Now, whenever I lead with that as an answer, there's the inevitable follow-up question of what I have against the Harry Potter books. Maybe I hate the books because I hate the name, and I have it all backwards.

Nope. The books are fine for what they are, as are the movies. But their popularity is completely out of proportion to their quality. In the sane world of *my* fantasy, everyone would have put their feet down and told Rowling and Warner Bros. enough already. Informed them that those eight movies were all we needed, so let's allow it all to come to a graceful end and then slowly forget all about it. Instead we have the prequels to keep the Potterverse alive in everyone's minds, and so my name will never be free of its association with that series.

Here, let me give you a contrasting example in the hopes that it will sharpen the distinctions I am making. You meet someone named Jareth with a "J". You Google the name to determine its origin, and you find that it was a character in *Labyrinth*, a fantasy movie from the eighties. But because the world isn't in the throes of perpetual Labyrinthmania, Jareth as a contemporary name has no particular valence. It's a curiosity and little more.

But Ollivander … I dread the moment that someone finds out my full name. It is an enduring testament to the inability of my parents, who are in most other respects reasonable people, to have treated pop cultural ephemera as disposable at the crucial juncture when they were deciding on the name of their first and only child. The only positive of it is that, much like that boy named Sue that Johnny Cash sang of, it has toughened me by making me brutally unsentimental. I am merciless in jettisoning emotional attachments. I am fully able to let the past be the past.

 Austria

    A Rom Holds ◊ A Nap S A Rom Holds ◊

 England

    A Bre → Gas ◊ A Stp Holds ◊
    F ENG S F Bel Holds ◊ A Lon → Nwy ◊
    F Lvp → IRI ◊ F NTH C A Lon → Nwy ◊
    A Par → Bur ◊ F SKA S F Swe → Den ◊
    F Bel S F ENG Holds
        Failure, Supp. disrupted
    F LYO → TYS -- Failure, Attack str. inadequate
    F Swe → Den -- Failure, Attack str. inadequate

 France

    F WES → Tun -- Failure, Attack str. inadequate

 Germany

    A Ber → Mun ◊ A War S A Mos → Lvn ◊
    F HEL S F Den Holds ◊ F Kie → BAL ◊
    A Ruh S A Hol → Bel ◊ A Ven S A Tus → Rom ◊
    F Den S F HEL Holds -- Failure, Supp. disrupted
    A Hol → Bel -- Failure, Attack str. inadequate
    A Tus → Rom -- Failure, Attack str. inadequate

 Turkey

    F ADR Holds ◊ F AEG C A Smy → Gre ◊
    A Bud Holds ◊ A Con → Bul ◊ A Gal Holds ◊
    A Mos → Lvn ◊ A Sev → Mos ◊ A Smy → Gre ◊
    A Ukr S A Sev → Mos ◊
    F ION → Tun -- Failure, Attack str. inadequate
    F TYS S F ION → Tun -- Failure, Supp. disrupted

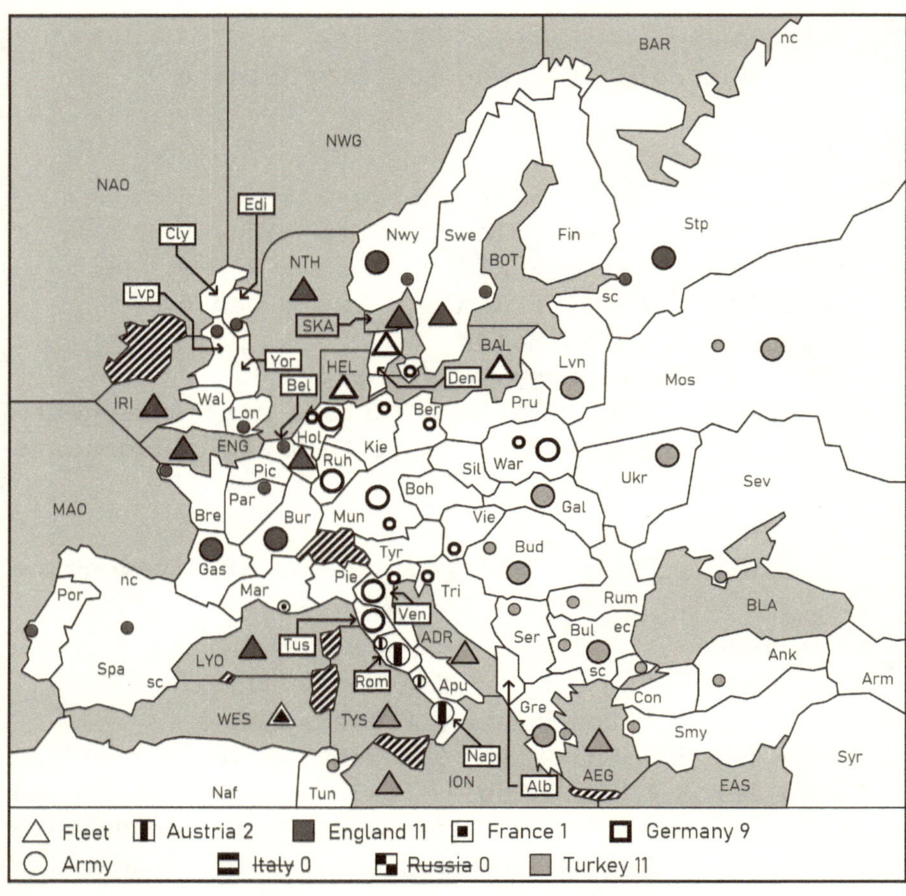

Figure 45 -- Game Map, Start of Fall 1908

Fall
1908

[Reactions to the orders of spring 1908]

Booker (France): When I looked at the board at the end of that season, I saw a stalemate. England could readily hold the line in St. Petersburg and the Scandinavian countries minus Denmark. Turkey would be unable to push westward past the Tyrrhenian Sea and Tunis.

This was futile. We would spend nearly another two hours and at the end of it would be a resolution that no one would find satisfactory.

Nestor had managed the play mechanics well. He had made some mistakes. But fewer than I would have expected, given both his relative inexperience and that he was handling the orders for both Germany and Turkey for nearly all of the game. That last is an assumption on my part, but I feel fairly safe in treating it as fact.

His report card for the other aspects was decidedly more mixed. One has to finesse the relationships with the other players. It is literally the name of the game. He had been botching his messaging throughout. But in the two minutes before the fall of 1908, his delivery was cunningly executed.

"Hey, yo, Booker. Congratulations on crowning the winner," he said once the laptop screen refreshed with the results of our orders for spring.

I ignored him. Jeffrey had misheard, and so he replied, "Booker's not the winner. What are you talking about?"

"*Crowning* is what I said. Lance's gonna keep him alive a little longer, then he takes Marseilles and d---s around until winter 1911. He'll have twelve. Take first place."

Lance stepped over to the mantel and leaned against it. He crossed his arms and observed Nestor coolly. "There's still some game left to play," Ollivander said.

"C'mon. You know there ain't enough." He turned to me. "You embarrassed to lose that way? Elimination's one thing, but you're like his pet *dog*. Makes you fetch for him until he puts you down."

"Don't be mean, bae," Vicki said.

"He knows I'm right." Nestor pointed at my forehead. "Watch how his eyebrow's twitching."

It was. That comment had perturbed me greatly. His aim had been true.

Nestor then addressed Lance. "It's a punk-a-- way to win, but at least you didn't cheat. You tell yourself that when it's over."

The day had been eventful in its own strange way. But it was only then, deep into the afternoon, that Nestor was finally able to get under Lance's skin. He uncrossed his arms and straightened up, his hands at his sides balled into fists.

"Stop it," Ollivander said. The anger in his voice was unmistakable. Everyone turned to regard him. His reaction was a surprise; even *I* had exhibited more emotion than he that day.

Nestor sported a triumphant grin as he looked from Ollivander to Lance and back again. Then he cocked his head towards one shoulder and rotated a thumb and forefinger in front of his lips before flicking that hand to the side.

Jeffrey (Russia): I'm looking at the board right now, and Nestor? He assumed incorrect, but if anyone else saw how he got it wrong back then, spring 1908, they weren't letting on. The only dot Nestor or Vicki could get off Lance was maybe St. Petersburg, but that was kind of a stretch. Maybe Lance could've got Denmark from Nestor? I don't know.

Imagine you're me or Evander. We can't do s---. We've already lost. No way are Cassie or Booker coming back, either. We all got to sit around because those three can't agree who finishes in what place. Yeah, we could say "F--- this" and go home, but then *we'd* be the d---s.

So when Nestor said that, he had a bunch of us on his side. Including Cassie. Well, kinda.

[Diplomatic phase of fall 1908]

Jeffrey (~~Russia~~): When the laptop made that ringing sound and it was fall, Cassie grabbed me by the hand and dragged me out to the sidewalk again.

"More cap talk?"

The front door opened behind us and Lance, Evander, and Booker came out to the porch. Cassie crossed the street. I took out my phone and called her. She saw my name on the caller I.D. and waved at me to come on over. I shook my head and she waved some more.

I gave up and went to her. "What?"

"Face away from them."

I saw how this was gonna go. I knew it would be easier to let her call the shots, so I put my back to those three. "Happy now?"

"You saw how Evander reacted?"

"Yeah, and?"

"How angry he was?"

"Cass, just tell me, all right?"

"Nestor made Evander angry. The only substantial point in what he said to Lance concerned cheating. That's what Evander was reacting to."

"Or he didn't like Nestor using 'punk-a--'."

"Uh uh. Evander's no shrinking violet to be offended by that."

"It's the cheating thing."

"Yes."

"Because you're hundred percent that Evander cheated in giving us the countries at the start."

"Yes."

"But Nestor said Lance *didn't* cheat. Why's Evander getting angry at that?"

Cassie grabbed my left arm with both hands and shook it. "Don't you get it? He was sending a message! *Lance* didn't cheat, but by implication, Booker and Evander did! And Nestor knows it!"

If I'd liked her right that moment, if I'd thought she was really my friend then? I would've told her to cut it the f--- out. Like, tough love or something. But I was kinda annoyed by the way she'd been acting all day. That's why I told her, "Let's go talk to Nestor, then."

"Huh?"

"What else are you going to do with that? You want to call them out? If you want, you can do that instead."

She stared at the sidewalk. "Five minutes, Cass."

Cassandra (Austria): What I hadn't told Jeff on the side of the street opposite Evander's house was how I had changed my mind on Nestor knowing. Unless he had somehow learned the truth in the preceding hour, he had fooled me completely.

What Jeff was proposing I do—daring me to do, really—was approach Nestor as a supplicant. I wanted something from him. I knew the stated price would be my final two supply centers; I told myself I could accept that.

The unstated price would be my abasing myself before him. I swallowed the spit in my mouth and said to Jeff, "Let's go."

Quick glances in each direction to make sure we weren't about to be run over by a car and I marched across, ran up the steps, and flung the front door open.

Jeff had stopped to talk to the assemblage on the porch. I shouted his name and he caught up as we made our way through the kitchen and out to the back. Where Vicki and Nestor were in each other's arms.

"You can't knock, boo?" Vicki asked.

"Sorry, Vicki," Jeff said.

"No, you're cool, I was talking to Cassie."

"Vicki, can Jeff and I talk to Nestor?"

Vicki kissed Nestor on the lips and went inside. When the door shut, Nestor said, "This must be important for you to be rude like that."

I didn't answer. He asked, "You want to step in, Jeff?"

"Not really. This is Cassie's show. I'm here to provide advice."

He pointedly looked at his watch. I took a deep breath to

steady myself. "I will give you both my supply centers."

That got their attentions, both of them. "In exchange for what?" Nestor wanted to know.

"Answers. You know something. I want to know what you know; I want to know how you know it."

They let out exasperated sighs. "How's this even gonna work?" Jeff asked.

"Yo, listen to your advisor, Cassie."

"You really don't want Rome and Naples?"

"If I thought for one second you'd go through with it, I'd give you those answers."

"You don't think I will?" I asked. "You believe I'll get the answers and renege on my end of the bargain?"

Nestor examined the roof above him and let his mouth puff up as he exhaled. He had been pretending to be in a hurry moments before, and yet, here he was, taking his sweet time. He faced me again. "I think you're gonna say I lie and keep holding Rome and supporting Naples."

Jeff clapped his hands together. "That's that, Cass. Can we go back inside?"

I shook my head no. "Then what else you got?" Nestor asked.

"Let me ask anyway. You can decide what you want to say."

"Rome and Naples?"

"You don't think I'll hand them over under any circumstance. So why promise otherwise?"

"Ask them quick."

Nestor (Germany): "You told me I would be thrown under the bus and I wouldn't see it coming. You told me it wouldn't be Booker who betrayed me. Later on, I asked if you meant Evander. You said you didn't understand what I was saying."

"There a question in there somewhere?"

"Were you pretending you didn't know the truth then? Or did you only find out later? And what tipped you off?"

I stand and stare at *la chica loca.* Jeff clears his throat and I check the time. "Two minutes left. Go inside and let me talk to Jeff."

"What? Why won't you tell *me*?"

"You say decide? That's what I'm doing. You get it from him later."

She's working on some answer to that in her head, and I tell her, "One forty," and that's when she gets going.

"I'm supposed to advise her on the game," Jeff says. "I don't want any part of this."

"Don't blame you. She's gonna hate you if you tell her this. I don't know what Evander's got to do with anything."

"It's ...." Jeff gives up trying to say what he was going to say. "Neither do I. She's got some idea. All right. That's what you want me to take back to her?"

"No. This next part? Between us. You tell Cassie, I say you're a liar. It's Vicki gonna slip that blade in. That's who I was talking about."

"Vicki?"

"I tell Vicki to support my attack on Cassie, she says 'Nuh uh.' Figured it out ten minutes ago it's because she wants them for herself."

"Really?"

"Add it up. She and Lance got eleven. Lance takes Marseilles, goes to twelve. Vicki needs two more to get thirteen. Who's got two dots and no way to protect them?"

Jeff groans. "Man, I really wish you hadn't told me."

"Thirty seconds. I knew it was coming. Didn't know exactly how. So now you make up some story 'bout what you and me discuss and feed it to Cassie."

I open the door and Jeff asks, "How do I do that?"

"Be creative. You'll think of something."

Lance (England): We went out to the front porch again. There wasn't much to say, but I wanted Booker to feel like he was involved.

Cassie and Jeff were already on the sidewalk, but when she saw us, she ran across the street. Jeff joined her eventually.

Booker watched those two go. "That seems to be a truly unnecessary precaution. Or am I missing something?"

"Not that I'm seeing," Evander replied. "So Lance, you want him to move to Tunis again?"

I tore my eyes away from Cassie and Jeff. "Um, yeah, for now. In spring of '09, you'll convoy my army from Gascony to Piedmont, unless we decide otherwise."

"And that's that," Evander said. We went back to watching them. They were facing away from us, but even still we could tell Cassie was excited about something and Jeff wasn't.

Then they ran back inside. Jeff had stopped to say "Hey", shoot the s---, but Cassie was on a mission and yelled at him to come along. I saw them go all the way back and out the door.

"She is planning to make a deal with Victoria."

I was going to ask Booker how he knew that, but then Vicki came in to the living room instead. Which meant Cassie and Jeff were talking to Nestor.

Booker's eyebrows went up. "*That* is unexpected."

[Another reason why Ollivander hates his name]

Ollivander (~~Italy~~): Okay, yes, I would hate it anyway, but what particularly annoys me about "Ollivander" is that the character sells wands. Rowling can dress it up with all the inane magical trappings she'd like, but that guy was the fantasy equivalent of some hick who inherited his dad's gun shop.

But wait, it's even worse than that, because his sole purpose in the series is to be reference librarian to Harry Potter and provide the backstory on some really, really awesome wand. And by the way, I'm not interested in hearing anyone's disquisition about how I'm oversimplifying and Garrick F---ing Ollivander is actually much more important to the series than I'm giving him credit for. You cannot make me give a s---.

You know what kind of secondary and tertiary characters I *do* like? The amoral dealmakers, those ones who sell opportunities. The apothecary who hawks love potions for a dollar and antidotes—of a sort—for a thousand. The middleman offering a million dollars if one presses a button that kills a stranger. The devil, granting wishes in exchange for souls.

That took a turn, didn't it? You're probably thinking I'm some sort of monster. Well, as much as I enjoy watching them at work, I don't aspire to be any of those. Once their offers are accepted, the outcome is predetermined. I can't help but feel it would be boring to wait for the denouement if you happen to know what it will be.

From a young age, I always thought it would instead be more interesting to experiment. Constrain people, put them in novel situations where their various drives and desires all vie for primacy. And then sit back and observe.

… Put whatever label you'd like on me. I don't value your opinion enough to argue the point with you.

 *Austria*

    A Rom Holds ◊ A Nap S A Rom Holds ◊

 *England*

    F Eng S F Bel Holds ◊ F Swe → BOT ◊
    A Gas Holds ◊ F IRI → MAO ◊
    A Nwy S A Stp Holds ◊
    A Bur → Mun -- Failure, Attack str. inadequate
    F LYO → TYS -- Failure, Attack str. inadequate
    F NTH → Den -- Failure, Attack str. inadequate
    F SKA → Swe -- Failure, Attack str. inadequate
    F Bel S F ENG Holds -- Failure, Supp. disrupted
    A Stp S A Nwy Holds -- Failure, Supp. disrupted

 *France*

    F WES → Tun -- Failure, Attack str. inadequate

 *Germany*

    F BAL Holds ◊ A Mun → Tyr ◊
    A Ven S A Tus → Rom ◊ A War → Sil ◊
    F Den → Swe -- Failure, Attack str. inadequate
    F HEL → Den -- Failure, Attack str. inadequate
    A Hol → Bel -- Failure, Attack str. inadequate
    A Ruh → Mun -- Failure, Attack str. inadequate
    A Tus → Rom -- Failure, Attack str. inadequate

 *Turkey*

    F ADR Holds ◊ F AEG Holds ◊
    A Bud Holds ◊ A Bul → Gre ◊ A Gal Holds ◊
    A Gre → Alb ◊ A Mos S A Lvn → Stp ◊
    A Ukr Holds ◊
    F ION → Tun -- Failure, Attack str. inadequate
    A Lvn → Stp -- Failure, Attack str. inadequate
    F TYS S F ION → Tun -- Failure, Supp. disrupted

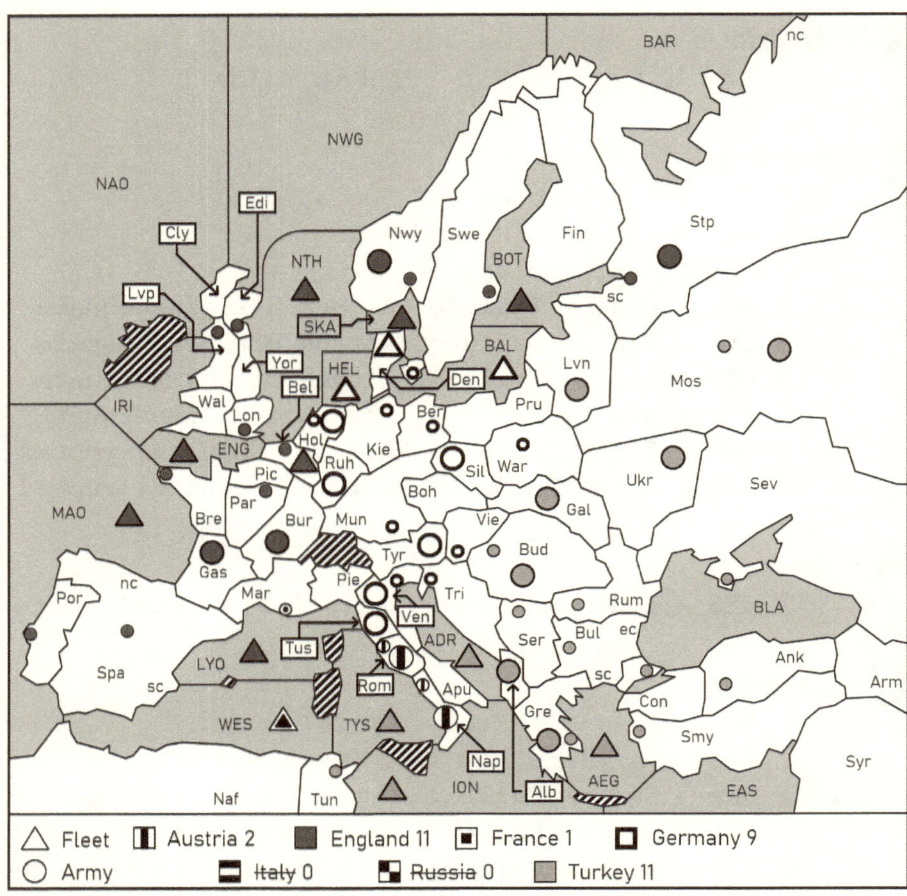

Figure 46 -- Game Map, Start of Winter 1908

Winter 1908

[Reactions to the orders of fall 1908]

Lance (England): "Wait, no one does anything?" Vicki asked.

"Everyone's got the same number of dots as last year," I explained. "No builds, no disbands."

"So … we skip winter?"

"It's a five minute break for everyone," Evander said. "Then spring of 1909."

Evander rearranged a few pieces on the board, but it was the same as last turn, almost. Vicki moved a couple armies to Albania and Greece. I moved fleets to the mid-Atlantic and the Gulf of Bothnia. Nestor moved armies to Tyrolia and Silesia. And everything else was a bunch of attacks that failed.

Cassie whispered in Jeff's ear and that time it was him leading her outside. Everyone was looking at everyone else, wondering what the deal was with those two. Except Nestor. All of a sudden he was really interested in something on his phone.

Out the window, I saw them on the sidewalk again, but this time they didn't cross the street. Jeff was doing most of the talking.

I heard Nestor get up from the couch. When he and Vicki headed off to the back porch, I asked, "What do you think they discussed with Nestor?"

Booker and Evander stood next to me and watched the Jeff-and-Cassie show. "I think it was mostly Jeff," Evander replied. "Right? Cassie was here a full minute before he and Nestor arrived."

Booker nodded. "It would appear she wants to know what was said in her absence."

"Terms of surrender? What else could it be?" Evander asked.

"Yeah, but … why now?"

"I agree with Lance. What could Cassandra possibly receive in exchange at this late stage of the game?"

He didn't have an answer. We kept staring out that window.

Victoria (Turkey): When we were on the back porch that time, I got out the phone and looked at the map. "Bae, why am I in Greece and … what's 'Alb' again?"

"Albania. It's psychology. You want those armies close to the front. Make Lance worry 'bout what you could do to him with them. The second him and Booker let up on the pressure with Tunis, you'd be convoying your army in. Get another one in North Africa later."

"But there's not enough time to do anything with those armies. They'll just sit there."

Nestor frowned. "I know. Like I said, Lance is gonna take Marseilles, knock Boring Booker out, and win the game. Twelve to eleven to nine. All we can do is make everyone else see how we would've won if we had more time."

"We can't do *anything*?"

He paced around, head down, still had that frown on. He was cute when he did that. "You're not going to like this."

"What?"

"No, forget it."

I got right in front of him so he couldn't not see me. "Tell me."

Nestor took a deep breath. "Take Naples and Rome off of Cassie."

"F--- you."

"I told you you wouldn't like it. I tried to keep quiet, but you wouldn't let me. This isn't on me, *querida*." He rubbed my shoulder then took me in for a hug. "Don't do it. Later on we'll remember how we could've beat Lance but we rose above. We'll laugh at it. Laugh at *him*."

My forehead was against his chest. I felt his strong, slow heartbeat and I let that sensation wash over me and calm me down.

Nestor (Germany): I'm thinking that's the end of it, she's not going Judas on Cassie. And then all of a sudden she says, "I mean, if I *did* do that, I'd lose Tunis anyway."

I make space between us for my phone. "Depends on how you do it. You're thinking of doing it in the spring, with your fleets?" She nods. "But you can convoy an army into Apulia from Albania. Or Greece, either one. Then in the fall you take Rome and I support you in. Then spring 1910 you take Naples. Take you one extra season, but you'll have them both."

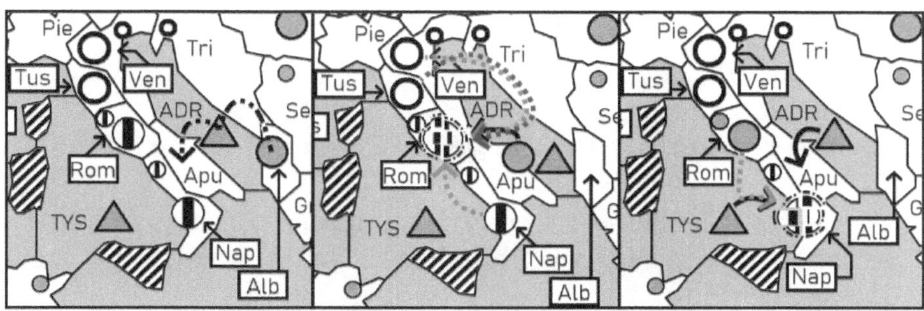

Figure 47 -- Plan to Invade Italy: [Left] Convoy to Apulia; [Center] Apulia to Rome, Forcing Disband; [Right] Tyrrhenian Sea to Naples, Forcing Disband

Vicki's looking down at the map. Screen's got her face lit up and she's like one of those pictures of someone opening up a treasure chest full of gold. She's biting the side of her bottom lip, thinking. I used to sneak peeks at her when she did that. I loved seeing it. I loved seeing *her*.

Cassandra (Austria): "Well? What did Nestor tell you?" I whispered to Jeff.

That drew some inquisitive glances. Possibly because nothing had occurred in the fall to occupy anyone's attention; the board was largely the same as it had been previously.

Rather than carry out an entire conversation in that manner, Jeff led me out to the sidewalk. "Nestor says he wasn't talking about Evander."

"Really?"

"He's got no idea what you mean by that."

"Do you believe him?"

"He could be lying? But no, I believe him."

"Did you tell him about the cap?"

"Not enough time."

I considered the information Jeff had provided. "You made the right call, not explaining it. If he doesn't know, there's nothing to be gained in enlightening him."

"Glad to hear it. Can we go back in?"

"I want you to take a quick glance at the living room window. Don't stare."

He did. "They're looking at us."

"Who are?"

"Booker, Lance, and Evander. Not even trying to hide it."

Which reminded me to ask Jeff, "Why didn't Lance take Holland?"

Jeff didn't get it, so I took out my phone and showed him. "He could have moved with his fleet in Belgium and supported with his fleet in the North Sea. So why didn't he?"

"He didn't know ahead of time what moves Nestor would make. He was probably expecting Ruhr to support Holland or Holland to support Ruhr. Two attackers, two defenders: nothing happens. So he takes a chance and goes for Munich instead."

"Which didn't work."

"Nope."

"He had to know it wouldn't work."

"No he didn't. What are you getting at?"

I took a second to get the wording right. "Lance isn't trying to defeat Nestor, and I don't know why."

"Yeah, that's probably true. He's up on Nestor and he's not going to get any easy dots off him, at least not in the years we got left. He's not going to risk what he's got trying."

I nodded. That situation felt weird, but I couldn't fault Jeff's reasoning. I brushed the toe of my shoe against the concrete and launched into it: "What else did you and Nestor discuss?"

"I … nothing. Why?"

I sighed. "You're lying, Jeff."

"What? No I'm not."

"You're bad at it. It's an admirable trait."

He looked away, not daring to make eye contact. He was going to stonewall me unless I came up with the right question.

"He told you who it was who was going to throw me under the bus, didn't he? It wasn't him, he said it wasn't Booker, and he affirmed to you that it wasn't Evander."

"It wasn't me either."

"Whom does that leave? Lance?"

He struggled to speak for a moment before replying, "All Nestor said was he didn't mean Evander. I'm out." And he went back inside.

Booker (France): Once Jeffrey made his way up the stairs, Ollivander suggested we commence the discussions for spring out on the front porch.

"Are we allowed to engage in diplomatic talks during the winter?" I asked.

"That rule exists to keep people from negotiating builds and disbands during the winter turn," Ollivander replied. "And I'm pretty sure that everyone else is strategizing as we speak. You know: more honored in the breach *et cetera*."

Lance waited until Cassandra was on the other side of the door before telling me to convoy his army from Gascony to Piedmont.

"You could've marched there in the same amount of time," Ollivander observed.

"Not without eliminating Booker. I would have been in Marseilles at the end of fall. Besides, this method preserves the element of surprise."

"Why Piedmont? Why not North Africa?" I asked.

Ollivander took out his phone and we studied the map for a short while. "Maybe," Lance said. "But go ahead and put in the convoy order anyway and I'll decide which one to do."

"If I do as you request, I cannot prevent Turkey from moving a unit into Tunis."

"That'd be something to consider in a longer game, sure. But Vicki won't have time to use it against me. Against us."

And a few seconds after that, spring had sprung.

[Booker's father's assessment of Ollivander]

Booker (France): Yes, my father did eventually clarify what he meant by the strange quality of Ollivander's banter.

He did so when I asked permission to spend the day playing the game at Ollivander's house; you correctly sensed that my answer to that question of yours was incomplete. He had me join him in his bedroom and closed the door behind us. A response that struck me as so disproportionate as to be ominous. I feared that it was a prelude to the delivery of some truly terrible news.

"Son, I've told you that I'm proud of you," he began.

"Dad, what's wrong? You're scaring me."

He dissolved into laughter. He assured me that no one had cancer; no one was going to prison; he and my mother were not about to get a divorce. I was relieved and then annoyed that he had worried me so.

"I'm sorry, Son. No, what I'm going to tell you is important, but nothing as *dire* as all that. Let me start over. Most recent time I told you I was proud of you was when you got into Princeton, remember?"

"I do."

"Your teenage years have been a relief to your mother and me. Staying out of trouble. Doing well in school. I want to take credit for it, but you barely needed my help in charting your path."

"Thank you?"

"You're wondering what any of that has to do with you going over to Evander's house and playing a game with him. Why I'm bringing it up now."

"Well, yes. I am."

My mother knocked then. "Talkin' to Booker," he said, loud enough to be heard through the door.

"Everythin' all right?"

"All good in the hood, baby. Be out in five." We listened to her footsteps recede. "When I told you about Stoicism and Buddhism long time back, I wasn't saying you shouldn't be happy or sad or angry. Just don't get overwhelmed by it. You observe and you let it flow past."

"I understood all that. Did you think otherwise?"

"I know you did. But there's this other kind of person who's the opposite. From the outside, you think they're being emotional. But it's an act: they're pretending because they don't feel anything inside. Like someone giving a speech in Chinese they memorized phonetically because they don't know the language."

"You mean sociopaths."

"I do. Anyway, you ain't gonna be running into people like that all the time, maybe once for every hundred standard-issue a--holes. Thing is, though, those people are dangerous. They ruin lives because they think it's *amusing*."

"Okay ...."

"You understand me?"

We sat there in silence until I made the connection. "You think *Ollivander* is a sociopath? Is that why you bring this up now, when I asked leave to go to his house to play a board game?"

"Don't know if I'd apply that term to him, but ... yes, I think he might be. Now, I'm not forbidding you from going. Just wanted to say it."

"He's ... he is my friend. And why now? I have been going to his house for years."

"Less and less. I wasn't sure why, but I was glad of it. Thought maybe you were outgrowing his company. And I'm telling you now because soon I won't be there to protect you, and I want you to examine your friend's behavior with new eyes when you go to his house for game day. So you can be prepared for the future."

It was a staggering thing to hear about one whose companionship you valued, and particularly to hear from one's father. Hearing his assessment, I asked the question I imagine is on your mind: "Why would you think that of him?"

"Think I beat around the bush in that car ride back home, said his banter had a strange quality or some such. Truth is, I got the impression he was acting most of the time when he was supposed to be showing empathy. Good at it, but still acting. It was the story about his cousin and the cat that did it for me."

Ollivander had returned for Christmas to England and was

visiting with relatives at his mother's sister's house. This aunt had a cat, a Persian, and the young cousins were drawn to it. One of whom had an allergy to cat dander. His mother warned him to stay away, but he was convinced he would be fine if he washed his hands immediately after petting it.

As it happened, he was not. Whether it was the breed or some aspect of its diet or environment, the allergic reaction was immediate and severe. This cousin started wheezing and, in his panicked state, had touched his face and eyes, which quickly became swollen and red. Ollivander imitated him and his impaired voice, and with his inventive dialogue and comic skill, he had everyone at the table in stitches.

"Not everyone, Booker. *I* was only smiling. I didn't want to call out your friend in front of everyone. Especially not in front of you."

"And that is why you think he might be a sociopath?"

"I won't press the point. Maybe it was a phase and he grew out of it. But that was the only time he came off real to me, and it was to laugh at the misery of someone else."

"Am I a bad person for laughing too?"

"Son, you got caught up in the moment. So did your mother and brother. Your friend didn't have that excuse." He got up. "Like I said, I'm not claiming he's still that way now. But you be on the lookout."

In honesty, his admonition had slipped my mind by that day. But I am not sure what difference it would have made had I remembered.

Austria

A Nap ◊ A Rom ◊

England

F Bel ◊ A Gas ◊ F ENG ◊ A Bur ◊
F LYO ◊ F NTH ◊ F BOT ◊ F SKA ◊
A Stp ◊ A Nwy ◊ F MAO ◊

France

F WES ◊

Germany

F BAL ◊ F Den ◊ F HEL ◊ A Hol ◊
A Sil ◊ A Ruh ◊ A Tus ◊ A Ven ◊
A Tyr ◊

Turkey

F ADR ◊ F AEG ◊ A Lvn ◊ A Mos ◊
A Gal ◊ F ION ◊ A Ukr ◊ A Bud ◊
F TYS ◊ A Gre ◊ A Alb ◊

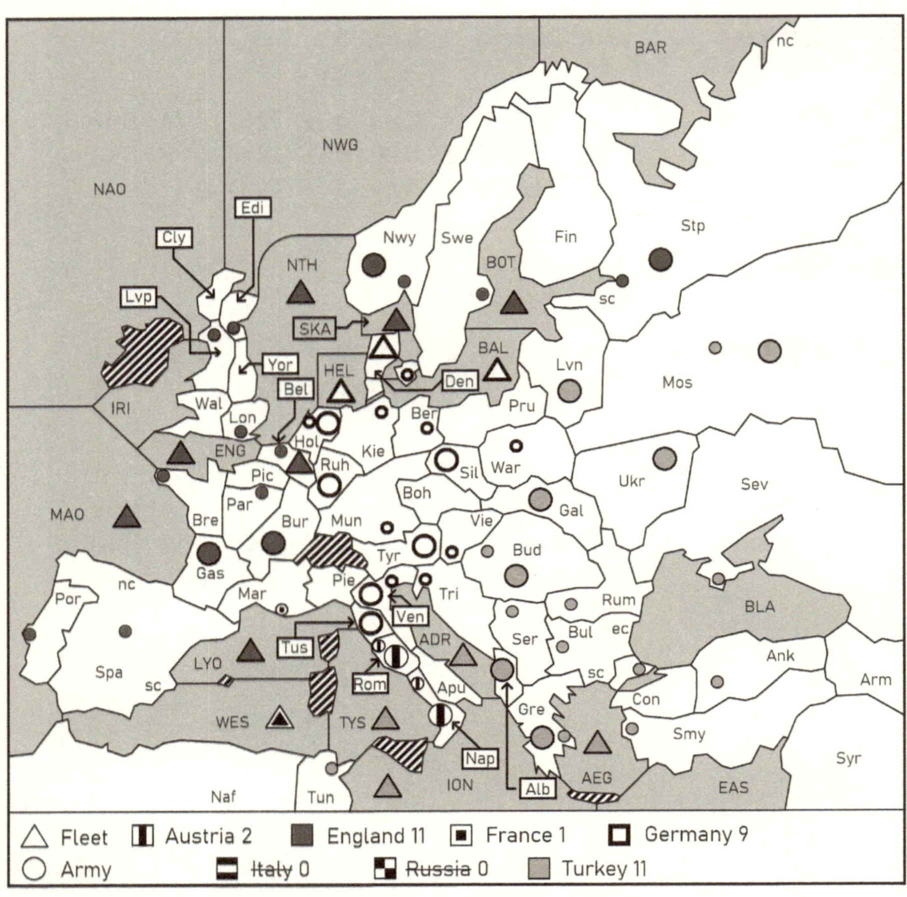

Figure 48 -- Game Map, Start of Spring 1909

324

Spring
1909

[Diplomatic phase of spring 1909]

Jeffrey (~~Russia~~): I don't know why I cared so much about helping Cassie keep her last two armies. She was ready to hand them over to Nestor if he answered that crazy-a-- question about bus throwing. I guess that had something to do with Evander and the baseball cap? But why she thought Nestor had some inside information about it, f--- if I know.

"You've got to talk to Lance."

Cassie was looking down at the board in the middle of the living room. Thinking too hard to hear me. I tapped her on the shoulder and said it again.

"Why?"

"He can help you defend against Nestor. Otherwise you lose both your dots by next spring."

She shook her head. "I just move my army from Naples to Apulia. He won't get in."

"What if he fakes you out and attacks Rome like he's been doing?"

"He won't. He brought that army from Berlin in order to have three units to attack my two."

I thought she was risking too much on her being able to read Nestor's mind, but on the plus side, she was thinking about her actual moves instead of all that other stuff. So at least I had that going for me, right?

Nope. "This isn't a normal game, Jeff."

"What, you mean in general?"

"Yes. But this instance of this game, the one we're playing right now, is unusual."

"This is your second time playing, Cass."

"Yes."

"So how would you know what's unusual?"

The look she gave me was so cold my nipples got hard. "The two absolute beginners are tied for first and in second place. Of the four experienced players, two have been eliminated and one is hanging on by a thread. This. Isn't. Normal."

"All right, all right."

"And Evander planned out who got what country." She was getting loud enough to make me nervous someone'd overhear. "And you know it."

I gave her half a minute to cool down. I mean, after she shot down my idea to talk to Lance, we had nothing to do before she put in her orders. "Do you want my help with anything?"

"How much time do we have?"

"Between five and six minutes."

"You're leaving out something that Nestor told you, and I want to know what it is."

I was f---ed. If I 'fessed up about how Nestor was sure Vicki was gonna hit her with a surprise attack, *I'd* be the one Cassie'd be mad at. If I kept my mouth shut, she'd hate me for not warning her.

Then the lightbulb over my head went on. "Let's ask Vicki."

"Huh?"

"You think Nestor's sitting on something big. If he told anyone, it'd be Vicki."

"I can't do that."

"Why not? You want to get to the bottom of whatever you think is going on, who else you gonna talk to?"

"No," she said. Shook her head *hard*.

"There's nobody left. Because I didn't leave a damn thing out with Nestor."

She stared at me. "You're getting better at lying. I almost believed you."

I gave up and went to the kitchen. Figured if she changed her mind, she'd pass by on her way to talk to her friend.

Ollivander (~~Italy~~): "We have another seven and a half minutes to discuss, if we want it," I told them.

Lance replied, "No, I'm good. See you soon." And went inside.

Booker stopped me before I could follow. "I wanted to ask you what you thought of Lance's plan."

"And you wanted to do it outside his presence."

"Of course. Well?"

"Moving to Piedmont makes sense. If he keeps Nestor from taking Rome or Naples, he protects his own lead."

"Now keep in mind that you are advising me and not him, and tell me once again what you think of Lance's plan."

Booker was careful how he spoke; you probably get that by now. His word choices were deliberate. So when he told Nestor his respect was a worthless currency, it was a big f---ing deal.

This wasn't as bad, but it was still quite cutting. It stung to be on the receiving end. I gave a chastened nod and said, "Whatever his motives are for keeping you alive, he *is* keeping you alive. This convoy plan of his will keep him from transiting through Marseilles and knocking you out of the game."

"And why would he care?"

I considered how to answer that. "He needs to have his fleets in place to step into the Western Mediterranean. For when you do go."

"I have another theory."

"Do tell."

"The moment I am eliminated, you and I are available to advise the other players. Nestor would have first pick. Victoria would have the other."

"I hadn't considered that."

"Whom do you think Nestor would pick?"

"I don't know."

"Is it really not obvious?"

It was. I waited a second to reply, "Probably me."

"And there we are."

"But it's not going to make a difference. Say Nestor picks me and Vicki gets you. What is it that you think you or I could say to help them? What are the orders that will break the stalemate line?"

Those moments when you actually see someone standing right in front of you come to a realization are rare, but that was one of them. His poker face had slipped. But Booker soldiered on: "I led us astray from the topic at hand. What can I do to survive through to the end of the game?"

"I think you know the answer. Talk to Vicki and see if she'll grant you Tunis. Because you won't see winter 1911 without it."

Lance (England): All of a sudden, the kitchen was the place to be in the spring of 1909.

Me and Jeff were on our phones, sitting at the table, waiting for the start of the order phase. Cassie came in, stood near the door. Jeff looked up and decided to join her.

We heard the steps coming from down the hall. Booker and Evander. And when they arrived, everyone was looking at everyone else, wondering what the f---.

Vicki and Nestor heard us and looked through the window. Vicki opened the door and asked what's up.

Cassie and Booker started talking at the same time. Booker stopped and gave Cassie the signal to go first. "I need to talk to you."

"As do I," Booker said.

"How long do we got?" Vicki asked, and a bunch of us told her four minutes.

"Two and two, I guess." She leaned out the door and said, "Bae? Can I get the porch?"

Nestor came in. "Booker first." Him and Evander went out with Vicki and the rest of us watched the clock.

Booker (France): I shut the door behind us and told Victoria, "I need a supply center."

"Can't give you one of mine, boo."

"I was thinking I would instead take one from France. You see, that army in Gascony will go to Piedmont this turn via a triple convoy. You can move your fleet in the Ionian Sea into Tunis, and your fleet in the Aegean into the Ionian."

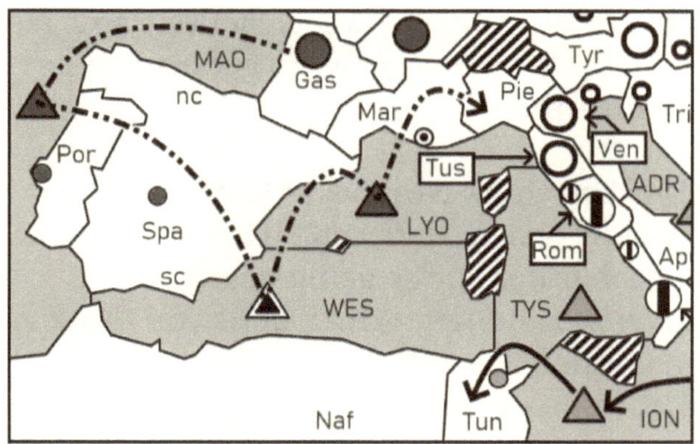

*Figure 49 -- Triple Convoy: Gas to Pie via MAO, WES, and LYO;
Turkish Fleet Moves: ION to Tun and AEG (Off-screen to Right) to ION*

"'kay? How's that get you a supply center?"

"In the fall, I will take Spain. You move your fleet in Tunis to the Western Mediterranean. Then you can support my fleet in Spain."

Ollivander held out his phone in order for her to study the map. She spent nearly a minute doing so. "What's in it for me?"

"You can break out of the Mediterranean with your fleets. It is a potential path to having the most supply centers by the time the game ends. You will not merely tie for first place, you will have it all to yourself."

"Time's up."

I opened the door. "Consider it. Please."

Cassandra (Austria): The moment Jeff and I were on the back porch, Vicki told me to hurry up.

Which had the effect of making me anxious and tongue-tied. "C'mon, girl. Spit it out."

"Nestor said someone was going to throw me under the bus."

"'Bus'?"

"Double-cross me. He said it wasn't going to be Booker, and it wasn't Nestor either, based on context. I asked if he meant Evander and he said no. Did he tell you who was going to do that?"

I thought I was ready for any reaction, any response she would have. I wasn't expecting her to get mad.

"You think it's me."

"What? No!"

"Who else? You think Nes meant Lance?"

"Lance couldn't have," Jeff said. "Him and Cass haven't even been next to each other on the game board."

"That leaves me and Jeff. Which of us you think was ready to do you dirty, Cassie?"

I looked at Jeff. A deer in the headlights, mouth agape and head shaking in disbelief.

"Everyone's going to the living room. I'm out, see you there."

I didn't move. Neither did Jeff.

[Order phase of spring 1909]

Jeffrey (Russia): My phone rang. It was Evander.

"Diplomatic phase is over. You and Cassie joining us?"

"Um ..."

"Tell him I'll be entering my orders from here."

"You heard that?"

"Yeah. Unless someone complains, that should be cool." And he hung up.

Cassie had her arms crossed. Staring at me hard. "Look, Cass—"

"Hold that thought. Let me do my orders."

I stood there, waiting for the hammer to come down. When she put her phone away, I said, "Cass, I wasn't straight with—"

"No, stop. I should have known. It was you."

"What was me?"

"You were the one who was in it with Nestor. That's why he demanded that he speak to you alone."

"Nuh uh. That's not it. What happened was—"

"He warned me you'd be the one to throw me under the bus. Why didn't I listen?"

"He did? When? When did he say that?" That shut her up. "Because I want to know when I even had the chance to screw you over in this game."

She mumbled something. "What? What was that?"

"All I remember was that it was before lunch."

"The only time we had a deal *you* tricked *me* into bouncing off Nestor in Vienna. And you want to know what he actually said? He said *Vicki* was gonna f--- you over. She's gonna try to take your last two dots from you."

"That's ridiculous."

"*That's* why I was pretending Nestor didn't talk on that. Because I knew you wouldn't believe me."

"All that time you had, and this is the lie you came up with."

I grabbed my hair on the sides of my head and this ... *noise* came out when I tried to speak. So I went to the other side of the porch, put my hands on the rail and breathed in and out, like fifteen times.

And when I was maybe halfway back to normal, I walked back to Cassie and said, "You want to say I've been up to something since almost the start of this game? Go ahead. Lay out what it is I did."

"I'm not going to talk to you when you're like this."

"Like what? Angry that you're accusing me? That's on *you*. Hundred percent."

"You're pretending not to believe that Evander has been up to something. And that's even after you know the cap's been moved."

"That's another thing. If I was in it with Evander, why the Hell would I bring that up?"

Cassie pressed her lips tight. "Don't have an answer to that, do you. Because it makes no sense. You'd rather accuse me than take one damn second to think."

"I don't want to talk about this."

"No, you want to insult me and get in the last word. Treat me like a dog."

"Oh, God. Stop being dramatic."

"I'm telling the truth. Nestor was right, wasn't he? You all let me hang around with you because you feel sorry for me. But if I ever try to have my own opinion about something, forget about it."

"Your—" Now Cassie was getting pissed too. She cleared her throat and made it sound like a growl, speaking of dogs. "Your 'opinion' is that I'm making it all up. Do you think I should meekly agree with you and let you gaslight me?"

"What the f--- does 'gaslight' mean?" I asked. That's when my phone rang to let me know I had a text. I took it out and read it. "Evander says the moves are all in." I looked at the map. I looked at the move orders. I looked back at the map. I looked at the move orders again.

Cassandra (Austria): Jeff started laughing. The way you might if you truly found something funny, but were laying it on thick on top of that. To make a point.

I had to ask. "What?"

He held up a finger while he stifled his guffaws. "Check … check … whew, boy. Check out the orders for spring."

I wasn't going to ask him to show me on his phone. So instead I pulled mine out. "I didn't move into Apulia."

"You sure didn't. That's because Vicki tried to do it too and you had yourselves a bounce."

He was right. I refreshed the screen, hoping somehow it was a glitch, but it didn't change. She was going to set herself up to seize my last two supply centers after she made that promise in the bathroom. She lied. And Jeff had told the truth.

He opened the door and said, "I told you so." And with those words, he left me out there to deal with it.

 *Austria*

```
A Rom Holds ◊
A Nap → Apu -- Failure, Attack str. inadequate
```

 *England*

```
F BOT  Holds ◊
F ENG  S F Bel Holds ◊ F LYO C A Gas → Pie ◊
F MAO  C A Gas → Pie ◊ A Nwy S A Stp Holds ◊
A Bur → Mun -- Failure, Attack str. inadequate
A Gas → Pie -- Failure, Attack str. inadequate
F NTH → Den -- Failure, Attack str. inadequate
F SKA → Swe -- Failure, Attack str. inadequate
A Stp S A Nwy Holds -- Failure, Supp. disrupted
F Bel S F ENG Holds -- Failure, Supp. disrupted
```

 *France*

```
F WES C A Gas → Pie ◊
```

 *Germany*

```
A Ruh S A Sil → Mun ◊ A Sil → Mun ◊
A Tus Holds ◊ A Ven Holds ◊
F Den → Swe -- Failure, Attack str. inadequate
F HEL → Den -- Failure, Attack str. inadequate
A Hol → Bel -- Failure, Attack str. inadequate
A Tyr → Pie -- Failure, Attack str. inadequate
F BAL → BOT -- Failure, Attack str. inadequate
```

Turkey

```
F ADR C A Alb → Apu ◊ F AEG Holds ◊
A Bud Holds ◊ A Gre → Tun ◊ A Gal Holds ◊
F ION C A Gre → Tun ◊ A Mos S A Lvn → Stp ◊
F TYS S A Gre → Tun ◊ A Ukr Holds ◊
A Lvn → Stp -- Failure, Attack str. inadequate
A Alb → Apu -- Failure, Attack str. inadequate
```

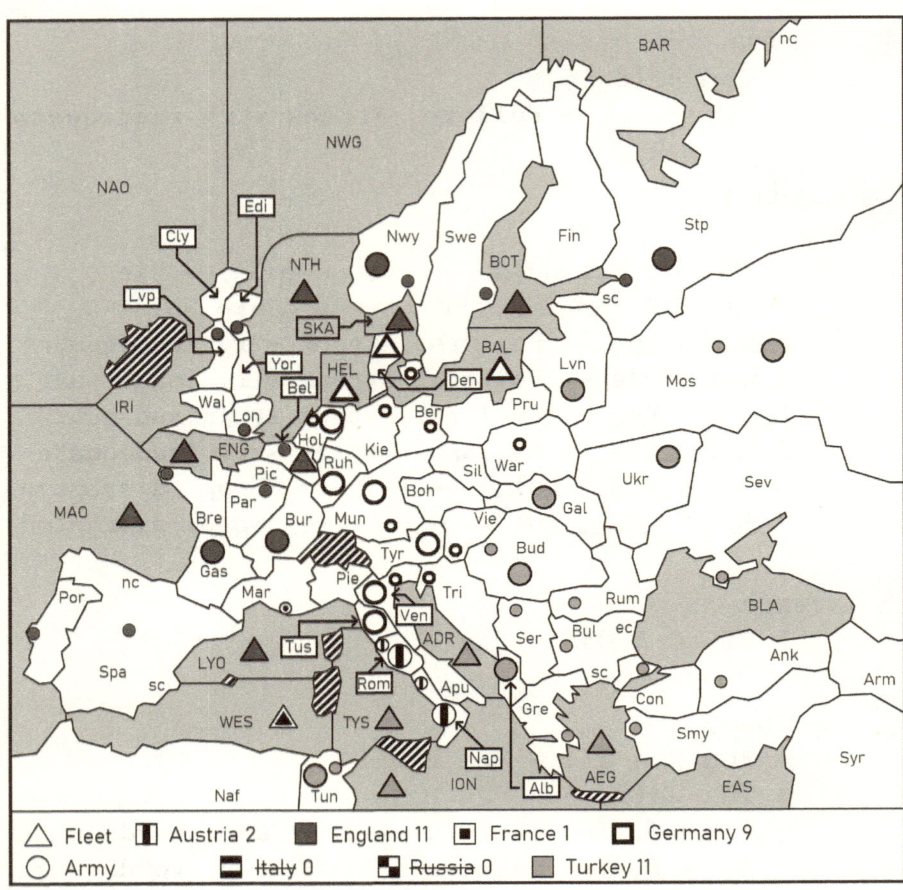

Figure 50 -- Game Map, Start of Fall 1909

Fall
1909

[Reactions to the orders of spring 1909, diplomatic phase fall 1909]

Ollivander (~~Italy~~): Thirty-four units on the board and only two moved that spring. Vicki got an army into Tunis from Greece. Nestor got his army into Munich from Silesia. Neither of those were terribly shocking to anyone.

It was the moves that didn't happen that was a big deal. Lance's convoy all the way around the Iberian Peninsula into Piedmont ran into Nestor's army coming from Tyrolia. I think we all—well, not *all*, obviously—expected him to move into Apulia then move from Tyrolia to Venice. Three armies to Cassie's two. Instead he held off.

Instead it was Vicki who made a move to establish a beachhead in Apulia. But Cassie successfully repelled her. There was a story there, one I was dying to hear.

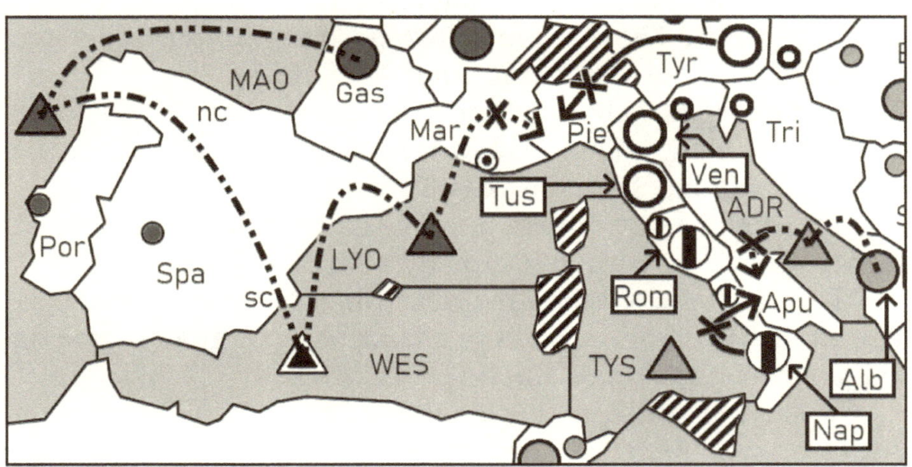

Figure 51 -- Bounces in Piedmont and Apulia, Spring of 1909

I wasn't going to get to do that just yet, though, because Lance was demanding answers from Booker. I was the last person out the front door, and I took a moment to watch Vicki and Nestor march to their usual spot on my back porch. Then, with a sigh and a heavy heart, I closed the door behind me.

Lance asked, "You want to explain, Booker?"

"Explain …?"

"Are you going to play dumb with me?" Booker crossed his arms and waited. "Fine, you want to explain how Nestor knew to bounce me in Piedmont?"

"I had no communications with Nestor about any move to Piedmont." I was thinking that I was wrong, and this *was* going to get interesting. Because of the next question coming.

"Did you tell Vicki?"

"I most certainly did."

If you were to judge from his reaction, Lance wasn't expecting Booker to admit it so readily and so unashamedly. He treated us both to some incoherent sputtering. Booker took it all in the way one who is safely ensconced behind a Plexiglas window might watch a monkey fling its feces.

After a while, Lance took a deep breath, and asked, "What do you think you're going to get out of it?"

"Me? Nothing. I provided that information to enable Turkey to retake Tunis. That, of course, would free it to push into the western half of the Mediterranean in later years."

"She would have been better off with a fleet there," I said.

"Agreed. Turkey should shift it to North Africa to allow the fleet in the Ionian Sea to move to Tunis."

"But then she can't take one of Austria's dots this turn," I pointed out. "Not without Germany's support."

"It is not at all clear to me that this was the ultimate goal. The bounce in Apulia smacks of a feint, with Germany agreeing to hold to avoid taking Rome."

He was way off there, but neither he nor I would know that until later on. "Why?" I asked him.

"To lull England into a sense of false security, allowing Turkey to take the Gulf of Lyon."

"Are you two going to keep talking about me like I'm not here? You know what? It doesn't matter. No more keeping you in the game."

"It is immaterial to me whether you eliminate me now or later. And now I must take my leave. I need to coordinate my final order with Turkey."

Booker left us on the porch. I asked Lance, "What do you think his first piece of advice to Vicki will be?"

"I guess it depends on if he's able to get her away from Nestor to give it."

Booker (France): The brief time I had spent with Lance and Ollivander had proven eventful for the remaining players. Nestor was sitting alone in the kitchen when I arrived; the others were outside, talking animatedly.

I briefly considered asking what I had missed. Instead I sat at the opposite end of the table and messaged Victoria.

```
Booker>  If you wish to move your fleet into
    the Gulf of Lyon, I can support it. Or if
    you prefer, I can move to North Africa to
    prevent England from taking it. Please let
    me know.
```

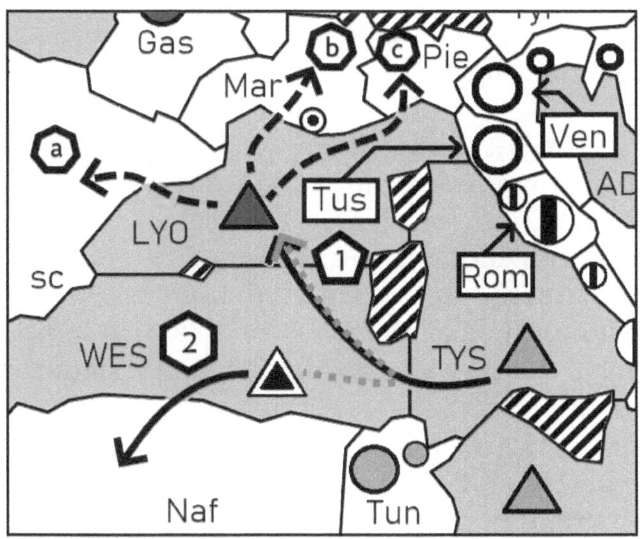

Figure 52 -- Booker's Proposed Orders: (1) Support Move from TYS to LYO, Forcing Retreat to (a) Spa.sc, (b) Mar, or (c) Pie; or (2) Move to Naf, Preventing English Move from MAO to Naf

"Who're you texting?" Nestor asked. Through the window we could see Victoria glance at her phone. "Never mind."

We sat for a bit and listened to them talk outside, barely loud enough to make out who was speaking, yet not loud enough to follow. "You think you made the right call?" Nestor asked me.

"Hmm?"

"Backing Lance. You *know* he's taking your last dot before the game's over."

"I do."

Nestor shifted in his chair. "You act all *logical*. Pretend nothing's personal to you. 'Cept there's no way you made the smart move not teaming up with me."

"I disagree. There is no reason for me to think I would have fared better trusting you."

He smacked his lips and leaned back. "You think not yelling and not making faces means you're not getting mad. It's *something*, I'll give you that. But it ain't everything, because I got all the way under your skin. And you dealt with it by running away and letting Lance take advantage."

I checked my watch. "Mm hmm."

"Too proud to listen. I give up, man." And once again it was quiet enough to hear the three of them argue.

Cassandra (Austria): I didn't know if Vicki would return to the back porch. But I was determined not to meekly allow her and Nestor have it all to themselves.

Through the window I was audience to their nearly silent one-act play. Nestor and Vicki arrived, noticed Jeff sitting at the table. Nestor mouthed a brief question to which Jeff pointed his thumb at me. Nestor then turned to Vicki and mouthed another brief question. Vicki shook her head, strode to the door, and realized Nestor wasn't following. She looked back at him and he shook his head and gestured no with his hands, crossing and then uncrossing them. And finally Vicki sighed and opened the door. Curtain.

"What now," she said.

"I'd like an explanation."

"Nestor! Come on out with me."

"No can do, *querida*."

"Jeff? You're her advisor."

"I don't want him in the conversation," I told her.

"Then forget it, girl. I'm not going to be alone with you."

"Fine. Jeff, get out here."

He remained where he was. "Jeff, would you mind joining us?" Vicki asked.

"Be glad to," he replied. I asked him to close the door behind him. He ignored me, I had to do it myself.

"Go ahead," Vicki said.

"Explain why you tried to move into Italy when you promised you wouldn't."

"I didn't do that."

"What? When"—I moved closer to Vicki and lowered my voice in a futile attempt to prevent Jeff from hearing—"we were in the bathroom. You swore to me."

"No, I said I wouldn't help *Nestor* take Italy off you."

It was a pure reflex action on my part to look to Jeff in the expectation that he would find Vicki's reply to be as outrageous as I did. But he wasn't about to provide any sort of moral support, not after our fight mere minutes ago. He instead fixed me with a withering stare.

I turned back to Vicki. "I would have given them both to you. I never asked you to keep me in the game. Why would you offer me hope just to cruelly snatch it away?"

She crossed her arms. "Didn't need them then. Now I do."

That did it. The dam broke and I started blubbering. In the state I was in, I had barely enough situational awareness to move away from the windows so that my shame would only be visible to Jeff and Vicki.

"Get a hold of yourself, girl." She was sneering contemptuously while Jeff was cringing with embarrassment at the spectacle unfolding before him. "It's just a game."

"A game? You don't … you don't know …" I wept for a while longer. The only word I clearly vocalized after that was "fixed".

"'Fixed'? Jeff, you know what she's talking about?"

"Honestly? Not really."

I flung open the door and ran to the bathroom.

Nestor (Germany): Like, ten seconds after I give up on trying to help Booker, Cassie's roaring out the back stoop like she's on wheels. Slams the bathroom door behind her and Lance and Evander peek out of the living room.

Lance goes to knock and Evander grabs him by the arm and tells him to let her be. They come on into the kitchen instead. Jeff's headed in too. I decide those four can have themselves a discussion group about it while I go to out to where Vicki is. And Cassie texts me from inside the bathroom.

```
Cassie>  Nestor, Rome and Naples are
    supporting each other. Unlike me and Vicki.
    Do what you want with that information.
```

I show it to Vicki. "Guess you two had an interesting conference and s--- out here."

And before I can, she cuts me off and says, "Don't ask."

"*Querida*, I got to, though, if it's gonna affect the game."

Vicki rolls her eyes. "It's nothing. She thinks I should keep her there in Italy forever, like I owe it to her. I told her Hell no and she's crying."

I'm nodding like I understand, but I'm thinking it's kind of a big deal. Those two were friends all through high school, and far as I knew they never fought. None of that teen girl drama bulls---.

But I figure those two will kiss and make up after. I tell her, "All right, take you an extra season. Move your army from Albania to Apulia. Support with your fleet in the Ionian if you think she's lying. Spring 1910, you smash her in Naples."

"And I get twelve."

"Meantime I take Rome, and that's it. You and Lance, you tie for first."

She's doing that thing, biting her lip while she thinks, but this time it's like she's *determined*. So when she says, "I want to win," I ain't exactly surprised.

"You want Rome too."

"Yeah."

"So I get to be kingmaker."

"*Queen*maker."

I smile at her and hold her face in my hands. "You and me. King and queen. This is just the start, because the world is ours."

She presses herself up against me and she says, low and soft, "Thank you."

Lance (England): There was maybe a little more than three minutes left when Cassie came back out of the bathroom. If I hadn't seen her crying before, I'd've never guessed from looking at her after.

Me, Booker, Evander, and Jeff were in the kitchen, waiting for the clock to tick down to zero when she stormed in and said, "I need to talk to you. Right now."

"Who?" Booker asked.

"All of you. I just need a minute on the front porch. *Please.*"

We looked at each other, waiting to see who'd go first, if anyone, and she started herding us out like we're sheep. Evander shrugged and he was first out the room. Jeff and Booker followed, and I thought to myself, "What the Hell, might as well," and took up the rear.

Well, the second she shut the door behind her, Booker told her she's got two minutes. "I only need one. Lance, here's how you can take first place."

"Listening," I said.

"Push Vicki out of TYS … what's that one short for?"

"The Tyrrhenian Sea," Booker answers.

"Right. Booker, you support him from the Gulf of Lyon into there. Lance, you move your fleet in MAO into North Africa. Vicki won't see it coming, her fleet will be crushed."

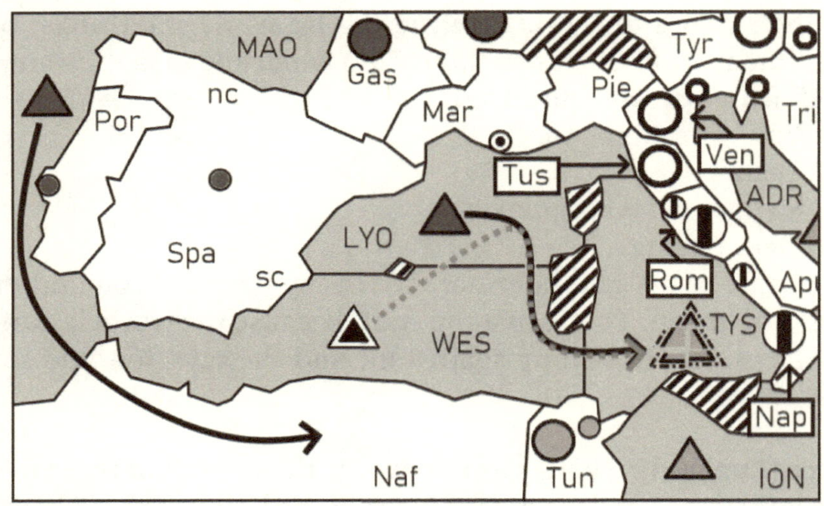

Figure 53 -- Fall 1909 Orders to Force Disband of Turkish Fleet in TYS

We took a few seconds to think about it while Cassie nervously tapped her foot. Booker asked, "To put it crassly, what is in it for me?"

"Tunis. In the spring. Lance, I'll support your fleet into Naples if I am able to do so."

"Hmm," Booker said, which for him was a definite maybe.

"And what's in it for you?" Evander asks her.

"I get to pick the winner. It's all I have left." Cassie opened the door. "See you in the living room."

Victoria (Turkey): "What was that message Booker sent you?"

"I almost forgot. Said he'd help support me, if I wanted."

"Yeah? Do you?"

"Not really, bae. Don't need it. Imma hold the line and take Cassie's last two dots."

Speaking of that crazy b----, I heard Cassie in the kitchen like a minute later. I felt Nestor twist so he could see. "What's going on, bae?"

"Cassie's back. Talking to those guys."

"Guess she got over herself fast. Forget about them."

"All right. Looks like they're leaving, anyhow."

Thirty seconds left and we were getting ready to go to the living room, and that's when I got these texts from her.

```
Cassie>  Say goodbye to your fleet in TYS. I
    just convinced Booker and Lance to team up
    against you.
Cassie>  Next spring they take Tunis.
```

"The f---?!" I shouted. I threw open that door and ran. Those five were in the living room, standing around the board. Cassie was cool as ice. I wish you could've seen it: five minutes—I mean, *not even* five minutes—earlier she was bawling her eyes out and there she was like it never happened.

I almost made a scene, right there, in front of everyone, when Nestor came up beside me and asked what was going on. I showed him what Cassie sent me and his eyes were jumping left and right, up and down, figuring it out.

Nestor said, "Okay, what you're gonna do is—" That's when the laptop buzzed.

"Order phase. You have five minutes," Evander said.

[Order phase of fall 1909]

Jeffrey (Russia): Cassie got hers in right away. You can bet the second she was done, she was staring at Vicki and Nestor.

"Why're those two freaking out?" I whispered to her.

"They're reacting to the news of Lance and Booker teaming up against her."

"How'd they find out?"

"Oh, I told her. Sent her a message."

Those two were trying to deal. Not "make a deal", I mean "deal with it". Nestor said he thought he had it figured out? But Vicki didn't think so, the way they were talking.

Booker only had one fleet to order, but he took his sweet time with it. Too fast for Vicki and Nestor, though. Like, five seconds after his phone was back in his pocket they came up to him and pulled him over to their side of the room.

Nestor was trying to smooth talk him, and Vicki was doing damsel in distress. Both of them were talking low, whispering practically. Booker we could hear: a lot of Nos and Sorrys. Then Vicki hissed "Fine", loud enough for us to make out and Booker took a seat on the sofa.

Booker (France): They asked to confer with me only after I had entered my order for the fall. I would not term it a blunder, as I had already come to a determination as to what that would be. They would not have been able to change my mind.

I am sure you can imagine how it went. They asked me if I had entered my order, and I told them I had. This was when I knew that they had caught wind of Cassandra's plan.

They asked me what my fleet would do and I refused to say.

"You said you'd help me!" Victoria complained.

"I asked you to let me know which of the two options I suggested you wished me to execute. You did not respond."

"You can't tell us *now*?"

"We can discuss it next turn, Victoria."

Nestor listed each of the possible orders available to me and attempted to read my reactions to each one. I believe I told you that I have a quite good poker face, and it did not fail me then.

They changed tack and showed me the message Cassandra sent to Victoria. Nestor wheedled and Victoria pled, but I politely refused to speculate as to how England would act.

I do recall something that may be of interest to you and your readers. Before Victoria angrily dismissed me, I glanced at our audience across the room. Jeffrey was staring, unabashedly and guilelessly. Lance's expression was the one I had seen when he held a very good hand and was silently hoping for a call.

Ollivander ... there is no other way to put this but to say that he was aroused. His skin was slightly flushed; his lips were parted; his chest rose and fell rapidly with each breath. I have little doubt that were I close enough to examine them, his pupils would have appeared dilated.

And Cassandra was observing Ollivander. What she saw had bestowed upon her an epiphany. What that was, I do not know.

You should ask her.

Nestor (Germany): All of a sudden my girl's freaking out. I'm thinking she's thinking she's late for putting in orders, but we got time.

So I catch up with her, all expecting she'll chill after I tell her she's early, when she shows me those texts from Cassie. Pisses me off. Not 'cause she's teaming up to hit Vicki. It's 'cause Cassie's been d---ing around most of the day, not playing the game, and all of a sudden it's all important to her.

Vicki's clutching my arm, wanting me to find a way to fix it, and I'm looking at the board and playing it out in my head. And I find the answer, and that's when Evander tells us we got five minutes.

"Hold in TYS and support with your fleet in the Ionian. Move from Tunis to North Africa to bounce Lance out."

"But when do I get Naples? And Rome?"

"Next year. Rome's still gonna be three on two after I support your army from Albania to Apulia. Same with Naples after that."

"How do I know Booker won't take Tunis if I do that? This could all be a trick Cassie's playing on me!"

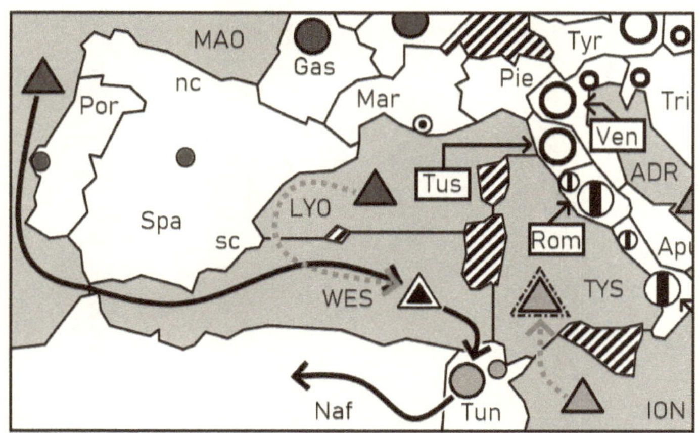

Figure 54 -- One Possible Outcome If England Does Not Move
MAO to Naf and LYO to TYS

And she's right. I remember … I remember I was proud of her

for seeing it.

I tell her, "It's possible. Fifty-fifty. You'll still take Italy, though."

"But if I lose Tunis, it'll be twelve-twelve with Lance! And if he takes Booker's last dot, he's thirteen!"

I got this idea that she gives Booker Tunis and takes Rome and Naples. It's twelve-twelve after Lance takes Marseilles, but it's a sure thing if we can trust him.

But when I look over to Booker, he's putting his phone back in his pocket. We call him over and he's already made his move. Won't say what it is, no matter how many ways we try to get it out of him.

So it's me and Vicki with the clock running down. "We'll keep fighting, *querida*. Spring 1910, we'll talk to Booker again, get him to help you with Tunis if we need it."

"But I'll *lose!*"

"You'll tie for sure. I'll make sure of it."

She's biting her lip again and I ask her, "You need help with your orders?"

"No, I'll manage on my own. We don't have a lot of time left. Take care of yourself."

 *Austria*

    A Rom Holds ◊
    A Nap → Apu -- Failure, Attack str. inadequate

 *England*

    F BOT Holds ◊ A Gas S A Bur Holds ◊
    A Nwy S A Stp Holds ◊
    F LYO → TYS -- Failure, Attack str. inadequate
    F SKA → Swe -- Failure, Attack str. inadequate
    F ENG → MAO -- Failure, Attack str. inadequate
    F MAO → Naf -- Failure, Attack str. inadequate
    F NTH S F Bel Holds -- Failure, Supp. disrupted
    F Bel S F NTH Holds -- Failure, Supp. disrupted
    A Stp S A Nwy Holds -- Failure, Supp. disrupted
    A Bur S A Gas Holds -- Failure, Supp. disrupted

 *France*

    F WES S F LYO → TYS ◊

 *Germany*

    A Mun S A Ruh → Bur ◊ A Tyr → Pie ◊
    F BAL → BOT -- Failure, Attack str. inadequate
    F Den → Swe -- Failure, Attack str. inadequate
    F HEL → NTH -- Failure, Attack str. inadequate
    A Hol → Bel -- Failure, Attack str. inadequate
    A Ruh → Bur -- Failure, Attack str. inadequate
    A Tus → Rom -- Failure, Attack str. inadequate
    A Ven S A Alb → Apu -- Failure, Order invalid

Turkey

    A Alb → Tri ◊ A Bud → Vie ◊
    A Gal → Sil ◊ F ION S F TYS Holds ◊
    A Lvn → Pru ◊ A Ukr → War ◊ F TYS Holds ◊
    F ADR → Apu -- Failure, Attack str. inadequate
    F AEG → ION -- Failure, Attack str. inadequate
    A Mos → Stp -- Failure, Attack str. inadequate
    A Tun → Naf -- Failure, Attack str. inadequate

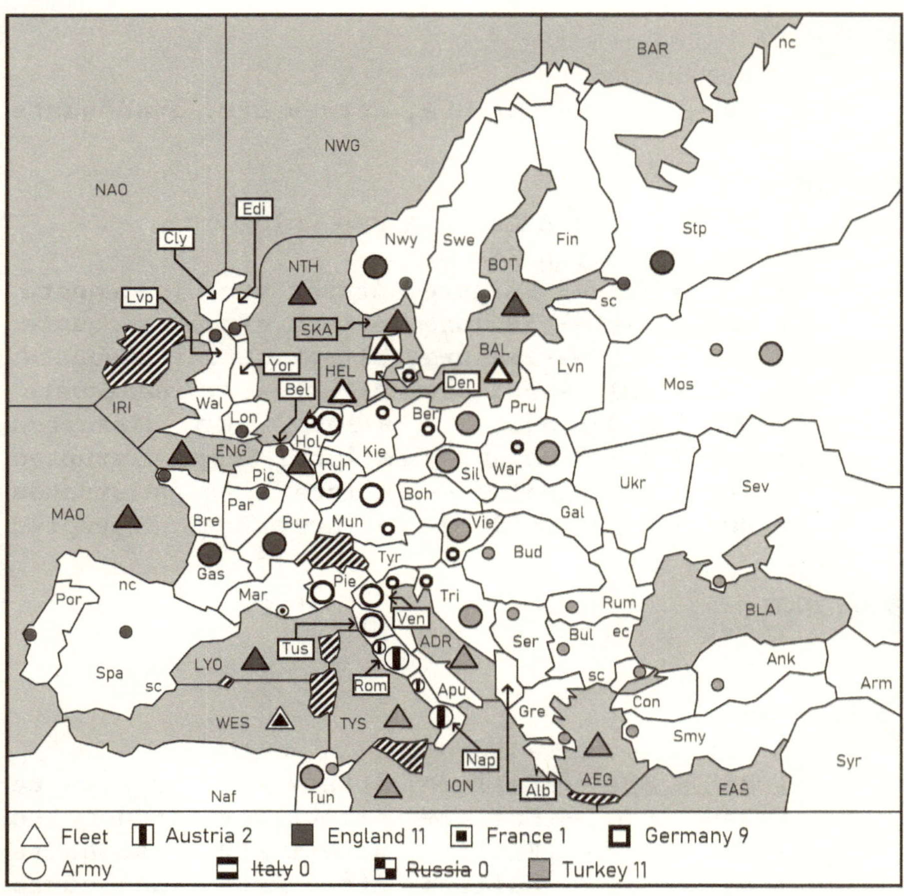

Figure 55 -- Game Map, Start of Winter 1909

Winter 1909

[Reactions to the orders of fall 1909]

Jeffrey (Russia): Evander got to see it first, sitting at the table, laptop in front.

People usually got their orders in with time to spare … yeah, except for that time I flipped the coin, right.

Anyway, not that turn. Vicki took it down to the wire. She was biting her thumbnail. You don't see that so often, girls with nail polish biting them.

And I'm wondering what's up. Yeah, sure, Cassie's in her head, but it's the same as before. Hold the line, get an army into Italy with Nestor's help. Then they take Rome and Naples down.

While we were waiting for Vicki, Booker zoned out. But Lance and Evander, it's like they knew it's going to happen. And Cassie figured it out too somehow?

Right, back to Evander. Those orders went through, and he nodded. Like he thought so. Cassie walked around to look over his shoulder, so I joined her and snuck a peek.

I said, "Holy s---." Like I heard it coming out of my mouth before I knew I was saying it. And Booker and Nestor come quick. Lance opens the map on his phone. Vicki, though, she's hanging back, staring at Nestor, looking worried.

Because Vicki doesn't know how badly he's going to react when he finds out she took three of his nine supply centers.

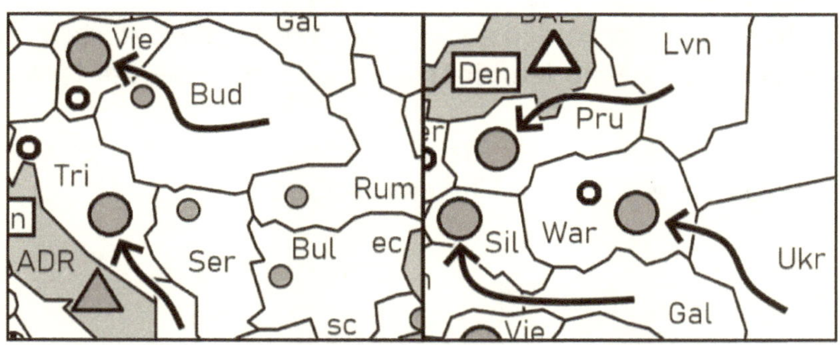

Figure 56 -- Turkey Takes Tri, Vie, and War Supply Centers from Germany

Nestor's jaw dropped and Lance started laughing.

Vicki took a few steps towards him and said, "Bae, look, I can explain …." Nestor had a hand up at her while he was mad-dogging Lance, who dropped his phone down to his side and laughed right in Nestor's face.

Vicki was like, Oh s---, and she got between them. Nestor was *shaking*, he was so angry. In that moment? I woulda bet he was gonna push her out of the way and put the hurting on Lance. Instead he grabbed the table with the board, flipped it up so the pieces flew all over the place and stomped out and slammed the front door.

She gave him a ten second head start and ran out after him.

And Lance threw up his arms like he was calling a touchdown and said, "Looks like I win!" He looked around, smiling, hoping someone else was happy about all that.

Booker took a couple of careful steps around the crap on the floor and said, "You're a f---ing child, Lance." Then he left too.

"Holy crap," I said. "Did Booker just—"

"Use a contraction?" Cassie asked. "I believe he did."

Lance dropped his left hand, the one with the phone, back to his hip and he shouted out, "Cassie! Up top!"

Cassie flicked her eyes at him and Evander. She said, "Read the room, Lance." Then she walked out.

Lance wasn't giving up on that high-five. I was tempted to leave him hanging but I couldn't bring myself to do it. So I held mine up and he slapped it and shouted, "Yeah! I'll be in touch, my man! Get you some cool s--- from Japan!"

I told him that sounded good to me. I bent down to start picking up those little wooden blocks. Evander told me not to worry about it.

Me and Lance made for the door. Lance said, "You go ahead, I've got to take a piss." And I went home.

After-
wards

[Ollivander and Lance's post-game analysis, part one]

Ollivander: I put my hands on my hips and surveyed the damage in the living room. When Lance doubled back, I told him, "Do me a favor and start cleaning up here." I took out the trash and wiped down the counters in the kitchen. Scrubbed the toilet in the bathroom. Took out the vacuum cleaner and got the floors.

I did the living room last. "The card table was a good idea," he said. "Imagine the damage Nestor would've done to a piece of real furniture."

"No doubt." I sat down on the couch next to him. "Did you record his reaction?"

He smirked as he took out his phone. The picture jumped about wildly. "I'm getting a headache watching that."

"If I'd made it obvious I was filming, Nestor would've caved in my skull. Still, I did get the look on his face when it dawned on him. Right ... here." He laughed. "Man, it's so good."

"And you can enjoy it over and over again."

"Oh yeah. I've got to hand it to you: your plan worked better than mine ever could have."

[Ollivander's proposal]

Ollivander: It was Karthik who suggested that Lance was still holding a torch for Vicki his senior year. You see ... really? I'm surprised Jeff remembered. What did he tell you?

... No, that's all correct. From the way he acted around us, it was as if a switch were thrown in his head freshman year and Vicki became just some girl. He was polite and friendly to her, and civil, if only just barely, to Nestor. And as Jeff told you, I wasn't the only one who thought so.

Some months passed between the time Karthik shared his supposition with us and the day I took Lance aside after school and interrogated him. He claimed not to recall staring at Vicki during the Homecoming assembly, but he couldn't categorically deny it: "I mean, yeah, I wouldn't put it past me to check out her a--." And he wouldn't admit to still being obsessed with her, but: "Look, if Vicki breaks up with Nestor tomorrow and asks me if I'm up for rebound sex, of *course* I'm going to say yes. F---, wouldn't you?"

"So it doesn't bother you that she's with Nestor?" I ask, and from his reaction, it's clear that I've hit a nerve.

"It bothers me that *anyone's* with Nestor. You know I found out for sure that he was the reason Juan heard about 'One-Nut Lance', right?"

"No. Why didn't you tell me?"

"I told Booker, and he said he believed me, but told me to let it go. Said there was nothing I could do with what I learned."

I put on a show of considering that: creased brow, pursed lips. I reckoned that my idea would be easier to sell were he to ask me.

He did. "You could get revenge. Or try to."

That garnered an eyeroll from him. "Yeah? How?"

That's when I proposed the game. "After all, to misquote Clausewitz, diplomacy is the continuation of war by other means. It's your opportunity to see him defeated."

"One, I'm not at war with him. Two, he'll never go for it."

"Probably not. But if he does, you'll get a chance."

"Okay, you see, this is why I'm not liking this. Only a chance?"

"It's not a game that lends itself to cheating beyond a certain stage. Lying, emotional manipulation, yes. Cheating, no."

It was when Lance asked, "Wait, what's the cheating we *can* do?" that I knew I had him hooked.

[Ollivander's scheme]

Lance: Evander laid it out for me. "I can fix it so that each player is assigned the country we want them to have."

The baseball cap, the one Evander used and the one Cassie found in the bathroom. It starts off with seven pieces, one for each country, tied in place with bits of string. In the middle is this bag with drawstrings. Evander picks up seven pieces in front of everyone and dumps them in the bag, closes it one-handed. Then he picks out the other seven pieces for each player.

"I'll be practicing over and over to make it look natural. You're going to provide the pretext."

"How?"

"You're going to start an argument over who gets which country by attempting to call dibs on France. Be completely ridiculous about it, because we *want* others to push back."

"What if people insist on picking themselves?"

"In the worst case scenario, you grab a coffee mug and put the pieces I take out of the cap into it for people to pick. Anyone feels around in the inside of my cap, it's game over."

"Yeah, no s---."

"But I have a way to discourage that. After I hand out the countries, I will float that very idea, that we start over and everyone picks their own country. You will mercilessly shoot down that trial balloon."

"Okay, but ... why would you hand out countries from your cap then immediately change your mind?"

"Because I will give myself the worst country."

"Italy."

"Italy. Italy's actually pretty playable, but we're working with the common consensus of amateur players here. Anyway, once that's done, the cap goes on my head and I'll get rid of the pouch and the thread loops in the bathroom."

Ollivander: Lance asked, "Wait, what about the rest of us?"

"Let's do the list of players first. You, me, Nestor, Vicki, obviously," I said. "Who else? Karthik?"

"He'll be in India, remember? I'm thinking Booker instead. He's played before, but not with me."

"Agreed. And Jeff and Cassie."

"So make me Austria and give Nestor Turkey. We run the Key Lepanto on him and knock him out of the game first thing."

"No."

"What? Why not?"

"One, it would be so blatant as to arouse suspicion. But even if it didn't somehow, Nestor wouldn't care, because he wouldn't have had time to build up his hopes of winning. He'll spend the rest of the day kicking back. Is that what you want?"

"No."

"Of course not. What you want is for Nestor to be betrayed last. It has to be effective and it has to be memorable. That's the art of the stab."

"But how can you guarantee it will happen?" Lance asked.

"I can't. We can maximize the chances by optimally assigning the powers to the right players. But short of mind control, there's no way we could."

"We could cheat some more. Figure out a way to eavesdrop? Mess with people's orders?"

"No. Even if I thought either or both of those would work, I still wouldn't allow it. We will select everyone's countries and we will manipulate others to steer to the desired outcome, but that is it."

Lance sighed. "This s---s."

"I should be clear. The reason I am proposing this is because I want to see what will occur. For me, this is an experiment. If I knew the outcome to a certainty, I wouldn't bother."

Lance: "Then what's the experiment? What are you trying to determine?"

Evander smiled. "I want to see if, given the opportunity, Vicki will stab Nestor. And if so, how he will react."

"Okay, that could be interesting. How do we get there?"

"You should understand that the odds are against the game even reaching *that* point. To have any appreciable chance of it coming to pass, we will need to engineer a three-way stalemate between you, Nestor, and Vicki."

"And how do we do that?"

We spent a good couple of hours in Evander's room with the game board open on his bed, going over every combination of players and countries. Well, not *every* combination, but lots of them. Eventually we came up with the assignments we used on that day. "It's a shame Cassie won't end up getting Turkey."

"Huh? Why?"

"Never mind, just thinking out loud," he replied. "Are you up for playing England?"

"Sure."

Evander locked eyes with me and said, "It will require you to shank Booker and Jeff. That's the only way you can build the stalemate line."

"If that's what it takes."

He nodded. "Good. I'm going to leave Italy open to invasion from the east. I'm wagering that Cassie will attack me rather than vie with Vicki for Greece and Bulgaria."

"Jeff's a wild card, though."

"He's got Turkey, Germany, and Austria breathing down his neck. Even if you weren't friends, he'd look to you for an alliance. Which will make it that much easier for you to steal Sweden from him. I'm more worried about France."

"When Cassie takes Italy from you, maybe I can get her to fight Booker."

"Draw his attention and units south and west. Your best play. Unless, of course, he turns on you first." Evander added, "But for my purposes, it's immaterial whether it's you or he who mans the trenches against the Hun."

"'Hun'?"

"Germany."

"What about Turkey?"

"It depends on how far west Vicki makes it, but I'm thinking she's not going to have a lot of units bumping up against England or France. Not until the end of the game."

And I said, "Wow. This could actually work."

"Yes. Then again, Nestor could surprise us and win it all."

[Ollivander and Lance's post-game analysis, part two]

Ollivander: And I tell Lance, "The setup came together cleanly. But the results were only one possible outcome."

"You said build a stalemate line against those two and Vicki would turn on Nestor. It actually happened and now you're saying it was just a guess?"

"I said she *might*. This wasn't a simulation operating in the domain of the deterministic. It wasn't even a scientific experiment where we can assign a p-value. We don't even know what the initial state of our reactants was."

"'Initial state'? What does that mean?"

I pull out my phone and check the time. "Among other things, it means that we are not privy to what went on between Vicki and Nestor between graduation day and today. But I'm glad you enjoyed yourself." I stood up and grabbed the vacuum cleaner. Lance got the hint and got off the couch.

"Sure did. Thanks for everything." At the front door, he stuck out his hand and I shook it. "So … I'll see you later?"

"Sorry, no."

"Oh. Why, are you going on vacation this summer?"

"No, I'm not," I replied. And then I waved goodbye as I closed the door.

[Cassandra's post-game analysis]

Cassandra: What I came to realize was my conception of "motive" was much too narrow, and that was why I spent the entire day running around in circles, pointing fingers everywhere and convincing no one.

Have you and Evander completed your interview? … And has he explained what his reason was for fixing the game?

… No, you can spare me the details: they are ultimately uninteresting. Whatever Evander tells you was his purpose behind his actions, the truth is that he was fomenting chaos. The game was an engine of destruction.

I hadn't thought on that day for many months until I read, for class my first semester here, the seminal paper "Deep Play" by the anthropologist Clifford Geertz. The title of which comes from a footnote to a specific translation of *The Theory of Legislation* by Jeremy Bentham.

The essay concerns the sociology of cockfighting in Bali.

"Deep play" in Bentham's work is a straightforward concept: he means it as a purely monetary wager that necessarily brings more misery to the loser than joy to the winner. And yes, Geertz finds that it is overwhelmingly a money-losing proposition for the owners of the roosters.

But "deep" for him has another layer. The violence of the fights is a reflection on their society. And so more is at stake than money. Their senses of self are ineluctably on the line.

I'm sure the analogy is clear. Had I already read it when I was asked why Evander would cheat only to be gone by 1903, I could have replied that his quick exit left him emotionally intact. Allowing him to coolly observe the rest of us desperately scrap in the arena of his making.

[The participants' interactions after the game]

Booker: My father asked me how it had gone and whether I had won or lost. I gave him an abbreviated version of the events of the day.

He was initially quite upset with Cassandra for having insinuated that I had cheated. But once I had finished with my telling, his anger had subsided, to be replaced with puzzlement.

"Son, do you get the feeling that this young lady's concern was misdirected?"

"But still justified?" He nodded. "I do not know. She was never able to articulate what was untoward about the day's proceedings. The end of the game, as abrupt as it was, is not evidence."

"Something to consider after you've had some distance on the matter?"

"Dad, I cannot imagine ever again thinking about this day."

As for the six others, the only one who has made an effort to contact me is Jeffrey. He sent me an e-mail, asking how I was liking Princeton so far. I told him I was enjoying myself, but schoolwork kept me quite busy. He wanted me to join Facebook so that he could "friend" me. I assured him I would notify him as soon as I did. ... No, I have no plans to join Facebook.

Lance: I texted Vicki Thursday morning, the day after it all went down. I said I wanted to meet with her in person to apologize. She left me on read. I followed her on Instagram, but she never replied to my DMs. Never acknowledged my likes. I gave up halfway through her European vacation.

I kept my promise to Jeff. Got him a bunch of figures from the anime series we used to watch. Some other cool stuff too. Came by his apartment to drop them off, but his mom told me he had an emergency and had to leave. She said she would make sure he got them.

He texted me thanks later. We played some Starcraft II online a couple times, but most of the summer he was busy getting ready for community college. He said he wanted to hit the ground running.

Evander never replied to my messages. Didn't bother trying with Cassie and Booker, and they didn't contact me either.

Jeffrey: I tried texting and calling Evander. He never got back to me. I even …. Okay, this is embarrassing, so don't laugh. I even went outside his house one day when I was pretty sure he'd be there, and he was. From across the street, I could see him through his windows, sitting in his living room. I texted him and watched him pick up his phone to look at it and put it right back down.

Lance, like he tried to make it like all that s--- he pulled during the game never happened? He came by with some stuff from Japan, but I convinced Mom to pretend I wasn't home and get him to go away.

We played a couple of games of Starcraft II online. I messaged him to say that the microphone on my headset wasn't working so I'd have an excuse for not talking to him. He wanted to get together IRL, but I told him I was busy getting ready for college.

He actually texted me and said, "It's community college. How hard do you really have to study?" That's when I cut him all the way off and put his presents up on eBay.

Ollivander: Jeff texted and e-mailed me in the days following the game, but I didn't reply. Same with Lance.

Nestor: I leave Evander's house and I'm walking fast to where the car is, three blocks away 'cause I couldn't find a closer spot. I had to f---ing *beg* my brother to let me borrow it. Said I wanted to give Vicki a nice time the last couple days before she flew off.

Whatever. I even turn around to make sure she's not running up after me. If I'd done her like she did me, I know I'd be sprinting to catch her. But she's not there. I take out my phone, check if I miss a call or a text from her. No.

Viejo asks me how it went when I get home. I just shake my head. Father asks who won. I just shake my head. My brother's surprised I'm back early. I just shake my head.

Next day, Thursday, I decide she's not going to Europe without talking to me first. I go to her place and ring the doorbell. No one comes to the door, but I hear people inside, so I ain't leaving. I ring that bell every five minutes. Sometimes I make it four or six, just to f--- with her.

I'm out there a half hour when the door opens and her father sits down on the stairs next to me. "She's not coming out."

"You know, I woulda just given them to her if she asked."

"What's that?"

"Vicki didn't tell you about the game?"

"She's a teenaged girl. She never tells me anything." He lets out this big-a-- sigh and says, "You know, Nestor, I've always liked you. You understood that, right?"

I don't know about "like", but I never felt any hate from him. He goes on, "You were good for her. What I worried about was whether she was good for you. But I was selfish the way every father is selfish. I didn't warn you."

I shift my a-- diagonal so I can see his face. "For real?"

"Yes. For real. Imagine I had taken you aside and told you to stay away from my daughter because I was afraid *she* would hurt *you*. How do you think you would have reacted?"

I don't want to answer, but he's waiting. "I wouldn't have bought it."

He looks out on the street and nods. "I overheard snatches of a phone conversation she had yesterday. She said she broke up with you and the way it happened she didn't even have to take the blame for it."

He's telling it true. There's no doubt in my mind. "It's cowardly. I don't care for it at all. But I can't force her to come out, Nestor."

Next thing I know, I'm home and in my bed. I don't remember anything in between.

But I'm over it and definitely over *her*. I'm in muthaf---ing *college*! Partying, hanging with the team, taking easy classes to keep my GPA up and me eligible. Because next season, imma play college ball. 2020's gonna be *my* year. Watch me take UConn to the top!

Victoria: I guess Lance hit me up on Instagram? But except for him, no. ... Oh yeah, that's right: Nestor wanted to talk the next day. I figured it could wait. I mean, it's not like we were going to be messaging while I was in Europe. Our relationship wasn't exactly built on conversation.

I didn't call him when I got back. Just totally forgot.

Cassandra: No, I didn't attempt to contact any of the other players. Nor did they attempt to contact me.

[Ollivander's final comments]

Ollivander: Your friend Cassie wasn't that far off. When you introduce a perturbation into a stable system, the outcomes fall into two categories: oscillation about an equilibrium or unpredictable chaos. As for "fomenting", it's a loaded word, but not an entirely unfair one. I was predicting instability. For bonds to break. Perhaps there were some relationships that survived the day, but not mine.

I've told you before: I am comfortable with endings. The game provided me the perfect excuse to jettison them all; I never considered any of them particularly worthwhile in the first place. I certainly see no need to maintain them now that I am in college, thousands of miles away, spending time with the people in my classes and the dorm. From here on out, my time in San

Francisco will be a week here, a long weekend there. I'll never have to see any of those six again.

Well. You have the chat transcripts. The audio recordings should be available in the shared drive; the e-mail I sent last week has the link. Kitchen, living room, both porches. ... The microphone on the back stoop was in the flowerbeds. Lucky for me she didn't think to look there, I suppose.

Her colloquies on the sidewalk and in the bathroom won't appear, and some whispered negotiations will be inaudible. Hopefully you'll be able to fill in any gaps with the participants' recollections. ... What do you mean, you already added my recordings "to the others"? Oh wait, I get it: the "others" are *your* interviews.

... What? That's ... who else was taping that day? Was it Cassie? It had to be Cassie. ... Hello? Hello?

[Victoria's statement at the outset of our interview]

Victoria: Oh yeah, right! Wow, I haven't thought about that game in, like, forever!

... Sure I'm up for talking about it! Why wouldn't I be? You know I won that day, right?

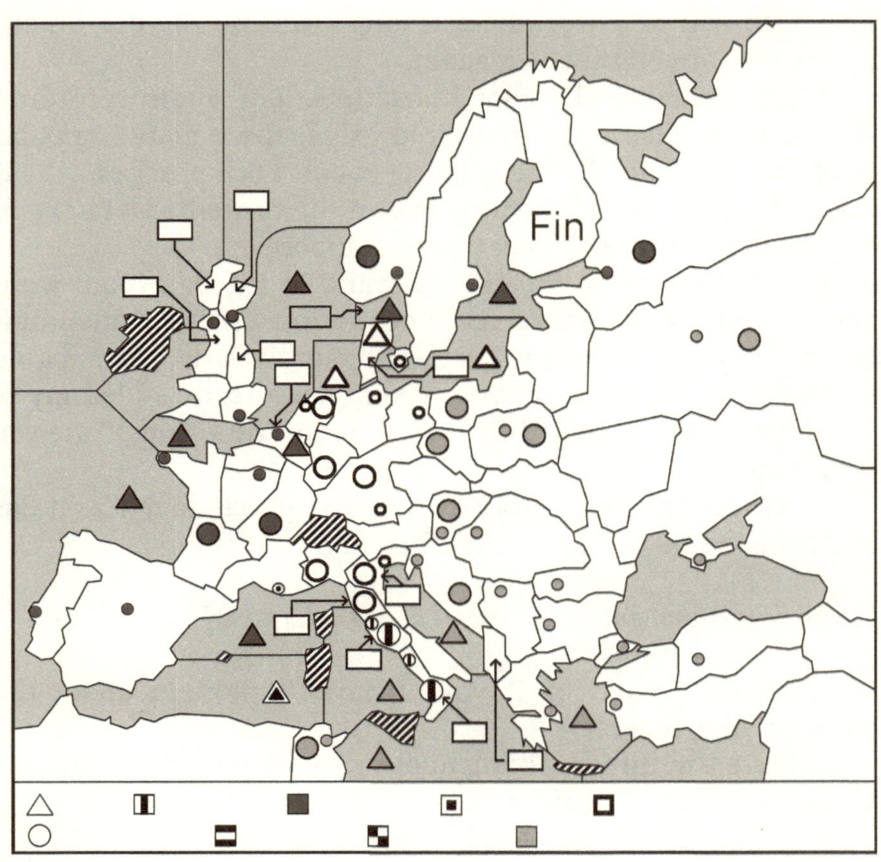

Fin

R. Jamie Langa is the author of
The Dream of the White Elephant.

R. Jamie Langa is a pseudonym.

@RJamieLanga
https://rjamielanga.substack.com

www.ingramcontent.com/pod-product-compliance
Lightning Source LLC
Chambersburg PA
CBHW030831110726
47900CB00006B/1838